"Lem Cobb is dead, Ben. You gotta come...."

It had been eight years since Ben had left Parish, Mississippi, and although some things had changed, it would take generations to alter something as ingrained as human behavior. Folks here were almost as fond of their eccentricities as they were their little local scandals.

He'd occasionally dreamed of his hometown, but they had been dreams of boyhood—days of innocence, days long gone. When awake, Ben's memories of Parish were of a darker nature, and he could have lived the rest of his life without being reminded of his past.

Now the city council wanted him to come home, to be the new chief of police, to investigate his friend's death.

At thirty-seven, Ben felt that life held few illusions for him. But nothing could have prepared him for the news that had brought him back—or the events that were about to occur.

"Ms. Myers never fails to give the reader a good, solid, entertaining story with fresh characterizations and dialogue that sparkles."
—*Rendezvous*

Watch for the newest blockbuster from
HELEN R. MYERS

Coming in May 1999
only from MIRA Books

HELEN R.
Come Sundown
MYERS

MIRA

ISBN 1-55166-436-4

COME SUNDOWN

Copyright © 1998 by Helen R. Myers.

MIRA and the star colophon are trademarks of MIRA Books.

Printed in U.S.A.

Heartfelt thanks to Dianne Moggy
and everyone at MIRA.
And to my editor Karen Taylor Richman—
my deepest gratitude and affection.

Count it the greatest sin to prefer mere existence
to honor, and for the sake of life
to lose the reasons for living.

—Emperor Justinian

_____ Prologue _____

Moss Lake
Parish, Mississippi
June 3, 1997

Lem Cobb ran like a blind man through the woods, his hands stretched before him, seeking, gauging. Sweat bled into his eyes, and although it stung, he was too terrified to give in to the need to blink.

Every step was a risk. Tree and shrub branches slapped at his face, his chest and his bare arms. Thorny vines raked across his skin and tore at his hair. He didn't know how much more he could stand; already each new assault was winning a bigger grimace or deeper grunt of pain from him, and every gasping breath sounded like a roar in the darkness, despite the frantic voice in his head that pleaded, _Quiet... quiet...you gotta be quiet!_

The ground, soggy from a heavy afternoon thundershower, sucked at his shoes. At times it pulled him ankle deep. Finally it dragged one completely off— the one with the broken lace. How many times had his mama told him to replace the damned thing? As he ran, he remembered her lectures...remembered too much.

He sobbed as a new wave of misery overwhelmed him. If only he'd listened. A fool, that's what he was; a stupid, dumbass fool who hadn't even had the sense to finish the sixth grade. God knew, every white man he'd ever worked for had taken pains to point that out to him. So had his mama, never mind that she'd never made it past the fourth grade herself. Well, it might be too late to do anything about that now, but at least he was bright enough to know these woods were only the beginning of the protection he needed.

He had to get to the lake and then swim across to Tilly's. Hopefully his lady had a few dollars she could spare. Enough to get him out of Parish, out of the county, as far away as possible. He might not be ready to get hitched or anything, but Tilly had a good heart and claimed to love him. His mama wouldn't approve of him using those feelings to talk the girl out of her hard-earned money, but what the hell? As least it wasn't the same as borrowing to bet on a dog-fight, or to buy beer. Mama would understand, once she knew it was a matter of life and death—only he would have to rely on Tilly to tell her because he wasn't about to stick around to do that himself.

He stopped, suddenly unsure of his route, and gulped more air to ease the burning in his lungs. Everything was so dark and overgrown, he couldn't be sure where he was, let alone which way to go. With his heart pounding in his ears like blows from a fist, he glanced upward, peering through the thick umbrella of oak and sweet gum trees, maples and hickories. They stirred from a breeze too weak to reach him, but strong enough that he could spot a few stars peeking out from slow-moving clouds. Not enough, though, to pick out a constellation, and the moon wasn't up yet, either. He tried to convince himself that was just as well since moonlight would be as much trouble as help.

Suddenly he heard men running and brush thrashing.

He spun around and his heart lurched painfully. "Jesus," he whimpered, bending at the waist to hold back a wail of terror. Not only were they still coming, they were getting closer!

Tears filled his eyes. Why couldn't they leave him alone? He hadn't done anything. He wasn't even sure he understood what he'd seen!

Terrified, he took off again. This time he chose the most impossible route, scaring the hell out of himself each time he lowered his bare foot into the mud. Had it been daylight, he'd have laughed, enjoying the chance to watch the thick muck oozing between his toes. Rich Mississippi mud had a slick, sensual feel to it that he loved. But not being able to see changed things, made him think of snakes and worse. Just the thought of stepping on a cottonmouth had him aching to take a leak—but no way would he risk stopping.

When he finally spotted the lake, he sucked back a cry of relief. Even without the moon, its calm surface glistened like the black pearl in his mama's Sunday brooch. Taking that as a sign, he raced toward the water as eagerly as he used to run to her.

One long stride from the edge of the water, his bare foot came in contact with metal. For an instant he tasted horror, knew the gut-chilling urge to recoil, all while understanding that few things in these woods would have been fast enough to succeed and that he wasn't one of them. Then the varmint trap slapped shut with the ferocity of a pit bulldog locking its jaws on prey. It didn't have the jagged teeth of bigger traps; this one's vicious bite came from velocity. And when agonizing pain shot up his leg and exploded in his groin, his heart and his brain, Lem screamed as he'd never screamed in his life.

A shudder worked through his body as if he was taking a massive electrical charge. Even so, he tried to fight, reached down to free himself, but it did no good. His struggles only threw him more off balance.

Too preoccupied and frightened to think of buffering his fall, he crashed headfirst into the sweet gum tree on the bank.

The two men who emerged from the dense brush a short time later spotted Lem straightaway, but seeing there was no longer any urgency, they kept their distance, studying him as he lay sprawled across the sweet gum's jutting roots. The tree's gnarled appendages resembled great arthritic fingers, and Lem appeared posed, one arm stretched toward the water as if in entreaty.

Finally, they edged closer. While one man held his rifle on Lem's still form, the other set his weapon against a tree and leaned over the body for a closer inspection. After considering the barely discernible rise and fall of Lem's chest for a few more seconds, he shook his head and straightened.

"Lucky son of a bitch is out cold. Never will know how easy he got off."

He slid his booted foot under Lem Cobb and rolled him facedown into the water. A startled frog croaked and abandoned a nearby lily pad to the interloper.

With a grunt of amusement, the man reached into his shirt pocket and drew out a pack of cigarettes and a lighter, and lit up. As he inhaled deeply, he watched the air bubbles rise and burst around Lem's nearly submerged head. The popping sounds mimicked the cicadas' and the tree frogs' chorus.

Only when the cigarette had nearly burned down to its filter, long after the bubbles had ceased, did the man face his companion again. Giving him a curt nod, he picked up his weapon and led the way back into the thick brush.

1

Parish, Mississippi
June 25, 1997

It was only midmorning, but Ben Rader could feel sweat soaking through his shirt. In another few minutes—thanks to the steamy air whipping through the open windows of his Chevy Blazer—the cotton would be clinging to him like an aroused woman. Such erotic thoughts should have been an agreeable diversion; after all, there were less pleasant ways to kill time than fantasizing about how it felt to be lying naked in bed with a cold beer and a willing female. Today, though, diversions of any kind were unwelcome.

With downtown Parish in his rearview mirror, he turned onto the farm-to-market road leading to the Maitland estate and considered pulling over to get a clean shirt from the suitcase in the back of the truck. Freshening up might make it easier to do what he had to do. Then again, who was he kidding?

In the end he decided Widow Maitland would just have to live with the sight of a sweaty man, since changing would be as much a waste as testing the air conditioner again. But damn this weather for adding to an already stress-filled homecoming; and damn this piece of mechanical crap for acting up not a day after he'd sunk over two hundred bucks into getting it fixed.

And damn you for letting yourself get caught up in this mess.

Hell, but it was hot. By noon the heat index would be edging into triple-digit territory and the radio station out of Greenville would be issuing an advisory to the residents of northwest Mississippi to use extreme caution when engaging in any form of physical activity. Of course, by then Parish would be virtually shut down anyway, the populace having retreated to verandas, covered storefronts or the most ancient of trees, like so many cattle lumbering toward their share of a patch of shade.

No one needed much of an excuse, let alone a recommendation to take things slow in these parts. Why, even as he'd exited the police station moments ago, the early birds had begun to collect in their customary array of cliques. Ben remembered well how it worked. With each newcomer's arrival, the topic of conversation would return to the current heat wave, just like a turntable needle caught in the groove of an old record: how if June was this hot, what would the rest of the summer bring? That would spawn a few moments of silence as everyone contemplated the possibilities, while straw hats, newspapers and embroidered cotton hankies worked overtime to cool vivid imaginations, as well as perspiring bodies. But move on they would because *gossip* was, irrefutably, the chief recreational activity in the community. At least until sundown. Ben believed that just as he knew *he* would be the second most discussed topic in town today.

No, some things never changed. It had been eight years since he left Parish for what he'd thought was the last time. And although there were indications of some improvements—for one thing, he hadn't seen the all-powerful Maitland name on every other store sign, and Hughes Hardware and Lumber had practically doubled in size, although only God knew why—it would take much longer, probably generations, to alter something as ingrained as human behavioral patterns. Besides, folks here were almost as fond of their eccentricities as they were their little local scandals. No doubt that was the real reason why Ben was here; screw what Fred had said about his special qualifications.

Ben yielded to a heavy sigh. He should have done it. Two weeks ago when Fred Varnell had called, he should have followed his first instinct and hung up on His Honor the Mayor. Even as he listened to the old fool plead, heard the surprisingly decent salary being offered, he couldn't imagine anyone intentionally choosing to move here. Short of facing a sentence at Parchman Penitentiary, what native would voluntarily come back? Being a detective on the Jackson police force might not be the culmination of some people's ambitions, but Ben had been content enough. Most important, when he'd been in dire need of a job, Jackson had been the first place where his name hadn't immediately raised eyebrows.

Sure, he'd occasionally dreamed of his hometown over the years, but they had been dreams of his boyhood; remembrances of days when he would get up before the moon set or the sun rose and take the launch out on the town lake to test wits against some largemouth bass; of lying in bed, listening to a world absent of human sounds, the music of crickets, bull-frogs or the less tuneful uproar of two raccoons arguing over territorial rights to his father's latest attempt at vegetable gardening.

However, when awake, most of his memories of Parish were of a darker nature, and those were the ones Fred's call had resurrected. Ben could have lived the rest of his life without being reminded of that fiasco. And yet to this day, his embarrassment wasn't so much over *what* his father had done, but *how* the old man had chosen to deal with it. As a result, he'd felt no pride or satisfaction when Fred told him that the city council wanted him to take on his father's former position, the job that as a boy Ben had stated would be his one day. At thirty-seven, life held few illusions for him. Even after Fred assured him that the old chief, Harry Wheeler, was retiring, Ben had resisted. He told Fred it would take more leverage than that to get him to uproot himself again...and damned if the son of a bitch hadn't broadsided him with a good one.

"Lem Cobb is dead, Ben," Fred had replied. "You've gotta come."

Fred explained that Lem had drowned over at Moss Lake, but even before hearing anything else, Ben had rejected the news, because Lem, the youngest brother of his childhood best friend, could swim better than a starving bass chasing down a fat pollywog. He had taught Lem himself one afternoon over twenty years ago when, tired of the younger boy's whining, he'd tossed him out of his boat and on top of a great old snapping turtle.

Dead. That he had to accept, but drowned...?

Only if someone had put a bullet in Lem's head first.

Reminding himself that he needed to keep his cool until he knew more, Ben let the scenery soothe him. A few hundred feet ahead, a squirrel darted across the paved road. Ben eased off the accelerator and watched the frisky animal successfully reach an ancient pecan tree.

Beyond the tree were well-tended cotton fields that matched those on the right side of the road. This was Ashworth land, and unless the season stayed too hot and dry, it appeared the family was in for a good crop this year. So what else was new? The rich always seemed to have the best luck.

Next to the Maitlands, Ben figured the Ashworths were still the wealthiest family in the county. He planned to stop by to talk to Vail Ashworth later, since Lem's body had been discovered between the Ashworth and Maitland estates. In the past, neither family had been strict about trespassers, and unless things had changed drastically, surely somebody should know or have seen something. He was determined to find out what. But before he started any serious investigating, he needed to pay his respects and find a place to stay.

After driving another half mile, he passed a sporty white convertible parked on the shoulder of the road. The white Mustang's top was down, exposing a strawberry red interior. Not far beyond it, he spotted someone walking. He didn't need any ID to tell him that she must be the driver.

A petite young blonde packaged as compactly as her car, she walked with an exaggerated sway of rounded hips sheathed in a skirt the color of cotton candy. But what had Ben clearing his throat wasn't the snugness of her skirt, it was that besides the high heels and purse she carried in her right hand, she had her panty hose slung over her left shoulder.

As if she could hear the gears grinding to a halt in his head, she glanced over her shoulder at him. With the same easy confidence, she swung around and used the hose to flag him down.

"Hell."

Instinct urged him to keep on driving. He was in no mood to tangle with jailbait. Unfortunately, twenty minutes ago he'd taken his oath as chief of police, so he had no choice but to stop. With another blunt comment for Fred Varnell's tenacity in tracking him down, he pulled over to the grassy shoulder and waited for her to reach the Blazer's open passenger window.

Although the truck's height limited his view, he could still tell she wore nothing under her half-unbuttoned, white knit top, and that she had the kind of breasts that promptly and acutely reminded him of having awakened this morning with his usual craving for sex...and that he'd gone without. Again. Already speculating as to whose headache she was, he nodded slightly.

"Problems?"

"Not anymore."

She gave him a smile that made her powder blue

eyes sparkle with mischief. As she tilted her head, her pale blond hair caressed her collarbone. The fringed style framed a heart-shaped face still childlike, despite an excessive amount of black mascara and equally overdone eyeliner. Ben wouldn't have recognized her as easily if it hadn't been for the cleft in her chin, a family trademark confirming her pedigree. The last time he saw her, she'd been a ten-year-old hellion with hair that had yet to grow out from a shearing inspired by God knew what rebellion. That would make her eighteen going on thirty now.

He ignored the invitation in her eyes and gestured with his thumb over his shoulder. "What's wrong with your car?"

"Well, I'm no mechanic, but I think it's out of gas."

As Ben studied her through the polarized lenses of his sunglasses, he thought about all the lectures he could give her regarding the dangers of hitchhiking, not to mention flirting with strangers—especially now. But he knew he would be wasting his breath. He hadn't been any different at her age. Call it a wild streak, explain it as a matter of being born in a place too confining for one's nature, whatever. People who strained at life's bit the way she did could be lectured to, threatened or punished; in the end they had to be left to learn their lessons at their own pace—and in their own way.

"All right, come on," he told her, pressing the button that released the electric door lock. "I'll drive you home."

She was inside before he could remove the folders and pads he had collected from the station. He jerked the things from under her bottom, hoping she would get the message, but she merely giggled and squirmed this way and that in a dubious attempt to assist him. Ben would have to have been blind not to notice the intent behind the effort: to provide him with the maximum opportunity to appreciate her firm, sun-kissed thighs.

"There now, that's better," she purred when she finally settled down. Positioned to face him, she draped an equally tanned arm across the back of her seat.

"Uh-uh." Annoyed that his imagination was drifting toward the subject of tan lines, Ben motioned for her to sit facing forward. "And fasten your seat belt."

"Oh, that's okay. My place is only a little ways down the road."

"I know. Do it anyway."

Instead of obeying, she eyed him with the shrewdness of someone twice her age. "What do you mean you know? We've never met. Believe me," she added, her smile aging her more than the cosmetics she wore ever could, "I would have remembered."

"It's been years. I only just moved back."

This time her laughter possessed an unmistakable sarcasm. "Sugar, no one moves back here, unless it's to be planted beside kin at the local ghoul yard...and, um, you don't look dead to me."

As she traced the shoulder seam of his shirt with frosted pink fingernails, Ben wondered if she had ever been up close and personal with anything remotely resembling dishwater. He took hold of her wrist and redirected her hand back onto her lap. "What I am, Miss Maitland, is too old to be used as an outlet for your boredom." He shifted so she could spot the badge on his left shirt pocket. "And since I'm sure you wouldn't indulge in behavior that might be misconstrued as a proposition, I know you'll want to refrain from saying or doing anything else that'll give me the wrong impression of you."

He watched Gabrielle Maitland's eyes grow wide, then narrow with renewed interest.

"Ben Rader." For a moment she abandoned her sex-kitten facade. "I should've recognized you."

"You were barely out of training pants when I left."

"I may have been young, but I wasn't blind." Like her smiles, her laugh was affecting. "You've got your daddy's looks all over again. People still talk about him. Nobody forgot that face—like storm clouds building on a hot summer afternoon. Why don't you take off those glasses so I can see if you inherited his dangerous eyes?"

The sex kitten was back with a vengeance; however, Ben wasn't the least bit tempted—not that his lack of enthusiasm seemed to dampen hers.

Once again she wriggled in her seat, tucked one leg beneath her and combed her hand through her hair. "When I heard old man Varnell was going to ask you back, I thought for sure you'd tell him to go to hell."

"And I thought your daddy would have packed you off to a convent ages ago."

The mask slipped momentarily, exposing a sad young woman. "He threatened to until the very end, but I guess he never found one he thought could keep me." She glanced out the front window. "I can't be-

lieve it's been a year already. For what it's worth, he
would have approved of you coming back, too.''

"Sure he would." Ben couldn't help his indiffer-
ence. After having been slapped on the back and having his hand grabbed by storeowners, the local mor-
tician and every past, present and aspiring politician,
he was fed up with any form of schmoozing—especially when he knew how brief his honeymoon was
bound to be.

"I mean it."

Maybe she did—and maybe he was just too cynical
for his own good. "Listen, Bree, I may not have been
Sumner's biggest fan, but I have to admit his death
took a lot of color out of this town.''

Blinking hard, she spent a few seconds attempting
to tug her skirt down to a more respectable level.
"Yeah, it did. He gave them a good show, though.
He was pure hell on wheels to the end." She shot
Ben a quick glance from beneath her vampish eye-
lashes. "I guess you heard he even married his private
nurse?"

After Lem, that was the second piece of news Fred
Varnell had shared with him. Ben slipped off his sunglasses and laid them on his thigh before reaching
into his shirt pocket for a cigarette. Regardless of
what he thought of gossip and gossipers, he needed
to keep track of what was what in town.

He eyed Bree over the flame of a throwaway
lighter. "How'd that go over with you and Justin?"

"Anything Daddy did was fine with us."

"Bullshit. How do you really feel about her?"

Instead of answering the question, she drew a long
breath, sucking cigarette smoke deep into her lungs

as though taking a hit off a joint. "Mmm...I love that smell, don't you? It's so...arousing."

"Don't waste your time, Bree."

She stuck her tongue out at him. "Spoilsport."

"Want to walk home?"

"Okay, okay. So we were nervous, is that what you're waiting to hear? Well, who wouldn't have been? The day Daddy phoned to tell us, Justin and I stayed up all night worrying about it. Needless to say, we anticipated the worst. At least I did." She wrinkled a nose a Barbie doll would envy. "My saintly twin brother kept insisting all that mattered to *him* was Daddy's happiness. Our Justin couldn't spot a gold digger if she stole his Jockey shorts while he was still in them."

"Is she a gold digger?"

Expertly outlined cupid-bow lips pursed as she considered the question. Ben wondered how many hours it took practicing in front of a mirror to achieve that petulant look.

"Why else would someone marry a man dying from cancer?"

"The word I got was that she was good for him."

"Maybe. Who knows? I'll tell you one thing, though, she's not easy to read." Bree shrugged. "I guess she's not so bad...in small doses."

"Be careful. That almost sounds as if you like her."

"I said in *small* doses. Don't think I'm about to nominate Eve as Stepmother of the Year or anything. In fact, lately, she's been a royal pain. But I am capable of giving credit where it's due. After all, I'm not sure any amount of money is worth the unenviable task of keeping the Maitland dynasty intact.''

As she spoke, she played with her hair, ultimately lifting it off her neck. The movement only pronounced the thrust of her already taut nipples, and Ben decided that it would be a wise idea to find out if any of his old girlfriends were single these days. The sooner the better.

"I hear she's young," he said.

"Thirty-two!"

To hide his twitching lips, Ben turned to flick cigarette ashes out the window. A moment ago she'd made a pass at him, and now she was suggesting that a woman five years his junior had one foot in the grave. It was too damned hot to follow an eighteen-year-old's rationale. He would just have to find out what he wanted to know about Sumner Maitland's widow his own way.

"So what are you doing with yourself these days besides pouring money into the gas tank of that hot rod back there, and driving up and down Main Street tormenting the local boys?"

"Whatever it takes to get through the day. And night," she told him with a sidelong look.

"Ever consider getting a job?"

She laughed. "Doing what? And where? Daddy put all kinds of restrictions on my trust fund. I have to live in this godforsaken place until I'm twenty-one, and even then I'll either have to have a college degree or a marriage license to touch it. Shoot, I'll probably end up the same way poor Lem did—planted before my time." She parted her sweater, inviting what breeze there was to caress her perspiration-free skin.

"Weren't you friends with his older brother, Luther?"

Ben managed to ignore the view she was offering by thinking of the scar near his hairline and how he'd earned it years ago. The six stitches had been a result of siding with Luther Cobb after three local boys claimed that Luther's catfish had come off their trotline—the first of several occasions when Ben found himself neck deep in trouble for siding with the wrong people. The scar also reminded him again that there had been no sign of Luther at his swearing-in.

"We hung around together," he said, telling himself he was a fool for letting Luther's absence matter.

"Rumor has it that's why you took this job. People say you don't think the coroner's report was right about Lem's death being an accident."

Ben had already ascertained that the coroner, a general practitioner that Parish shared with a handful of other equally small communities, was a half-blind, senile fossil who would impress everyone if he could successfully differentiate a hemorrhoid from a testicle. He crushed out his cigarette among the dozen butts already in the ashtray.

"This town couldn't survive without its rumors. Now be a good girl and fasten that seat belt." He slipped on his sunglasses and started the engine.

Vinyl squeaked as Bree once again repositioned herself. "Sure thing, Chief. And, listen, if there's ever anything else I can do for you...well, I hope you know you only have to ask."

Ben kept his eyes on the road. "Kid, the only thing you can do for me is to remember that I don't waste energy telling people to do things twice."

* * *

The front door of Cobb's Market burst open and both Luther Cobb and his wife, Racine, looked up from the greens they were rinsing and bundling. They beamed bright smiles of welcome—until they saw that the newcomer was only their youngest boy.

Succumbing to his fatigue, Luther dropped his head and returned to the chore at hand. He felt bad enough without watching the light of optimism grow bleak in Rae's eyes. For two weeks now, ever since the store's grand opening, they had been waiting for their so-called friends to bring some business their way. After all, those had been the very people who had encouraged the idea of a *brother* competing against the other grocery store in town. So far, though, less than a handful had dared let their dollars back up all the backslapping and amen-ing he and Rae got in church. But worse than watching his life savings being thrown out along with the dead or dying produce and meat, what Luther hated most was watching what failure was doing to his wife's spirit.

Except for his mother, he had never met a woman with more faith and perseverance than Racine Johnson Cobb. And even though he was three years her senior—and there'd been times when that seemed like thirty—he supposed he had always been drawn to her. But it hadn't been until after he'd graduated from high school and found a job working at the lumberyard that he began to make plans regarding the popular and bright Rae.

For another full year he kept an eye on her. He brooded that she might take up with someone else, someone who hadn't needed to repeat the third and fifth grades. Later he worried her mother would move

Rae and her sister to Tupelo or Jackson—something the woman always threatened whenever money got too tight. Not until the end of Rae's senior year had Luther decided he couldn't bear to wait any longer.

One afternoon he'd made certain he would be the one available to load ninety-four-pound bags of concrete onto Bum Poag's pickup truck. The school bells had sounded, but for the longest while there hadn't been a sign of Rae among the young people wandering by.

Luther had worked slowly, prolonging the job for as long as he could, until storm clouds came out of nowhere and thunder rumbled. That's when Mr. Hughes himself had come out to warn him that he would beat his black ass if that concrete got wet. But Luther barely paid him any mind because as he carried the last sack balanced on his shoulder, Rae had appeared.

She'd strolled down the sidewalk with a girlfriend, laughing and hugging her books to the full round breasts that had been keeping him hard and harried for what seemed an eternity. When she pretended not to be aware of him, he tossed the bag onto the truck and dismissed Bum with a wave that earned him a one-finger salute in reply. But Luther hadn't cared because he soon learned from the whispering and giggling going on behind him that Rae was as conscious of him as he was of her.

That weekend her mother finally allowed her to go on a date with him, and that Saturday night he and Rae just about destroyed what was left of the shocks on his old pickup truck playing slap and tickle. Two

weeks after her graduation, lovesick and hornier than
a brand-new parolee, he'd made her his wife.

Eighteen years and four sons later he was still crazy
about the woman, but he knew if he failed her in this
venture, it would finally kill something between them.
Always sensitive to how well she had done in school,
and of how she'd once dreamed of a business career
somewhere far off like Atlanta or Dallas, he was painfully aware that she deserved better than what he had
managed to provide. At the least, she didn't need to
be putting in twelve-hour days here, then another four
to six keeping their home, as she did now.

He straightened to relieve the ache in his lower
back—the only reward for his own long days at the
store, then keeping the farm going—and once again
told himself he must have been out of his mind to let
Eve Maitland push him into opening this place. He
was no businessman. He was a simple farmer, a share-
cropper no less. He didn't know how to get his no-
account friends and neighbors to come here to trade,
short of hog-tying them and dragging them over. He
was also afraid of taking any more risks. Every night
he crawled into bed bone-assed tired and wondering
if this would be the night he and his family got burned
alive in their home for daring the unthinkable. Every
morning he rose praying that today wouldn't be the
day when a stray bullet came through the storefront
window and killed one of them. He had been crazy,
all right. He'd shown no more sense than a lonesome
bull suddenly let loose in a pasture of willing heifers.

"Pa! Papa! Guess who I just seen at—"

"Close the goddamn door, boy!" Luther snapped
as Noah, his youngest, raced through the beam of

sunlight spearing into the store. The boy's bare feet squeaked as he braked to a stop on the scrubbed and waxed wood. "You think this is a dinin' room for flies or somethin'?"

"Luther," Rae whispered. "Don't be cussing in front of the child."

"Yeah, well, just 'cuz this stuff is rottin' here, don't mean every bug in Parish is invited to a free meal on me."

Noah retraced his steps and shoved the door so hard the bell his mother had fastened at the top nearly ripped from its bright red ribbon. Oblivious, he once again charged toward them. At six he was a small child who'd inherited his mother's gentle eyes, her subtly rounded build and her upbeat disposition. But Luther knew that even for Noah, this much jumping could mean only one thing.

"What's got you all wound up, son?" Rae asked, as though knowing Luther wouldn't.

As always, Luther had to admire the way she spoke to the boy. She never slipped up, never let her fatigue or annoyances get the best of her—and this was the child she'd once hoped would be a daughter.

"I seen him. I seen Ben!"

Luther jerked to attention and pointed the water-hose nozzle at him. "That's *Mr.* Rader to you."

"That's right, dear," Rae added more kindly. "It's not polite for young people to call their elders by their Christian names. And the correct phrasing is 'saw.' 'I *saw* him. I saw Mr. Rader.'"

"It's Chief now, Mama. And you know what? They gave him a badge and a gun!"

"Can't be no cop without one." But as sarcastic

as Luther tried to sound, he had to wonder how Ben had felt holding the weapon that had ended his father's life. It had to be the same one; this town was too cheap, let alone poor, to have dished out the dollars for a new one.

"He only put on the badge," Noah replied, thrusting out his small chest. "I seen—*saw* him put the gun in his truck. And you know what else, Pa? He's way bigger than in those pictures you and Mama got."

"Imagine he's shavin' more regular, too," Luther mumbled, unable to completely repress a smile. For a moment he allowed himself to remember old times, the childhood that had been far more carefree than adulthood ever would be, though he'd been poorer than he was today. Simplicity, that was the key, the lesson he seemed unable to learn.

"How come you didn' wanna go watch, Papa?"

Luther scowled at the rubber band that snapped from his rough handling. "You finish your chores like I told you?"

"I'm fixin' to do 'em. But how come—"

"Do them now!"

As soon as he began reaching under his apron to unbuckle his belt, Noah's eyes widened with alarm and he scampered toward the back of the store. Only when Luther turned back to the cart did he see the dismay and reproach in his wife's eyes.

"Did that make you feel better?"

He grimaced. His insides always burned like sandpaper on a raw wound when she used that tone on him. "Don't start with me, woman."

"Don't you call me woman. We're equal partners

in this, Luther Cobb, and I have a right to my say. What's more, the boy asked a legitimate question."

Legitimate. Lord, the words his wife used. "You know damn well why I stayed here. What *was* ain't got no bearin' on what is. Today they made Ben Rader the law 'round here, and the way I see it, that makes him a whole different person. A person I don't know no more."

"Don't bother giving him the benefit of the doubt."

The bell in the back sounded, signaling a delivery he already knew he couldn't afford. "You're the one with all the hope and dreams in this family, Rae." He threw the hose on top of the box of greens and stalked toward the storage room. At the doorway he glanced back at her. "Me, all I got is a dead brother and a business that's about to go belly up. I ain't got time to give no white man nothin'."

2

"Child, what I tell you about workin' in the sun, especially when the heat's this bad?"

Eve Maitland stopped weeding the flower bed and sat back on her heels to watch the sturdily built woman who had burst from the house and was marching across the veranda as though leading an infantry charge. "Well, it was only a matter of time," she said under her breath.

No doubt about it, their two-week break had come to an end. But it was good to see the speed with which Mama Lulu was moving, even though sunlight highlighted the increase of gray in her bunned hair and emphasized her crow's-feet and laugh lines. The sexagenarian was apparently back to operating at full throttle.

As she stomped down the stairs and the hem of her cotton print dress lifted, Eve caught a glimpse of knee-high stockings and almost grinned. But spotting the hell-and-brimstone in the woman's dark eyes, she cleared her throat instead and set her hand cultivator on top of the basket beside her.

"How far off was I?" she asked the teenager sprawled a yard or so away.

Papers rustled as Justin Maitland twisted his arm

to inspect his watch. "Ten fifty-three. She's a good half hour earlier than what you expected."

"She must have decided to tackle Bree's room before straightening yours or mine and spotted us from the window." Eve hadn't considered the possibility of that.

With a philosophical shrug, she brushed her hands together and began pulling off her gardening gloves. "I know what you told me, Mama Lulu," she called back to the scowling woman. "But these petunias are going to get as leggy as ivy vines if they're not pinched back, and the weeds are ready to overtake the beds again."

"Plenty folk available t'pinch petunias and yank them weeds." The older woman shook a wide-brimmed straw hat at her as she scolded. In her other hand was a tall frosted glass of iced tea. When she reached her quarry, she thrust the hat at Eve, her zealot's eyes daring a refusal. "If I told you once I told you a dozen times, skin like yours'll freckle if you ain't careful. Why you wanna let the sun bleach that pretty red hair for anyways?"

Eve did her best to repress an appreciative chuckle. Freckles and sun-bleached hair were the least of their housekeeper's concerns, although after thirty-five years of running the Maitland household, Lulu May Cobb did have some fixed ideas about the proper behavior for the people in her care, and none of them included seeing the lady of the house on her knees like some field hand. But Eve knew that wasn't really what had Mama Lulu's blood stirred.

As Lulu shook the hat at her like some voodoo priestess about to burst into a chant, Eve accepted it and put it on. Nevertheless, it did little to appease the disapproving woman.

"Guess you think your days ain't full enough between overseein' the businesses and all." She shook her head, her moon face as shiny as it was exasperated. "I swear, it is one of the Lord's better-kept secrets why he gave so much drive to some folk and nothin' to others."

Certain Mama Lulu wasn't looking for a response, Eve pretended to suddenly notice a missed wilted blossom and pinched it off. One of the most valuable lessons she'd learned in the eighteen months since coming to Maitland Hall was discerning that if Mama Lulu wanted insight into why things were the way they were, the housekeeper would turn to her well-used Bible for an answer. From Eve she wanted cooperation.

As the older woman had pointed out to her on more than one occasion, Eve knew her slender build wasn't unlike that of the first Mrs. Maitland, who had expended most of her energy giving birth to the twins, only to spend the final eight years of her life in bed, "Waitin' for gentle Jesus to carry her home," as Lulu put it ad nauseam. Despite frequent reassurances, Eve had yet to convince Mama Lulu that she was made of tougher stuff, or that Jesus had more important things to concern Himself with than chauffeuring *her* to an early paradise.

She also knew it wasn't affection, magnanimity or even professional pride that made their housekeeper hover over her as though protecting the last heir to a throne—although Eve had to admit they were getting along better than either of them had initially expected.

No, Mama Lulu's motivation was based on nothing more virtuous, and nothing less preoccupying, than all-out fear.

Enlightenment hadn't come quickly or easily; however, Eve had come to the conclusion that the otherwise feisty housekeeper lived in a perpetual state of dread, fearing that one day she would find herself the last authority figure left at Maitland Hall. Better to spend the rest of her life on arthritic knees scrubbing the kitchen floor with a toothbrush, or to go back to washing clothes with a scrub board, than to have to deal with Miss Gabrielle Marcine Maitland by herself. That prospect carried about as much appeal as living long enough for a front-row seat to Armageddon. And, Eve concluded, it was shades of that private terror that had the wily character riled now, not the gardening or the sun.

So what had Bree done? Eve wondered, scratching at an itch under her chin with the back of her hand. Apparently, a few weeks was the girl's limit for staying out of trouble, despite being asked to respect this dear soul's vulnerable state of mind over the loss of her youngest son.

Still clucking over Eve's flushed cheeks, Mama Lulu held the glass of tea with the same insistence that she had held the hat. "Go on, take it."

The tea looked photograph-perfect in the perspiring julep glass with its chipped ice and a sprig of mint from Mama Lulu's own pampered herb garden. Nevertheless, Eve shook her head. "You know I don't like that stuff. Give it to Justin."

They had been around and around the subject of iced tea before, and it remained the one concession

Eve refused to grant. Memories of times when nourishment and warmth were luxuries prompted her to prefer her tea hot and strong, even in the heat of summer.

"Crazy Yankee," their majordomo muttered, although she did hand the glass to the boy. But when she saw the twinkle in the teenager's clear blue eyes, she narrowed her own. "What's so funny?"

No doubt about it, Mama Lulu had discovered something objectionable in Bree's room. Maybe it was some crust from the cherry pie that had disappeared mysteriously from the kitchen a few days ago, Eve mused, or some half-eaten chicken legs. Heaven help her stepdaughter if it was something worse.

After receiving word about Lem, Eve had drawn both Justin and his twin aside to explain that during this difficult time, they should try to make things as easy as possible for the woman who had served the family for so long. Of course, Bree's idea of consideration followed a unique logic.

Instead of showing up on time for dinner, she was missing meals entirely. When she finally did come home, she would steal into the kitchen, snatch something from the refrigerator and dash off to the sanctuary of her bedroom. Rarely did she finish what she took, and she never made an effort to return the remains or dirty dishes to the kitchen.

Eve shot Justin a speaking glance. The look agreed that they needed to try to avoid antagonizing Mama Lulu any more than she already was, otherwise there would be muttering going on in the house for the rest of the day, not to mention slamming doors, windows and anything else the woman decided to fixate on in

retaliation. Adding injury to censure, they would all
suffer as some of their least favorite recipes appeared
on the dinner table. A true egalitarian when riled,
Mama Lulu could be as generous at sharing her displeasure as Bree could be inventive at exhibiting hers.

"I'm about through here," Eve said, to draw the
woman's attention away from Justin. She beamed at
Mama Lulu, who pulled a plain cotton hankie from
between her heaving breasts and began fanning herself with it. "Why don't you sit down for a minute
and join us?" She nodded, indicating the white
wrought-iron bench encircling the nearest magnolia
tree. "Justin's been sketching me while I've been
working. You can tell me if I'm likely to get a swollen head or not."

"You're giving me too much credit," Justin told
her, ducking his head. "I still haven't got it—you—
right yet."

"Well, what you waitin' for?" Mama Lulu muttered, crossing strong arms under her massive bosom.

"It's her fault. She's too animated to get down on
paper easily."

"Excuses. That's the one thing you and your sister
got in common besides blood." But her expression
betrayed her affection for the boy. "If your stepmama
says you's good, that be that, hear? Leastways, let me
think somethin' good 'bout you while I'm scrubbin'
my fingers raw tryin' to get them grass stains outta
that shirt."

Justin bolted upright and grimaced when he saw
the blotch of green on his left elbow. "Damn...sorry,
Mama Lulu. I thought I'd rolled up the sleeves
enough."

"You gonna be lots sorrier if I hear any more cussin', young man. And speakin' o' sorry, where'd that no-account sister of yours? I found another broke plate in her trash basket. Them dishes made it through two generations of Maitlands just fine, but the way she's workin' through 'em, y'all gonna be eatin' outta one pot by Christmas."

Eve watched Justin pay particular attention to the sprig of mint in his glass and wondered how two people could look so much alike and yet be so different. Barely checking the impulse to reach out and brush his baby-fine hair from his forehead, she thought again of how when Mama Lulu was on a tirade, she often accused him and his sister of being two of a kind, but nothing could be further from the truth.

As identical twins, brother and sister had inherited the same fair coloring from their mother, Marcine, as well as her fine-boned features; so much so as to make them appear like angels in their sleep. But awake, even Eve—with a reservoir of personal and professional experience to season her—was occasionally left shaking her head over the contrasts between the siblings.

Granted, Justin had his weaknesses; for instance, when it came to making excuses for Bree, he could be nothing short of exasperating, especially since his sister rarely paid him back in kind. And despite romantic good looks, he wasn't the most confident individual Eve had ever met, thanks to years of bullying and browbeating by his father.

At the same time, her stepson was one of the most considerate, introspective people she knew, intrinsically kind, and possessing a truly gentle soul. Eve ached for him, and worried about the trouble and heartbreak she knew that kind of sensitivity could bring.

As for Bree…she sighed at the mere thought of the girl. Bree had inherited all of the piss and vinegar in the family. At least that's how Sumner used to put it. It took only days living under the same roof with her stepdaughter for Eve to conclude that the description came as close to being accurate as anyone was apt to get. However, there were times when even that seemed a conservative summation of Bree's character.

"Justin was still in the shower when I heard her go out the front door," she told Mama Lulu on behalf of her stepson. She knew that since their recent graduation, Bree had grown increasingly restless, and that restlessness was creating an ever-widening chasm between brother and sister. Justin would resist doing or saying anything to add to the situation.

Mama Lulu snorted. "Fine. Ain't my china. Only, nobody better say I don't keep a clean house!"

"No one would think of suggesting that."

"You will if she keeps on sneakin' half the kitchen up to her room. Might as well put up a rent sign in the yard for all the roaches and mice that'll be linin' up on the front walk here. And every one'll have their hands out and their mouths open."

Eve almost laughed at the image. "All right, I hear you. I'll talk to her when she—" The sound of an approaching vehicle stopped her. Just as the others did, she looked down their curved driveway lined with pecan trees. A chest-high azalea hedge made it difficult to identify visitors unless you were on the second-floor balcony, but she already knew it couldn't be Bree. She couldn't hear that recognizable mixture of sounds—roaring acceleration and blaring music—which usually heralded her stepdaughter's departures and arrivals. But when the unfamiliar blue-and-white Blazer came into view, she remained at a loss.

"Justin?"

"Beats me."

"Lord, bless my soul." Mama Lulu pressed a hand to her bosom as the truck came to a halt before the front walkway. An incredulous smile lit her dark face. But as quickly as it came, the smile turned into a scowl. "Wait a minute...what's that girl doin' in there with him?"

Eve had spotted Bree, too; however, well experienced with the girl's talent for showing up where least expected, or desired, she decided it would be less wearing to simply wait for an explanation than to speculate. What interested her more was finding out who had the ability to temporarily remove the grief that had been shadowing Lulu May Cobb's eyes.

Rising, Eve pulled off her hat.

She'd used the word *hard* before to describe men; Sumner, for one, hadn't been a teddy bear, even in his most congenial moments. Yet the word took on a stronger, more elemental meaning with this man.

The stranger was well over six feet and stood taller in his boots. For the most part, he had a body like the men who worked for the area timber companies, except that his hips were trimmer, his belly flatter. Impressive, Eve thought, eyeing his badge, and a bit disturbing.

As sunlight reflected off the metal, she ran through a mental list of the law officers who had attended

Sumner's funeral. No, he hadn't been one of them. Her years at the hospital keeping patients straight in her mind had made her competent at recalling names, and even better at remembering faces. That left her with only one other possibility: he had to be the man everyone in Parish was whispering about. As she struggled to remember his name, Mama Lulu stretched out her arms and rushed forward.

"Ben."

Ben Rader. Yes, that was it. So, here was the man taking over Harry Wheeler's job. Now she had a hint as to what all the fuss had been for.

He smiled—at least that's what Eve decided to call the subtle shifting of that wide compressed mouth— and, removing his sunglasses, tucked them into the breast pocket bearing the badge before stepping into Mama Lulu's embrace.

"It's been a long time," he said.

"Too long. My, it's good to have you home."

Intrigued, Eve stepped closer. Although his hat covered part of his face and cast the rest in shadow, she could see enough to tell he had the kind of sharp features that drew the eye, the kind of face women would be attracted to. She wouldn't go so far as to call him good-looking, but an artist would love him as a subject. What was the word she was looking for...? Dramatic. That didn't quite capture it, but she would bet his eyes were compelling. No matter what their color, they would be flinty.

Mama Lulu murmured something Eve couldn't hear and laid her hand against the lawman's cheek. He replied just as quietly, then turned his head and pressed a kiss into her palm.

Eve found her breath hitching in her throat. How tender—and completely incongruous to expectation. Here his looks suggested a temperament altogether too explosive to be on the right side of the law, yet he was exhibiting an affection more in keeping with someone of Justin's disposition.

"If I'd heard about Lem sooner," he said in a more conversational tone of voice.

Mama Lulu nodded. "You don't have to tell me what I already know. Oh, Ben." She sobbed softly. "He made his mistakes, but he was my boy. I already gave two husbands to the earth, but my baby... What they're sayin' about him ain't so. This wasn't no accident. No, sir."

"I promise you, I'm going to do my best to find out what really happened."

She touched his badge. "I heard you was takin' Chief Wheeler's place, but I didn't dare believe it. Now I can see with my own eyes."

"Got sworn in less than an hour ago," Ben replied, one corner of his mouth dipping again. "No doubt there'll be a few noses bent out of shape over the news."

Mama Lulu answered that with an imperious toss of her head. "Most of the gossips in this town are the people who got the least right to talk. You don't pay them no mind, hear? Aw...let me look at you." She pushed him to arm's length and eyed him from top to bottom. "My...you're your daddy all over again."

"That's not saying much, considering how he ended up."

"Ben!" Lulu cast a distressed look over her shoulder and spotted Eve. "Bless me, but my manners are slidin'! Come meet the lady of the house."

Eve tried to be discreet as she brushed her palm against her thigh before extending her hand. "Chief Rader."

"Mrs. Maitland."

Finally getting to meet Benjamin Tyrell Rader's gaze reminded her of the time her hair dryer shorted out and the cord began to melt and smoke near the plug. She'd grabbed at it instinctively, only to earn herself a nasty jolt and a painful burn for her stupidity. If her subconscious was trying to warn her that too much contact with Chief Ben Rader would be equally foolish and hurtful, she didn't need the reminder. She was female enough to acknowledge an interesting man when she saw one, and wise enough to let it end there.

It did please her to know she was right about his eyes, though. They were compelling, a dark brown that was almost the color of pitch or—if it had a color—sin. Flinty, to be sure. When they made a slow survey of her face and moved downward, she felt a warmth permeate her body that would have been pleasant if it wasn't so laughable. After all, it was hardly a look to waste on a size-six woman covered from throat to thigh in a man's size sixteen-long dress shirt and rumpled jeans that all but hid what other few curves she possessed.

Don't forget the wagging tongues in town.

She hoped she wouldn't have to straighten him out on a few things. After having spent too much time since Sumner's death convincing the male population of this and neighboring counties that the "Widow

Maitland'' wasn't looking for, and wasn't even mildly interested in, a husband, lover or any combination thereof, she had neither the time, nor cared to waste the energy, going through all of that nonsense again with him.

"If you think this getup is something," she told him dryly, "you should stop by when I help Mama Lulu sort things out in the chicken house."

"That might be a sight to see."

Withdrawing her hand from his firm grasp, Eve glanced around him to consider her stepdaughter, who was leaning against the truck and suggestively caressing the Blazer's chrome trim. Eve wondered how much of Bree's conversation with Ben Rader had been about her.

"I hope there hasn't been any trouble?" she said, frowning.

"Relax." Bree sauntered over to them. "You're not going to have to write a check to keep me out of jail or anything." She smiled up at Ben. "Eve's developed quite a reputation for being generous—with everyone, that is, except her late husband's children."

For a moment Eve fantasized about shaking the girl until Bree's pretty blond hair resembled the mop on a troll doll. Not a good sign. That made twice this month alone that the kid had triggered such a ground-zero instinct in her—and Bree was supposed to be behaving herself. "Maybe you'd better hold off on the theatrics, dear. We don't want to shatter any lingering illusions Chief Rader may have about the family on his first day back. Instead, why don't you tell us where you've left your car this time, and do we need to call for a wrecker?"

"Very funny. It's down the road and only out of gas. Wasn't it sweet of Ben to offer me a lift home?" Bree rose on tiptoe and gave him a lingering kiss on the cheek. "Thanks again...for everything."

She made a graceful pirouette, her hair fanning out around her and stroking his arm in the process. When she reached her brother, she paused only long enough to lift the glass of tea out of his hands before continuing up the sidewalk and steps.

Mama Lulu placed her hands on her ample hips and muttered under her breath even after the screen door closed behind the girl. Eve exchanged looks with Justin and rolled her eyes. By the time she turned back to Ben Rader, he was wiping lipstick off his cheek. The pained expression on his face had her wanting to like the man despite what her instincts were telling her.

"Be glad she wasn't wearing the industrial-strength she usually uses," she told him. To Mama Lulu she added, "Don't you think the chief looks as if he could use something to wash away the ah, dust?"

"Good idea." The older woman lifted thick eyebrows at Ben. "Beer? Tea?"

He rubbed his jaw, his look wry. "Since I'm not really on duty yet, I wouldn't turn down a beer. Thanks."

"I'll fetch it," Mama Lulu said, heading toward the house. "Y'all come out of the sun and set a spell. Eve, honey, how about a nice cool glass of my lemonade?"

"Why not."

Once Mama Lulu shuffled out of hearing distance,

Ben eyed Eve with greater curiosity. "I get the strongest feeling you would prefer a beer, too."

"Probably because it's true."

"Then why didn't you say so? You're not striking me as the kind of woman to pull any punches."

"I'm glad you noticed." She gestured toward the porch with a sweep of her hat, inviting him to accompany her. "However, I'm also not in the mood to do ten minutes on how it isn't proper for a lady, specifically *the* lady of Maitland Hall to be indulging in alcoholic beverages at this unseemly hour. You've been away from Parish for some time, but I'm sure you still remember how Mama Lulu feels about appearances. Most of all, though," she added after his guttural agreement, "I'm trying to set a good example for the kids, since I asked them to go easy on her for a while."

They walked side by side, their shadows leading the way. Eve found it a relief that hers managed to look far more casual than she felt. But their shadows also reinforced her awareness of the differences in their size. Above average height to begin with, high heels would put her on eye level or better with most of the men in the area. It was unusual to find someone she would have to look up to without them. But Ben Rader did more than that; he made her feel something even Sumner with his acerbic wit and combustible temper had never achieved, although he'd tested her as hard as anyone could try. *That* she could do without.

She needed something else to focus on and was grateful Justin hadn't followed Bree inside. She paused and slipped an arm around the teenager's waist. "Do you remember my stepson, Chief Rader? He's newly graduated, with honors, from Parish High." She beamed her encouragement to the boy, who, in response, bowed his head and began fidgeting with his pad and pencils.

"I remember," Ben Rader said, extending his hand. "Justin."

"Sir."

There was no missing the sudden tension in the boy, and Eve mentally kicked herself for instigating the moment. Dominant men always sent Justin into retreat, and if she'd kept her wits about her, she would have remained sensitive to that.

His condition was one that had begun years before her arrival in Parish. Being born the son of an autocratic, demanding father had played the key role in its development, but she didn't discount the high-school athletic coaches who'd believed a boy wasn't normal if he wasn't sports-crazy. As a result, Justin had been exposed to ridicule and persecution as the males around him had attempted to change his mind. Eve hated the posturing and brainwashing that she'd noticed from day one, and her deepest regret was that she hadn't arrived sooner to help the boy.

She gave him a reassuring pat on his back, and then released him, to continue the rest of the way up the stairs to the pristine, pillared veranda. But her thoughts were anything but sublime....

Sumner, be grateful you're where you are and that I didn't know then half of what I do now.

The shade provided by the wide porch helped soothe her bristling temper. This was one of her favorite places, exactly what she'd envisioned when she first listened to Sumner describe home as he lay in his hospital bed waxing nostalgic about the house and the land that made up Maitland Hall. As traditional, the veranda circled the entire house and was adorned by great pots of plants, most of them flowering.

Eve tossed her hat onto the rattan couch and sat down on one of the matching chairs grouped around a glass-topped table. After only a slight hesitation, Ben Rader cautiously lowered himself onto the next flowery cushion.

As she expected, Justin held back. His gaze skittered from their guest to her. "I guess I'll go put this away," he said. As he gestured to his work, he made sidesteps to the screen door, not unlike an anxious softshell crab wanting the protection of the deep sea.

Eve didn't try to stop him, but as the door banged shut behind him, she wished Mama Lulu would surprise her and add a generous splash of vodka to that lemonade.

"You'll find I tend to have that effect on people."

"No," she murmured, still mostly lost in thought. "It's not you."

But no sooner were the words out than one of the three cats that freeloaded Mama Lulu's kitchen scraps awoke from a nap on the railing. Rather than wander over to Eve for some stroking, as the calico normally did, she arched her back and hissed at him, then spun around and scurried down the steps.

Now Ben Rader won her full attention.

She lifted an eyebrow. "Then again, maybe I shouldn't jump to conclusions."

"I told you so."

"My, you sound pleased."

He crossed one leg in male fashion. "Intimidation has its usefulness. But it's not going to work as easily on you, is it?"

His choice of positions put unusual stress on a certain area of his jeans—for more reasons than one. Although her mouth went dry, she managed a smile for the double entendre. "You're continuing to impress me with your perceptiveness, Chief Rader."

"I don't think either of us tends to miss much, Mrs. Maitland." He glanced around. "So, how does Parish compare to— That was a Chicago hospital where Sumner's specialist was located, right? The one where you two met and...fell in love?"

Even though Eve knew the instant his gaze swung back to her, she forced herself to continue her own slow scan of the landscape. She needed the extra time to tame her inner turbulence.

Sumner had enjoyed playing mind games with people, too; and while she hadn't been fond of that predilection, she had indulged him, since his condition left him with damned few options for entertainment. Most of the time the incidents were harmless. When pain began to give his humor a brutal edge, she would simply make sure the venom was directed anywhere but at his children. She'd recognized it as nothing more than a dying man's attempt to prove that while his body had been decaying, his mind had still been virile.

In comparison, Ben Rader was the picture of health. To Eve, that sharply reduced his right to toy with someone's feelings, or to maneuver for psychological one-upmanship.

"I think we're both fully aware of how the Maitland estate compares to what's beyond its property lines,'' she replied, nodding toward the unseen borders.

The first time she'd stood on this veranda and looked out at the dew lingering on the front lawn, the sun filtering through the trees, she had compared the manicured utopia to what she used to look at from the one-room apartment she'd lived in before. Although no longer impoverished herself, she'd continued to be surrounded with it because of where she'd worked, and so she'd dealt with a view of an interstate highway, where cars raced by as if intent on escaping the ugliness of urban decay and strife. On the basketball court below her apartment, more drugs were sold than hoops shot—and there had always been a game in progress on that slab of asphalt. Yes, the contrasts between her past and present were profound, as stark as those between Maitland Hall and any number of shacks and decrepit cabins in the area.

''It's always nice to live on the right side of the fence.''

Eve eyed her fingernails that were somewhat dirty despite the gloves, then the slender gold band she still wore on her left ring finger. It was far less than what Sumner had offered. ''You have to know, don't you? You're unable to get a handle on the woman who married a man more than twenty years her senior and dying of cancer, and you want to insist I fit the shallow conclusions you've already drawn.''

''In order to do my job, I need to know who the people are in this town. That includes its wealthiest and most powerful woman. Nothing more, nothing less.''

Right. "Then let me make it easy for you," Eve drawled, lifting her gaze to his. "There was no pretense of love between Sumner and I when I accepted his proposal. Eventually, however, I did come to feel genuine fondness for him—not that I expect you to believe that, nor do I care.

"I married him because he needed someone. Badly. He was going to die. He needed someone who could stomach that and who would stay on afterward for Bree and Justin's sake. He wanted a person emotionally stable, someone strong enough to put up with the son of a bitch that he could be at times. He figured only a person like that could ensure that everything he'd achieved didn't get chipped away by attorneys or smooth operators after he was gone."

"And after only a few weeks in the hospital, he could tell you were the right girl for the job?"

Eve didn't miss a beat. "I have my own effect on people."

"Touché, Mrs. Maitland."

"You might as well call me Eve. I can tell I'm going to call you several things besides Chief Rader."

His laugh was brief, but it lingered in his eyes. "I don't doubt you will...Eve."

"Good. Now that we have that out of the way, why don't you tell me what else is on your mind." When he lifted both of his eyebrows, she shrugged. "As considerate as it was to stop by and offer your condolences to Mama Lulu, I suspect there are other reasons for you being here, otherwise you'd be inside with her. Or gone."

"It could be that I remember what a great cook Mama Lulu is—and that it's almost time for lunch."

"No, you're fishing...and I have no patience with people who aren't direct, or worse yet, try to deceive me. So out with it. Why are you sitting there wasting your time with not-so-subtle small talk?"

"Two reasons," he replied smoothly. "First, I want to ask if you'll rent me my old house down the road leading to the lake. I understand you own it now. And second...I wanted to see for myself if you're capable of committing murder."

3

Silence spread between them like a blight, and yet unlike anything so debilitating, the very air reverberated with energy. As Ben watched shock blossom in Eve Maitland's cheeks and anger blaze in her unusual, smoke-green eyes, he wondered how deeply she would make him regret having opened his mouth.

He'd surprised himself. Granted, he needed to get to know her as well as he did anyone who'd had contact with Lem or his family, but that wasn't what this was about. This was about cracking her gutsy control and confidence, and knocking her off balance. Not because he'd been told she was the type who could put a man in his place and he wanted her to know he liked it fine where he was. No, this was about not wanting to settle for polite dialogue or having only a portion of her attention. For some reason, he wanted to look into those bewitching eyes and know they saw only him.

A very interesting phenomenon.

Very nuts.

He needed to snap out of it, but no matter what happened next, he wouldn't completely regret having caused the fire he felt simmering inside Eve now. How could he, when he found himself approving of the results so much? She had been too pale, never mind that she was a natural redhead; and to hell with the stereotypical consensus on southern magnolias' complexions. Nobody over the age of five deserved skin like Eve Hudson Maitland's. He'd been caught staring more than once, and worse, losing the battle about wondering if she was that perfect all over. Heaven help him, she stirred strange memories. No, one memory. His first trip to New Orleans....

He had been all of eighteen. What an exercise in hormonal indiscretion that had been. It was the weekend he'd experienced his first hard-liquor drunk, got laid by his first prostitute and survived his first knife fight. It had also been the first time his wayward Baptist butt had crossed the threshold of a Catholic church. The images came so sharply, he could still taste the musty flavor of the place, feel some divine melancholia that had reached for him from the dark corners. It had seeped through him like blood soaking linen, permeating his spiritual dissatisfaction. He'd stood in that tomb-quiet cathedral before a life-size sculpture of the Virgin Mary and relived in blinding flashes those twenty-four hours of sheer primitive indulgence.

Until he'd discovered his T-shirt was wet with his own sweat and tears.

Until the face of the woman he'd used to purge his disappointment and frustration, and that of the Virgin's, had been one and the same.

Until, shaken to his core, he had run out of the church faster than he had ever run for any high-school football coach.

For hours afterward he had wandered aimlessly. To

this day he didn't know how he'd ended up in front of the Marine Corps recruiting office. Dazed and almost relieved, he'd walked in, and less than two months later he had reported to boot camp.

"Exactly what do you think you're doing?"

Ben forced his mind back to the present and the woman glaring at him. Her blush had deepened to a persimmon pink, and the shade clashed with her fiery hair and brought the dry reminder that, enviable complexion aside, she probably wasn't any closer to being a saint than he was.

But what exactly was she? So far he had sought only a handful of opinions; just enough to figure out that there would be plenty more, and that the community would be splintered. Folks were firmly entrenched in their various judgments that ran the gamut from adoration, awe and bewilderment, to suspiciousness, resentment and dislike. Except for Bree's evasiveness a short while ago, he had yet to fail at getting at least one definite viewpoint regarding the mistress of Maitland Hall.

"Having a smoke," he finally replied, reaching into his shirt pocket. To his chagrin the package almost squashed flat between his fingers. He counted by touch, determining he was down to his last…three. Since the day was young, this was not good news.

"You know perfectly well what I mean."

"Answer my questions and I might tell you."

"Question. A singular inquiry from my perspective, which can only have one response, considering the rest of what you said. In fact, if it wasn't for my regard for Mama Lulu, all you would get at this point would be an invitation to take your arrogant behind off this property."

Ben lit the cigarette, wishing Mama Lulu would make tracks bringing that beer. The feisty Mrs. Maitland about had him reduced to feeling as dry as a thirsty tick trying to feed on week-old roadkill.

He exhaled a long breath. "Do you ever answer a simple yes or no to anything?"

"Not to a question like that! Do you seriously think I'm capable of murder?"

He wasn't about to go into what he was *seriously* thinking.

She must have seen the amusement in his eyes because her own narrowed with new annoyance. "You provoked me just to see how I would react!"

"Are you going to deny it took your mind off your other problems?"

"If you think I'm going to thank you for that—" She frowned. "Wait a minute. You agree with us. You don't think Lem's death *was* an accident, either!"

"Keep your voice down." Ben glanced toward the screen door. Besides not wanting Mama Lulu to hear, he had no idea who else might be within earshot. "Let's say I believe that varmint trap would have seriously injured Lem, but he shouldn't have drowned in any six inches of water, unless he had help."

"And it's your plan to go from door to door until you insult someone into a confession?"

There went that mouth again. No wonder young Bree was all bent out of shape; the girl had real competition in her stepmama—and in all the ways that mattered to a young female. "Whatever it takes."

"I don't think I like your method of investigation, Chief Rader."

"You'll get used to it." He decided her eyes were the shade of Spanish moss, or a pine shrouded in morning mist, and Ben found himself torn between wanting to learn the secrets in their mysterious depths, and finding out whether her mouth would taste as tart as her words. "So are you going to rent me the cabin or not?"

"What cabin?" Mama Lulu demanded, easing the screen door open with her well-cushioned backside.

She carried their drinks on a gleaming silver tray, and its ornateness reminded Ben of another reason why he couldn't let his imagination get the better of him. Rising, he relieved Mama Lulu of her load. "The old homestead." He set the tray on the glass-topped table, aware of and amused by Eve's intent scrutiny. No doubt she was wondering at a redneck jerk showing consideration for another human being, especially a colored servant. "I just told your boss lady that I want to rent it."

The housekeeper exchanged glances with her employer. "Ben, that ain't no place for you. There be too much sadness there."

"I'm not going to be put off by a few ghosts, Mama Lulu."

"Well, you should be—and by the mice and rats, too. In case you forgot, we got some bigger'n 'coons. And the hands say squirrels got in through them broke windows and have been tearin' up everythin' the kids ain't. The place is a mess, I tell you."

"So I'll clean it up." He took her hand and led her to the chair he'd been sitting in. Not caring whether

Eve would approve or not, he gently urged the woman who had been like a foster mother to him to sit, then hunched down beside her. "Listen to me. That cabin's only a few hundred yards away from where Lem died. I haven't been here long enough to get out to the site yet, but I don't doubt the area's been pretty well trampled and picked over by now. I don't hold out much hope that it'll prove helpful to my investigation. What might, though, is staying close. Maybe something will come up that will give me a clue as to why he was there that night."

"I think what Mama Lulu has been trying to avoid telling you," Eve said almost as gently, "is that I'm having the cottage torn down soon."

The announcement came like a kick in the belly, sharp and stunning. Ben reached for the beer. Ignoring the glass Mama Lulu had provided as a courtesy, he raised the bottle to his lips, closing his eyes against Eve Maitland's canny inspection. He didn't want to share his feelings, especially not with a woman who was spawning too many contradictory emotions inside him.

Tearing down the old homestead. He hadn't thought of the possibility; nevertheless, he should have once he'd heard it was now Maitland property. Besides, the place hadn't been any monument to architectural brilliance even when he and his father had lived in it. The roof had leaked in heavy downpours, and the doors and windows were draftier than a picket fence in a January blizzard, no matter how often he and the old man had caulked them. Still, it was difficult to accept the idea of the cabin no longer existing. It was as foreign as...

Losing one's parent?

Ben drank deeply, emptying half the bottle before recovering enough to speak. "Never thought you'd get the Lotts to sell." Sumner had been worse than a bird dog on a fresh scent about trying to get their previous landlords to give up the tiny acreage, simply because it stood between Maitland and Ashworth property and the families lived for those opportunities of one-upmanship. "But why tear down the cabin?"

"The Junior League refused to put it on their spring tour of homes," Eve drawled. "Haven't you been listening?"

"I was born in that house."

"A sixteen-year-old girl died from a drug overdose in that house."

A hummingbird zipped past Ben's head. It might as well have been a bullet between his eyes. Stunned, he managed to shift onto the chair beside Mama Lulu.

"That's one bit of information someone forgot to pass on."

"So I see." Eve's gaze never left his face. "In that case, you'd better know something else. The outside world has found Parish, Mississippi. I won't go as far as to suggest we have a drug epidemic, but the availability and usage is here. There are also rumors of something more complicated going on, but nothing's been proven and no one's dared to point fingers."

"Who was the girl?" Ben asked, remembering the laughter and contentment that had filled those four walls back in the days when there had been just him, his father and Blue, his Labrador-rottweiler pup.

"Cassy Ann Wheats."

"Sonny Wheats's girl?"

"His eldest."

Ben thought of the youngster he'd known, who used to accompany her father to town in the dilapidated truck that had coughed and wheezed like a chain-smoker in the final stages of emphysema. Although her face remained a blur, he could remember that she had been a chubby child with unevenly cut, yellow-white hair. Painfully shy, she'd hidden behind her father's huge overalls whenever someone spoke to her.

"The kids have been using the house as a love nest for ages," Eve said, reaching for her lemonade. "I'm told it's not only the remoteness that makes it appealing to them, but supposedly the girls are turned on by the idea of lying on the same beds Cole and Ben Rader slept in."

Ben shot Mama Lulu an apologetic look. Because he'd hung around her kids so much, she knew better than most that the acorn hadn't fallen far from the tree where he and his father were concerned. But considering what she'd been through lately, she didn't need to be reminded of things like that.

"What are your plans for the land?" he asked not all that politely, to let Eve know what he thought of her timing. "More cotton, or maybe a catfish tank in the hopes that people will forget the Raders ever lived there?"

"Trees." Eve reached for a napkin to soak up the moisture quickly building around her ice-packed glass. "It's my understanding that before the cabin was built, this entire area was dense forest. I want to replant a portion of it. I'm concerned that Perry Ashworth may cut down more of his woods for additional pasture. If he does, we'll have to look hard to spot a tree between here and town. That doesn't strike me as entirely wise, either, since we're also in tornado country.''

"Perry?" Ben didn't hide his smirk. "Since when did he hang around Bellemere long enough to give a damn one way or another?"

Eve exchanged a perplexed look with Mama Lulu. "Since Vail died."

Good God. "Vail Ashworth's dead?"

"It happened Christmas '95 just after Sumner's cancer was diagnosed. I wasn't here, of course, but I understand it was a terrible accident. Vail, as you might recall, shared Sumner's fondness for cigars. The authorities believe he set one down the night he was in the stables checking on one of his mares that had been about to foal. He must have forgotten about it, or maybe it fell, who knows. In any case, the hay caught fire. Perry thinks he must have been knocked unconscious as he was trying to get the horses out. He and a number of them died in the blaze."

Ben couldn't believe it. He also couldn't imagine Perry Ashworth running Bellemere! That weasel Fred Varnell—what else had he kept mum about?

He crushed out his cigarette in the large crystal ashtray. "Well, I guess I'm out of luck then."

"Don't be in such a hurry." Mama Lulu turned to Eve. "How about the ol' foreman's place?"

"That's practically at our back porch!" Eve sputtered.

"You got a whole orchard between here and there. Besides, it has its own gate. I think you should take him over and show him."

"Mama Lulu, really—"

"Pay the dust no mind, hear?" the housekeeper said to Ben. "I'll have it all cleaned up in no time."

Ben set his bottle on the tray and waited for Eve to respond. He was game if she was. He had to stay somewhere, and the location was now ideal for more reasons than one. Eve wasn't allowing herself to see. "Look at it this way," he told her quietly. "My presence in the area could keep what happened from happening again."

Mama Lulu uttered a sound of distress and leaned over and covered Eve's hand with her own. "Two weeks ago you told me if there was anythin' you could do, I only had to ask. Well, I'm askin'."

The sound of a vehicle engine had Bree scrambling off her bed and hurrying to the window. When she spotted her stepmother getting in on the passenger side of Ben's Blazer, her grip on the lace drapes threatened to tear them. "Where does she think she's going? Justin, come look. Eve's going off with him!"

They'd been talking, and now he left his post at the doorway. But by the time he joined her, the truck was already pulling away.

"They're probably going to get your car," he said.

"Then why's Ben cutting a U-turn and driving around back?"

"*Ben?* You sure have your nerve."

"Is there any other way to get what you want?"

"He's practically a stranger, and old enough to be your father."

"Barely. And so what? I like mature men."

"You like anything in pants."

With the truck about out of sight, Bree crossed her arms and leaned back against the window frame. "Look who's suddenly brave. I didn't hear you saying anything about age when Daddy married Eve."

"That was different. More of a business thing. They didn't get married to—"

His embarrassed pause had her bursting into laughter. "Screw?" she drawled.

Justin's face turned an angry red, but Bree doubted he would explode, as she might if their situations were reversed. For all that they shared genetically, he didn't have her passionate nature or innate curiosity about life.

"You really are turning into a first-class vulgarian, Bree."

She snorted at his archaic phrasing. "Well, pardon me, m'lord, but that's what you meant, and Daddy always said you should call a spade a spade. What's more, how do you know he and Eve never did it?"

"You know I don't, but they slept in separate rooms, didn't they?"

"Big deal. There was a connecting door."

"That was only so Eve wouldn't disturb us in case there was a medical emergency in the middle of the night."

His chin was beginning to jut slightly. Like hers it was accented by their father's infamous notch, and she drew her index finger along it and crooned, "Yeah, like if Daddy was suffering from a massive hard-on."

He brushed her hand away. "You're disgusting, and I'm not going to listen to any more."

Stone-faced, he started for the door. Bree followed

as far as the first bedpost, and used it as a ballast while swinging herself back and forth. "Poor baby, why are you always panicking at the first mention of sex? C'mon, Justin, stay! I think it's precious that you're still a virgin."

He spun around. "Who said I was?"

She tilted back her head, enjoying the feel of her hair brushing across her shoulders. Advertising experts might be saying that visuals were the stimuli of the decade, but she found touch the most erotic. "Me. Good grief, who knows you better? Why, you barely get near a girl and you break out in a cold sweat."

"That doesn't mean anything. And even if it did, there's nothing wrong with waiting f-for the right person."

Hearing the faint stutter had Bree grinning even more. He almost had that cured, but every once in a while she had the most irresistible urge to see if she could make him do it as easily as their father could. "Uh-huh. You know what your problem is? You were born two hundred years too late. Get real, kiddo. Do you think Daddy saved himself for Mother? I happen to know he wasn't fifteen when he did it for the first time, and you know who with? Bitsy Jean Carstairs."

"Lorna Carstairs's mother? You're full of it."

"He told me himself." She giggled at his expression, which went from incredulous to disgusted. "Okay, so I was curious and asked. But he didn't mind talking about it. He said she wasn't always as fat as she is now. He called her 'voluptuously nubile.'"

"You're making that up, and that proves how disturbed you are."

"If I am, then so are you, twin dear," she called after him as he continued across the hallway and into his own room. When he didn't respond, she hurried after him. "Listen, Justin, I'm only trying to help. If you don't do something soon, all those repressed hormones of yours are going to really start affecting your brain. Why don't you let me help?"

"Leave me alone!"

Bree chased him across the hall, catching his door before he could slam it shut. Of course, she knew she could always unlock it if he did—a skill she'd taught herself ages ago, but didn't want him to know about any sooner than necessary.

She pushed with all her might, until he relented and let the door swing wide. It struck the inside wall and she stumbled into the middle of the room before finding her balance again. Justin raked his hands through his collar-length hair and retreated to the far side of his immaculate room, looking more hunted than angry with her.

"Listen to me." Bree spoke in a loud whisper, in case Mama Lulu had heard the loud noise and came to investigate. "I could fix you up with someone. Someone who's really interested in you."

"Who?"

As she'd always suspected, everyone had their vanities. "Marcy Varnell. She says she used to get wet just watching you practice with the school tennis team."

This, she thought, had to flatter him. Besides being almost a year older than them, Mayor Varnell's only daughter was attractive enough for her to consider the girl the only real competition in the county. But instead of seeming intrigued or grateful, her brother reacted with outrage.

"You have the filthiest mouth— If you want to act like a slut and socialize with them, go ahead. But stop assuming that everyone else wants to live down on your level!"

Bree set her hands on her hips, but only because she liked the pose. "Fine, but don't cry to me when people start wondering if maybe it's not girls you're into."

"Get out."

"Hey, it's not as if I care. I'm open-minded enough to accept you, even if you turn out to be gay."

For a moment it looked as if Justin might come after her. But to her disappointment, he relaxed his clenched hands and folded them across his chest. "Do you know what I think?" he said, his tone speculative. "This isn't really about me. You're simply bored and looking for something else to focus on because you're worried that Eve's won yet another round."

"What on earth are you talking about?" She managed to keep her cocky grin, but as with everything else, her brother was about to cease being a source of entertainment for her.

"First Daddy fell for her, and then Perry Ashworth?"

Bree toed the navy blue throw rug behind Justin's orderly desk. God, what a neatnik, she fumed. Not even the damned fringe was rumpled. "Daddy never lost his head over any woman. He used them just as he did all of his assets. And there's nothing between her and Perry."

"Maybe not as far as she's concerned, but from what I've seen and heard he'd like there to be. Then—" he stepped closer "—not minutes after you *introduce* Chief Rader to your charms, he drives off with her?"

Bree shoved his leather desk chair at him. "Stuff it, Justin. Perry's like me, he enjoys flirting, but it's all in good fun." And that was the problem, Bree thought, a wave of misery washing over her; no matter how she tried, she couldn't get Perry to take her seriously. She hated the possibility that she might be wasting her time trying. Not after waiting all these years.

"Maybe you're right," Justin said, catching the chair and rolling it back to where it belonged. "But Chief Rader doesn't strike me as being cut from the same superficial mold. He seems the type to be pretty direct…and he seemed pretty direct about the way he was looking at Eve."

"Asshole."

"Just stay out of my business and I'll stay out of yours."

"Ooh…my nail polish is chipping, I'm shaking so hard," she taunted, wiggling her fingers at him. But when he came at her, she did back up.

He pushed her the last step into the hall and slammed the door in her face. As she listened to the lock turning, Bree smirked, then returned to her room.

"Sanctimonious runt," she muttered.

How dare he finish ruining her day. And what if he was right? Could Ben Rader be interested in Eve?

Damn, what was so special about that skinny pain in the butt anyway? Here she'd had the most delicious brainstorm for how to finally make Perry jealous, too.

"It's not fair!" she cried, throwing herself across her bed. Nothing was fair. First her father, then Lem... "Oh, why did you have to go be stupid when I need you more than ever?"

Eve continued to bristle even as Ben Rader's truck rounded the peach orchard, and the increasing heat only made it worse. Not even the visual reminder that this year's crop had escaped a late-spring freeze and was promising to be the best in ages was doing anything to soothe her. All she could focus on was that she'd been manipulated—for a good reason, of course—but *managed* nonetheless. And now she was going to have Chief Ben Rader hanging around like an unsettling precognition.

"I should warn you there'll be no air-conditioning," she said, determined not to let him get to her again. "Our present foreman, Dewitt Nellis, came to us with his own trailer and parks it up by the barns. I gave him the window air conditioner for his office."

"No problem. I prefer fresh air to recycled anyway."

He turned onto the narrower path forking to the right before she could give him directions, and it irked that despite his long absence, he probably knew the property as well as she did.

"That might be difficult," she replied, "since the screens on the windows aren't in the best shape."

"Next you'll be telling me the indoor plumbing no longer works and offer me Sumner's bedpan."

She was beginning to think the tenderness he'd exhibited to Mama Lulu had been an optical illusion. "Give me a few more hours and I think I could learn to despise you," she said with a serene smile.

"That long? I must be losing my touch."

Eve focused on the white two-bedroom cottage ahead. It looked like a misplaced appendage of the big house with its black shutters framing the two front windows and the four posts along the long porch. Although no building on Maitland land was allowed to get overly neglected, this one seemed particularly barren and lonely because it had remained unused for some time. The lack of greenery didn't help. On several occasions she'd made a mental note to look into planting some shrubs out front, maybe some rosebushes, but now she was perversely pleased that she hadn't gotten around to it. If he was determined to inflict himself on them, she wouldn't make him any more comfortable here than necessity dictated.

God, you're being a bitch. The man's here to help!

Disgusted with herself almost more than she was annoyed with him, she was out of the truck before Ben shut down the engine. Heading straight to the front door, she reached for the key on top of the frame. Not the best hiding spot, but then this was private property and well monitored. Besides, there wasn't anything worth stealing in the—

Where the devil is the key?

As she slid her hand along the narrow board, Ben appeared beside her and began a search from the other end. He found the key and handed it over, only to reach around her and grab hold of the screen door.

"Pardon me," he murmured, his breath a hot caress against her cheek.

All she would have to do is turn her head slightly to the right, and their lips would have touched. Unable to deny she was curious to know how that would feel and hoping he hadn't noticed how she'd all but stopped breathing, she quickly unlocked the door.

Darkness, heat and dreadful stale air greeted them. It brought back memories of too many nights when she had walked up the grimy, poorly lit stairs of her apartment building after her shift at the hospital, never knowing if she would make it safely or not. Not the most pleasant of memories.

Intent on putting those thoughts and her awareness in their proper places, she dived into an inane monologue, pointing out the obvious: living room, kitchen, dining nook, bathroom, bedrooms. Although furnished, the pieces were third- or fourth-hand and covered with enough dust to write a novel, let alone a bit of fun like, "Clean me!"

"As I said, it's not much." She slipped her hands into her pockets to keep from drawing a trail of animal footprints on the dining table, a habit she'd acquired entertaining the kids in the children's ward. "Hardly what you can be looking for."

"But you don't know what I'm looking for."

Suggestive words, echoed by a glint in his dark eyes. She wondered if he flirted with all females, and how he could do it now at such a serious time. "Obviously I don't." Nor, she told him with her eyes, would she give him the satisfaction of asking.

He smiled. "How much?"

She considered naming a ridiculous figure, an amount that would guarantee him going elsewhere; however, that had been Sumner's way, and one she disapproved of. He had charged people appalling amounts for the simplest things, and since his death—to the dismay of the family accountant—she often tried to make amends for that by asking too little. Would her conscience allow her the moral back-sliding to do an abrupt reversal?

She hedged. "What do you think is fair?"

The figure he named was too high, and she knew he'd done it on purpose. But why? To test her, or was he that serious about his need to be here? Her gaze fell on a cracked window that she hadn't noticed before and her decision was made. So much for her career as a highway robber.

Naming a figure that was half of what he'd offered, she added, "If you're convinced this is what you want?"

"It's nothing close to what I want. But it'll do. For now."

She'd endured less innuendo at hospital Christmas parties. Determined to clear her head with sunlight and fresh air, she gestured toward the door. "We can go back to the house and draw up a formal lease. I have some forms that—"

"A handshake will do."

He stepped closer, his hand extended. She eyed it with as much pleasure as she would a cottonmouth; but knowing there was no way to avoid this, she gave him her hand.

Strong fingers closed around hers, and the contact

made her extreme⋯ ⋯
tween her breasts, o⋯ ⋯ sweat trickling be-
bra, and that her camisole w⋯ ⋯ was wearing no
from Sumner on their wedding nigh⋯ Sheer. A gift
request to watch her put it on. ⋯owed by a

The beginning of a very unorthodox relationship.

What did Ben Rader ask from his women?

"You have great eyes. Very expressive," he murmured. "But if you keep looking at me that way, we're going to have a huge problem."

She pulled her hand free. "If that's everything, you'll have to excuse me. I have a great deal of work to see to."

"Eve."

She told herself that she had to retrace her steps from the door anyway to hand over the key she'd forgotten to give him, that he'd won nothing from her. But it felt like a surrender anyway.

"What I was trying to say is that I feel it, too. And I'm tempted as hell to see how far it goes. But I don't need the complications any more than you do. If you'll keep your distance, I'll keep mine."

She slapped the key into his palm. "Do that."

She was already on the porch when he called after her to wait for him. "I'll drive you back!"

"No thanks! I've already been taken for one ride too many today."

She was acutely aware of his gaze following her as she made her way up the dirt road, and she cursed him for making her feel as if she were walking in someone else's shoes. But she swore at herself more for acting like a just-hatched chick.

She notice . . . the road several paces ahead,
and still ma . . . red her favorite vulgarity and wished
laugh, she . . . stumble into it. Hearing his low
Ben Rade . . . the longest case of impotence in history.

4

Ben's laugh ended on a soft, "Well, hell."

He'd found himself a place to stay, all right, but at what cost? He'd upset Lady Eve to where she now wanted his balls on a platter, young Bree just wanted them, while the rest of Parish expected him to prove they were made of pure twenty-four–karat gold and yet tungsten steel-strong. He couldn't have created a bigger mess for himself if he'd volunteered to be a human guinea pig at a college science lab.

Shaking his head, he returned to his truck to retrieve his things and carried them into the left bedroom, the larger of the two. The heat was most oppressive back here, which convinced him he'd better drive back into town and hunt down some kind of fan if he planned on getting any sleep tonight. Even sleeping buck-assed naked, as he usually did, would fail to provide any relief in this sauna. Bad enough the smell of the place suggested dust and mold spores were hard at work creating a new life-form.

Mama Lulu couldn't get here too soon. But when she came, she would use the opportunity to talk more about Lem, ask about the reports he'd taken from the station to read later tonight, grill him for information he didn't have yet and probably wouldn't share with her if he did. Deciding it would be kinder to make himself unavailable, just as it would be easier on her not to have to navigate around him, he left his bags by the bedroom closet and headed back to the sports utility truck.

As he drove out the gate behind his new home, he reminded himself of another few reasons to return to town. He needed to see about getting a police radio for the truck, and a phone for the house. But most of all, he had a few more people to see before the sun set on this first day back.

A crow could fly from Maitland Hall to Bellemere in two or three minutes. Driving took closer to five and he spent the time steeling himself to deal with Perry instead of Vail. Any way he looked at it, their reunion would be strained. If only he could picture the guy as more than the smug jerk he remembered from high school. It would be easier to dial 1-900-PSYCHIC and ask them what had happened to Lem.

Although two years his junior, back in school Perry had been called Mr. Slick, and he'd always had his choice of girls regardless of their ages. His scene had been tennis, not football, basketball or even baseball; and the girls had added insult to injury by gushing how on him even sweat looked classy. Ben and the rest of the football jocks knew the closest Ashworth ever came to really sweating was when one of the guys on the team threatened to feed him his black convertible piece by piece after the prick had made a play for the tackler's girl.

Back then, Ashworth had been the only kid in the state who drove without having qualified for a hardship permit. Ben would gripe on and on because his old man never hauled Perry's butt into jail or impounded the car. He just wrote Slick one ticket after another, all of which Vail paid without complaint. Not until Ben saw the badly needed new patrol car that extra revenue paid for did he understand his father's logic. The city council alternately headed by Sumner, then Vail, were always squeezing the last penny out of every community-budgeted dollar. Chief Rader had quietly, methodically, shown them what they could do with their miserliness that somehow never extended to their own life-styles. He even paid for the personal license plate reading Perry out of his own pocket.

Thereafter, Ben's own approach toward dealing with politicians and businessmen would always reflect that lesson.

He pulled into Bellemere's photogenic driveway, aware of the bad taste the past still left in his mouth. Wishing he'd kept his mind on business and had interrogated Eve a bit more about her neighbor, he parked between the house and front pasture. Not quite as large as the Maitland mansion, the Victorian two-story made up for that with more ornamentation, elaborate gardens and an incredible bronze stallion that rose on two legs to swipe at the air and anyone approaching the front steps.

Like Maitland Hall, Bellemere was one of the dwindling number of working plantations around, enhanced by miles of freshly painted fence corralling the dozens of Thoroughbred horses that ran on lush green pastures and slept in stables that would be a paradise for the street people he'd come across in Jackson, as well as for some Parish residents residing in the shacks between here and town. It was clear that at least on the outside the estate continued to be run with discipline and competence. He never would have believed Perry Ashworth had it in him.

A movement to the right of the house caught his attention. He didn't recognize the man who had come out of the nearest stable and was approaching him. Lean and sun-bronzed, and wearing a refined what-the-hell-do-you-want look, the guy could have been mistaken as any farm laborer by an inexperienced observer. But Ben took note of the man's immaculate denim shirt and jeans, the expensive snakeskin band on his straw hat that matched his boots, and concluded he was more likely the foreman or a friend. An in-law perhaps? No one had said anything about Perry getting hitched.

"Help you?" the man asked as Ben came around the vehicle and stopped before him.

"I'm looking for Perry Ashworth."

"He's not here."

The man had a drawl, but it wasn't the Mississippi variety. It was harsher and had a twang to it.

"Do you expect him back soon?"

"Maybe." The stranger's gaze zeroed in on the badge. "You Rader?"

"That's right. Who are you?"

"Blanchard. Foreman."

And a man of few words. Ben thought of apple-cheeked Swede who used to run the place for Vail. Gregarious and considered a near magician for his way with horses, Swede used to carve small boats out of the trees felled in Bellemere's woods and launch them in the lake for the local kids to find. Times had obviously changed, and not necessarily for the better.

Ben matched the man's prolonged stare. "You're not from around here."

"So?"

"Just an observation. I'm making the rounds, introducing myself to all the large property owners inside the city limits."

The man's thin lips didn't alter their sullen slant as he scanned the pastures on three sides of them. "Some city. Reckon this won't compare anywhere close to Jackson."

In other words, the news about his return had reached here, too. No wonder Perry wasn't around. Ben took some satisfaction in the idea that Ashworth might be reluctant to face him again.

The pleasant idea lasted all of seconds, until he heard the sound of hooves pounding the thick turf. Turning, he saw a horse and rider take the five-foot board fence separating one pasture from the next. Complementing the grace and power of the white stallion, the rider showed enviable form as he leaned low and forward on his mount. Having never been on anything more spirited than the Cobbs' old plow horses, Ben had to give credit where it was due.

Perry Ashworth brought up the stallion and grinned down at Ben. White teeth challenged the brightness of his dress shirt and riding breeches. Add a hat and coat, Ben mused, and the S.O.B. could have posed for one of the ancestral paintings said to line the stairs of the great house. Knowing Perry, there was probably already one of himself up there.

"Well, well. You always said you'd get that badge,

Rader. I suppose that ends the bet as to whether you were full of it or not.''

"I hope you lost a small fortune."

Perry laughed softly. "Only to myself. To what do I owe...this pleasure? Since we were never buddies, I have a feeling this isn't a social call."

"Nevertheless, we need to talk." Ben didn't see a reason to say more before the foreman, and purposely ignored the man. "Is now a good time?"

After a slight hesitation, Perry dismounted and without a word handed his employee the reins. The two were of similar height and build, except Perry moved with a smoothness and precision matched only by his horse.

With a grim parting look toward Ben, Blanchard led away the stallion.

"I was only kidding, you know," Perry said, stripping off his gloves. "I really didn't doubt you'd come back. There always was something of the fatalist in you."

"You know why I'm here."

"Yes, well...that was a shame about Lem." Perry bowed his head, the sun highlighting the blond streaks in his brown hair. "I gave him work whenever I could, but he was one lazy son of a gun. Not nearly as industrious as the rest of the family."

True enough. "What was he doing behind your place the night he died?"

"Copulating with turtles, what do I know? He had my permission to move around the place, even when he wasn't on the payroll. He fished harder than he worked, that's for sure. I assume he was doing that."

But there was no mention of any fishing equipment

in the reports Ben had glanced at thus far. "Do you authorize the use of varmint traps?"

"No...and may it please the court, the one that tagged him wasn't exactly on my land. Could we be sure to note that?"

"Touchy, touchy. It was close enough to justify asking. He was also wearing only one shoe when he was found. Any of your people come across the other one *on* or *near* your property?"

"It rained several times since then. Parts of those bottoms become like quicksand after a while."

"Are you saying that no one found anything?"

Perry uttered a sound of exasperation and spread his arms wide. "I didn't know he'd lost the damned shoe until you said so. And do you have any idea how overgrown it is down there? Of course you don't. You're just back and haven't seen squat, so let me enlighten you. It would take a dozer a week to break a path through the vines and wild brush alone."

"The coroner cited evidence of scratches and cuts—on the parts of him that the turtles hadn't begun chewing on."

Perry screwed his aristocratic face into a grimace. With his hair swept back from his straight, clean forehead, he looked like a character out of F. Scott Fitzgerald's *The Great Gatsby*. Remembering the required reading in high school, Ben thought again how he'd come away from the experience having no more use for Fitzgerald than he did for Ashworth.

"Thank you so much for thinking I wanted to hear that," Perry drawled. "Listen, pal, if you want to play Sherlock Holmes over an accidental drowning, you do it on your own time with your own people. I don't care if your reports say he had the tattoo of one of my horse's hooves on his ass, I'm not wasting my men or my money on the damned shoe of a guy too dumb to watch where he was going. Hell, what's the point?''

Ben almost told him, but he suspected Perry already knew the other theory buzzing around town, and decided it would be more entertaining, and maybe even fruitful, if the rumor became like a burr under Ashworth's skin. He intended to do the same thing with Dewitt Nellis and everyone at Maitland Hall, too, until something shook loose somewhere. But right now it was Perry's reaction that interested him. It wasn't like Slick to show this much agitation.

''What happened to the money-is-no-object guy who used to flash twenty-dollar bills at the girls so they would go through the cafeteria line for him?''

The smile curving Perry's well-defined mouth didn't warm the chill out of his blue-gray eyes. ''I did ultimately learn one or two things from my daddy. I no longer pay for what I can get for free.''

In other words, he'd gone from being an arrogant prick to a cruel and self-serving one. Ben wasn't surprised. ''Well, your philosophy sure failed you regarding the Lott property. I hear the Maitlands finally got the place.''

''For the moment.'' The indifferent shrug followed like a comma. ''I prefer to see that as a temporary situation.''

That piqued Ben's curiosity, as well. ''Not unless the not-so-friendly war between the Maitlands and Ashworths is history.''

''Let's put it this way,'' Perry replied smoothly,

"the viscosity in the venom between the Maitlands and Ashworths has undergone a refreshing change. Have you met the Widow Maitland, by chance?" Before Ben could reply, Perry chuckled. "Ah, I can see you have. She is a piece of work, our Eve. Has Parish completely rattled. The old-timers haven't shown this much moral outrage since Grant finally outmaneuvered us at Vicksburg."

"You're damned cheerful about it."

"That's because I haven't lost my boyish sense of humor—or my appreciation for a beautiful woman."

Ben didn't welcome the tightening in his belly. Careful to keep his expression impassive, he refocused on Bellemere's foreman over by the stables. "Since we're on the subject of bullshit, who's Blanchard?"

"A valued employee."

"That I can tell by the creases in his jeans. I mean where is he from?"

"Texas."

"Huntsville Penitentiary?"

Perry wagged a glove at him. "Play nice, Ben. I'm willing to let bygones be bygones, why can't you?"

"Probably because it feels right to leave things the way they were." He nodded toward the woods behind and to the left of the house. "Keep your people out of there until I tell you otherwise. I'll be looking around."

"Should I ask for a warrant before you trespass?"

"If you insist, I'll get you one. But if you put me through the trouble, it will allow me to search every inch of Bellemere if I choose. Your call."

"As much as I'm enjoying this reunion, I'm not

sure I'd like to have you underfoot that much. All right, then. Do what you think you must—the new broom sweeping clean and all that," Perry drawled. "The question is who are you out to impress? Our illustrious mayor? He occasionally makes an attempt at being a leader, but more and more he hides in that bottomless flask of vodka he hides from Mrs. Varnell. The rest of the city council? The faces have changed somewhat since Sumner and my father ran things, but basically they're still a jaundiced bunch who'll never do more than flap their mouths, unless there's an opportunity to stick a knife in someone's back."

"It's reassuring to know the democratic process continues to thrive in Parish," Ben replied, not about to answer Perry's question. Besides, the answer wasn't as clear to him as it had been two weeks ago. About to leave, he thought of something else. "It was a shock to hear what happened to Vail."

"The old fool. It needn't have happened." Perry slapped his gloves against his thigh, and then offered Ben a melancholy smile. "You'll find much has changed, Ben."

"That's what everyone keeps telling me."

"So where are you going to hole up? I own a few rent-houses in town. I could—"

"I'm at the Maitlands'."

The suggestive phrasing, although not intentional, earned him a startled look.

"Are you? It would seem Eve's sympathy for Mama Lulu knows no bounds." Once again he slapped the gloves against his leg. "And quite a step up from what you're used to. No wonder you're walking around like the only stallion in a pasture full of mares and geldings.''

Ben was enjoying himself too much to correct him. "Worried, Slick?''

A vein pulsated near Perry's right eye. "I told you things had changed. I don't believe you grasped that one of those changes is my relationship with the Maitlands, thanks to the arrival of Eve. She may be spirited and occasionally willful, but in the right hands, she would be quite the asset.''

"Hell, you sound as if you're planning to breed her to one of your own horses," Ben muttered in disgust.

"No. To me.''

"And what does she think about that?" Ben asked, against his better judgment.

"We haven't discussed it. But Eve's a pragmatic woman. She did, after all, marry Sumner.''

"Which set her up for life. Why give away all that money, let alone the control?''

Perry tugged at an earlobe, his expression wry. "That's an indelicate question, Benjamin. For all her spirit and passion, try to remember she is a lady.''

He'd heard enough. "If she wants you, it's no skin off my nose. Just make sure your people stay out of my way, and I'll stay out of yours.''

"When put like that, I do see how we might actually get along this time around.''

If he wanted to believe that, Ben would let him. All he cared about was answers, and he would get them no matter what it took.

"Luther, please. Eat your sandwich, hon. You can't keep working around the clock the way you do without putting something in your stomach. You'll get sick.''

It was almost two o'clock in the afternoon, and Luther did feel as if there was a deep pit growing in his stomach. But he knew that if he ate at this point, a half hour later his insides would be on fire. It brought him less grief to stay hungry.

''In a minute, baby,'' he told Rae, his head deep in the wire bread racks. ''I gotta check the dates on these burger buns. I think that son of a weasel Clooney cheated me again and left some of the out-of-date stuff.''

''Mr. Clooney must be in Greenville by now. Knowing this minute if he did or didn't gyp us isn't going to change anything.'' When he made no response, Rae set her hands on her hips and sighed with exasperation. ''At least get off your feet for a while. I'm about to start the paperwork at the front counter, so I'll watch the register.''

''Ain't anything in it to watch,'' Luther muttered, fully aware of how little they'd taken in so far today. That was the real reason his mood had gone from bad to worse.

''That's an ungrateful thing to say. Mrs. Yates and Mrs. Jacks both rang up nice orders today.''

The hamburger buns were okay, but the hot-dog buns were borderline. Luther silently cussed the deliveryman before straightening. ''Whoopee, two ol' women spending what's left of their social security checks. And in an hour the summer school kids'll be in with their dimes and quarters to buy a cold drink and candy. Look out—we're gonna need two bread sacks to carry all our money home tonight!''

Rae crossed to him and stroked his back, large, slow circles as soothing as her voice. "We didn't open the store to get rich, Luther. We opened it to give ourselves and our family more choices."

"We got choices, all right. We can choose to be a little broke now, or a lot broke later."

Rae stilled her hand and tilted her head forward to check his expression. Her large, soulful eyes caressed his face as her hand had his back. "What are you trying to say? Are you ready to quit already?"

Hearing her speak the words opened some dam inside him. "We'd lose every penny we'd invested, but we'd still be able to give back some of the loan money. A month from now would be a different story, and I don't know who'll hire me around here seeing as I was tryin' to take away business from some of 'em."

Rae shook her head. "We're not quitters, Luther. You just have to have a little more faith."

Where did she get hers? Or her naiveté for that matter? Luther hung his head, exasperated that he couldn't make her see, yet sorry that he'd almost yelled at her. "Baby, you gotta—"

The door opened and the bell sang as it danced across the glass. He and Rae jumped apart like two kids caught necking. In the next instant, Rae gasped and launched herself to the front of the store. For his part, the pit in his belly filled with a combination of anxiety and dread.

"Ben...*Ben!*" Rae rushed into Ben Rader's arms, and laughed girlishly as he swept her off her feet and planted a lusty, growling kiss on her cheek.

"Damn, you don't weigh an ounce more than when

you married that big lummox, honey. How'd you manage that and give birth to all those big strapping boys?"

"Aw, Ben. You always did know how to make me feel good. Put me down and let me look at you." Back on her feet again, Rae leaned back to beam up at him. She skimmed her rough but long-fingered hands over his cheek and chest. "You are a sight for these eyes, Mr. Chief of Police. Welcome home."

Luther didn't have to see his wife's face to know there were tears in her eyes. He could hear them turn her low, musical voice into a huskier whisper. Hell, he had a lump in his throat, too. He didn't want to feel this much, and spun away to adjust some perfectly straight cans to delay the inevitable.

"Thanks, Rae," Ben said. "The one good thing about all this is getting to see you again."

"Always the one with the smoothest line," she said with another chuckle. "But as soon as I get over being so happy to see you, I'm going to box your ears for not keeping in touch."

Although he'd tried not to look, Luther saw his old friend duck his head and grimace. That sheepish bullshit would work on Rae, but Luther had stopped being gullible years ago.

"Hell, sweetheart, I'm no letter writer."

"Uh-huh. And they don't have phones in Jackson?"

"You wouldn't have wanted to talk to me. Not for a good while. I was too angry."

"I know it. We both knew. You should have trusted that we did, and would have taken everything into consideration, Ben." Rae glanced over her shoulder. "We still understand, that's why we're glad you're back, aren't we, Luther? Luther. Stop being such a big fool and come say hello."

Might as well get it over with, Luther thought, forcing his feet down the aisle. Then his gaze slammed into Ben's, and suddenly he was a kid again, and loneliness, betrayal, disappointment, joy...they all raced through him like a dose of salts, leaving him weak. It was almost like being forced to relive every day since Ben left all over again.

"How you doin'?" he murmured to his childhood friend.

The smile Ben had kept so strong for Rae wavered, sadness filled his eyes. "Hey, Luther."

Rae looked from one of them to the other. When neither said another word or made a move, she threw up hers. "Stubborn jackasses. You two shake hands, or hug, or something, or so help me, I'll take the broom to both of you! You were best *friends!*"

He didn't know whether he made the first move or Ben did, but something cracked and yielded, and in the next instant the two of them were clutching each other's hand in a death grip. Then Ben pulled him off balance and they were hugging. Hugging and shaking...or maybe he was the only one shaking. It didn't matter anymore, he simply shut his eyes tight against the pain.

"I'm sorry, man," Ben whispered roughly. "I'm so sorry."

Luther understood. He was talking about more than Lem. He was talking about abandoning their friendship, about not being here to share in the joy when the boys were born and celebrating their various achievements, as well as to help them through the shock, confusion and grief after Lem was found. It was a lot to deal with, let alone forgive.

"You son of a bitch," he muttered, adding a rough shake to say even more. "You big, tough old—"

Ben laughed. "Nothing like the pot calling the kettle metal."

"Me? Ha. I'm a has-been. That's what bein' married and havin' a swarm of kids'll do to you."

Rae slapped at his arm, and said to Ben, "Are you hearing this? To think I could have had any man in this county and then some."

"Didn't I tell you that you were beautiful but blind?" he asked her. But he seemed relieved to have something to laugh about. "It's good to see you both, though."

Luther took a deep breath to settle the remaining butterflies in his belly. "You, too. Guess you been out to see Mama?"

"About an hour ago. She looks good...all things considered."

"Women are stronger than men in those ways," Rae said. "We have to be. But Lem's death broke something in her, Ben. She tries not to let it show, but I see it. So does Eve. Did you get a chance to meet Mrs. Maitland?"

"Can anyone in this town have a conversation for more than three minutes without mentioning her?" He slipped off his hat and raked his hand through his hair. "Even Sumner had to work a lifetime to achieve that kind of impact."

Rae chuckled and sent Luther a pleased look. He

didn't know what she was looking so happy about; it wasn't as though Ben had complimented the woman.

"You hang around long enough," he told Ben, "you'll answer your own questions. This—" he indicated the store with a toss of his head "—is 'cuz of her. Talk about wearin' a silk glove and carryin' a cattle prod."

"That sounds like her."

"Oh, you two!" Rae took hold of their arms and pointed them toward the back room. "She didn't suggest anything you hadn't been daydreaming about yourself, Luther Cobb."

"Ain't denyin' it. But that's why they're called daydreams. You ain't supposed to take 'em serious, 'cuz you know they're over your head and don't work out."

"They sure won't with that kind of attitude."

Luther strode away. Halfway through the curtained doorway, he braked and glared over his shoulder. "Excuse me for worryin' about my family and their future."

"You're frustrated and disappointed, not worried. People haven't thrown their money at you in droves and you're feeling cheated." Rae appealed to Ben. "Talk to him. Tell him that he's having a male panic attack."

As expected, Ben balked. "Hey, don't drag me into this. I have enough troubles of my own without making myself a target in the middle of yours."

Luther saw his wife's expression go from amused to sympathetic. Before she could start on Ben the way she coddled and loved on the boys and him, he signaled his friend to follow him. "Come on. Rae'll watch the store while we talk. You still like your coffee to talk back at you? Well, you're in luck. We drink lots of that kind these days. Sometimes, it's the only way to stay awake.''

"You don't have plans for dinner, do you, Ben?" Rae called after them. "Say no, because you have to come out to the house and see the boys."

As expected, Ben made excuses, but Luther wouldn't stand for any, either. "You might as well come. Rae's got it in her mind to show you off and there ain't gonna be no peace for any of us till she gets her way. Besides, if you don't come, I'm gonna get accused of chasin' you off."

Ben sat there surrounded by boxes of unpacked peas and tomato sauce, beans and rice, beans and beans. A strong smell of rotting potatoes and overripe onions competed with ammonia-based cleaners. Luther tried to see the place from his friend's perspective and it wasn't reassuring.

"You'd have every right," Ben told him. "I know I haven't been a good friend, leaving as fast as I did that last time and staying out of touch for as long as I have...."

"You're back now, ain't you?"

For a moment they stood there looking at each other. So much remained between them, it would have been easy to slide into the prolonged silence of strangers; and yet the flood of memories continued filtering through, refusing to free them completely.

Ben must have felt the tie, too, because he relaxed and nodded. "Okay. I'd like to come out. But you'll have to let me bring the beer. Does Moe Mobley still sell booze out of the back of his feed store?"

"More'n ever now that he don't have Mr. Sumner to pay off." Luther motioned to the Formica table and chairs they'd brought from the house, and went to pour their coffee. "But you better let me pick it up, since you're not supposed to know about it."

Ben's laugh was low, but rich with appreciation. "You're right. I'll leave you the money. Well, I guess that's one business venture going on in this town that Mrs. Maitland won't poke her nose into."

"Are you kiddin'? Moe said one night he was lockin' up and here she comes casual as you please tappin' him on the shoulder. Didn't waste one minute gettin' to the point, either. She told him that if he promised her he wouldn't sell to the kids, she'd let his business be. Said it was better that folks got their stuff local and stayed off the highways when they been drinkin'."

"A pragmatic woman," Ben mused.

"Say what?" Luther carried the chipped mugs to the table and sat down opposite the town's new chief of police. He liked that it didn't feel so different, after all.

"I was just remembering what Perry Ashworth said."

"Dunno about that, but she got a sense of humor. Moe asked her how much her knowin's gonna cost him, and she grew real quiet. Then she asked him what old Sumner used to charge. When he told her, Moe said she called Mr. Sumner a 'blood-suckin' polecat.' You get Moe to tell you that story and I swear tears'll be spillin' down his face before he's through, he likes it so much."

"I'll make a point to pay him a visit to the *front*

of the store real soon,'' Ben said, setting his hat on the extra chair.

Between them was the plate with a thick meat loaf and cheese sandwich on rye. Luther motioned to it. "You eat yet? Help yourself if you want."

"Good as it looks, I'll save myself for dinner. One thing I didn't forget was what a fantastic cook Rae is.'' Ben eyed his steaming coffee, looking oddly sober all of a sudden. "So why did you give me that look when I mentioned Perry Ashworth?"

Luther's smile died. He didn't want to reply, not yet. He wanted to hang on to this moment for a while longer. But there was Lem's face to deal with in his sleep…and Mama's when he was awake….

He sighed. "'Cuz Lem worked for Perry sometimes when his other stuff wasn't bringin' in much."

"What other stuff?"

Luther knew that look, dreaded it. "Shit, Ben. You're the law."

"I'm asking as your friend. You want me to walk out of here, walk those streets blind? I've been back less than a half day, Luther, and do you want to know how many surprises I've already had? Tell me now…I'll pick up my hat and get the hell out, no hard feelings…but are you or are you not going to be someone I can really talk to?"

5

There were some questions you never answered right away. You might not understand why, but you felt the weight of their importance, like those sacks of concrete he'd hauled for Bum Poag all those years ago, bearing down on you. Like the day he signed that promissory note and took Eve Maitland's money to open the store. Like the day Rae told him it was time to get Mama on account Theo was coming, and he'd run almost crying because he was excited, and scared, and feeling a failure for not being able to afford to take Rae to a hospital....

Luther had heard a saying once: If you come to a fork in the road…take it. It was a funny saying. Until it was your turn. He was at a fork, and even though it was Ben sitting there staring him down with those direct, honest eyes, he felt more like getting up and heading for the toilet than anything else.

"Shit," he said again.

"You think I don't know Lem wasn't always earning legal money?" Ben asked quietly.

Lem approved of shortcuts. He'd liked the good life, sitting in a bar and buying his buddies a round of drinks, buying his girls flashy clothes or big bottles of cologne. He liked to pull out a wad of money from his hind pocket and watch people's eyes glaze over, their mouths salivate. It didn't happen often because money was like water through a cracked cup for Lem, but he lived for those moments.

"He's gone, Luther. There's nothing I can do to him now."

"Ain't him I'm worryin' about. I'm worryin' about the guy he used to collect for—and that's just for the stuff I knew Lem was into. He didn't tell me everythin'."

Ben nodded. "So what are we talking about? Gambling? Drugs?"

"Gamblin' for sure."

"Who's the guy who's got you nervous? No, let me guess—Blanchard over at Bellemere."

Luther frowned. "Don't know much about him. He's a tough dude, all right, but he don't come into town much, and when he does, he does his business over at the bank or hardware store, maybe the feed store once in a while, but that's about it."

"But Lem was over there a lot, that's what I heard."

"Sure. Mr. Perry gave him work when he had to look legit for ol' Chief Wheeler. But the real reason Lem hung out there was 'cuz of all the guys Mr. Perry worked."

"I saw. There'd probably be a mass exodus if anyone did a green-card check."

"Work ain't easy to come by here any more than anywhere else, but people like Mr. Perry bring in folk who've had it worse yet, and who still think they're rich but are workin' for less than minimum wage. They think they got a deal, 'cuz he gives 'em a bed to sleep in, but he takes some of that pay back on room and board. Lem played both sides of all that."

"Are you saying Lem had more than a few enemies?"

Luther knew what Ben had to be thinking. "It's gonna make your job tougher, but yeah, that's exactly what I'm sayin'."

"Thanks heaps. I took one look at Blanchard and wanted to reach for my handcuffs."

"He's one scary dude. Mean eyes."

"Didn't strike me as the kind Vail would've had around. What happened to Swede?"

"Perry fired him. Said he'd cost him a good horse." Luther shrugged because information had been scarce. Swede had just vanished and that was the story given.

"Do you think Blanchard might know something about what happened to Lem?"

"*All* I know is Lem was scared of the dark. Come sundown, you'd find him in lots of places, but the woods…? Uh-uh."

"We don't know he went down there at night. He could have gone down earlier to check on some trotlines."

"Bree Maitland was one of the last people to see him, and it was at sunset when he was unloadin' a feed truck at Bellemere."

Ben straightened. "Whoa. What was she doing there?"

"Mama says the girl's in heat and has her eyes set on Mr. Perry."

"Ashworth made it clear he was after Eve. What's going on, a game of musical beds?"

No matter how much he sometimes resented listening to Eve Maitland, Luther wouldn't slander her. "Ms. Maitland's been a fine lady. Opinionated, but fair. That's all I got to say."

"Well, you've given me plenty more to chew on," Ben told him. "Guess I'd better backtrack somewhat and have a longer chat with Bree. I still want to know about the guy Lem was collecting for."

Luther shook his head.

"What's that mean? You can't or won't?"

"Never seen more than a top-dollar set of treads peeling through town. Don't even know if the dude be here for Lem, except the boy was always either happier or sadder after the car drove off." Luther leaned forward and said more quietly, "Don't say nothin' to Mama, okay?"

"Come on, Luther. She'd guessed he was no angel."

"Guessin' it and havin' the facts spread around town are two different things."

"Okay." Ben studied him several seconds. "Then tell me about how this place came to be. You never said anything about wanting to start your own business."

"Well, that was before Rae...who'd been listenin' to Eve. She said times were changin' and more folk had the right to make a profit than were. When she insisted on financin' us outright to make sure we wouldn' be left high and dry, well...we couldn't say no."

Ben looked understanding. "An offer like that would turn anyone's head. The problem comes when the rest of the community doesn't come through with their support. Is that what I sense is happening to you two?"

Luther snorted. "We're gettin' hung out to dry." Since he'd come this far, he saw no reason to stop. If anyone would understand, Ben would; he'd never seen skin color. At least he hadn't before. "I keep gettin' this feelin' nobody wants us to make it."

As expected, Ben looked troubled by the news. "Have you had problems? Been threatened?"

"Nothin' bad. But there's been looks and words said when I go 'round town. It don't help that a few church elders came with us when we went to Mayor Varnell and demanded a better investigation about Lem. Some see that as us gettin' uppity. Now the church folk are afraid they'll get in trouble tradin' here. I swear, it's gettin' so I can't sleep no more."

"I'm here now, and I promise you that I'll get this resolved."

"All I want is peace for Mama, okay? We barely saw Lem the last month of his life. Me, I lived five, ten minutes away from him, and I didn't take the time to find out how he was doin' 'cuz I was angry for him moochin' off her."

"Hindsight'll kill you, pal. Let it go. Whatever happened, he made the initial choices that triggered them. You have to accept that."

Maybe. It was the not knowing that drove Luther nuts. "Do the reports say anything? Have you read 'em yet?"

"Only glanced through some parts, and they're spare at best. This is a small town, Luther. Good investigative work costs money. It wasn't spent on

Lem. Now I'm going to have to do things the hard way. Bear with me."

"I'm scared, Ben. And I'm pissed."

"Good. Stay that way. It'll make you more observant. From now on, I want you to be an extra pair of eyes and ears for me. Except for you, Rae and Mama Lulu, I'm not sure I can trust another soul in this town—and your mother's affections for the Maitlands may be shading her opinions. Anything and everything you see and hear, no matter how inconsequential, I want to be told. Will you do that for me?"

Luther knew what he was taking on, but when he nodded, he felt lighter somehow.

"Even if someone tries to push you out of here one way or another?"

"Shoot. If business don't pick up soon, I'll lend 'em the matches myself." His smile was short-lived, though. "You gotta understand one thing. I won't risk my family. Or the farm. I gotta know Rae and the boys'll have somethin' if— Well, you know."

"I promise that I'll do everything in my power so things never get to that point," Ben said, extending his hand again.

Luther took it, gripped hard and prayed he was right.

By the time Ben left the Cobbs' farm, the sinking sun was turning delta country multi-shades of amber. On impulse, he'd stopped briefly at the station. By then the dispatcher was off duty and the small community was in the hands of Norm Friedman and Ron Scranton, the two night-shift officers; he'd wanted to see if things were going as smoothly as the dispatcher,

Dewey Pearl, had assured on the phone earlier. Finding that they seemed to be, he headed west and let his foot rest heavily on the gas pedal.

The seductive early-evening air threatened to finish what Rae's cooking and a few beers had begun. Replete with corn-breaded catfish, fried pickles, buttermilk biscuits and the various other homemade treats she'd set before them on the picnic table, he felt like the fattest of spoiled house cats. But it sure beat the grub he'd been ingesting at Jackson's various fast-food joints; and it had been a far more pleasant evening than he'd anticipated spending on his first evening back in Parish.

He rolled a toothpick over his tongue and sped past a moss-covered pond where a dilapidated dock was bowing under the weight of dozens of snowy-white egrets. The scene belonged in a coffee-table book. In fact, everything had taken on a picturesque quality so that even the line of shacks outside of town looked less desperate. It was nature's idea of cosmetics making it easier on the eyes, if not the mind. Similarly, he and Luther had reminisced tonight, but not so thoroughly as to raise any more painful memories.

The day was ending on a sigh, and he was grateful for that. Tomorrow he had some shaking up to do, maybe some butts to kick in order to get a true picture of the Parish Police Department, as well as of the town as it operated today. Manure could very possibly hit the fan by the time he was through. For the rest of tonight, however, he wanted nothing more than to smell Old Man River seeping up through the soil, trees, everything, its scent as inebriating as bourbon, as riveting as holding a cane pole between his fingers. That should finally reconcile him to being back here.

He owed Luther and Rae for his detour into nostalgia. Watching them together, seeing for himself that they continued to be nuts about each other, meeting their four sons, who were a testament to that love... Once the boys got over gawking at him as if he were another Lazarus, he'd discovered they were a lively, bright bunch. Gentle with their mother, which was always a good sign. Affectionate with their father, which didn't hurt, either. Undeniably opinionated and irreverent, he amended with a crooked grin, but a decent lot, and full of potential.

The eldest, eighteen-year-old Theo, had impressed him with his honesty. On summer break before starting his first year of college, he seemed a fine, hardworking boy. Intent on getting himself into pro football, he seemed on the right path, considering his full scholarship into Old Miss—something neither Bree nor Justin Maitland had managed. "I want to help my folks get out from under the bank's thumb," he'd said. Then, with an unabashed, devilish smile, he'd added, "And to drive down Main Street in the meanest, shiniest pickup money can buy."

Micah, seventeen, was more like Rae, bookish and thoughtful. About to start his final year at Parish High, he had given up the chance to go on a field trip to the nation's capital in order to stay home and help run the farm while his parents got the store on its feet. A tough choice, Ben thought, remembering the dreams he'd seen in the youngster's eyes; dreams of government and making a difference.

No scholar, and hardly wearing a halo, thirteen-year-old, smooth-talking Calvin had provided the big laughs of the evening with his comical monologue about ending the seventh grade without a girlfriend, as well as the pleasures he took in persecuting six-year-old Noah.

"Now *he* sounds like yours," Ben had said, ribbing Luther.

He grinned again thinking of how his childhood friend had kicked him under the table for that.

And what could be said about Noah? The pup was pure high octane. Ben could have stayed the rest of the night watching him outjive his brothers. Only concern that Luther and Rae would be dead on their feet in the morning convinced him to leave when he did, but not without telling them how glad he was to have turned down the mayor and city council's offer of a more formal celebration.

As soon as he parked beside his new home, he immediately noted signs that Mama Lulu had been busy in his absence. There were crisp white curtains framing the cleaned windows, a new straw mat lay at the front door—a strong hint to wipe his feet before traipsing on the freshly wiped-down floors, no doubt. Every room probably smelled of pine cleaner—no, herbs, he mused as an afterthought, because unless things had changed, Mama Lulu was *old* South, and that meant trying to avoid encounters with the spirit world as much as with germs. It would be like her to protect his worthless soul, as well.

Not quite ready for that attack on his olfactory sense, he glanced in the direction of the woods. The sun was well behind the trees now, almost gone, but the sky remained a bright orange and would for another half hour. Light enough for a quick walk and a glimpse of the lake.

Unconcerned with traffic, he kept to the middle of the paved road. As he'd remembered, the pavement stopped at the end of the old Maitland property line. After that, the road began a natural decline. Potholes in the hard earth were as numerous as ever. Some southerner had once called the weather down here a demigod; thinking of the violent downpours that had caused these and the innumerable ruts throughout the state, Ben figured that was as good an explanation as any.

When he spotted all that remained of the oak on his left, his heart made a little skip. The tree had been ancient when he and Luther built a tree fort in it more than twenty-five years ago. Lightning had since severed one of the great limbs, leaving it looking wounded, but more stubborn than ever.

He glanced across the road at what had been their favorite view. The best wild blackberries in the county had grown there. Now honeysuckle smothered every spare inch of earth and reached for trees the way aggressive kudzu grew out of control elsewhere in the South. Just the thought of the sweet honeysuckle flower that bloomed on and off from April to November had Ben sucking in a deep breath for a hint of the fragrance. In town, some folks burned their yards yearly to keep the vines from getting so dense that the sweet odor became narcotic.

How his memories flowed. People were right when they said time didn't stand still in Dixie, but that it didn't rush past you, either.

Things *had* changed around here. But not so much

as to make him forget to stay to the left when he came to the fork in the road. He walked a few dozen more yards and stopped. He needed a moment to let his eyes adjust to the increased darkness, although the woods here weren't quite as dense as if he'd turned right at the fork. Then he saw it.

The place was every bit the disaster Eve Maitland and Mama Lulu had warned. Although the frame of the house still looked solid enough, the screens on the small porch were mostly torn, the front door hung on one hinge and most of the windows were smashed or blown out. He could just imagine what it was like inside.

Mosquito paradise.

The graffiti bothered Ben. It covered the peeling siding, and even the posted No Trespassing signs. He had no doubt worse things were written inside. But whoever had come in the powder blue compact parked directly in front of the steps didn't seem to mind.

He'd already started across the overgrown yard when he first heard then saw two people stumble out onto the porch. They giggled and groped at each other, oblivious to everything in their avid love play. The girl was close to Bree Maitland's age, and her hair was as fair, but frizzy. Her companion was a skinny boy who slung his T-shirt around the girl's neck to bring her to him for a long, sucking kiss. Their enthusiasm threw them off balance and they almost toppled back into the house, had it not been for the girl grabbing the door frame.

Were they drunk or high on something else? The

thought that they hadn't even waited until after dark
had Ben guessing on the latter. He cleared his throat.

Lost in their youthful lust, they didn't hear him.

"Yo! Hot pants!"

The girl uttered a brief squeak and they broke apart,
only to gape at him with dazed, guilty eyes. Their
flushed faces looked pale in comparison to their
kiss-swollen mouths. The boy recovered first; whispering something to his companion, he grabbed her
hand and launched them both toward the car.

Ben could have stopped them, but he didn't want
to ruin his pleasant evening by watching the boy
sweat blood and the girl cry until her carefully applied
mascara turned into raccoon rings around her eyes. It
would serve him better to let them sound a warning
throughout the community that it wasn't safe to come
here anymore. His gift before lowering the real boom.

They raced away, the girl slouching low in her seat
and hiding her face, the boy's Adam's apple bobbing
as he gulped for air. Ben wondered if he'd looked as
goofy when he was their age and had gotten caught
in the act by one of his father's men.

Probably worse.

Hooking his thumbs into his pockets, he refocused
on the house. He didn't want to go in, not now; however, if the kids had been smoking or something, they
might have left evidence that could provide clues as
to what he was dealing with here, maybe even where
the stuff had come from. Of course, the smell alone
would probably put his dinner in jeopardy.

"That's why they're paying you a king's ransom
in salary, pal."

Uttering a one-word critique of his humor, Ben headed for the stairs.

"Blasted kids!" Eve braked hard, stopping the golf cart near the house she'd leased to Ben Rader, and glared at the car racing down the road. Those young idiots had been at it again, ignoring the signs she'd had put up warning against trespassing on private property.

So much for hoping that having the chief of police around would stop them. And where was he? She shot a disgusted look at the blue-and-white Blazer. At some point after she'd met with Dewitt about a potential infestation problem in one of the fields, Ben Rader had returned; but except for the truck, there wasn't a sign that he was around or that he'd heard the kids racing by. Mama Lulu should see this—then try to convince her again about why having the law around was such a good thing.

"Who needs him?" she muttered, turning the cart around. "I'll jerk those beds out of that dump myself and set a match to them, even if it means starting a fire that brings in every volunteer firefighter in the county!"

She drove at maximum speed, impatient with the silly machine that Sumner had bought for her after she'd drawn the line at learning how to ride. Since his death, Perry had offered to teach her more than once. But she was one ex–city girl who thought that climbing onto the back of a creature that outweighed her by nearly half a ton was not something she intended to try anytime soon.

As she pulled up to the miserable shack, the trees

and increasing darkness made it difficult to identify too many details, but she could see there wasn't any other vehicle around. That didn't necessarily mean she was alone, though. What's more, she belatedly reminded herself, no one knew she was here.

But those kids still needed to be stopped.

Although feeling a bit less brave than she did a minute ago, she turned on the cart's headlights, found a flashlight and dug around in the storage compartment for the throwaway lighter she'd confiscated from Bree during one of her numerous attempts to stop the kid from smoking, then she hurried into the house.

Even in the increasing darkness the place looked worse than the last time she'd been here. The living room was strewn with new paper containers from the Dairy Mart, and with empty beer and soda cans, and bottles. The flashlight beam picked up an outrageous number of condom packets, the foil glistening like dropped gems. She didn't, however, take any satisfaction in knowing that at least the kids—some of the kids—were practicing safe sex, especially not after stepping into the bedroom where the stench of spilled beer and semen, along with the slightly sweet, sickening aroma of grass assaulted her. It retriggered her rage at stupidity and waste.

No more. Not here.

She reached for the side straps on the stained mattress, but before she could gain a good hold, she was snatched from behind and spun around. In the next instant she was looking into some giant's dark, furious face.

No giant, she amended, in the midst of a possible heart attack. Ben Rader.

Weak with relief, she dropped her head against his chest.

"What the hell do you think you're doing?" he asked.

Trying not to wet my panties.

Fortunately, she'd always been one to rebound quickly, and she released the two handfuls of shirt she'd been clutching, only to give him a smart punch with both fists. "Never mind what I'm doing, where did you come from? You're at the house!"

"Obviously not."

He let her go, although clearly not because she'd hurt him. Even so, Eve took some satisfaction in having made him back off. "Well, did you have to scare me gray?"

Between the darkness and the hat that dipped low over his forehead, she could feel his gaze. It lingered on her hair, which was loose because she'd showered before dinner and brushed it dry out on the balcony—a small ritual Sumner had often enjoyed. Ben Rader made her far more self-conscious than Sumner ever did.

"That works both ways, you know."

"I saw the kids driving away from here and my temper got the best of me. You must have seen them earlier and walked down to investigate."

"No, I was just walking. Didn't have a clue that they were here."

"Did you talk to them? Tell them to stop using this place?"

"You don't tell kids that age anything. You change the situation, or their environment, so that they make decisions for themselves."

His cynical response triggered her own sarcasm. "In case you haven't noticed, that was the theory behind those signs outside."

"And what were you planning to do just now, take away their beds?"

"It couldn't hurt."

"It wouldn't help. They'll only do it on the floor...or against the wall. Don't tell me a redhead could forget that passion isn't particular? When it strikes, its demands are immediate."

Did he think nonsense like that could shock her? Clearly he wasn't thinking about whom she'd been married to. What's more, her occupation and childhood had provided more education than he could probably imagine.

"What's the matter?" he drawled when she failed to answer. "Is the subject matter offending your feminine sensibilities?"

"Exactly what is it about me that's giving your less than charismatic side a nasty itch?"

"Red, you don't want to get me started on my itch."

"You're right. What I do want is to keep everyone out of here until I can get this place torn down."

"Well, you'd better hurry, because nothing less will keep them away." He glanced around the litter-strewn room. "And for what it's worth, you have my enthusiastic support."

Eve heard the bitterness in his voice and wondered how it must feel to see the old homestead in this shape. "I guess this is a particularly unpleasant sight for you."

"Why do you think I'd rather concentrate on riling you?"

He took her elbow and escorted her out of there. He didn't stop in the living room, nor on the porch. Only when they were on the trampled grass did he pause; then it was to reach for a cigarette.

Her insides humming from her own adrenaline surge, as well as the energy she felt pulsating inside him, Eve beat him to it by lighting her lighter and offering it to him. She studied his grim profile in its flame as he cupped his hands around hers and bent close.

"How many is that over your limit for the day?"

"Save the lecture. I've got plenty of my own memorized."

"That's not why I asked. I was merely trying to gauge what kind of day it's been for you."

"I lost count after leaving your place this morning."

"In other words, things here—in Parish, I mean—are worse than you expected."

"In other words, my old man and I weren't saints, and weren't interested in being saints, but—" he gestured at the house "—I doubt he'd like knowing he'd inspired that. God knows, it makes me want to puke."

Eve watched him purge a long stream of smoke. Now that the flame was out, she couldn't see his face very well, but she didn't need to; it was his voice that told her how upset, even devastated, he was. That made it surprisingly easy to forgive him his previous rudeness. It definitely rekindled her curiosity about him.

"You can't take responsibility for this," she said.

"We're all responsible."

She believed that herself, but it was a shock to hear it coming from the mouth of a man rumored to have become a cop because he enjoyed wielding power. Well, she amended, not everyone thought so. "Mama Lulu says you and your father were close."

He hesitated, and she sensed that wasn't a subject he liked to talk about. But then, he seemed to be having difficulty being back in Parish, period.

"Once, yeah," he said slowly. "For the most part. Until close to the end...or maybe that helped cause the end, I don't know anymore."

"What about your mother?"

"What is this? It's a little late to be interviewing me for my stability as a tenant."

"Humor me. I can't walk away from a knot that needs unraveling, either."

He muttered something that sounded suspiciously like, "Just my luck," then looked up, beyond the canopy of trees, as if his memories were written there, but in handwriting too small to read. "She died when I was barely more than a baby. She'd contracted scarlet fever as a kid and it weakened her heart. I don't know that she should have risked pregnancy, but she wanted a child for my father, so she had me."

Despite a dispassionate tone, Eve heard the echo of the bewildered, lonely boy he had been, a boy who still controlled a portion of the man. She thought of his mother, too, tried to imagine loving someone that much as to not care about her own mortality. Then she thought of Ben being raised by a rawboned, tough cop much like the man he'd become. The opportunity for hero worship would have been incredibly strong, but so would those for conflict. The latter had ultimately pulled father and son apart, that she knew from hearsay. But who had been the woman who'd acted as the catalyst? Eve had never cared to listen to the gossip before. Unfortunately, she didn't know Ben well enough to probe more deeply into his wounds now.

"Ancient history," Ben said before she could think of something else to say. "Do me a favor and forget I said anything."

Oh, yes, he was in fast retreat, and she knew there was only one of two ways to deal with that. She chose the most risky. Humor.

"You can't be serious? I have a feeling you do one impulsive thing, say one deeply personal statement a year, and that was it. As the only witness for miles around, I probably have a civic obligation to remember every utterance."

The headlights from the cart picked up a bat that disappeared into the safety of the Spanish moss draping from a majestic oak. In the distance an owl hooted.

If Ben Rader noticed any of that, he didn't let on. He was clearly trying to decide how to react to her.

"I'm beginning to see another reason for Sumner wanting you."

Another...wanted... Either he enjoyed being provocative or it was natural to his personality. Not one to shrink from a challenge, she smiled. "There were more than two. Stick around long enough and I'll make your head spin."

"Something tells me you could. What about your childhood?"

No, he didn't like being in the spotlight, while she was growing ever more used to it. People had been sieving through her past since she'd moved here. Southerners were far more interested in pedigree than most people, and she'd learned to deal with that by keeping things simple. For example, she explained she'd lost both parents when she'd been a child. Only that wasn't wholly the truth. Since she had a feeling Ben Rader would double-check if he sensed she hadn't been completely honest, she chose to be as explicit with him as she'd been with Sumner.

"My childhood would have made good fiction for Dickens...or for your Faulkner. My father was a petty thief, who was in and out of prison for as far back as I can remember, and when my mother went to my spinster great-aunt for help, the only way Aunt Cora would take us in was if Mother divorced him. She did, but she also soon decided that Aunt Cora's eccentricities didn't prove a .fair exchange, so after about four months she ran off with a guitarist."

"Leaving you behind?"

"He wasn't much of a guitarist."

"How old were you?"

"Ten. Aunt Cora introduced me to a psychologist who explained to me that the tenth year is a crucial one between mothers and daughters, and that it would be better for me in the long run if I just worked through my feelings of abandonment right away. One thing I had to give my aunt—she had fascinating people flitting in and out of her life. What the psychologist failed to mention was that the years that followed would be fairly attention-getting, too."

"Because?"

"For one thing, instead of postcards from the happy couple, we were visited periodically by the FBI. You see, Mother and her guitarist became quite the political activists."

"Ah. You and Mom had more in common than you first suggested."

She'd never looked at it that way, but had to allow a low, satisfied chuckle. "Well, I tend to draw the line at turning flagpoles outside of VFW halls into missile launchers."

"Good idea. It's not kind to mess with senior vets. VA hospitals tend to be stingy at doling out sedatives. Did you see much of her?"

"No. And if she wrote, Aunt Cora didn't tell me. There was nothing to suggest any contact, though. Even after Cora died and I was sorting through her personal effects, I didn't find anything." Eve paused a moment, trying to pick up on some emotion, but as usual her past left her feeling as though her history belonged to someone else.

"Did you like this Aunt Cora?"

"Now that's a cop question. You mean love, and the answer is not always. And before you start justifying yourself for asking the way you did, I'll tell you that I didn't always like her, either. Not until I was old enough to understand what it cost her to take me in. Thereafter I was forever grateful.

"You see, Cora never married—by choice, I should add—and she had a full plan for her life, when my mother and I came along. She had to make considerable changes, to expend a great deal of energy on me, energy that she'd expected to direct elsewhere."

"Such as?"

"Who knows? She was an intensely private woman. When she developed cancer and learned her illness was terminal, she burned reams and reams of journals and letters in her office. I have no idea what was in them, and the curiosity *ate* at me for some time, but the older I get, the more I respect and admire her passion for privacy.

"What was telling was that she asked for her considerable collection of books to be donated to a small impoverished library outside of Chicago, and the house went to a friend who turned it into a home for battered women. Only afterward did I learn that Cora had been born in that house. Now, she hadn't inherited it, mind you, she bought it with money she'd earned cleaning other people's houses." Eve shook her head. "If only those walls could have talked...."

"You never filled in the holes?"

"No. As far as I can tell, she never married and had no family, except us. My mother—her niece—and me."

"What did she leave you?"

"A good mind and the sense to figure out that I needed a trade if I was going to support myself."

"So you decided to become a nurse?"

"It was an evolutionary thing. Between my mother and Aunt Cora, I deduced it might be a letdown to expect a man to be there for the long haul. Later, Cora suggested that if I had any maternal instincts, they would be better served by taking care of other people's 'mistakes,' as she put it. I discovered I had an affinity for the work."

When Ben took a long drag on his cigarette, the

burning tip attracted a dainty moth that quickly veered away from its heat. "And along came Sumner and his juicy bankroll. Is that why you're turning this town inside out and upside down with your plans and your changes? You feel a little guilty for finding things cushier than you'd expected or imagined, and now you're willing to devote a little more time to the things your great-aunt only began to achieve in death?"

"Good grief, now I'm an apologist? You've met my stepchildren. Suffice it to say that my commitment is first and foremost to them. But that hasn't made me blind to Parish's needs."

"Sumner managed to overlook them."

"I can't explain Sumner. But I can say that he figured out the old Kingfisher, Big Daddy type of control was self-destructive. Only by then it was too late for him. He often said that his one regret would be not witnessing the stink I would cause adjusting for what he'd done."

"No doubt just looking at you lengthened his life span by several months."

Eve grew very aware that her dress was sleeveless and that her ice-blue shift delineated far more than this morning's outfit had. "Considering how you warned me off earlier today, I find that comment...contradictory."

"So never let it be said we don't agree on something. I just wish I could decide whether you're the Pollyanna some people think you are, or an extremely fine-tuned Delilah."

6

"That's it?" Eve fought back an incredulous laugh.
"Heaven forbid that I should have a few more di-
mensions."

"I'll be watching for them. But so far that's the
gist of the picture I'm getting."

No wonder he was in such a dour mood. "Maybe
you're collecting information from the wrong people.
Did you visit with a great many this afternoon?"

Ben eyed her in the darkness. "Perry Ashworth.
The Cobbs."

And he'd come away with that character profile?
"None of them would describe me the way you just
did."

"They didn't. The conclusions are my own. But
you have to know that Luther isn't thanking you for
the mess you've convinced him to take on."

Eve was a bit concerned, sure. Business was slower
than she'd expected it would be. But she believed
Luther would discover why and make the necessary
changes in his own time and way. If she made any
suggestions without being asked, then she would be
no different than Sumner.

"Did he cite something specific? A problem at the
store, I mean."

"No. Only that he's questioning the wisdom of having listened to you."

Eve relaxed. "He says that at least once a day. Luther's a born worrier."

"Is drinking more than he should something to shrug off, as well?"

Eve frowned and stared hard at her bare toes peeking through the straps of her sandals. She would have put on canvas shoes if she'd known she was coming out here, and worn slacks. Now she would probably spend hours scratching at mosquito and chigger bites. Then again, since she would be awake anyway, brooding over Mama Lulu's family, the bites would be as useful as any worry stone.

"If he's driving himself crazy fretting over money," she told Ben, "he doesn't have to. I promised that I would carry his note as long as he needed, and I meant it. For goodness' sake, his mother has been a part of the Maitland family for years. It's the least we can do."

"You think he wants that? You were raised by a person who seemed to have understood pride. Leave the man his. He has to be able to face his boys and Rae, and feel he was the one who pulled things together for them."

"But he is!"

"No, *you* are. You and all that money you threw at them."

Although he had stirred some doubts in her, Eve held fast to her convictions out of sheer necessity. "Mama Lulu thinks I did the right thing."

"She would volunteer to become a slave again if it meant helping her family. For all you know, she might be thinking of retiring, but she won't, now that her son owes you and the bank more than what either of her late husbands probably earned in their entire lives!"

He wasn't telling her anything she didn't know, but his accusations, *insinuations,* stung nonetheless. Concerned as much as she was annoyed, she squared her shoulders. "This is all so enlightening. And what's Perry Ashworth saying about me?"

Ben dropped his cigarette and crushed it into a clear patch of earth. "He warned me off."

Now she knew he had to be toying with her. "Say that again?"

"When he heard where I'd be staying, he made it clear I'm to keep my unrefined hands to myself."

Perry was charming, debonair and wickedly funny, but Perry was not seriously attracted to her. Surely she, more than anyone, would know if he was?

"That's...ludicrous!" Embarrassed for practically sputtering like a mindless twit, and for letting Ben control the conversation for as long as he had, she gestured to the cart. "I'm going home. If you want a lift, get in."

The nerve of the man, she fumed as he followed and scrunched his considerable frame onto the bench beside her. This is what she got for being curious. What upset her most, though, was how easy it was for him to get under her skin, to probe deep nerves. She was shocked at her urge to lash out in retaliation, to say things without caring what damage or hurt she would inflict. God, she thought, driving through the tunnel of trees that suddenly seemed as small as a rabbit's hole, he'd even made her forget the death and danger that existed here.

The man was bad news for her equilibrium. She was Eve Maitland, *Mrs.* Sumner Maitland. The lives of dozens of people, a fortune, rested on her shoulders. She could not afford to make a fool of herself over one brash, crude and rude cop, no matter what her hormones were telling her.

As she turned sharply into the gated drive, she took minute satisfaction when he had to grab the rollover bar to keep from falling into her. She would have been happier yet to find a mud hole and toss him into it.

The headlights illuminated the foreman's cottage. "Mama Lulu and two of our part-time helpers spent most of the afternoon here," she said, her jaw aching as though she'd been clenching her teeth. "I'm sure you'll be pleased with the results."

"I'm sure."

"Don't patronize me. She'll ask if I ran into you and if you are."

"Then tell her I'm thrilled. Couldn't be happier."

"She said she had a fan brought down, and put some food in the refrigerator."

"If you'll tell me what I owe you, I'll drop off a check at the house on my way into the station in the morning."

"Don't even think it. I don't want it, and Mama Lulu would be upset with me if I took it."

She braked and waited for him to get out.

Do not look at him again.

"You really are too good to be true."

She spun to face him. "Understand this...I'm not

too anything. All I am is a woman trying to keep a promise because I saw something of value worth saving here. Don't talk yourself into some silly male competition thing, either. You were right this morning about it being a bad idea to pay too much attention to chemistry. I've told Perry basically the same thing, that's why whatever was said between you two during your talk was about you, not me, and I resent like hell being blamed for it.''

She was almost breathless when she finished.

"Is it my turn?''

"I'd prefer you just get out so I can go home.''

"In a minute. First let's get something else out of the way.''

Before she could stop him, he leaned over and, clamping a hand to the back of her head, he crushed his mouth to hers.

It should have hurt, and did. It also infuriated her, but heaven help her, she couldn't move. Cliché or not, now she knew what the butterfly impaled by a straight pin knew, a complete helplessness as she was caught by Ben's power and heat. She could do little as he forced her lips open and thrust his tongue deep. He was bold, and hungry, and that's what entrapped her most, made her respond to the blatant thrusts, had her melting, melting, until she knew if he didn't stop, she would slump against him, maybe even climb onto his lap and beg him to take her right there.

When he tore his mouth from hers, he couldn't suck air into his lungs fast enough. She couldn't tell him it served him right because she couldn't breathe, either.

"Two other things," he all but growled. "First, stay out of those woods, especially after dark."

She couldn't find her voice to agree or tell him to go to hell.

"Second, if you're serious about not wanting to start anything, don't wear that dress around me again. It's twice as provocative as anything I could do or say."

Although well used to stress, Eve didn't get much sleep that night. Before a hint of gray seeped through her partially opened shutters, she gave up, groping in the bathroom medicine cabinet for aspirin to relieve the throbbing in her head. A long shower followed, which provided faster relief, but when she arrived in the kitchen, she wasn't surprised at Mama Lulu's narrow-eyed look.

"What's wrong with you?"

"Good morning to you, too. The coffee smells extra good. Why don't you pour me a mug to go and we'll head for town early?"

"Why? Devil on your tail?"

The woman was closer to the truth than she knew. "You have a good deal of shopping to do, and I have things planned myself. I'd like to get back as soon as possible to return some phone calls I didn't get to yesterday."

"That don't answer my question."

"Sinus headache," Eve replied, reaching for the phone to have her sedan brought up front. It was a legitimate excuse—one of the few negatives resulting in her move south—although not valid in this instance. "Now, do I get the coffee or not?"

She got the coffee, and they were on their way ten minutes later. What she wouldn't tell Mama Lulu was that she needed to see Luther and Rae. If they were having new doubts about the store, she wanted to hear it from them. Of course, getting a private moment to talk with Luther's mother sniffing around would be easier said than done.

"Looks like they're barely gettin' started themselves," Mama Lulu said a short time later when Eve parked before the store.

The market was at the end of the oldest row of stores in town. Luther had painted the trim with a fresh coat of white, and although it stood out clean and bright against the others, it also had Eve paying closer attention to its location. Today, Ben's critical comments held more weight, and she couldn't deny that maybe the shop was farther away from the major flow of traffic in town than she'd realized. Maybe almost isolated, which would make the Cobbs somewhat vulnerable if there was trouble.

"I'll come inside with you and say hello before I go down to talk to Mayor Varnell," she told the housekeeper. "Of course, if you think you can't manage, I can always rearrange my itinerary and stay with you."

"Been shoppin' for this family longer than you've been on the planet. Exactly what you think I can't handle? Besides, Rae'll follow me around like a second shadow, you know that. And—" Mama Lulu froze and gaped at one of the several handmade signs in the windows. "Will you look at that? What's that boy doin' sellin' fryers at that price? How's he expectin' to make a livin' givin' stuff away?"

Eve bit her lower lip trying not to agree. Not only were the chicken prices low, they and everything else advertised ranked in the fire-sale range—more proof that what Ben had said held merit.

"It's probably some clever promotional idea Luther came up with," she said hoping the older woman believed it. "Don't scold the second we walk in."

Mama Lulu eyed her dolefully as she settled her black vinyl bag over her forearm. "I'm his mama. If I can't give my opinion, who can? Mornin', children," she called as they entered. She raised a hand as though giving a benediction. "Get me a wagon and oil that register! We're here to shop!"

Looking more tired than Eve felt, but pretty in a denim jumper and red T-shirt, Rae smiled in welcome and came around the counter to embrace her mother-in-law. "How are you today, Mama? You look fine, just fine."

"My arthritis is actin' up in my knees. It's gonna rain again."

"The weatherman said only twenty percent chance, Mama."

"Fool man. What's he know? It's gonna, I say. The ache's bad."

Eve exchanged looks with Rae. Her housekeeper had said nothing earlier.

"I have aspirin in the back," Rae said with a dismissive wave to Eve. "Can I get you juice or water with them, Mama?"

"Don't hurt bad enough for drugs. What you can do is tell me what that boy o' mine's doin' sellin' chicken cheaper'n air?"

Eve wanted to do an about-face and walk out. So

much for any hope that Mama Lulu would attempt any form of diplomacy.

"Well, Mama," Rae said with impressive patience, "those chickens aren't getting any fresher sitting in the showcase. They need to go before we can't even sell them for soup or, worse yet, dog food."

"Dog food!" Mama Lulu's full cheeks dimpled as she pressed her lips together. "We'll see about that. Luther! Where you at, boy?"

She stalked through the curtained doorway, leaving Eve and Rae alone. Eve offered immediate apologies.

"You didn't need that first thing this morning, but I had to talk to you."

"Oh, don't you worry. She's not going to say or do anything we haven't already dealt with ourselves."

That was the opening Eve had been hoping for. "Rae, what have I done to you and Luther? When I came to you about opening the store—"

The taller woman silenced her by patting her shoulder gently. Eight years older, Rae had a quieting quality about her that Eve envied.

"Business is slow, that's all. We have to give ourselves a chance. We can't blame folks for being cautious."

Before she could say more, there was a cry from the back. It was a toss-up to Eve whether she or Rae reacted first, but within seconds they were rushing through the draped doorway. Just beyond the curtains they stopped at the sight of Noah standing inside the back door, arms akimbo looking...

"What on earth...?" Rae breathed.

The small boy sobbed softly, plucking at his striped T-shirt, clearly not wanting it to touch his body. There was no telling what covered the shirt—for that matter, what covered most of him.

"I didn't do it, Mama! I'm sorry!"

Rae hurried to him and began peeling him out of the offensive garment.

"Lord have mercy," Mama Lulu said, covering her nose with one hand and pressing the other to her bosom. "What is that all over him? Eggs?"

"If they are, they're rotten ones," Luther muttered, sniffing and grimacing. "Damn, Noah. You get into a fight with a dyin' chicken?"

"No, Papa. I just sat out back like you told me."

"Uh-huh. And that mess dropped from an airplane?"

"I ain't sayin'. They told me they'd kill me if I told!"

"They who?"

The boy shook his head vehemently. "They'll do it. They said they could get me in my own bed if'n they wanna. Don't ask me no more, Papa!"

"No one abuses and threatens my baby that way," Rae muttered, pausing in the middle of peeling the boy out of his equally messy jeans. She strode toward the front. "I'm phoning Ben!"

"Mama!" Noah screamed.

"Wait, Rae." Luther caught her by the arm. "Let's get the full story before we send Ben on some wild-goose chase."

His wife uttered an incredulous sound. "Are you serious? My child has been assaulted. Defiled! I will not stand by while you interrogate him, looking for a way to sweep yet another problem under the rug."

"What do you— I don't do that!"

"Yes, you do, Luther, and I can handle it most of the time, but not when it comes to my children."

Everything Eve knew about Racine Cobb indicated that she was an independent thinker, and a strong woman, but this stand against Luther—before his mother, no less—shocked even her. Wanting to give the family privacy, as well as help where she could, she stepped forward. "Let me go. Noah needs you, Rae. The police station is on my way to Mayor Varnell's office, where I was headed anyway."

"Oh, but this isn't your problem," Rae said. "In fact, I think *we* should take Noah down to the station."

"Well, if there is someone watching..." Eve gestured toward the back and then to Noah, leaving the rest for everyone's imagination. "I'll tell Ben to try to look casual about it, okay?"

For his part, Luther appeared extremely embarrassed, and not a little upset with his wife, but he nodded. "That would be good. Thank you, Eve. Ms. Maitland."

The situation was worse than he'd feared.

As Ben sat in his office, his desk covered with a mound of unanswered mail, un*opened* mail, unprocessed offense and arrest reports, and unfiled complaint reports—all of which he'd scooped out of the deep drawers of what was now his desk—he accepted that he'd been had by Varnell in yet another way. There was no way in hell that he could begin to straighten out this mess and still do an in-depth review of Lem's death. He didn't want to think about what surprises were in the other cops' desks, let alone behind the locked door of the property and file room. In fact, right now he didn't care if Dewey ever found the key to it. If the guy appeared with the thing, he was of half a mind to make him swallow it.

To be fair, his descent into gloom had begun well before arriving here; in fact, it had begun last night when, unable to sleep—thanks to Eve Maitland—he'd picked up Lem's file, thinking he might start some serious digging. Only now did he realize what a miracle it was that the file hadn't been shoved down some other black hole in this dump. Then again, considering how little it contained was reason enough for old man Wheeler and the rest of the mental midgets beyond his closed door not to worry about it being seen.

After maybe three hours' sleep he'd given up and come down here at around six this morning to give the place a real inspection, not just the cursory once-over done yesterday while Harry was still on the premises. Ten minutes ago he'd held his first department meeting, making it clear that he doubted anyone on the payroll was capable of responding professionally to a fender bender, let alone anything more serious.

Apparently, his predecessor had been content to rely on Sumner Maitland for advice and direction when it came to matters of the law in Parish. If Sumner had wanted an abusive husband to sleep off a drunk in jail so the wife could fulfill her obligations as a cashier at Sumner's grocery store, then that's what happened; and maybe the paperwork would be processed on the arrest, and maybe it wouldn't. If Sumner was angry over a slacker's continued delinquency on a debt at Maitland's bank, an officer was told to drive Sumner to the bum's home, where the old shylock either broke a headlight on the guy's vehicle or something equally effective until payment miraculously appeared.

After Sumner died, Wheeler had been like an armless man sitting before a computer keyboard. Too weak to take control of his own department, let alone oversee the town, the citizens of Parish were left to resolve their problems themselves. Sure, calls were responded to—the officers had to keep the patrol-car batteries juiced somehow—but little progress was made otherwise. The mess on his desk was proof of that. He had two full-time day patrolmen, a combination desk sergeant–dispatcher and one full-time and one part-time night officer that combined weren't worth one Jackson detective's salary.

"Christ," Ben groaned, rubbing his face with both hands.

Maybe Parish had never been the Garden of Eden—when one individual wielded as much power as Sumner did, and even Vail Ashworth, in a slightly more subtle way, justice tended to have a certain slant to it—but this was ridiculous. It was a wonder there weren't lynch mobs running in the streets. Even Luther's fear of finding a cross burning in his yard no longer sounded melodramatic. And that was why he couldn't just throw down his badge and get the hell out of Dodge.

But things had to change. Immediately.

He'd given the men outside an hour to decide if they wanted to stay on or turn in their resignations. If they stayed, they had thirty days to process the proper paperwork for every call received so far this month, and from here on they were to have all reports filed daily before going off duty. From the look on Jack Haygood's and Buck Preston's faces, the men would use most of that hour in the head and the rest of it on the phone with Norm Friedman and Ron Scranton who pulled the evening shift, warning their buddies of what they had to look forward to. For his part, Ben hoped they all quit; but he also knew that Varnell and company wouldn't okay the pay raises he would need to attract more qualified people to replace them.

Thinking he might as well have a hangover, he wondered if the commotion outside his office meant the men were tripping over each other to escape. But before he could summon the interest to investigate, someone was knocking on his door.

"At your own risk!"

Eve Maitland entered.

Tempted to raise his hands in surrender, he closed his eyes instead. It didn't erase the image of the sleek woman in a breezy white shirtwaist dress, and all that marvelous red hair swept up into a loose chignon. If last night he'd briefly labeled her a Pollyanna, this morning with her head high and smoke and fire in those stunning eyes, she looked more like Joan of Arc ready to take on the Prince of Hades. How angry would she be if last night he'd done more than kissed her? No wonder his men had sounded as though they'd been falling all over themselves out there.

Opening his eyes, he leaned back in his chair and rubbed his face with both hands. "It figures. Some people get icing on a cake, I get a slice of the knife across the jugular for good measure.''

Eve shut the door behind her. ''Finding mutiny in the ranks, Captain?''

''Ranks? I have no ranks. What you passed on your way in here was the harvest of your beloved husband's reign in this town.''

''Well, I have more good news to pass on. The Cobbs need you. Noah's been hurt.''

He sat forward, his sarcasm instantly replaced with concern. ''How bad? What happened?''

''I think he'll be all right, at least I didn't see any bleeding or bruises. But he's a mess, and he's almost hysterical. As for what happened, I'm not sure. He won't tell his parents, because whoever dumped or dipped him into the crud he's covered with threatened him if he told.''

''Sounds as though he ran into a bunch of thugs-in-training.''

''If so, they're not far from graduating. They threatened to break into his house and get him in his bed.''

Swearing, Ben reached for his hat and holster on the credenza behind him. ''We used to pull pranks like making someone stumble into an uncovered outhouse hole. We even threatened to beat a guy's ears back into his head for snitching on us once, but promise that...?''

He followed her out of his office. Buck Preston sat hunched over an ancient electric typewriter while Dewey flipped through a dictionary.

''Where's Haygood?'' Ben asked, wondering if the

one with the most experience had been the only member of the squad to quit. It would be just his luck.

"There's a cat stuck in a tree over by the senior citizens' building," Dewey said, offering a weak smile.

Ben slipped on his hat, hoping that Eve Maitland would have the courtesy to wait until she got outside to burst a seam laughing. "I'm over at Cobb's Market checking out some juvenile delinquency. Call the coroner's office to see if he's available sometime this afternoon."

"For what, Chief?"

He opened the door for Eve, and ignored her snicker. "To see me. What else?"

"He can't," Buck Preston told him.

"He's fishing," Dewey added.

Buck nodded. "Won't be back until he restocks his freezer. The one at his home, not the office," he said with a pleased grin for the gruesome joke.

Ben let the glass door close behind him.

Outside, the humidity was rising as fast as the heat, but Eve's high-heel sandals tapped an energetic tune on the sidewalk as she walked beside him. No sense to ask if she'd had trouble sleeping last night.

"You *are* having a bad day."

And she looked so happy about it. "I'll recover. I see you drove here. Do you want to ride over there with me, or do we turn this into a parade that will attract everyone in town curious to see what's going on?"

"This may come as a surprise to you, but having heard the threat myself, I already thought about the danger in attracting too much attention. Why don't we stand here a moment longer and appear to be having a polite conversation—if that's at all possible— and then I'll go over to talk to Fred Varnell.''

''Oh, sure, tell him. That should really keep things under wraps.''

The fire in her eyes grew lethal—a look completely at odds with the serene smile curving her delicious mouth. ''I'm going to talk to him about a library. I'll pick up Mama Lulu at the market after I'm through.''

So he'd just put his foot in his mouth. He still didn't follow. ''A library? For who?''

''The *children*. Maybe if we had a safe, entertaining place for children to go, things like this wouldn't happen. A library could schedule activities throughout the summer—storytelling for the youngest, maybe guest authors eventually for the adults. We could hold exhibits featuring local artists and historical memorabilia...things like that.''

It would never catch on. As a boy, he remembered Sumner had tried to start a newspaper—''to give the place some culture,'' he'd said. It had been one of his few financial failures. No one wanted to pay for information they were already getting free and faster via gossip, and no one wanted to buy ads for what was clearly visible in shop windows. Culture, the citizens made clear in no uncertain terms, was about as useful as hip waders in the desert.

''Who's going to pay for this?'' Ben asked, imagining the uproar if a tax increase was even hinted. ''Don't make that face. You're the one who said we should stand here and make nice.''

She cleared her throat and stood a little straighter. ''Surely we can arrange something. I'm going to talk to Perry, too. If he hears the Maitlands are willing to finance a portion of the expense, he might agree to match our donation. Perry doesn't involve himself in local politics the way Vail did, but he does care about the town.''

"Please. Not on an empty stomach.''

"What's that supposed to mean?''

"Absolutely nothing. Go on, have your fun. I'm sure you'll get everything you want. If it doesn't work out, try undoing a third button on your dress. That should have Varnell forgetting he turned down my request to hire another cop and replace my oldest patrol car. Even if he says no, I doubt Ashworth will.''

"You—'' She broke off and, smiling, nodded to the Hispanic couple who hurried by, their eyes downcast. "Why are you taking your rotten mood out on me?'' she whispered. "I'm not the one who behaved badly last night.''

"No, if you'd been any better, neither one of us would be out of bed yet.''

She shook her head, her look telling him she refused to be baited. "This isn't about me. This has to do with you not being able to get hold of the county coroner. You've seen something in his report on Lem that demands an explanation.''

It was fine with him if that's what she wanted to think. It was far easier for him to handle than the truth that was just beginning to claw at him. "That,'' he said pointing at her feminine nose, "you need to forget you heard. I don't need any slipups around Mama Lulu and her getting her hopes up.''

"I'll make you a deal. Take back that crack about my dress.''

Instead, Ben stepped off the sidewalk, reached into the open window of his truck, released the glove compartment and shoved in his gun and holster. It gave him the time he needed to keep from answering honestly.

"I apologize."

He regretted his lewd comments, his relentlessly sexual stream of consciousness and his inability to keep either under control around her. Most of all, however, he regretted that he must never again let himself yield to the temptation of those bewitching lips. Eve Maitland was one enticement he couldn't afford. He might have to carry his father's gun, but he wasn't about to repeat his disastrous history with women.

"Ben...go see about Noah."

He went, hoping he could help a little boy more than he was liable to help anyone else in this town.

Justin stayed behind the safety of his locked bedroom door until he heard Bree take off on her horse, the gray gelding unenviably named Mr. Darling. Confident she would be heading toward Perry Ashworth's, he snatched up his sketch pad and pens and took off in the opposite direction. Eve and Mama Lulu had left earlier, which was also a relief. They wouldn't like the idea of him choosing to work at the lake, even if it was some distance away from where all the trouble had been happening. Not having to fabricate a lie was much better.

As he let himself out the kitchen door, a hummingbird shot past him, attracted by the red insulated tote he'd picked up from the pantry and filled with

bottled water, some cheese and fruit. Belatedly he
thought about a hat, but decided he would try to sit
in the shade of a tree to save himself a trip back
upstairs. Unlike his sister, he listened to Mama Lulu's
lectures about sunstroke and Eve's about skin cancer.
His caution left him somewhat paler than most of the
guys around, and had been an embarrassment in
school, especially during gym. Fortunately, those
days were behind him.

Circling the long way around the orchard, he managed to avoid the barns and the workers in the fields
behind them. By the time he was on the dirt road
leading toward the northwest corner of the lake, he
felt like a kingfisher doing acrobatic dives over the
water—free and a little reckless.

The sun baked through his short-sleeved shirt, the
azure sky burned his eyes and the fields sloping toward the water were dense with wildflowers that had
him grinning with anticipation. Today he would have
this corner of the lake to himself…except for whoever
was home in the few houses on the left side of the
shore.

Shacks, he amended, settling near, though not under, a red maple tree. The three rough cedar buildings
interested the artist in him, while their impoverished
and neglected condition filled him with distaste. Just
because people were poor, did they have to be slobs?
He liked that wind and weather had turned the wood
siding gray, and that flimsy architecture had some of
the walls tilting toward opposing axes. It was the
yards that offended him. Each was an obstacle course
of litter, abandoned vehicles, discarded furniture and

appliances. How could anyone live surrounded by such a mess?

Well, not everyone did, he amended, seeing the back door of the first house open. A young girl emerged. She was one-third of a family that had moved in earlier in the week—an odd family consisting of an old, feeble man, and another guy maybe Eve's age. Ever since he'd watched the girl try to salvage one bit of the yard for a garden, he'd felt sorry for her. Her father, husband—or brother, maybe?—made that a challenge at every turn. When he wasn't throwing things right where she was working, he stomped through it, laughing at her as she tried to ward him off with frantic hand signals.

The guy was a pig. The girl was speech- and hearing-impaired.

Justin hunched lower in the tall grass, hoping that like the other times these past few days he would remain undetected. He wanted to sketch her again. There was something vulnerable and skittish about her that reminded him of a traumatized deer. All arms and legs, and a mile of thick brown hair that she continually used as a wrap or blanket to hide herself, she might easily have been mistaken for a child, but she worked harder than any adult he'd ever seen.

Today she wore the same cotton shift she'd been wearing when he first saw her. It had to be at least two sizes too big for her, and the small flower print was fading against the cream background. She carried a big shallow bowl with several things in it.

What really got his attention, however, was how slowly, how stiffly she moved. It had nothing to do with her being barefoot; Justin guessed she had tough little soles because she was always going around without shoes. No, this was different; she wasn't feeling well today.

Making her way to the lake, she tucked the items in the bowl into her deep skirt pockets and with difficulty scooped up a bowl of water. She carried it to the side of the house, the side with no windows and full sun, and set the container on a board resting between two makeshift sawhorses. Then she retrieved soap and a comb from her pockets.

He understood now. She was going to wash her hair.

Concern overrode his elation. Not only did she keep glancing around to make sure no one was watching, but she seemed...so drained. Maybe she had a summer cold, or could this be her time for cramps and all that? Those days could certainly turn Bree into a witch. In any case, the girl's cautious movements tugged at something inside him as he continued to watch the sun play on her creamy skin, her hair—so unremarkable in color, but wonderfully abundant. Then she began unbuttoning the front of her dress.

His mouth went dry.

Would she do it? And here he'd resigned himself to thinking he would have to wait until college before having the opportunity to draw a nude—not that finding a model had ever been the problem. Bree said she knew girls willing to expose themselves to him. But they would expect sex in return. The mere thought of having his performance graded afterward, then reported to his sister, was enough to convince him to wait.

The girl awkwardly slipped her arms out of the

sleeveless dress and let it fall to her waist. The knot forming in Justin's throat was matched by one growing deep in his belly, and an ache stirred even lower, yet all he could see so far was hair.

At last she scooped up the wild mane and bent forward to wet it. The sun baked down on her delicate spine, delineating her thinness, the dancer's grace in each movement of her long arms. But her breasts were what mesmerized him, small and cone-shaped in her current position, the nipples were a tawny rose.

Once she had her hair wet, she straightened and reached for the soap.

A soft gush of air burst from his lips. She was round as an apple now. Enchanting. Perfect. When she raised her face to the sun, her breasts lifted, too. He'd never seen an offering more simple and honest, or beautiful in its innocence.

Then she winced, reached down and cupped her right breast.

Justin gnawed at his lower lip, filled with pity even as his gaze worshiped. He wished there was something he could do to help her, but that was out of the question. The poor kid would probably be mortified to find out she was being watched.

With a long, shuddering sigh, she turned a bit more to the sun to inspect the spot herself. Justin saw tears on her wan face, but what had him choking back a cry of outrage was the ugly bruise across her tender flesh.

What kind of animal did that to someone so sweet?

7

Ben heard the sound of water even before he pushed open the screen door. As Rae had told him, Luther had their son out back and was hosing him down. He had to wait to do more than nod in greeting because the boy was wailing in protest against the hard spray.

Luther adjusted the nozzle to a fine spray and aimed at the child's wide-open mouth. "Cut that out! You'd think I had you buck-ass naked and was shootin' rock salt for all the racket you're makin'. You want Mama doin' this? She'll strip you sure, and rub you all over with girly-smellin' stuff."

"Uh-uh!"

"Yeah, she will. She'd like nothin' better right about now than to make you smell like a birthday cake. Now go on to the bathroom and get outta those wet things. Put on my extra shirt behind the door. Your mama'll drive you home directly so you can get changed for real."

"Everything okay, pal?" Ben asked as Noah dashed by him.

"Uh-huh."

Not surprisingly, the youngster didn't look at him, let alone stop. From what little he knew about what happened, Ben couldn't blame him. Being assaulted was bad enough, but being threatened, then embarrassed like this would make anyone uncommunicative. Luther seemed sensitive to that, as well. He, too, busied himself with re-coiling the hose, until the screen door slammed shut.

"You didn't have to come out, Ben. I reckon you got enough to keep you busy, this bein' your first full day on the job and all."

Ben frowned. Had he heard him correctly? "Eve Maitland told me what happened. How could you think I wouldn't come over?"

"Aw, there ain't no problem. Just a misunderstandin', that's all."

Ben glanced around at the line of Dumpsters, parked vehicles and storage sheds that was, along with the drainage ditch beyond, Noah's playground. "Really? I heard Noah was pretty upset. So were Rae and Mama Lulu when I came through the store."

Luther nodded, his smile sheepish. "You know how them women are. Rae especially. Noah's her baby. He tears a nail and she'll be wantin' to haul him to the hospital."

"I see." He would have had less difficulty believing him if his friend would meet his gaze.

"Yeah. Him and some kids got into a name-callin' contest, best as I figure it. He's been babied by us and his big brothers too long. He's gotta learn not everybody's gonna let him shoot off his mouth and get away with it."

"Well, I guess that's a lesson we all have to learn. But I heard someone threatened him. That's a serious thing, Luther."

"Don't think they meant to use the words they did,

Ben. And you saw how Noah can act. He's better'n some of those kids on TV. Could be he colored things some. Wish I could've saved you a trip, man.''

Ben studied his friend for a moment. ''No problem. Glad that things worked out. But you let me know if the situation changes.''

''Sure. Right away.''

He was lying. About how much and why, Ben wasn't certain, nor did he know what he could do about it without voicing the accusation. But that would create a chasm they didn't need in the still-fragile territory of their friendship right now. All he could do was wait, be there for Luther and his family and hope Luther's trust grew to what it once had been.

''At least I get the chance to thank you and Rae again for last night,'' he said.

''Shoot, wasn't nothin'. We enjoyed it ourselves. Now, you don't be a stranger, hear?''

''I won't.'' Ben checked his watch. ''Listen, if you're sure everything is okay here…?''

''Hey, you got things to do. Don't worry about us.''

''I'm heading over to the lake before the heat gets too bad.''

Luther sucked in a deep breath, but nodded. ''You didn't tell Mama that, did you?''

''Absolutely not. What do you take me for?''

''Sorry. Guess I'm a bit more hungover than I thought.'' He offered another vague smile and faked a punch to Ben's middle. ''I can't keep up with you single guys no more.''

''I've got news for you, my partying days are over,

as well.'' Ben pointed with his thumb over his shoulder. ''And if it's okay with you, I'll go around the building instead of going back inside. This way I won't have to lie to Mama Lulu.''

''Fine. See you 'round.''

Luther stood there until he couldn't see his friend anymore. Then he stared hard at the ditch, and up and down the alley. A plumber's repair truck was pulling up to one of the stores at the end of the building. This was the third time since they'd leased the place, and it wasn't good news. But that wasn't what had him wanting to punch something or someone for real.

When he turned back to the store, he saw Rae standing on the other side of the screen door. With her hands on her hips and that look in her eye, he knew she'd heard more of his conversation with Ben than he would like.

She came outside. At least he could be grateful that Mama wasn't about to get an earful.

''How could you?'' she whispered harshly. ''Are you out of your mind?''

''I did what I felt was right.''

''Our *son* could have been seriously injured by those two drug-addict punks—you heard what he confided to us after Eve left. They were taking something down in that ditch. And you stood there and told the chief of police of this town that your boy is a liar?''

He hadn't used that word, but he knew it would do no good to split hairs with his wife; in her current mood, she was liable to scalp him. ''Sounds to me it was just grass, Rae. You think they would've gone on home with their mamas' groceries if they was high on coke or somethin'?''

"Who knows? It made them crazy and mean enough to break a dozen eggs over my baby and push him into dog poo!'' She fisted her hands and set them on her hips. "I don't care if Hughes Lumber is the most successful business in town next to the bank, Trevor Hughes and Grover Meece need to know their boys are in trouble.''

"Go on and tell 'em then!'' Luther let his anger match hers. "Then make sure you watch Noah every minute from now on to make sure them boys don't get him for snitchin'! That's what you got to look forward to if you do. And what if Trevor and that pit bull of a manager of his decide to pay us back for sharin' this good news? Maybe they'll tell folks we're lyin' and spread rumors about us or our place? You wanna lose what little business we have?''

"Oh, so it's more acceptable to lose face with your son?''

"No. Hell! I'll explain it to him. I'll talk to him as soon as I get home tonight. Damn it, Rae, you're supposed to help me here, not add to my trouble.''

"You don't have trouble other than what you're making yourself, Luther. But all right, we'll do it your way. Only, how many times are you going to turn the other cheek, ask your family to do the same thing, before we're allowed to have the same rights as everyone else in this town?''

"Rae...Rae!'' Luther called after her as she strode tall and straight back into the store.

She ignored him and the screen slammed hard behind her.

Swearing under his breath, he kicked his thick rubber heel against the cinder-block wall. The pain that shot up his leg was almost welcome because she was right. Not only was he doing a lousy job supporting his family, he was compromising on principles. Why couldn't she see, though, that he'd done it all to protect them?

Heaven had to help him. He had no intention of continuing to let his family be the only guinea pigs for an entire town resisting civil rights. They'd already risked too much. He wished Rae could see that. He wished he could explain to Ben. He wished he didn't feel so alone.

"I'm tired of riding alone. Come on, Perry, ride with me." Bree offered a pretty pout to tempt her handsome neighbor as he accepted yet another clipboard to review.

"You've been riding for almost two hours," he replied without looking up. "I'd think your bottom would be nicely sore by now."

So he had noticed her out on the course. He'd appeared in a constant state of preoccupation with one thing or another, and she'd begun to believe she'd wasted her time coming out here this early in the day. "But I'm not, and you said you wanted to put Lancer through his paces."

The chestnut was one of Perry's newest acquisitions, and the stallion stood impatiently waiting at the stable, tugging at his lines and pawing at the concrete floor as if adding his agreement. Perry glanced back at the horse before returning to his reading.

"Trying to cast a spell on my stock as well as on me?"

Bree leaned forward to stroke Mr. Darling's mane the way she would have liked to run her hands through Perry's ever-perfect hair. "Would it work?"

He finished making a notation on a second sheet, then tucked the clipboard under his arm and eyed her with amusement. "You're being more than a little naughty today, Miss Gabrielle. What would Eve say if she heard you flirting so outrageously?"

"Who cares? I'm eighteen."

"And a lovely specimen of feminine puberty you are. But you should be practicing on boys your own age, or shopping for your college wardrobe."

"Don't patronize me, Perry." Bree stripped off the band that had kept her hair in a casual ponytail. "You know full well that I'm bored by people my age. They're silly and unimaginative. What's more, I have enough clothes to fill every suitcase at Maitland Hall if I was interested in packing them, which I'm not. That form of exile is just Eve's way of getting me out of her hair. What good did a nursing degree do her?"

Perry's throaty laugh won another snort from Lancer. "Need you ask?"

She supposed that wasn't her brightest question. It was what frustrated her most about being this age, that sometimes she spoke as though her mouth and head were entirely disconnected. "Well, I already have money and position."

"Not nearly enough for a little carnivore like you, sweet. And it will take discipline to make something out of what Sumner left you. Eve knows that. You could learn from her.''

"I'd rather learn from you," she purred, letting her eyes clarify the invitation. She'd never been this direct, but what did she have to lose? She didn't care who noticed, and she was fed up with him bringing up Eve at every opportunity. "For once, stop trying to play hard to get. You made your point, but the novelty has worn off. We could have fun, you know."

"Dear heart, in case you haven't noticed, I'm already having fun."

"More fun."

"You're a delightful child, but an infant nonetheless." He reached up to rub Mr. Darling's nose before starting back toward the stables.

Furious, Bree kneed her mount to cut off her host. "Turning your back on a guest isn't polite."

He had stopped, but he also lost the affable smile. "Bree, it's not going to happen. I'm not going to bed you. I'm not even going to kiss you. I like my women experienced…and discreet. You're neither."

"The hell you know! For your information I rid myself of my virginity on my fifteenth birthday!"

"Fingers don't count, darling."

Already embarrassed, she wanted to strike out with rage, when Skeet Blanchard appeared from behind a truck, snickered and disappeared into the stables. She despised men when they were in groups like this. They always acted so arrogant and superior. Get one alone, though, and they became like whimpering puppies begging for attention. But she wasn't about to give up; she'd invested too much energy into making Perry Ashworth notice her. Besides, if he'd meant what he said about not being interested, he would never have let her have virtual run of the place.

Inspiration had her slipping off her mount. She signaled a young groom and handed him Mr. Darling's reins.

"Watch him for me, sugar," she whispered. She added a saucy wink, then, while glancing into the barn to make sure Perry wasn't watching, she released Lancer.

Skeet was the first to notice her, but by the time he murmured a warning to Perry, she was on the stallion and setting her heels into his ribs.

The Thoroughbred took off like a bolt of lightning.

"Bree!" Perry ran out of the barn after her. "Gabrielle, get your ass back here!"

Out of the reach of any of the hands, she urged Lancer across the immaculate lawn, past Perry's precious statue and laughed at him over her shoulder. "Make me!"

Being on top of a magnificent animal like this was both exhilarating and a bit frightening. Lancer made every other horse she'd ridden a carnival pony in comparison. All energy and will, he stretched every limb, every muscle, for an extra length of ground as though he had the memories of his ancestors' charges at the Kentucky Derby to inspire him.

Bree had to duck low to miss a cedar branch, and then hang tight as Lancer took a natural draw with minimal effort. When she was able to risk glancing back again, she saw that, as she'd hoped, Perry had grabbed a mount from a trainer and was giving chase. She laughed with glee. He'd chosen Madrigal, a gorgeous black mare, but no match for Lancer.

Perfect.

Bree directed the stallion into the woods, following the dirt trail that ran throughout those parts of Belle- mere not fenced for pasture. At the road separating the estate from her family's, she made a sharp right. Lancer didn't like that much, but she kept her seat, and at the fork made him hold to the right, away from the old Rader place. She'd decided she would wait for Perry at the lake. Lancer's trail was easy enough to follow on this clay. She would walk the stallion until Perry caught up, then invite him to join her for a swim. She had on some of her best lingerie. Surely when he saw it, her, he would forget those stupid comments about her being too young for him.

That careful planning came to an abrupt end when she had to bring up the horse because of a familiar blue-and-white truck blocking her way. As she fought to stay on the protesting horse, Ben Rader came out of the woods. Almost as breathless as her mount, Bree swept back her hair and grinned. She couldn't have planned this better herself.

"Why, hello! What are you doing down here? Not the best hour for fishing, is it?"

Ben swept off his hat and dragged his forearm across his sweaty forehead as he eyed Lancer, who pawed at the ground and whinnied at him. "More important is what are you doing on that monster? Tempting fate?"

"I can handle him all right."

"Does the horse know it?"

"Funny man." She eyed his muddy boots, and the stickers and seedpods that clung to his jeans and shirt.

Her grin faded somewhat. "You went to have a look, didn't you?"

"Been down there yourself?"

She shuddered at the thought. "No way! But I've heard a few kids tried to find the spot. Maybe one or two made it all the way. The others were either chased off by mosquitoes or snakes. Is it spooky?"

"Do you believe in ghosts, Bree?"

She frowned. "I don't know. Lem did."

"Maybe that's what I felt, Lem's ghost...and maybe it was his voice and not the breeze that made me think I'd heard your name."

Despite the hot sun baking down on her, she shivered again. *"What?"*

"We need to talk."

Before she could reply, she heard hooves signaling Perry's arrival. Exhaling her relief, she plastered her confident smile on her face and plucked her sweat-soaked blouse from between her breasts. "My, it's sultry, isn't it? How did you sleep last night? It can't be bearable in that hut. Why don't I talk to Eve about getting you into one of our guest rooms?"

"You have a dark sense of humor, Bree. And why are you—"

Perry drew up, cutting him off. One look at the ominous threat in his blue-gray eyes and she decided she wasn't wholly sorry for running in to Ben, although she didn't like the idea that he wanted to talk to her.

"Hi, slowpoke. I was just talking to Ben about the heat. Don't you think it's too warm to traipse through those woods?"

Perry swung his gaze to Ben. "You didn't waste much time."

"Told you that I wouldn't."

"Any luck?"

"Better than yours seems to be running."

As Bree tried to decide whether or not she should take that remark as a personal insult, Perry responded with a slight bow and faint laugh.

"You've got that right," he added. He shifted in his saddle as though trying to see if Ben was carrying anything.

Ben reached for a cigarette and calmly lit it. "Don't waste your time."

"Come on, Benjamin. This is more or less my backyard."

"It could all be if you played your cards right," Bree said in a singsong voice. "Of course—" she sent Ben a seductive smile "—I am open to all offers."

"My dear," Perry drawled, "you'll be lucky if you make it back to the stables with your hide intact."

Although she couldn't deny a bit of concern at the edge she heard in his voice, she waved with airy dismissal to Ben. "He's grumbling because I gave Lancer the real run this sweetie's been wanting."

"Give him the horse," Ben said, "and I'll drive you home."

She wanted to ask him how stupid he thought she was, but that would mean exposing their earlier dialogue to Perry, and she didn't want to do that, either. She did, however, notice Perry didn't look pleased with the suggestion at all. *That* she liked.

"Why, Ben, that's sweet. But not to worry. Perry

only pretends to care more about his horses than he does me, isn't that right, darling?"

"What's right, *darling,* is that we'd better get back before Skeet sends out a search party after us."

"I did leave my horse at Bellemere," Bree told Ben, "and it is time for Perry to feed me. I missed breakfast and all this exercise has made me famished. Let's talk later about that room and...things."

Afraid he might say something to ruin the moment for her, she spun Lancer around and launched him back toward the trail she'd taken earlier. She heard Perry follow soon afterward. He didn't, however, reach over and take Lancer's reins until they were well out of view of the road.

Bree had no choice but to let him stop the stallion.

"What room?" he snapped.

So she could rouse the passion in him! Pleasure energized Bree and made her bolder. "Ben's not comfortable at that shack Eve rented to him. I think we should have him stay at the house until we can get the cottage in more livable condition."

"Eve approves of this?"

Eve...Eve...Eve... Bree thought Perry's mind-set exasperating. "She may not have come to us with a refined sense of hospitality, but she's learned a thing or two since. Now, what about lunch?"

"No."

"Taking back an invitation is not gentlemanly behavior, Mr. Ashworth," she said, warming to her coquettish teasing. It always turned the boys in school and the hands working their place into tongue-tied clods.

"I didn't extend one, and I won't."

"Perry..."

"You've overestimated your value to me once too often today, Gabrielle. When we get back to the stables, I want you to take your horse and get lost. And don't come back to Bellemere until you've outgrown your penchant for manipulation and childish pranks. You're an accident waiting to happen, and I'll be damned if I'll pay for your stupidity."

Who did he think he was talking to? Blinking hard at the unwelcome tears threatening to blind her, Bree jerked her reins out of his grasp, at the same time giving Lancer a sharp kick. As the horse burst into another run, she heard Perry swear and call to her, but she ignored him.

He wanted her gone? Well, fuck him. He could eat her dust as she left.

By the time she reached the stables, she had the tears under control, but she was shaking with fury. She dismounted and slapped the winded horse's reins into the hands of a bewildered groom.

Perry arrived seconds later. "Doug, take this one, too," he said to the blemish-scarred teen. Then, before Bree could gather up Mr. Darling's reins, he grabbed her by the upper arm.

"Ow! What do you think you're—"

"Shut up." He pulled her into the stable and yelled, "Out!" to the man hanging tackle.

The man took off without a word.

It was all Bree could do not to slip on the concrete floor as Perry dragged her farther into the barn, and into the tackle room. When he slammed her against a wall, gear rattled, metal bits sang out like angry wind chimes and pain had her gasping for the breath he'd knocked out of her. All of that, however, was nothing to the shock of having him wrap a hand around her throat.

"If you ever pull a stunt like that again, I'll wring your silly little neck."

He looked as if he meant it, but convinced he had to be fighting other impulses, as well, Bree arched away from the wall to press her hips against his. "Are you sure you wouldn't prefer punishing me some other way?"

Perry narrowed his eyes, their color growing more like cold steel than frosty blue. But as she felt him stir against her, she laughed in breathless triumph.

"See? Deny it all you want, but I turn you on."

"Think so? Give it your best shot."

Did he think she wouldn't? The adrenaline still pumping from her exciting ride would have been enough to provoke her. This latest challenge sent a dizzying power through her, and she slid her fingers over his crotch, rose on tiptoe and traced his lips with her tongue. She meant merely to tempt, but the thrill of finally getting to touch him the way she'd dreamed triggered something primitive. With a moan, she wrapped her other arm around his neck, pressed and rubbed herself against him; she drove her tongue into his mouth, desperate to show him everything she had to offer. He tasted as clean as he always looked, and smelled a divine combination of French cologne, horse and leather; and when she felt him grow big and harden in her hand, she could barely resist climbing onto him, wrapping her legs around his waist and riding to quick satisfaction.

Lost in her own pleasure, she was slow to realize

what he was doing when he disengaged himself from her and backed a step away.

"Enjoy that?" he asked, his tone conversational.

"Yeah, and so did you." She lowered her gaze to the bulge in his riding breeches, and her pride almost matched her desire for him.

"That's where you're wrong. I get harder collecting my winnings at the races. And you're also wrong to think you're ever going to get this," he added, touching himself. "My horses show more finesse at foreplay than you do."

Bree didn't think he could hurt her so much, so deeply, twice. Backing away from him, she came up against the wall. It reminded her to keep her back straight and her head up.

"You bastard. Keep mooning over her. But one day you'll realize *I'm* the one with real power at Maitland Hall. As soon as I'm twenty-one, things change, whether your precious Eve likes it or not."

"That's a few years away yet. A number of things can happen between now and then."

"Never what you want," she sneered, determined to hide her pain from him. "Try to get off thinking about that!"

She didn't need this. As she walked, Eve checked her watch for what proved to be the third time in thirty minutes. Nearly eight o'clock and still no sign of Bree. In future, the girl wouldn't leave the house without leaving a full itinerary—and that wasn't going to happen any time soon. For the next several days—at least until after the Fourth of July festivities—she could consider herself grounded!

Good grief, where was she? Not even Justin had a clue; he said he'd been busy sketching here and there all day. After Bree missed dinner, Eve had gone to the barns to ask Dewitt if he or anyone had seen her since returning Mr. Darling to his stable. Dewitt found young Rod, who'd cooled down the gelding, even though Eve had made it clear on previous occasions that Bree should do it herself.

"Miss Maitland came charging through here around noon," he told her, "and there was no missing that she was pretty upset. When she drove away, she kicked up enough gravel and dust that she even had old Mr. D. skittering around, and you know how calm he is."

More or less. Eve did her best to stay away from that gentle creature, as she did any four-legged beast that she had to look up to. But she'd thanked Rod for his honesty, and turned down Dewitt's offer for a ride back to the house because walking in the fresh air beat pacing from room to room in the house.

Unfortunately, she had to take the long route back, instead of cutting through the orchard. Thanks to several late-evening showers, the mosquito population was heavier in there at this time of day. For obvious reasons, she also wanted to be closer to the county road. That took her directly past the foreman's cottage, but at least fate was kind in that Ben wasn't home yet, so she wouldn't have to add to her indigestion by having another confrontation with him. As it was, Mama Lulu's recent affection for using rue as a diet staple was beginning to aggravate her stomach lining. But no sooner did she congratulate herself than she saw a familiar vehicle coming around the bend.

One look as he braked beside her and she knew his day had matched hers in its decline, and although his eyes were hidden by those inevitable sunglasses, he didn't appear any happier than she was to be meeting again.

"I stopped at the house because I needed to talk to her," he said as though they were continuing a conversation after only a brief interruption. "Well, her and Mama Lulu."

Eve could understand his need to see Lulu, but Bree...? "What's wrong now?"

"First things first. You've looked everywhere?"

"Her usual haunts on the property. Except for riding, she's not an outdoors person. I've also made calls to her friends." Those she knew. Bree could be quite secretive when it suited her. "Hopefully, they're telling me the truth."

"She was at Bellemere earlier. I ran into her and Perry down by the lake. What did Ashworth say?"

Eve didn't miss the note of disapproval in his voice. "I haven't talked to him. I didn't think it necessary, since I knew she'd already left there."

"Maybe she went back. She was flirting. Pretty heavily."

"Oh, no...poor Perry."

"Don't waste your sympathy. That's one guy who can take care of himself."

"You don't get it. He's been very generous to her, and he's always an attentive host. I hate that she would take his goodwill the wrong way. I'm also upset that he didn't feel he could call and tell me about it."

"Could be he's keeping his options open. If things

don't work out with you, he'll switch over to heiress junior.''

"I thought we'd been through that?"

"You didn't believe me. I figure if I tell you enough times, maybe you'll start paying attention."

"And I'm telling you that Perry's been wonderful to us."

"To Justin? To Mama Lulu?"

He had her there. Except for the time Perry stopped by to pay his respects after Sumner died, she doubted he and her stepson's paths had crossed. And Mama Lulu did say she thought Perry "as smooth as a water snake." Eve had been disappointed with that pronouncement; however, one had to allow that Mama Lulu was always suspicious of men who were more beautiful than most women.

She sighed. "When I get back to the house, I'll call over there. Thank you for passing on the information."

"You can thank me by hopping in. I think you should be face-to-face when you ask Ashworth what happened."

8

"Considering the mood you're in," Eve said, "I wouldn't inflict you on someone I even mildly disliked, let alone a friend."

Ben smiled, although he didn't care for the term *friend* being applied to Ashworth. "You're definitely getting that southern-belle, kiss-my-grits attitude down pat."

"So why isn't it effective on you?"

"My skin's tougher than most. Or else I'm getting addicted to your variety of venom." He tilted his head toward the passenger side of his truck. "Come on, Red. If you go to the house to wait, you know you'll only walk a hole into the hardwood floors."

"I hate that nickname."

"Hop in and you can tell me how, when you were a kid, you used to wrestle little boys to the ground to make them stop calling you that."

"I'd rather have cramps."

She almost made him forget it had been a bitch of a day. Later he could call himself a glutton for punishment, but for now he wanted more of this—the mental dueling her company would guarantee—while he continued the distasteful probing into this town's dirty laundry. He knew exactly how to tempt her, too.

"Aren't you even slightly curious about what I want to talk to Bree about?"

He could tell her annoyance with him had made her momentarily forget about that. "You didn't want to tell me before."

"Women aren't the only ones allowed to change their minds."

Narrowing her eyes, she circled the truck and climbed in on the passenger side. "You'll have to stop at the house again," she said as he shifted into drive and headed toward the side gate.

Ben braked, but said, "No need to change on my account." He wasn't wild about the jeans and man's denim shirt she now wore, but he didn't want her dolling up for Perry, either.

"I had no intention of changing. I need to tell Mama Lulu where I'll be."

Not wanting to upset her so much that she wouldn't come back out, he switched subjects as he cut a sharp three-point turn and drove back toward the house. "So how did the meeting with Varnell go? No doubt he took to your idea like kids to ice cream?"

"He wasn't enthusiastic at first. But when I explained how we could finance the library, he—damn."

"What?"

"Between one thing and another, I forgot all about talking to Perry," she said, her fingers against her lips. "If Fred called him this afternoon, he's not going to know what's going on, and as good-natured as Perry is, he's not going to like that I volunteered his financial backing without discussing things with him first." Eve shot Ben a worried look. "Maybe you'd better stay here. You're apt to upset him, and I need him agreeable.''

''Just bat those green eyes at him, and I have a feeling he'll come through.'' Ben dug out a cigarette, but settled for simply holding it between his lips.

''Can you say anything that isn't sexist?''

''What's sexist about pointing out that no matter how much you try to hide behind outfits like the one you're wearing, you *are* female and we men notice?''

She shook her head. ''First, you accuse me of dressing provocatively, and now I'm hiding. Before this conversation disintegrates completely, why don't you tell me why you needed to see Mama Lulu? Did something else happen to Noah, or is this about you going down to the lake?''

''Noah's fine, as far as I know. Luther explained how you'd overreacted a bit.''

''I *what?*''

''Thanks for confirming what I suspected. Between the time you came to get me and my arrival there, Luther had a change of heart about involving the law. He turned it into some boys-will-be-boys skirmish.''

''That child was terrified!''

''Rae and Mama Lulu seemed pretty rattled themselves. But if Luther insists he has things under control, there's not much I can do.''

As he stopped in front of the house, Eve asked, ''How did Mama Lulu react to that? When we drove home earlier, she was convinced you were going to do a full investigation.''

Yeah, ''full,'' as though he had nothing else on his plate. As much as he hated to admit it, even a cute kid like Noah getting bullied didn't compete with the rest of what he knew and sensed was going on in Parish. "For the time being, let her think what she wants. Besides, that's not what I came to see her about."

"Lem?"

"As I suspected, things are a mess down there. Everything's been trampled over pretty good. Part of that couldn't be helped, what with the investigative team and the coroner's group. But inevitably, there's the human-nature factor, some people react to yellow tape like ants to sugar. But I stopped by to ask Mama Lulu for a list of Lem's friends. I thought I'd check and see which of them might have gone down there."

Eve frowned down at her clasped hands. "Maybe you haven't figured this out yet, but Lem was generally considered an okay guy...and heaven knows he had an eye for the ladies, but...he didn't appear to have what you would call *close* friends."

"That's the conclusion I'm coming to from my talks with Luther and Mama Lulu."

"So where does Bree figure in? You said you needed to talk to her, as well."

Ben wondered if she was a good actress or had she somehow been kept out of the loop on this? "When statements were being given, Bree came forward voluntarily and said she'd been at Bellemere at sunset the night Lem died. She's listed as one of the last people who saw him alive. She said he was helping to unload a truck of feed, something not reported by anyone else at Bellemere."

"I had no idea."

"I can see that."

"But there's more, isn't there? I can see there is."

"Shortly after leaving the station this evening, I was stopped by Harry Wheeler. He looked as though he'd aged a decade in the twenty-four hours since his official retirement."

"Everyone wondered why he quit so abruptly. Sure, we were complaining about the lack of investigation, but he did seem to enjoy his job otherwise."

"He's not a happy camper now. It seems that when Lem's body was found, he had two thousand dollars on him. He said it was recorded on the original reports."

"What do you mean the *original* reports?" Eve twisted in her seat to face him fully. "How many versions are there?"

"Good question. The only one I've seen says that he had a wallet with thirty-six bucks on him and a half-dozen useless credit cards."

Eve held up her hand. "Wait. Wait. This is too…" She opened the truck door and climbed out. "I'll be back in a minute."

"Not a word of that to Mama Lulu."

She shot him a look that told him what she thought of his reading of human nature, and hurried inside.

Ben settled in his seat and lit the cigarette dangling in his mouth. So, she hadn't known about Bree; what's more, the news about the money had rattled her every bit as much as that kiss yesterday. That won her a number of points with him, not necessarily a good thing, and gave him a slightly better picture of things—an extremely welcome thing.

He knew what he needed to do next. It would mean using her to get at Perry Ashworth. That wouldn't endear him to her, but hopefully the end would justify the means. It was Bree who Eve should really worry about. What else did the kid know? What trouble would it bring to her family?

"D'you know what you're doing?"

Not about to let him know her insides were liquefying from nerves, Bree turned on her hundred-watt smile for the giant glaring at her and wriggled to a more relaxed position in the dark, leather-upholstered interior of the Lincoln. "Sure. You're Moxie Larouche. You were Lem's friend. I thought we could talk."

"First of all—" the huge man slipped a stainless-steel emery board he'd been using on his thick nails into his silk suit jacket "—nobody calls me Moxie except my mama. It's Mox, and maybe even Mr. Larouche to you. Second, Cobb was no friend, he was a business acquaintance…a trying one. And third…I don't talk to babies."

Mox Larouche's car was customized, his clothes designer-made, tailored for a large-boned, steroid-enhanced body, and any one of his diamond rings would adequately post his bail if he was arrested. Until today Bree had only heard stories about him, and seen him from a distance. If she didn't want this to be their first and last encounter, she had to hang on to her composure. *And you can,* she reminded herself. After all, he might be a successful bookie; however, *she* was a Maitland.

"I'm not a baby. I was a customer of Lem's." She shook her head the way models did so her hair would caress her face and shoulders. She thought that always gave them a sexy confident look. "A good one.

That's how I got your number. I was with him several times when he phoned in my bets to you. You know that.''

"Do I?"

"You also saw Lem and I together a few times when he needed a ride to meet you here to—"

Before she could finish, the giant lunged across from the driver's seat to clap his hand over her mouth. A scream locked in her throat; her heart pounded in a frantic attempt to escape through her sternum.

"What the fuck're you doing? You wired?"

At first she thought he meant drugged or drunk and vigorously shook her head, or at least she tried to. Mox's great paw threatened to push her through one side of the leather seat and out the other.

"Show me."

Then it hit her. He wanted her to prove she wasn't wearing some kind of listening device, that she hadn't turned informer. Thinking of the scenes she'd seen on TV when guys lifted their shirts to expose their stomachs, she tugged her black T-shirt from her jeans to expose a few inches of tummy.

"Higher."

Those viper eyes told her that she shouldn't ask him to cut her any slack simply because she was new at this. What the hell? she thought. It wasn't as though she was braless. In fact, she wore less swimming. With a smirk, she gave him a better peek at the French lace that made up the underside of her demi-bra, then tugged the shirt down in place.

Muttering a crude expletive, Mox reached into the scooped neck and bra, and groped within each cup.

"Not bad," he said, withdrawing just as quickly.

He settled back in his seat. "But I prefer 'em bigger myself. Something to fill these."

Outraged, Bree eyed the hands he cupped between them. "Yeah, well, good luck finding a cow that hasn't been milked in a week."

"Watch your mouth, or I'll start on those britches next. 'Course, I don't guess I need to bother. There's barely room for you in 'em."

If he reached for her again, she thought she might have to call the whole thing off. Only the thought of having to go home a failure had her sitting up and thrusting out her chest. "I never thought of you as the anxious type, worrying about wires and cops."

He had to weigh at least three hundred pounds, and Bree figured his great bald head accounted for fifty pounds of that. Lem said that Mox Larouche never used outside muscle to collect past-due accounts. One look at Mox and you changed your mind about not having the money you owed him. No one was ever stupid enough to think about turning him in to the law.

Her comment had him laughing, which exposed several gold teeth. "Anxious. You're something else, kid." In the next instant he was sober again, and he pointed a hot link-size finger into her face. "Now cut the crap. I don't like leaving Memphis without a good reason, and the only good reason is money. Cops out here in the boonies see my out-of-state plates and this car, and they know I ain't here to sightsee, so this better be good. What do you have for me?"

"Me. I want to take Lem's place." As he made a face and reached for the ignition key, she stayed his hand. "Hear me out. I know how it's done. What's more, I know a good number of Lem's regulars."

Mox narrowed his eyes. "How's that? Were you two screwing?"

"No! He was a friend, that's all." She would supply the cash and he would get the beer or wine and they would sit out here or somewhere away from town and talk, complain about the things that were holding them back and plan what they would do once they got out of Parish. "How do you think he got to Memphis most of the time?"

"Who cares? He owed, I collected. That's all that mattered. And he wasn't that reliable. Seems to me, you were the reason a few times. Why should I go through more of that?"

"Because I'll bring you more business than Lem did."

He laughed. "Right. You wanna make money? I know a guy who'd probably give you all the work you could handle."

"Don't treat me like some brainless tramp. You're only getting a small percentage of the money you could make out here and you know it."

He pushed out his thick lower lip and shrugged. "What do you know about it?"

She and Lem had discussed it, how some people, people in her circle particularly, wouldn't do business with him. They'd talked of becoming partners. "I know you were pushing him to get a car and travel to the neighboring towns to bring in more business. I know you even offered to finance it for him, but he wouldn't do it because you wanted to charge more than any finance company would."

"Why shouldn't I have made a decent profit? Who else would loan him the money? You?"

She would if she could have gotten her hands on that much. But just like her winnings, her allowance went for clothes. "Okay, if you don't care, why did you bother with Lem in the first place? And why did you bother agreeing to meet me out here in the middle of nowhere?" She gestured toward the tinted windows. The sun was setting fast and long shadows from ancient live oaks crept over the sedan parked beside the dilapidated barn. They were miles outside of Parish. This monster of a man could kill her and her body might not be found for weeks, if ever. She couldn't think of that, only success. Success meant power, and power would mean freedom.

"I wanted to get a look at the baby-voiced hotshot who said she had valuable information about Lem. But if that's it—this business-arrangement idea—this meeting is over. I don't deal with kids."

"I'm eighteen, for crying out loud! Besides, what's age got to do with anything? Being young is an asset, if you ask me."

"Who do you think you're talking to? Some jerk from the government? You think I care about affirmative action and equal opportunity? Listen, I like your sass, okay, though I think it would eventually get on my nerves, but I have two rules. One, I never do business with a woman, and two, I don't deal with kids." He raised his hands as she began to protest again. "See? Already you're gonna give me lip. You know what I would do to Cobb if he'd given me the hassle you are?" Mox punched his fist into his palm.

Bree didn't want to think of that fist anywhere near

her body, but she wasn't a quitter, either. "I understand it's in your best interest to act tough with me, Mr. Larouche, and I respect that. But I'm not just any female or any kid. I'm Gabrielle Maitland. Surely the name means something to you?"

"Yeah. It's one more reason we ain't gonna be doing business. First thing that happens is that you get nailed and the law offers to cut a deal to protect your family's reputation. Guess what happens to poor Mox? I get a ride down to Parchman, and sweet cheeks, I ain't going back there. So get out of my car, and go be the debutante your mama wants you to be."

"I can't believe you're turning me down! Lem wasn't as ambitious as I am. And soon I'll be going away to school. That's new connections because I'll be commuting."

Mox rubbed his face and a sound, more like a groan, rumbled from between his fingers. "I don't know where you're hiding 'em in those britches, but you've got balls. You wanna keep 'em, get the hell out. Now."

When she didn't budge, he reached into his jacket, pulled out a gun, which fit too well between her thighs.

"Maybe you didn't hear me." He leaned over to open her door, and shoved with the gun. "Get lost. Forget my name, my number, my license plate. I get so much as a sniff of a cop hanging around me, and I'm gonna blame you, understand? You won't like the crew I'll send to clean up this little problem."

She'd gasped as steel assaulted her tender flesh, and when she hit the packed ground, she cried out against the sharp stones digging into her bottom; but her reflexes remained good. As he gunned the car's engine and pulled out of there kicking up dirt and rocks, she rolled to safety and scrambled to her feet.

"You son of a bitch!" For good measure, she picked up a rock and threw it after him as he raced away.

Hurting and humiliated, and wishing she'd first asked him if he had anything for a quick buzz, she brushed at her clothes. "Well, fine. In the end you'll be the loser missing out," she muttered. "Who needs you, you hear me? Who needs anybody!"

"Do you know what strikes me as most profound and sad about Bree? She really does need and want to be loved."

Eve had returned to Ben's Blazer and they were almost at the end of the driveway. Until now she'd remained silent about Ben's latest news flash. But she didn't want to get to Bellemere without knowing more, or without Ben understanding how she felt about her stepdaughter.

He slowed to check for oncoming traffic. "That's about as useful as saying everyone wants to be happy."

"You're right." Eve sighed. "Do you think she's connected with that missing money?"

"No. There's one piece of good news for you and bad news for me. I'm afraid that problem lies in my office."

"Oh, Ben."

"Don't worry about it. I knew I'd inherit some trouble, and I'll take care of it. I'm just grateful Harry decided to tell me. The only reason I'm telling *you* any of this is because Bree may know something about where Lem got the money, so don't ask me to go easy on Ashworth or any of his people if I sense they're hiding her or keeping information about her from you.''

"Why would they do that?'' Eve wasn't around Bellemere enough to know his crew very well, but she couldn't imagine Perry being anything less than helpful and supportive.

"They may not. I'm just warning you in case they do.''

"Maybe we'd better change the subject before I regret agreeing to this.''

"Go ahead. Pick one.''

"What do you think Lem was doing with that much money?''

"I have no idea.''

Nor did he want to guess; she could hear that unspoken thought follow the first. She didn't blame him. Lem liked the good life and money didn't slip through his fingers, it poured as though from a hundred-year flood. Mama Lulu said he'd admitted to gambling every once in a while even though he knew it upset her terribly, but that was a good bit of money to win. Had he stolen it? If so, from whom?

"If the money was legally his,'' she said tentatively, "do you think you may be able to get it back?''

"You're thinking how useful it would be to Mama Lulu.''

"She would give it to Luther for the boys' schooling.''

"That's what I figured, too. Don't get your hopes

up, though. Chances are, Haygood's already spent it.''

''You know who took it?''

''It's his report.''

Perry was coming out of the stables when Ben pulled up before the house. At first he seemed annoyed at the sight of the Blazer, but then he saw her getting out. After a brief lift of both aristocratic eyebrows, he smiled.

''I should have called,'' she told him as he approached her and took both of her hands.

''Nonsense.'' He kissed her on both cheeks. ''I'd even tell one of my expectant mothers in the throes of labor to take five just to visit with you.''

''No wonder horses don't like me.''

''One of these days I'll convince you otherwise.'' He studied her face. ''But this isn't a social call. You look troubled. What's up?''

Eve noticed how he virtually ignored Ben. ''I can't find Bree. After she came home from riding, she took off in her car and no one's seen her since. We were hoping that you might have an idea. No, actually, Ben told me that she'd made quite the pest of herself here earlier today, and I was hoping she'd come back to continue. Forgive the wishful thinking, Perry, but it would be easier to take her by the scruff of the neck from here than to have to search through half the county for her.''

''Bless your heart.'' He released her, only to encircle her back with one arm to give her a tender squeeze. ''That girl's determined to test you at every turn.''

''It appears so. Any suggestions?''

"It's a cliché, but the idea of a convent appeals."

Although she smiled, she said, "I meant, did you have any suggestions about where she could be?"

"I'm afraid not."

"How was she when she left here?" Ben asked. "From what I saw, you didn't much care for the way she was handling your horse."

Perry shot Ben a look of sheer resentment.

"*Your* horse…?" Eve knew Perry's protectiveness of his stock. She doubted he would ever willingly let Bree on one of his high-strung beauties. "Perry, she got on one of your horses?"

"Lancer." Despite an obvious unhappiness with Ben, he seemed willing to have a philosophical attitude about the experience. "I'm afraid I did have to give her a stern talking-to, Eve. But it's over with now and fortunately there was no damage done on either side."

"You should have called and told me!"

"She's a kid, testing her wings. Forget it."

Instead, Eve laid a hand on his chest. "How can I do that? You've been beyond generous with her. When I think of her abusing your goodwill—"

"Hey…my choice." Perry covered her hand with his. "I've told you before, I'm here to help any way I can. If that means a little stressful baby-sitting, so be it."

"That's touching, Slick." Ben came around the Blazer. "I know it's nowhere near as interesting to make points with the law, but how about helping me?"

Eve couldn't believe his rudeness. "Ben, really. There's no need to—"

"It's okay, love. Our new chief isn't used to seeing the Maitlands and Ashworths getting along so well, that's all."

Ben stopped before Perry. "I have no problem with that. It's having to wade through your bullshit that's tough."

"Stop it!" Eve stepped between the two men. "Don't make me regret accepting your help, Ben."

Ignoring her, he reached into his shirt pocket. "What about it? If I show you this, are you going to tell me if someone from your crew smokes these?"

He took out a small plastic bag, and inside, Eve saw what she assumed was a cigarette butt. Perry eased her out of his way and took it for a closer examination, but Eve wanted Ben to know he didn't deserve the courtesy.

"This is ridiculous—and insensitive. Considering what happened to Perry's father, you must know how he feels about his employees smoking. And why didn't you tell me about that thing when I asked you before if you'd had any success down there?"

"I think I made myself clear," he asked quietly. His eyes, however, warned her that if she said much more, she would be sorry.

She shut up, but she wasn't happy about it.

Perry handed back the bag. "Eve's right. I'd fire anyone I caught smoking around the stables. Some may enjoy the habit for all I know, but they don't light up around here." He nodded to the package Ben tucked back into his shirt. "You shouldn't have any problem finding your man, though. That's an exclusive blend, isn't it?"

"So far, the closest supplier I've been able to find

is in New Orleans. You wouldn't by chance have someone working for you who's been there recently?''

"Offhand I'd have to say no. But I also don't monitor the personal lives of the people who work for me.''

"What about business contacts, sales reps, delivery people?''

"They come and go. It's possible that a number of them smoke, but if you're suggesting anything of theirs ended up down— Where did you say you found that?''

"Guess.''

For several seconds the only sound was the plaintive call of mourning doves heralding the end of the day. Eve loved to sit on the veranda at Maitland Hall and listen to them. She wished she was there now.

"I don't think I like your tone of voice, Chief Rader,'' Perry replied at last. ''If you're suggesting something, I wish you'd say so. Then I can call my attorney, who will feel compelled to phone Mayor Varnell to ask the reason why we have to put up with your less-than-professional investigative tactics.''

The amber sunset did nothing to soften Ben's darker, less refined features. ''Save yourself a phone call, I'll be happy to tell you. I don't believe in coincidence. This,'' he said, pointing to his pocket with his thumb, ''was caught between a leaf stem and stalk of a swamp plant as if someone had flicked it away.''

"There you are then. Surely someone who had something to hide wouldn't be so careless?''

"Unless they were overconfident that the butt would get lost in the undergrowth.''

"Like a cop maybe? Or someone attached to the coroner's office? Or one of who knows how many people who've been to the lake to satisfy their morbid curiosity?"

Ben focused on Eve. "She's not here. Let's go."

He had to be kidding. Eve stiffened. "Under the circumstances, I don't think so. Besides, I still have to talk to Perry about—"

"Do it tomorrow." He took hold of her arm and opened the passenger door. "We have a girl to find, and the darker it gets, the tougher that will be."

Perry appeared on her left side. "Eve, if you're going to continue looking for Bree, I'll be more than happy to take you. Besides, you said you needed to talk…?"

She began to answer Perry, but Ben tightened his grip on her arm. Suddenly it was all she could do to breathe, let alone speak.

"Tomorrow," Ben all but growled at him. After Eve got into the truck, he slammed the passenger door behind her to punctuate his message.

As Perry appeared in the open window, she discreetly rubbed her right arm, but summoned a reassuring, if brief, smile for her neighbor. "Maybe it's better this way. I will call you in the morning. But if you hear anything from her—"

"I'll call immediately, of course. Take care. Please."

His frown spoke eloquently of his concern and displeasure. Almost suffocating between his emotions and the angry ones radiating from Ben as he climbed in on the driver's side, it was a relief when he had the Blazer heading down the driveway and fresh air rushed through the open window to cool her overheated skin. Nevertheless, she exploded as soon as she knew they were out of hearing distance.

"You're impossible!"

"Yeah, well, apparently you never heard of the practice of going home with the guy who brought you to the dance." And by the way his jaw was working, he had much more to say than that.

"This isn't a date, and you used me! Why didn't you tell me about that cigarette butt?"

"I had my reasons."

"Which are?"

"The element of surprise, for one. You made it clear that given the chance, you'd blab it to Ashworth first thing. I thought you said you two were only friends?"

"We are!"

"Uh-huh. Friends who can barely keep their hands off each other."

This was ridiculous; he sounded worse than a jealous lover. Preoccupied with that, as well as with the insulting connotations of his previous accusation, she was slow to realize he'd turned left toward town.

"I want to go home."

"We are *going* to locate your errant stepdaughter."

"I'll walk home and look for her myself. Please stop and let me out. This is the last time I'm going to say it politely."

When he ignored her, she reached over and turned off the ignition.

Swearing, he jammed on the brake, and because she'd failed to put on her seat belt, that sent her flying forward. Thanks to his terrific instincts, she hit the arm he thrust out, and not the windshield or dash, but nothing could save her from wrath.

"You fool!" As the momentum of the truck bounced her off the back of the passenger seat, he took hold of her upper arms and brought them nose-to-nose. "Never, *never* do that again!"

"Then don't ignore me!"

It was an insane thing to say when they were gasping for the same snatch of air, and losing focus from being too close to see anything but themselves in each other's eyes. She wasn't surprised when the remark won a brief, harsh laugh from him.

"*Ignore* you! Who gets the chance?"

She recognized his intent and opened her mouth to gasp, "Don't." But she wasn't fast enough, and his grip was uncompromising. Before she could even replenish the air in her lungs, he'd angled his head and locked his mouth to hers.

This was what she didn't want to happen again. She didn't want to be reminded of how good it felt to have a strong male body against hers, particularly *his* body, to feel his energy and heat; but he, it, assaulted and enveloped her, burning through to the long-denied hunger she kept so well under control. It didn't matter that she fisted her hands and resisted drawing him closer, her mouth and mind cooperated.

"God help me, I want you."

His gruff whisper sent her careening—no, flying. *God help us both.*

Suddenly she took a blinding blow to the head. Her cry was muted by his long string of expletives.

They'd crashed, really crashed this time.

When she trusted that the truck would stay still,

and the worst stab of pain eased to a deafening throb, she opened her eyes to see Ben way above her giving his shoulder a quick rub and then reaching for her.

"Are you okay?"

"What happened?"

"We rolled into a tree."

And even though he helped her back onto her seat, Eve could see he thought it was all her fault. She gingerly fingered the right side of her head and eyed the big oak through the windshield. "There's proof positive."

"No kidding?"

"I meant proof that we're too old to act like kids with raging hormones."

Shooting her a speaking look, he got out and checked the bumper. Eve used the opportunity to angle the rearview mirror in her direction to check for any visible signs of injury. She didn't find any, but she did notice two strategic buttons on her shirt had come undone. Not undone, she realized with increasing misery, but broken off. Swearing again because it would now be obvious—as if he hadn't already guessed—that she wore nothing beneath it, she began searching for something to keep her presentable.

Ben returned, took one look at her situation and dug under his seat, finally drawing out a first-aid kit. "There should be a few safety pins in there," he said, handing it over.

"Thanks. What's the damage?"

"A bump in the fender and a crack in my resolve."

Funny man. "Then we can call it a draw."

"And pretend this didn't happen?" he asked, his tone challenging.

Eve tried to sit as straight as possible as she searched through the kit, but she could feel his gaze moving over her like hot breath. "I guess that *is* asking a bit much."

"So would using the argument that we haven't known each other long enough for this to be happening."

"I'm not going to have an affair with you, Ben."

"Say that a few times for me while you're at it."

How could someone she'd just wanted to take a swing at make her smile. "I won't have to if you remind yourself that you don't even like me. Correction, you don't *want* to like me."

"But I'm fast developing an excruciating affection for your body."

She lifted an eyebrow. "Sex for the sake of sex?"

"Trust me, it's the only kind of relationship I'm interested in. Ever."

Eve wanted no part of love, either. It would be one complication too many at this stage of her life. But it would take someone far more naive than her to believe being Ben Rader's lover would be easy.

"Why don't I simply apologize for overreacting," she said, staring at the plastic container of safety pins. Her fingers were too unsteady to reach for them.

"Coward."

He had that right. She didn't like the feeling, either, but considering her options.... "That's not to say I'm not disappointed you behaved the way you did with Perry, but I'll accept it's old territory between you two, and none of my business."

"Look at me, Red."

She sighed, but did as he asked.

''The matter's under control for tonight, but I think we'd better get used to the idea that we have a big problem developing between us.''

''And I'd rather we stay...friendly antagonists.''

The left corner of his mouth twitched. ''If you mean that, then hurry up and fix that shirt.''

Muttering under her breath, she snatched the container of pins. She'd just removed the lid when he reached over and, with a finger under her chin, lifted her head.

''One more warning—if you change your mind about wanting an affair, don't you dare go to Ashworth. Come to me.''

9

"What do you say? Will you?"

As usual with boys his age, Donny Reynolds was too eager to wait for an answer. He also ignored the inconvenience presented by the console in Bree's car and began fumbling with her T-shirt. She watched the former senior-class president's intent expression and thought of who she wished was doing that. Perry wouldn't have been so clumsy that he took longer to get the thing out of the waistband of her jeans than it took to perform brain surgery. But then, Donny was only with her because she was furious with Perry.

To think that until a few hours ago she'd believed only girls enjoyed playing hard to get. Well, Mr. Full-of-Himself Ashworth had taught her a thing or two. And grown men were definitely less easy to manipulate than boys. She would have to plan carefully and weigh her options before deciding how to retaliate.

In the meantime, she'd been entertaining herself by stealing Connie Craig's boyfriend away from her. Bree thought of how the ex-captain of the cheerleader squad would squeal when she found out. Imagining the scene was almost as pleasing as the cool, evening air caressing her increasingly bared skin, especially when joined by Donny's warm, humid breath. Not that she intended to let him enjoy himself too much.

"I don't know, Donny. This might not be a good idea." Bree wiggled a bit farther against the driver's door to make him think she was trying to get away from him. "Maybe you're only using me. I don't want you thinking I'm easy."

"Me? Never, Bree!"

She almost giggled at how his voice cracked and his hands shook; but she would knee him where it hurts if he messed up her hair while slipping her top over her head. All she needed was explaining a new hairdo when she got home. But she forgave him his clumsiness once he finally had the shirt completely off her and was pressing his face in the valley of her breasts.

Donny's groan sounded something between pleasure and pain. "If you would've given me a hint that you liked me, Bree, there would never have been any Connie. You're the one I've always wanted."

She barely listened to what he was saying; boys his age were so uninventive when talking to a girl. But he was a better kisser than most, and she enjoyed the way his lips vibrated against her skin when he spoke. Closing her eyes, she whimpered softly to encourage him, before adding, "I'll bet you say almost the same thing to her every time you two make up."

"No way! Besides, it's over with her for good this time. I swear it!"

He was as cute as a cocker spaniel. But his mind-set was as transparent as cellophane wrap.

"We'll see. Tell me what she let you do."

"Not much besides necking and some touching through our clothes."

"Poor Donny, that was cruel of her. But then, she isn't as pretty as I am, either, is she?" she cooed, cupping and lifting herself to deepen her already generous cleavage. She wished he would have thought of that himself; on the other hand, her car hadn't been designed for petting, and she certainly had no intention of doing anything more athletic. She simply wanted to burn off some of her frustration and give her ego a bit of bolstering.

The boy groaned and pressed his open mouth against the firm mound swelling over her lacy bra. "Nobody is, Bree. You're not just pretty, you're beautiful."

He laved her with his tongue, but only the exposed part of her breasts. Bree bit back a sigh of frustration. Did she have to teach him *everything*?

"Oh, Donny." She moaned and arched against his mouth, hoping he got the message. "That feels so good, it makes my nipples ache."

His breathing was beginning to sound like Mr. Darling after too hard of a run. "Want me to show you how much better it can get?"

The damned snap was right in front of his nose, what the hell was he waiting for, a signal from his former football coach? "You're not being a big ol' bragger, are you?" she teased, brushing his dark blond hair off his forehead.

"No! I didn't mean to insinuate—"

Bree touched a finger to his lips. "I'm only kidding. I like you—" she ran her fingertip over his moist lower lip, then brought the finger to her own mouth to lick "—just the way you are."

After giving her a quick, wet kiss, he began wrestling with the closure. After several seconds passed with no success, Bree turned her attention to the first stars coming out in the cloudless sky. She'd parked behind the town water tower's maintenance shed. It was her favorite place to hide when it was too early to go home. This evening she wanted to avoid Maitland Hall more than usual. Thanks to Perry and that pig Mox, the prospect of sitting around that huge mostly empty dining table while Eve questioned her and Justin about their day and tried to interest them in current events was more than she could bear.

At last Donny succeeded in opening her bra. But nothing else happened.

Bree glanced down to see him gaping at her. "What's the matter now?"

"Damn, Bree. I've never— You really are something."

He fell on her as if he was starving. Had she compared him to a puppy? Then he was a mongrel. She wouldn't have minded his enthusiasm, but did he have to knead her like Mama Lulu worked dough for their bread?

"Easy, honey. Easy. Ouch! Now, listen, buster, you're no newborn and I'm not your mama. Be careful with those."

"I didn't realize…"

"Shh…" She drew him toward her again. "Don't talk. Just try again. Do you like to play make-believe, Donny? I love to. Let's pretend I'm a fresh-baked slice of sweet, sweet cherry pie and there's a luscious, melting scoop of vanilla ice cream keeping me from you. What are you going to do about that?''

"Man, oh, man." Donny gulped. "I'm gonna get it all or die tryin'."

And he gave it his best effort, she had to credit him with that. Unfortunately, his focus was on pleasing himself, and when he urged her hand down to his bulging zipper, she thought it only fair that he reciprocate. Only, after three tries she realized he couldn't concentrate on two things at one time, at least not when his pleasure was involved.

"Well, screw this," she muttered, pushing him off her. It was bad enough to be rejected by Perry, she fumed, fastening her bra and reaching for her shirt, but if that was the best this jerk could do, she might as well go home and make herself come while showering.

"Bree? What's wrong?"

Although it was nearly dark now, Bree could see Donny's stunned and pained expression as she keyed her car's engine, but she couldn't care less. She wasn't feeling all that great herself.

"I forgot an appointment."

"At this hour?"

"It's a family thing, okay?" She would tell him she'd had a psychic moment, that her stepmother had died, if that's what it took to get free of him. Switching on the car's headlights, she spooked a rabbit across the field. It looked as startled as the boy beside her.

"Well, I guess if you have to be there... Wish you'd have remembered this sooner, though."

"I'll look into getting a social secretary."

She dropped him off with a minimum of promises, none of which she intended to keep, and turned the car toward Maitland Hall. How she wished she had the means to keep going, but even when she'd gambled through Lem, she could barely get from week to week, what with her luck running from hot to cold just when she was beginning to build a nice tidy sum. There was no way she could live on her allowance alone. And if there *was* work for her in this boring little town, it wouldn't provide what she needed to meet her needs and interests. No, Eve had her exactly where she wanted her—under the proverbial thumb.

Preoccupied, she was momentarily confused when her car began to lurch. But she quickly realized what was wrong and swore as she checked the fuel gauge.

"Oh, for...not again!"

She couldn't believe this could happen to her twice in a week; however, the car's gas tank was indeed empty, and she wasn't even on the right side of Parish! Damn Donny for living way off on that farm northeast of town. And damn this piddling town for closing the only gas station so early. It was barely past nine, for pity's sake!

Aware she had a long walk ahead of her if someone didn't show up to give her a lift, she let the car roll as far as it would go before parking on the shoulder. Then, after setting the brake and groping around in the dark for her purse, she glanced up at the sky to see if she had to secure the top. Hardly. It was a still, clear night; the sky had deepened to an indigo blue and was wonderfully radiant with the brightest stars that reminded her of the most divine rhinestone-studded gown she'd seen recently in a magazine.

"That's something else I'll be doing without," she muttered, getting out. If she ever needed a drink or something, she needed it now.

As she slammed the door, she was caught in the headlights of an oncoming vehicle. When it stopped beside her, she remained slightly wary but hopeful. Considering what had happened earlier, she wouldn't have put one cent on her chances that he would stop, yet here he was.

"Well, well," she purred, "you're a gentleman, after all. Now, what can I do to convince you to give me a lift home? I'm afraid I've let myself get too low on fuel again."

"Do you mind a small detour first?"

She brushed her hair behind her shoulders and gave him her brightest smile. "There's nothing scheduled that can't wait. What did you have in mind?"

"What do you mean what do I have in mind?" Luther said, wounded because Rae had now brushed his hand off her thigh for the second time since leaving the farm. For the six weeks they'd been making this trip, today was the first day they'd been alone, and even though it was for a somber cause, he would be damned if he behaved until he absolutely had to. Moments of privacy like this were hard to come by for them, but Rae seemed intent on making a point. "I'm lettin' my wife know I'm glad she's with me, that's all."

"Mister, you know full well that I started my thing this morning, so whatever you're really thinking, you're out of luck."

Luther sighed. "You sound like you got cramps or a headache."

"No, I'm still upset over what happened to Noah, and I'm hoping we did the right thing leaving him in Micah's care. His intentions are good, but I know him. He'll try to help Theo on the roof, too, and then Calvin's likely to take advantage. You know that boy can be nearly as big a torment to our baby as those boys were yesterday."

"I talked to Theo, and he gave me his word that *he'd* keep an eye on Calvin."

"You did?" Although they had a solid commitment never to go to bed with angry words between them, this was the first real smile Rae had given him since yesterday, and this time when he put his hand on her thigh, she covered it with hers. "Thank you for that."

Encouraged, Luther continued, "Sure. They'll be okay, even if they have to take him up on the roof with 'em."

"Oh, that's reassuring."

For his part, Luther was proud that their older boys had suggested reshingling the house themselves. He'd bought the material for the job back in the early spring before he'd committed to opening the store, but the way things were going, it would have been next year at the earliest before he would have had time to tackle the project.

"It's gonna get hotter than they think today," Rae added, lifting her cotton top from her already glistening chest. "I'm going to call at eleven and tell them to quit for the day or else— *Luther!*"

He saw it at the same moment she cried out. They

were coming down the alley to the back of their store, and there was no way to miss that something was terribly wrong.

"Sweet Lord have mercy!" This couldn't be happening.

Someone had paid them a visit since they'd locked up last night, and now it looked as though a considerable amount of their inventory had been thrown outside. Food, shelves, paper...Luther could barely identify some of the mess. What was equally shocking was that the rest of the stores appeared untouched. Only they had been singled out.

He parked in the middle of the alley and left the engine running. "Stay in the car," he told his wife. "If somebody's still inside there—"

"Nobody's in there. And I'll bet nobody around here knows what happened or saw anything, either."

Her tone matched her defeated stare, and that scared him almost as much as this scene of disrespect and waste. But not trusting his voice, he remained silent and eased out of the truck.

As an afterthought, before entering the store, he picked up a sturdy piece of wood from a broken crate that had a nail sticking out of it. If Rae was wrong, he wanted a chance at whoever had done this, before he turned them over to the law.

If he'd been told to imagine being vandalized, he couldn't have pictured what he saw once inside. As bad as the alley had been, the stockroom and store were a wreck—shelves tipped over, canned goods dented and wrappers torn off so the contents couldn't be easily identified without opening them, and as if that wasn't enough, the walk-in refrigerator had been left open all night. Not only could he guarantee they'd lost a small fortune in meats and poultry items, but the overworked compressor sounded as if it was working on its last few breaths. He didn't want to think of what their next electric bill would be.

This would finish him off for sure.

"They left us with virtually nothing."

Luther started. Numb, blood pounding in his head, he hadn't heard Rae follow him. "I told you to stay outside!" he snapped.

She ignored him, too shattered by what surrounded them. "Every morning I rise and say to the Lord, 'I have faith that you'll show us how folks in this town are decent and fair. That they'll give us a chance,'" she whispered, her eyes brimming with tears. "But I swear, there's an awful wickedness in some of them. I can't explain it, and I'm getting too tired of pretending it isn't there."

What could he say in response to that? Luther touched her short hair, wanting to give comfort but afraid that if he embraced her right now she might shatter in his arms. "I'll call the police."

"If the phone is working. If there's anyone there who's awake. The whole damn town had to be in a coma not to hear this."

Yes, she was in bad shape, and that made him more determined to hang on himself. "It's working," he called from the storeroom, and dialed the number Rae had taped, with the other emergency numbers, beside the wall phone. Along with too many other important things, 911 service had yet to reach Parish.

He got through on the third ring. "Uh, yeah...this is Luther Cobb over at the market. *Cobb's,*" he ground out after the smart-ass on the other end snidely asked which one. "Look, mister, we been busted into. You gotta send somebody over right away."

Hanging up, he returned to his wife, and even though she still looked ready to fall apart, he put his arms around her. She might not want to be touched right now, but he could use a hug.

"It'll be okay, baby. We're okay. That's all that matters."

"Why, Luther? Just tell me why people have to be so mean? What poison gets in their hearts that they can do this?"

He could barely bring himself to look at her. She was so beautiful with her regal features and fine café au lait skin. Seeing her enduring hardship was tough enough; this was almost too much for him. "I don't know, baby. But it don't mean nothin', hear? Ain't nothin' matters except that we got each other."

"I'm so glad Noah isn't seeing this. I'm afraid it would—" With a gasp, she grabbed his arm. "Luther! Do you think the boys who gave Noah such a bad time did this?"

He hadn't given it much thought, hadn't gotten past the whys yet. But now that she'd brought it up....

"I don't know. But I'll tell you this. If they did, whoever did it, they better hope the police finds them before I do."

"What you gonna do?"

"I know what I'm angry enough to do," Eve told Mama Lulu, "but Bree would probably phone the nearest TV station and accuse me of child abuse."

Mama Lulu had stuck as close as the devil's advocate while she'd paced and fumed and had strode around the kitchen. Now the housekeeper joined her at the base of the stairs, her hands on her hips, and like Eve, scowled at the upper landing.

"She ain't no child, and this wasn't her first time comin' home smellin' of liquor."

"But this is the first time she dragged in this late and needed help getting to her room. And as much as I don't want to face it, that wasn't only liquor we smelled on her, was it?"

"All the more reason to let her sleep it off."

True enough. But as Eve combed her hands through her hair to massage a prolonged headache, the suggestion did nothing to ease the outrage she'd felt since someone had dropped off the girl at nearly three in the morning. She'd been as concerned as she'd been repelled by the stench she'd experienced too often with patients coming into emergency. Lucky for Bree, she'd been too far gone to explain what she'd inhaled or ingested.

"That kid is like a puppy. If you don't correct her as soon as she does something wrong, in a few days you might as well be talking to this newel cap," she said, nodding toward the most ornate part of the balustrade. "Especially this time. She's crossed a line she can't afford to cross again."

As she started up the stairs, Mama Lulu grabbed her by the wrist. "Now wait a minute, hon. Come have a bite to eat first. You been up almost all night and you ain't ate yet."

"Aggravation has gnawed a hole straight through my stomach, Mama Lulu. I'm afraid that at this point, food would only prove it." Eve gently but firmly removed the housekeeper's hand and continued on her way.

"Well, what you gonna do once she's woke?" Lulu called after her. When Eve didn't reply, she added, "Remember, she bites!"

"Not if she wants to keep those teeth."

"Lord bless us...."

Eve could appreciate the older woman's dismay, but Mama Lulu needed to respect what she'd been through, too. Last night, Ben had brought her home after they'd searched all through town and the surrounding area for another hour. Then she had paced and worried the rest of the night—worried about her head-spinning situation with Ben, too—until hearing that truck, or whatever it had been, roar away. Eve still had no idea where Bree's car was and planned to phone Ben as soon as she came downstairs to ask him if he and his people would keep an eye out for it.

From the beginning, Bree had challenged her authority, and Eve had cut her more slack than anyone deserved. All she had ever asked was that her stepdaughter meet her halfway. Last night the girl had proved she either wouldn't or couldn't. Enough was enough.

Bree's bedroom door was unlocked. Eve had made sure of that herself last night after stripping the girl to her underwear and dragging a sheet over her limp body.

"Rise and shine!" she called, crossing to the bed.

A door opened behind her, and Justin cleared his throat. "She's still out cold. I checked on her about an hour ago. I was afraid she might not be alive."

"She's about to wish she wasn't."

"Are you going to need help?"

Eve shot him a wry look over her shoulder. He was dressed in a short-sleeved dress shirt and jeans, neat and sweet-faced as ever, and as usual he had his sketch pad and drawing supplies tucked under one arm. She knew he wanted badly to escape, and she couldn't blame him. He and Bree might occasionally share the unique mental rapport many twins exhibited, but their contrasting personalities usually caused Justin as much emotional distress as it did everyone else who had to deal with Bree. Sensitive to that, Eve shook her head.

"No, dear, it's all right. You go on and do whatever you had planned. But you might not want to stick too close to the house. Things are bound to get noisy around here for a while."

He took off as if she'd suddenly yanked a hypodermic needle out of the pocket of her jeans. With a sigh, Eve turned back to her stepdaughter.

Such a pretty girl, and such a mixed-up, directionless one. "Bree. Time to get up." She shook the girl by the shoulder, and when that didn't get more than a slight movement from her, Eve lightly tapped the teenager's cheeks. "Come on. Plug in the brain. Either you get up voluntarily, or I'll drag you to the shower, and then it won't be pleasant lukewarm water you'll rouse to, but me using the scrub brush. Bree!"

Nothing short of a SCUD missile was going to budge her, so Eve yanked back the sheet and shifted the girl's legs over the side and let her feet drop to the floor. Ignoring the teen's moaned protest, she then pulled her by the arms to get her to sit up.

A rubber toy had more form.

"Work with me, kiddo." She used her own body to lift Bree's and hugged her to her side as she proceeded to half carry, half drag her out of the bedroom and to the main bathroom.

Maybe it was the cooler tile floor, but Bree awakened enough to begin finding her footing, only not well. "What're you...? S-trrred."

"No doubt. But guess what, sweetie? All the violins are rented out for people who really deserve them. Nobody's interested in how rotten you feel now, and your fatigue is nothing compared to the worry and exhaustion you've heaped upon this family. I'm going to help you see that and stop it."

In the shower stall that Sumner had added to the huge room when the children were small, Eve sat her stepdaughter on the bench and turned on the cold faucet all the way. Of course, she wouldn't get the icy stream she wanted since it was the last day of June and the only chilled water available was in the refrigerator downstairs. Until October, and maybe even November, the cold-water tap would emit nothing cooler than pee.

The force of the spray was another matter entirely. When it struck her face, Bree gasped and sprang up screaming. "You rat! What are you *doing?*"

Although she got soaked in the process, Eve fought the girl's attempt to escape and pushed her down on the seat again. "Nice to know last night's stupidity didn't turn you into a complete vegetable. Now let's cut a deal—you strip and take a shower, and I'll give you privacy. Fight me, and I'll treat you like a three-year-old."

"Bitch."

Eve shook her head. "Young one, I've been called worse by some noble, special people I didn't have a choice but to hurt. Do you think the whining of one spoiled little girl fazes me? Choose. Now."

For a moment the girl looked ready to launch into her like some transformed being in a werewolf movie. Then she brushed off Eve's hands. "All right, I'll do it."

Eve muttered a low, "Sing hallelujah and raise the flag." Although dripping wet and secretly still worrying for the girl, she backed out of the shower stall. "I'll see you downstairs," she said, sliding the door closed. "We'll talk."

Although she'd wrapped herself in one of the white bath sheets, she left a trail of water as she retreated to the master bedroom. It might have been premature, but she changed into dry jeans and another of Sumner's ridiculously expensive custom-tailored shirts. After sweeping her drenched hair into a careless French braid, she headed downstairs, thinking she might be ready for more than coffee.

Instead, she found Mama Lulu talking to herself as she moved around the kitchen filling a tote on the table. Eve eyed the woman's purse beside the canvas sack and surmised their housekeeper was in a hurry to be somewhere. That could mean only one thing.

"What's happened?" she asked as Lulu added a jar of her personal herbal-tea mix to the bag. Whenever she did that, Eve knew the trouble was serious.

"I called the store to say hello. Found out somebody broke in there last night."

Poor Rae and Luther! Eve couldn't believe their run of bad luck. "Are they all right?"

"No. Everything's trashed. Eve...I gotta go."

"Of course you do."

"I'll call for a cab. Just wanted to be sure you understood first."

"Forget the cab. I'll buzz Dewitt."

"You can't take him from his work!"

Eve expected the refusal, and it would do no good to offer her one of the cars. Mama Lulu had never learned to drive. "Then I'll take you over there."

"And leave her by herself?" the housekeeper asked, nodding upstairs.

"It's one way to see if she's willing to change." She didn't quite believe her own words, but Mama Lulu was family, too, and needed support more at the moment, not the added burden of guilt. "Let me get my purse and I'll be right with you."

"Wait!"

The anxiety in Mama Lulu's voice had her pausing in the doorway. "Yes?"

"If things are as bad as they sound, I'll wanna stay. Will that be a problem?"

What a question. She ran this place as efficiently as any four-star hotel. The question was whether she would want to come back to the disaster that was likely to result from her absence; but Eve smiled and shook her head anyway. "I already assumed as much. We'll miss you, but we'll cope for as long as you need to be away."

Knowing better than to worry that Mama Lulu would abuse that trust, she hurried for her purse. She couldn't help thinking of Ben. He would be at the store for sure, which meant no matter what, she couldn't stay long. She needed a few days before she would trust herself to be around him again; she needed time to build up her resistance to what he'd stirred in her last night. Otherwise...

There could be no otherwise. As Bree had made perfectly clear, life was, indeed, complicated enough.

What the hell...?

Ben frowned as he spotted Luther storming into the police station. Only a few dozen yards away himself, he abruptly parked the Blazer vertically in the parallel-parking area and raced after him. Something was up, and he had a hunch he needed to forget that his eyeballs felt dipped in salt rock, and that his body was humming with more sexual frustration than when, as a marine, he'd pulled a sixteen-month assignment to one of the Arab emirates. Friend Luther had the look of a guy intent on getting his pound of flesh, and that was a dangerous way for a black man to behave in this town.

He got through the first of the two sets of glass doors and immediately heard the cussing and threats. But he wasn't prepared to see Jack Haygood with his gun aimed at Luther. As his stomach rolled the way it had his first time at sea, he prayed the asshole didn't have a nervous trigger finger.

"Just answer me!" Luther cried. "Why didn't anyone come?"

"On the ground, Cobb, or so help me, your ma'll be mourning more than one of her mouthy bastard sons!"

If anything, Luther stood taller. "I am a citizen of

this community. I have a right to ask the question. *Why?*''

At the sight of Haygood pulling back the hammer on his revolver, Ben yanked at the second door so hard the whole steel frame shuddered. ''Drop, Luther!''

In the silence that followed they could have heard a mosquito slurp its breakfast in Biloxi. Nobody seemed to believe that he'd ordered his friend to the ground, especially Luther, who slowly looked over his shoulder to give him an incredulous look. But a moment later he did as Ben directed. Not all the way, of course, and not without making Ben sense that he would not easily forgive him for that order. Ben couldn't care less; a man had to be alive to be pissed.

The command had the desired effect. Haygood relaxed and pointed the barrel of the gun toward the ceiling.

His hands on his hips and adrenaline raging through his system, Ben growled at his men, ''What the hell are you doing?''

Dewey Pearl pointed at Luther. ''He threatened Jack!''

''Why?''

'''Cause he's pi—ticked off that Jack didn't—''

''I can speak for myself, Pearl,'' the other cop snapped. But despite that declaration, Haygood seemed in no hurry to offer any justification.

''Well?'' Ben demanded.

''It was a misunderstanding, that's all.''

With a feral growl, Luther started rising. Ben stepped forward and put a hand on his shoulder, staying him. "Put the gun away, Haygood, or so help me they'll need anesthesia to remove it at the hospital."

"Chief—"

"Do it!"

Giving Luther a venomous look, Jack holstered the gun. "I should've known. You're only interested in hearing that nigger's side."

"I'm not interested in sides, period. I want facts and I want them fast."

"Cobb's Grocery got burglarized," Dewey rattled off before anyone else could speak. "Luther here phoned in the call close to an hour ago—"

"*More* than an hour!" Luther intoned.

"Er, maybe," Dewey said, his bulging eyes darting every which way. "Point is, he came barreling in here like a crazy man. What were we to think?"

"We waited for over an hour," Luther said, enunciating each word, but speaking this time to Ben alone. "Is that what's meant by protectin' and servin' the community?"

"You know better than that." Ben turned to Haygood, who was beginning to look less and less confident. "All right, what's your excuse?"

"If you have your mind made up, I don't see any point—"

"Haygood!"

The craggy-faced man turned as red as the fire extinguisher on the wall behind him. "This ain't right, Chief. He's taking advantage of knowing you! You should've heard him talking all uppity like, demanding we get over to his store as if we had to do what he says that second or else."

"Did he tell you why he needed you?"

"Well…"

"Correct me if I'm wrong, but he is a taxpayer, right? You are paid by tax revenues, correct?"

"He could have been blowing things out of proportion, damn it."

Ben had heard enough, even if he didn't already have adequate reason to shut down one of the department's most experienced officers. "Hand over the gun."

The cop's mouth dropped open. "Are you shittin' me?"

Ben drew his own weapon and aimed it at him. "If you want to continue, we can discuss the two thousand dollars you took that was found on Lem Cobb's body."

For an instant, Haygood looked close to losing his breakfast, but he surprised Ben by laughing. The sound was awkward at best.

"You're crazy. Read the report. Cobb had only a few bucks on him and a couple of credit cards canceled by the issuer."

"That's the report you typed up after you decided to take the money yourself. I have a witness willing to come forward and testify to that effect. Dewey, take his gun and lock him up," he said, not taking his eyes off Haygood. "By the way, where the hell is Buck?"

"Uh, down at the bank where, uh, he usually is while the drive-in tellers get settled," Dewey said. "You know, those girls come in early and don't feel comfortable about being alone with all that money, what with the unemployment rate inching up and the

increase of bank robberies, not to mention the crazies
out there with their car bombs and firebombs and—''

"I follow the news occasionally, myself, Pearl,"
Ben said to shut him up. "I didn't ask why but
where." He was relieved to learn that at least one of
his crew had a legitimate excuse for not responding
to Luther's crisis more quickly.

"Chief, are you serious?" Dewey asked, his gaze
bouncing from Ben to a shaken but still angry Haygood.

"Dead serious. Do it, Dewey. And since we know
what a cop thinks about being sentenced to prison,
I'll keep you covered as you take him to the back."

Out of necessity, Luther had to be ignored for the
next minute or two. But once a recovered and swearing Haygood was safely in one of the cells, Ben said
to Dewey, "I'm going to lock up his weapon and then
I'm going over to the market. You keep the outer door
to this area shut and ignore anything he yells, understood?"

Dewey nodded, but had yet to close his gaping
mouth. "Chief? Are you sure about…you know?"

Ben crossed to pick up his dropped holster. For the
first time since taking office, he slipped the revolver
back into the holster and fastened the belt around his
waist. Regardless of his feelings toward this gun and
its history, he knew where it belonged now.

"I'm sure."

Not trusting himself to say more, he detoured to
his office, locked away Haygood's gun and badge and
ushered Luther outside. Only when they were on the
front green did he really allow himself to look at his
friend.

"You okay?"

"What do you think? Here I was thinkin' all I had to cuss you out for was orderin' me to hit the floor, and then you come out with *that*. How long have you known about Lem's money, man?"

"A few hours, and I'm still trying to get to the bottom of it, so whatever you're thinking, don't." Seeing that mollified Luther slightly, Ben continued, asking, "Now, what happened at your place?"

Luther exhaled heavily. "The store's destroyed. Rae's practically hysterical. Our life savings are wiped out, and you got the KKK running the police department!"

"Hey, he's behind bars, and he'll stay there."

Luther would not be appeased. "You shoulda got rid of all of 'em the minute you came back. They're bigots, the lot of 'em."

"That's easy for you to say. I had to appease the powers that be, who made it clear I had to work with what I had until I could prove changes or additions were imperative to the safety of the community."

"What do they want as proof, Haygood to shoot off my balls?"

"Considering the way you charged in there, a jury might have been coerced into seeing it as self-defense."

It was such an outrageous response he wasn't surprised when Luther started reaching for him. But just as quickly he backed off, only to rub his face with his hands.

"God. This town is gonna drive me crazy yet."

Ben squeezed his friend's shoulder. "Come on. Let's see what we can do."

On the way, he had Luther tell him as much as he knew about the break-in. What Luther described outraged him, and yet the vivid descriptions didn't come close to reflecting the utter destruction he found upon entering the store. He saw Rae crying in Mama Lulu's arms, and Eve was there, too, already working with all four of the Cobb boys, sorting through the refrigerated items and removing the foodstuffs that wouldn't be safe to sell.

He should have known Eve would be here, standing up for the Cobbs despite her own weighty problem. After embracing Rae and Mama Lulu and giving the boys an encouraging word or two, he managed to murmur to her, "Did she get home?"

"Yes. Around three."

What she didn't say was that she was exhausted, that things were worse than ever at home and that she didn't know how to react to him any more than he could figure out how to respond to her. They exchanged one more look that wasn't near long enough to suit him but that said too much. Then, tearing his gaze away, he continued through the store, studying the brutality of the devastation.

"It's nothing short of rape," he murmured in conclusion.

"You understand." Rae went into his arms and burst into fierce, wracking sobs. He stroked her back, but as soon as possible passed her over to Mama Lulu because he didn't want her gratitude, and he was feeling dirty and ashamed of this abominable waste, ashamed that he could have grown up in a community that could breed such cruelty.

He headed toward the back and Luther followed

him. Together they went outside, where the ugliness came to a halt in a final explosion of solids and liquids in the alley. Ben knew the first and most important question he had to ask his childhood friend.

"Why did you lie to me yesterday?"

"What are you talking about?"

"Yesterday, when your son got roughed up. You called it a misunderstanding. Today there's this. What happened that you decided I should be kept in the dark? Or haven't you had enough yet?"

"You can't assume— This wasn't done by the same kids! Shoot, we should be that lucky to have only two punks in this town." Swearing, Luther began walking away, but after several yards he spun around. "It's Parish! It's always *been* Parish. The faces don't matter. This place has always bred more evil than good."

"You don't believe that. Apathy maybe. Greed for sure. But outright evil...?"

"Don't tell me what I believe! *I* stayed. I didn't run away. I earned the right to say what I'm sayin'!"

He was right. But Ben also knew that sometimes people stayed because they didn't have the courage to find out if things could be any different somewhere else. "You want to beat me up for choosing something else, Luther? Here I am."

Luther swore again as Ben spread his arms wide. "You'd like that. Then you could arrest me and not have to do anything about anything."

Incredible words, and lame logic, but understandable under the circumstances. Over his friend's shoulder Ben saw people coming out of the stores down the row.

"Where were all of you when this happened?" he shouted. "Get out of here and mind your own business!"

It would be a pleasure to go from store to store later and question everyone. It would certainly give him the opportunity to get a better handle on who the agitators were in town and who were the cowards, as well as find out if there was anyone who really wanted to change things, not just do a face-lift in the community. But he wouldn't want to guess the odds on the latter.

"You're gonna hear about that," Luther muttered, as good as reading his mind.

"Yeah, well, I'd hate for you to feel like the only punching bag in town."

Luther let his head hang. When he finally met Ben's watchful gaze again, the anger was gone, but not the bitterness. "I don't know about you, but I'm ready for people to ignore me again."

10

The dew had barely dried on the tall grass and wild-flowers when Justin settled in his favorite spot by the lake. As he'd hoped, the pickup at the last house was gone, despite its being the day before the Fourth, with many people already beginning to celebrate the holiday around the lake. Already he could see an increase in activity on the more populated side east of him, but thankfully things were still quiet where he sat. He hadn't, however, seen any sign of the girl yet.

He knew she was home; what he didn't know was if she would come out. In the last three days he'd only seen her for a few minutes here and there, and then for one longer stretch of time yesterday when she'd worked in her garden. But he could hope, and he could fantasize, and if worse came to worst, he could draw her from his memory. Just being close was all that seemed necessary to trigger his creativity where she was concerned.

She was becoming his world, filling his mind and inspiring his dreams. No one had ever affected him this way; not his parents, although Bree had accused him of a particularly macabre fascination as he'd sketched his father weakening and drifting away from this world; not even Bree herself, who demanded focus, if only for the relentless and disruptive energy that emanated from her.

But the girl in the run-down shack affected more than his art. She trespassed on his carefully erected boundaries, permeated his invisible armor to reach his spirit, but gently, like the brush of an angel wing. He found himself consumed with the need to know more about this frail, wounded creature who lived in a world of isolation and deprivation. She was making him as much a prisoner of hers as she was a prisoner of that house. And that allowed him to ignore all those pangs of guilt for leaving Eve to cope with Bree on her own.

And he'd made a decision while walking here today.... If it was at all possible, he would find out the girl's name. He didn't know how yet, only that he must, because he couldn't forget the bruises he'd seen on her young body, or her grief. Something very wrong was going on over there, and everything inside him insisted he discover what it was.

He had a plan. The most natural way to prompt a reaction would be to have her spot him, but he'd decided to hide until she came out, in case his presence kept her indoors. Of course, if she objected, he would go away, but he hoped she would be as taken by the idea of being sketched as most people he met tended to be.

While looking for a clean page in his pad, he passed a pencil sketch of his sister in a pensive mood resting on her window bench. He'd done that right after Lem's funeral and someday he wanted to do a full oil portrait of it because she so rarely let anyone see that side of her.

Looking around for something that might be interesting to draw while he waited, Justin heard a noise. It was her! She emerged from the back of the house carrying a basket of wash. Since he'd resigned himself to waiting, he couldn't believe this stroke of good fortune. But his pleasure was quickly checked as he noticed how she moved.

Today she walked with a veteran laborer's gait, her shoulders rounded and her step halting. She might as well have been an old woman who'd carried one too many baskets of laundry. Although she never really acted as youthful as she was, this proved all the more disturbing. Her hair also reflected her misery. Nowhere as clean as she usually kept it, it hung in a matted mess almost obliterating her face like Rochester's mad wife in *Jane Eyre*. Not sure what to think or how long he had before she disappeared inside, he abandoned his plan to pique her curiosity in a more romantic way and simply stood.

When she spotted him, she was attempting to shake out a pillowcase to hang on the sagging line that hung between two young trees. She clutched the wet material to her chest and peered at him through the narrow gap in her hair, her fear palpable as she struggled to gauge his threat and her choices. When she made the sensible but negative response to start backing toward the house, Justin impulsively started toward her.

"Don't run away!"

She didn't do that, but she did fling the cloth back into the basket and search around for something in the grass. When she swooped down and came up with a length of rusty pipe, Justin understood that she saw him as a serious threat, but even then he didn't expect her to come after him. Wrens made noise and put on a nervous show to scare off predators. None he had ever encountered were what he would call aggressive. And yet she came at him...across the grass, over the dam, carrying the pipe like a hammer.

He told himself there would be no shame in running. He was guilty of being a voyeur, of stealing her privacy. Nevertheless, convinced she was in trouble, he couldn't stop watching her. What could one bit of a girl do to him? Then when she halted yards away and growled at him—even though she sounded like the puniest pit-bull pup in a litter—he almost changed his mind.

"It's okay. I'm only here to draw. See?" He held up his sketch pad. "I didn't mean to scare you."

She shook the pipe at him again.

So he'd been right about his hunches. She couldn't call him a choice name or two. She couldn't scream for help. She lived in a world of silence and he was locked out. But he hadn't come this far to quit now, and so, following another hunch, he pointed to his ear and then at her.

The results were amazing. She dropped the pipe as if struck by lightning.

"So I'm right, huh? Poor little thing, you can't speak or hear, can you?" he said, pointing to his mouth and then at her.

She lowered her gaze, and even though he'd guessed the truth for some time now, he was deeply shaken. After all, how could he hope to find out what had happened to her if she couldn't hear his questions, not to mention answer him?

"You know what?" he said abruptly. "We won't let it matter." He smiled, hoping he looked reassuring. "Hello?" He ducked and waved to get her attention. Then he printed, "It doesn't matter."

She looked intrigued, and to keep her attention he wrote his name. When he saw her expression grow more animated, he offered her the pencil.

At first he expected her to brush it away, but after a tense moment or two she took the pencil from him. It gave her trouble and she was clearly embarrassed about the condition of her hands, which were nicely shaped but work-roughened. However, she did manage a childish scrawl.

Go.

"So much for my fantasy about the artist always getting the girl." He offered a weak smile, wishing he could communicate that he wasn't good at humor, had never cared about getting the girl, let alone being a heroic figure, or anything like that. All he wanted to do was figure out a way to help her. How could she expect him to go when she looked so…tragic? He flipped back a page on his tablet and showed her what he'd been sketching over the past several days. It was a big mistake.

She gasped and croaked a terrible wail. That would have been disturbing enough, but then she fell on him and began to struggle for the drawing.

"Wait. What are you doing?" He struggled with her to save his work from her ruinous grasp. God, she was crazed! Bree's temper was nothing compared to this.

He finally managed to fling aside the pad and get the girl flat on her back. "Stop it!" he yelled, keeping a firm grasp of her wrists. "I'm not going to hurt you."

Of course, she couldn't understand, or respond. When she burst into strangled, hysterical sobs, he wanted to cry himself. Desperate, he sat back and drew her into his arms, rocking her and whispering soothingly. He prayed, too, prayed that she would let him help, that she would give him a chance.

Reminded of an incident in his childhood when a storm had raged outside and his father had forbidden him to cower with Bree in her room, he closed his eyes and hummed a lullaby Mama Lulu used to sing to them. Maybe this girl couldn't hear him, but surely she could feel the music vibrate in his body?

It happened slowly, but she did grow quiet. When he looked down again, he discovered she was watching him. There was no sign of trust, but neither did he see any sign of dread or disgust, either.

Her stillness gave him the opportunity to study her cut lip and the bruises that reached from the collar of her worn dress up along her throat. He fought to repress a rush of outrage, but he couldn't help thinking that there was only one way wounds like those could have happened.

"I'm sorry," he mouthed. *For all of it.*

He would have been grateful just to see her nod in understanding. When she touched her hand to his heart, he felt as if a steel hand was closing around his throat. Suddenly, he could barely breathe. Dear heaven, she didn't look much more than fifteen or sixteen now that her hair was swept back and he had a chance to really look at her. Her features still possessed the soft, rounded curves of youth, and it was only the sadness in her eyes, the lack of hope that had first suggested he might be several years off. Which guess was closer to the truth?

With a sigh, he looked around, trying to figure out a way to ask, to make these exchanges easier. "I wish I knew how much you're really understanding."

She reached up and turned his face back toward her. She frowned, but touched his lips then pointed to her eyes.

"I don't under— Oh, wow! You read lips?" When she nodded, he laughed and felt as if a giant wall between them was being whisked away. "That's terrific! That's great!" With a hundred questions rushing through his mind, the only one he could get out was, "How? I mean, how did your neck get bruised?" He indicated the marks.

Before he could stop her, she was rolling away from him and rising to her knees. The most heart-wrenching sound came out of her as she signaled that he should go. Clearly, he'd asked the wrong thing again.

She had the sweetest face, not at all like the girls from school, who by thirteen could make themselves up as expertly as runway models, and appeared so sophisticated.

But beyond the grime and the shadows of fatigue or worse, she had the softest skin, the most eloquent brown eyes. And even though it was a mess again, and dull from poor rinsing, her hair's length and volume drew the eye. Given a good washing in a decent shower, and pampered with some of Bree's pricey shampoo and conditioner, he knew the lustrous ash-brown waves that would be his reward. God forgive him, but he wanted to paint the scene, to paint her wearing nothing else.

"Will you tell me your name?" he whispered, afraid she was good at reading minds, too.

Glancing down, she pointed to her skirt. The dress was a simple cotton thing, with straps that had been torn and resewn several times. The flared skirt fell to midcalf. As for the faded print, it was small and fussy. She pointed to it again.

"Flowers...?" What were they specifically? "Rose."

She shook her head and pointed again. It was ridiculous, unless her name was cotton or beige; he couldn't see anything else except— He met her expectant gaze. "The stems and leaves...is that supposed to be a lace design? Lace? Lacey? Lacey!" He laughed as she nodded eagerly.

He held out his hand. "Hello, Lacey. I'm Justin Maitland."

She didn't react the way other girls did when they heard his name, their eyes glazing over as if they'd read one too many financial-statement zeroes. Either the kid wasn't from around here or she'd been locked in a closet all of her life. What else would explain her apparent unfamiliarity with his family name?

The tentative way she gave him her hand left him with the strongest feeling that she didn't reach out to too many people, certainly not to many men. As humbled as he was relieved, he released her hand and retrieved his sketch pad.

"Do you understand what I do?"

Although her expression grew pensive again, she nodded.

"Do you mind? That I come here, I mean?"

She glanced back at the house to consider his view and bit her lower lip.

Justin reached out to touch her hand. "I mean no harm. I'm not a—a Peeping Tom." He could tell the explanation meant nothing to her. "What is it you're afraid of? The man you live with?"

Lacey leaped to her feet. Justin stood, too. "Please. "I only want to help."

She shook her head vehemently and pointed, once again indicating that he should go.

He couldn't. Didn't she understand they'd touched, he'd felt her trembling and had tasted her fear? He saw the hopelessness in her eyes. Even if he could walk away from her, her image would be imprinted forever in his mind's eye.

When he didn't budge, she snatched up his things, his pens and pencils and bottled water, shoving everything at him. *Go,* she signaled more insistently than before.

"All right." Afraid to lose the progress they'd made, he accepted that he had to be patient, to earn her trust. "I'll go this time. But I'll be back."

With another keening cry, she bolted. Her gait was awkward, and she stumbled several times, but she never stopped, and she never looked back. Justin knew because he watched her the entire way. Even after she disappeared into the house, he stood there absorbing the moment. He'd never felt more alive or more afraid in his life.

In spite of all the work there was to do, the day dragged for Luther. By late evening he and the family had succeeded in cleaning up the worst of the mess at the store, and the refrigeration people out of Greenville had come out and done some work that was, thank goodness, covered under the warranty; but he'd gone home that night aware the Fourth of July would bring very little reason to celebrate.

He insisted Rae and the kids stay home the next day, while he spent much of his holiday waiting for the locksmith Eve insisted come up from Jackson. His landlady had assured the man that she didn't care what he charged on a holiday, better locks for the rear door and a security alarm at both the front and back entrances were to be put up immediately. Although the locksmith was a widower with no children, he took his sweet time getting there; nevertheless, Luther couldn't say the man worked any slower or faster once he'd learned he was helping out a black grocer. The guy proved to be a totally unbigoted crook.

The deliveries of fresh dairy products and meats didn't start coming until the following day. That's when they learned some of their suppliers were refusing them an extension on their existing debt. Others simply dropped them. But Rae stayed busy on the telephone, calling different sources, and by evening they had enough inventory to know that the next morning they would be ready to reopen again.

One last time, he told himself, and then no more. It wasn't something he needed or wanted to discuss with Rae, either. He'd made up his mind—and Ben's news about Lem's money had helped him decide.

As warned, he hadn't seen much of Ben for the forty-eight or so hours after the break-in. Ben was busy checking with the proprietors of the other businesses on their block and elsewhere, when he wasn't raising hell at the station and with the city council. When he did stop by, as expected, he reported that no one had seen anything, and no one had any information about the break-in.

"Well, why should people stick their necks out?" Luther asked when Ben stopped by to share the grim news. "They don't know us or owe us anythin'. Besides, most likely it's true they'd been home tucked safe in bed when the break-in happened. We sure were. And even if they hear anythin', one friend ain't gonna talk against another friend for no black man. Tell me about the money," he said, wanting to change the subject before he got riled all over again. "What was Lem doin' with that kind of cash?"

"Come on, Luther. You knew he was into bookmaking, though from what I gather it was in a small way."

"Hell, to hear him talk, he was a superhero with connections in everythin'. Don't mean I believed him, especially since he was broke all the time, and usually hidin' from somebody or other wantin' to whip his ass."

"That's what I would have guessed myself. Especially after I talked to Bree Maitland." Ben explained how he finally had time yesterday to interview her. "She insists that as she was leaving Bellemere that night, Lem asked if he could borrow ten bucks to buy dinner. That would back up what we'd both said about him—only, does a guy with two thousand on him beg for pocket change?"

"If it wasn't his two grand..." Luther frowned,

trying to make sense of his brother's behavior. "You think he met somebody down in the woods?"

"It's not impossible, but it seems unlikely. Why the need for such secrecy? Bree said he'd mentioned that he usually paid up somewhere on the outskirts of town, close to a highway. Those woods offered no easy access for someone in a fancy car. And if he did meet with someone, why didn't they take the money?"

"Could be they never found him?" Luther asked. He was trying to follow Ben, but was getting confused.

"That's the most logical explanation, except again, they wouldn't have met there in the first place. It's not even logical to contemplate that it was all a setup."

"What do you mean, a setup?"

"A hit. It's not uncommon for a guy doing a contract killing to *steal* the victim's wallet to make the cops see the incident as a random mugging. But I've never heard of anyone doing the opposite, literally donating money when a death already looked like an accident."

"Besides which, drugs and guns and stuff get planted on people to make 'em look dirty, right?"

"And unfortunately, Lem didn't need the help. This was like putting a diamond crucifix on a penniless Catholic."

Now Luther saw, and he wondered who would make such a mistake. No one Lem hung around with would let him get away with a hundred bucks, let alone a few grand. "Then the money had to be his, and steppin' into that trap was an accident."

"You want to believe that, don't you?"

"Yeah. Except for what Bree said...and Mama will remind me that he was scared of the dark. Damn, this isn't making any more sense than it did before."

"There's one other explanation," Ben said, his gaze steady.

"What's that?"

"The money could've been planted as a gift to you."

"To *me?*"

"To the family. To keep your mouths shut and let it go."

"Jesus."

Luther was glad that he'd insisted Rae stay home with the boys. Thanks to his conversation with Ben, by the time he reached the farm, his head felt like one of those creatures in the science-fiction movies Noah liked to watch where the monster pulsates and swells until it finally explodes. His head felt about ready to do something that nasty and painful.

What a relief it was to turn into his driveway and see the frame house. It needed a coat of paint again, but that was nothing. When they'd moved in shortly after Theo was born, the place had been in shambles. He and Rae, and even the boys, had worked hard to make the decaying farm house a decent home. What two thousand dollars would do to improve things!

Needing a few minutes before he could face his kids or Rae, for that matter, he wandered out to the edge of the yard to consider their land. This had been a forty-acres-and-a-mule package that had originally belonged to a freed-slave ancestor on his mother's side. Through savings and relentless negotiating, Luther had increased the size to ninety-seven acres. Today the boys had an old '57 Massey-Ferguson tractor to help them plow the fields. It remained tough work, but the crops looked well-tended, despite his long absences. They stuck with sorghum because it was less labor-intensive than cotton, and they sharecropped another hundred acres adjoining their own, which paid the taxes and what little insurance they could afford.

He circled the barn to inspect the reshingling job on the back of the house that his older two boys had been working on despite this latest crisis. It struck him that he hadn't thanked them for any of their efforts yet, and that just added to his sense of guilt. What kind of father was he becoming that he couldn't find five minutes to show his gratitude to his sons for doing what he should be doing himself? This farm wasn't their choice, it had been his. They were here out of love, and he was taking that love and feeding off of it. What was he giving them in return?

He sensed Rae approaching well before she wrapped her arms around his waist and pressed her cheek to his back.

"You're home earlier than you thought you'd be. I was hoping that might happen."

"Everythin's done that could be. Nothin' to do now but wait and see how tomorrow goes."

She kept still for a moment, then circled him to search his face. "What's happened? Something else has, I heard it in your voice and I see it in your eyes."

He would never get used to her tolerance for trouble, her compassion for those grieving. "Haven't you had enough? What else should there be?"

"I don't know," she said quietly, "and I have had enough. But you forget, my love, being married for over eighteen years gives a wife a certain advantage. You can't keep secrets from me as well as you once could." She laid a soothing hand against his chest and massaged gently. "When I called to check how you were doing, you cut me short because Ben had walked in. What did he say that upset you? I know that has to be what's bothering you."

"Yeah, I guess. Be prepared, 'cuz he's pissed off everybody on our block and then some."

Rae broke into a cheeky grin. "I say good for him."

"You would. Our second grand openin's gonna be one long party, I can see it now."

Rae shrugged. "They're not good neighbors, Luther. Who among them came to pay their respects, offered to help clean up? Nobody did. We would have been there this fast—" she snapped her fingers "—with our sleeves rolled up if it was the other way around. As far as I'm concerned, they can't be shamed enough."

Luther let that be. She deserved her chance to just talk, but he knew that no matter what a person's sin, she'd be wherever there was a need if a call was voiced. Instead, he concentrated on the sun creeping lower over the distant Mississippi River. The orange sky deepened with every few seconds he stood there. It helped ease his inner chill somewhat.

"Did Ben go to Hughes's, too?" she asked, once winded.

"Yeah."

"Did you tell him what we thought?"

How could he? He didn't know himself about the connection between Noah and the Hughes and Meece boys. Not for sure. "No. And anyways, if Trevor Hughes and Grover Meece know anythin' about what their kids have been up to, they wouldn't admit it."

"You can't assume that, and Ben needs to know!"

That's exactly what he expected her to say. Wanting nothing more than to find a hole and crawl in, he gripped her by the shoulders. "If we give him names, and he pushes for results, it's our butts that're left exposed."

"Ben's our friend, he'll protect us."

"Like he did the other day? He was barely in time to help me, Rae. You think I'm gonna risk all of you?"

He clutched her close, needing her to understand. Some things weren't worth any risk.

As expected, Rae fought him. Pushing at his chest to see his face, she snapped, "Are you still not through with that? Once, you would have trusted him with your life."

"We were kids. Risks didn't have the high price tag to 'em they do now. Besides, we've been apart a long time, baby."

"Ben is Ben."

"All I know is, the other day I couldn't get a cop out to the market on an emergency call! Right in the middle of findin' out why, I'm told Lem had a bunch of money on him when he died, only that was kept from us 'cuz a greedy cop stole it and changed the reports."

"What?"

"Tonight Ben says Haygood spent it. At least that's what Ben says."

"It was probably dishonest money, anyway."

"Come on, Rae. Mama could have used it to pay on the funeral."

She stepped out of his reach. "What aren't you telling me now, Luther? And why didn't you tell me about the money sooner?"

It had shaken him bad, that's why. How could she have forgotten that he wasn't as fast a thinker as good old Ben, that when it came to important things, he grew very quiet and withdrawn.

She must have seen his answer in his face. "And so you're going to lock out Ben because you can't compete. You think he's keeping things from you, so you're going to pay him back in kind."

"Don't talk to me as if I was Noah!"

"Stop acting his age!"

"Woman, I don't know that I can trust him like I used to. What's he given me so far to prove I should?"

"He's *here!*"

"Giving me news after the fact!"

She spun away from him uttering a deep groan. "The man is working in the dark, Luther. When are you going to see that? After we lose everything? Damn your stubborn hide…you are not going to protect your pride or fear of failing at the cost of my babies, do you hear me?"

"Rae, if you'd just listen…"

"No, *you* listen." Hands on her hips, she glared at him. "I'm going inside to finish getting our dinner. When it's ready, we're going to sit down and have a proper meal, and then I'm going to clean up. Afterward, I'm going to wait for you in our bedroom. You'd better show up, mister. And you'd better be ready to tell me everything that's been going on with Lem, the store and anything else I may not know about, or else...."

He didn't want to hear more, but he forced himself to challenge her, fascinated with this wild woman that stood before him. "Or else what?"

"You don't want to find out."

This was a bad idea after the pressures of the last several days, but Ben decided that blaming Haygood offered a fair start toward purging the anger within him. If the jerk hadn't finally admitted what he'd done, if there wasn't proof he'd spent most of the money he'd stolen from Lem, Ben wouldn't be in this mood. But here he was out at the town cemetery, the one location he'd insisted to himself time and again since returning to Parish that he had no interest in revisiting.

Fred Varnell deserved some of the blame, too, for convincing him to leave Jackson in the first place, as well as for mocking his commitment to principle. "You're as bad as your old man was," the mayor had snapped during their most recent phone conversation, the one where Ben had asked for restitution for the Cobb family.

Ben could have let the mayor's insult pass. But it was when Varnell made that crack about another Rader destined to end up with fresh flowers being put daily on his grave that he'd whispered—no, growled, *"Enough."*

So now he was standing here wishing he wasn't.

The cemetery covered about an acre of land on the northeast edge of the city limits. Flat and treeless, it epitomized his idea of dreaded final resting places with its plastic geraniums and dime-store miniature flags. As he parked, Ben reaffirmed his commitment to have himself cremated. Better to be useful compost in a forest somewhere than this.

His father's grave was all the way at the back, in the shadow of a larger monument that hadn't been there when they'd buried him. In fact, Ben was surprised his father's marker remained visible, since it was only one of those small flat jobs. But, no, the grass was neatly trimmed, revealing the spare identification Coleman Rader. There was something else, too, and it had Ben frowning...a glass bud vase to the left of the name, which held a single bloodred rose.

Wrong.

Whoever put it there was dead wrong, and he had a sudden and violent urge to kick the vase and send it and the flower flying. He didn't want to feel those old emotions, didn't like having any reaction to this place. Damn Varnell for saying what he did to compel him to come out here, and damn whoever was responsible for that ludicrousness.

Ben spun around and started back to the truck. That's when he spotted the woman. She stood at the house diagonally across from the cemetery, the only house within a quarter mile or so, and she was so thin and gray she was about as substantial as smoke.

He didn't like the feeling he got looking at her, and he grew increasingly uneasy when she crossed the road and headed toward him. When she closed within a dozen yards, he understood why.

It was her. She was still here.

He likened his reaction to driving at top speed into a brick wall. In a way, he had—an emotional one.

Why had she stayed after all these years? Her reputation had been ruined.

"Hello, Ben. Welcome home."

"I have nothing to say to you."

Although she bowed her head and nodded, she maintained her brave smile and glanced toward the grave. "I told him that you would be back. He would be pleased."

"I don't give a shit."

"So you're still angry. Even after all this time."

"Uh-uh. I only came because I heard about the flowers and I couldn't believe your audacity."

She gestured toward the grave. The movement embodied sheer helplessness. "I loved him. It's the least I can do."

Old fury sprang from Ben as if it had never had the chance to be purged. "You could finally leave him alone, just as you should have then."

"I tried. We both did. But…" She smiled gently. "Haven't you ever met someone, felt a connection that was…irresistible?"

He couldn't listen to any more. *"No,"* he snarled, and stormed past her.

11

An hour and many miles later, Ben pulled into the main entrance of Maitland Hall. He accepted the move as the second stupid thing he'd done tonight. Nevertheless, he felt a wave of relief when he spotted Eve on the veranda of the great house. It would have been much tougher to have to knock on the door.

Only after he parked and killed the Blazer's engine did he hear the music roaring from upstairs. Every few bars or so the racket was accompanied by Bree singing the chorus. That told him why Eve was out there tolerating the heat and braving the mosquitoes.

"So she's still angry with you," he said upon reaching the top of the stairs. He knew she'd grounded the girl, but had thought by now she would have given up her role as jailer.

"Whatever gave you that idea?" After the droll reply, she told him that the uproar had convinced Mama Lulu to allow herself to be picked up by one of the ladies from her church. The women were planning on making peach cobbler, blackberry tarts and candied watermelon rind for their next bake sale. Justin was protecting his eardrums and his sanity by using earphones as he worked in his room. "I'm beginning to wish I had my own pair to bleed her out with a little Yo-Yo Ma or Mandy Pantinkin. Unfortunately, the only other set is up in her room.''

He was unfamiliar with the names she'd mentioned and wondered if they were real or made up to test him. ''You could always open the cage door and let the songbird fly. She might surprise you and calm down. It's been three days.''

''Trust me, Dr. Freud, not this nightingale.'' She shrugged. ''It's all right, really. Challenges have always been a hobby of mine. Far less strenuous on the eyes than working crossword puzzles.''

Ben lifted the bottle he'd picked up on his way over. ''Sounds like thirsty work. Care to freshen that up?''

Already holding a glass half-full of some iced-down amber liquid, Eve eyed the bottle. ''What's your poison?''

''Bourbon. You *are* in the South.''

''Mmm, but I'm afraid my blood hasn't thinned enough to tolerate that stuff.'' She stretched one long bare leg to toe aside the fern on the coffee table to show him a tray laden with a bottle of Scotch, a crystal decanter of ice and three other matching glasses.

The number didn't please Ben. ''Expecting company?'' If she told him Ashworth was due, he wasn't sure he could be a good sport about that.

''Not that I know of. Unless you're staying...?''

''I'd better.'' In a better mood than when he'd arrived, he settled on the chair beside hers. ''Your reputation will go to hell if it's reported that you were drinking alone.''

Amusement added a familiar wicked light to her

intelligent eyes. "Tonight I'm not sure I give a damn."

"My kind of woman." Ben chose a tumbler and scooped it into the bowl of melting ice, then filled the remaining space with bourbon.

"In a flirting mood, are we?"

"It beats trying to be reasonable, or sympathetic, or helpful, or..."

"Another bad day at the office, dear?"

He eyed her from her elegant bare feet to the distant hem of her cutoffs, barely visible beneath a white silk shirt. It was an exceedingly *un*lady-of-the-manorlike outfit, and he wholly approved, especially since the miles-too-big shirt was unbuttoned to where it exposed far more than creamy throat.

"A terrible day. Can I lay my head in your lap and tell you about it, or is that likely to get me chased off your porch with a broom?"

"A broom is Mama Lulu's modus operandi, as you people have been known to put it. But if you think you'll need keeping in line, I could call over to the kitchen at the Baptist church and have her shuttled back."

Rolling his eyes, he took a deep swallow of his drink.

Eve chuckled, then asked, "How are the rest of the Cobbs?"

"Luther says they'll reopen the store tomorrow."

"You don't seem happy about that."

Her immediate, sincere concern invited honesty, while the bourbon and the coming night worked their own effect on him. "Sure I am. I guess. Hell, I don't know. Something's going on, but he's keeping it from me, I feel it. No one wants to tell me anything in this stinking town. I'm supposed to explain a death, stop vandalism, eradicate drugs from the community...but no one wants to give me the answers I need to do any of that. Nobody wants to get involved, except you, of course,'' he added, lifting his glass in a wry salute.

"In the wrong way, of course.''

"Of course.''

She smiled at their nonsense, only to grow serious again. "I'm sorry to hear you're still having trouble convincing Luther to open up to you.''

"Oh, he's friendly enough...but things aren't the way they used to be between us.''

"You've been gone a long time.''

"We were the best of friends.''

"You left him. What's more, Jackson's not exactly going on a death march with the French Foreign Legion. You could have called, visited on your days off or during a holiday.''

Was there anything she couldn't find out? She damn well knew more about him at this stage than he knew about her. "Maybe I've been wasting my time going from business to business trying to uncover new information. Maybe I should have come straight to you.''

"Now don't go getting your male pride in a knot. The conclusion was an easy enough one to come to.''

She was willing to let him off the hook, but that didn't relieve the urge to justify his absence. "I kept my distance because I needed the time and space.''

"I think that was tough on Luther.''

"It wasn't a picnic for me.''

"Okay, but as you said yourself a moment ago, this

is the South. How many white friends do you think he has?''

Not liking the direction she was heading, Ben smirked. "Leave it to a Yankee to turn this into a racial issue."

"Everything is about race down here. People insist on it."

"Not when you have a Maitland in your corner, bleeding heart or otherwise. Then you don't need any other friends."

Eve shook her head. "Luther doesn't consider me a friend. He has trouble dealing with the idea that Rae and I get along as well as we do. And when you add to that the mystery of how someone is suddenly—just because you've returned with a clear agenda, I might add—doing more than complaining about a black man competing with white-owned businesses in town, yes, I would imagine it's difficult for him to be as trusting as he used to be."

She might as well have kicked his chair out from beneath him. "Wait a minute…you think what happened over at the store is because of *me?*"

"What does the police procedural manual say about coincidence? I grant you that shop owners aren't thrilled with the idea of competition, particularly competition encouraged by the family who, in most cases, they pay rent to—''

"Nice of you to acknowledge that can of worms you've opened."

"But," she added as though he hadn't spoken, "until you got back, there wasn't this level of trouble. Why should Luther thank you for that?"

No, no trouble. Just his brother getting himself

killed. Ben wasn't about to accept her ditsy argument. "I don't need his thanks, I need his cooperation. He won't let me talk to Noah to find out who roughed up the boy, and he won't share his hunch about who trashed the store, and I know he has at least one."

"Maybe things will improve when the family gets Lem's money back from Jack Haygood."

With a sigh, Ben pinched the bridge of his nose, knowing full well what was coming. "They're not going to get it back. At least not yet. Not much of it anyway. Haygood says he spent most of the cash on one of the gambling boats during his last weekend off."

"Then can you blame Luther for being upset?" Eve cried. "Now Haygood's going to be prosecuted for stealing what everyone will see as ill-gotten money…"

"You don't know where the money came from," Ben said, wishing he hadn't let her sit in on his conversation with Bree. "Besides, what am I supposed to do, let him go and send out the message that two wrongs make a right?"

"Oh, please. You know I don't think that, I'm merely saying that Luther must be fearing what else might happen if he starts naming names. Once you follow up on the leads, wouldn't people assume he was the source? In fact, maybe that's what's happening. Maybe the family is undergoing a punishment of some kind for their friendship with *you*."

"Uh-uh." The ice in Ben's glass tinkled merrily as he pointed at her with the tumbler. The sound didn't come close to reflecting his mood. "You encouraged him to buck the system. Don't try to combine Lem's troubles to those Luther and his family are suffering. That grocery store means revenue out of the pockets of other businessmen, and it was your late husband who taught people how to play dirty to keep that from happening.''

''Don't remind me. During my first weeks down here, I think my hair stood continually on end as I watched Sumner act like a cross between Big Daddy and the Kingfisher. But if there's one message I'm determined to bring to this community, it's that revenue is earned, it's not a protected right.''

Ben grunted. ''Mrs. Maitland, ma'am, you really should consider running for political office. Why, you'd make taking poison sound as harmless as sniffing magnolias.''

''Go ahead and be sarcastic,'' she chided, stirring her drink with her index finger. ''You're just sore because an outsider, not one of your own, is doing the right thing.''

He would rather watch her lick Scotch off her finger. She had a bad habit of doing a number of casual things that his mind registered as provocative, and a list of them tended to taunt him when he was supposed to be sleeping, or else filtered into his dreams.

He glanced up to the porch above them. The music had changed from heavy metal to gangsta rap. ''I'm beginning to feel sorry for Bree. She doesn't stand a chance against you.''

''And here I thought you came over tonight because you needed a drinking buddy. Instead, you want to probe for weaknesses.''

''I can't do both?''

''It all depends what your goal is. The danger is

that by the time we say good-night, I may have lost my respect for you.''

"Provided she had some to begin with," he said to the calico cat observing them from a safe distance. "As for goals," he added to her, "I tend to avoid them. Have for years."

She stopped the glass midway to her lips. "That's an untruth if ever I heard one. And if you want to drink with me, you have to observe the rules. Take it or leave it."

"Honesty being one of them?"

"The only one, actually."

He thought about reminding her that she'd already made it clear she had no use for his, and he wasn't naive enough to trust he would get complete honesty from her, no matter what she insisted. "I'd just as soon go through boot camp again."

"While I have always thought that honesty can be a rather interesting extension of foreplay."

"Call me old-fashioned, but I prefer the real thing. Then again, I am open to inspiration."

"An easy man—what a novelty."

Ben grinned. Regardless of whether it was the bourbon or the woman that was beginning to take the edge off the daggers slicing at his insides, he was glad he'd yielded to impulse and ended up here. "If you find one who tries to convince you he's not, you'd better call for a plumber."

"Now *that* was honest."

"Does that mean I can stay?"

Rae sat on the edge of the bed and gazed into the dresser mirror at Luther lying behind her, one arm over his eyes. Except for the towel wrapped around his waist, he was naked, and his body still glistened from the heat and from the shower he'd taken fifteen minutes ago. Since then, he'd been doing what she'd demanded earlier, telling her the things he'd been keeping from her—about Bree's unexpected and un-orthodox friendship with Lem that had resulted in helpful testimony for Ben; but most of all, what Ben thought the money had meant.

"Say somethin'," he said at last. "I'll take you bein' mad at me easier than I can stand this waitin'."

"You've been pretty good at making me wait, yourself."

He sat up and stroked her back. "I'm sorry, baby. I thought I was helpin'. I didn't want you worryin' more than you already were."

"I needed to know these things, Luther. How can I protect my children and support you, when you don't tell me what's happening?"

"What good's this latest bad news gonna do you?"

"At least I understand why you try not to give Ben any more information or opinions than he gives you! I don't agree, but I see that you're afraid what happened to Lem and what's happening to us may be connected."

"It's gotta be."

"How do you figure that?"

"'Cuz we're not telling Ben to let it go. And maybe he's found somethin' else he ain't tellin' us about that's scarin' somebody bad, makin' them think we're greedy or ungrateful."

Rae shook her head. "Come morning, I'm going to go to the police station myself and announce that we don't want the money, and neither does Mama Lulu. It doesn't take a genius to figure out that it's bringing bad luck to anyone who has it, so good riddance, I say. Maybe when *that* gets around town, we'll be left alone.''

"It's not enough," her husband replied with a sigh. "Ain't nothin' gonna be enough until Ben stops goin' into those woods, and askin' questions.''

"Or he finds out who did these terrible things." She turned to hold him close. "Tell Ben about the Hughes and Meece boys, Luther. Ask him not to approach the family for now, just to watch them.''

"I can watch them myself."

"No, you can't. Tell him and he might share what else he knows. Promise, Luther.'' Rae lifted his hand and pressed it over her breast. His big, rough palm warmed her through the cotton dress and her bra.

He exhaled, the sound more of a shuddering sigh. "I love you.'' He awarded a hotter kiss against the side of her neck. "I love you so much. You and the boys are my life. Don't lose faith in me.''

Her sweet, sweet man. She closed her eyes against her own fear and tilted her head to give him better access to her neck and throat. She might not agree with everything he said or did, but when he whispered to her like this, held her as though his strength could only come from her love, she couldn't refuse him anything, didn't have the heart to stay angry with him.

When he reached for the buttons on her dress, she began to melt inside. "Luther, I still have my period.''

"Is the bleedin' bad?''

"No, but I'd have to use the bathroom first...if you're wanting to..."

"Do you want to?"

She eased out of his arms thinking about the front door that needed to be checked, the final instructions she wanted to give to the boys, the coffee machine she hadn't set for the morning. If she thought about what else waited to be done, she would never get to bed, or have the energy to make love, and so she pushed those thoughts away and smiled at her husband. "Close your eyes for a few minutes. I'll be back shortly."

"You're empty."

As Ben poured himself a refill, the music from upstairs changed again. This tune was country-western, and the volume was lower than what they'd been listening to up until now.

"She's on the phone," Eve said at his quizzical look.

"You're getting to know her quite well."

"She's angry not complicated."

They'd been covering a good deal of territory so far, but this one interested him, too, because Bree remained a part of his investigation. "What's she angry about, besides the obvious?"

"Life. Particularly as it applies to her. The rules have been changing rapidly for her and she isn't prepared. All this—" she indicated the estate "—gave her a somewhat false sense of security. Sumner made it worse by treating her like something between a princess and a china doll. By the time he realized his mistake, the damage was done, and now she's not prepared to be anything more than a rich man's toy."

"Since when do girls like her consider that a negative?"

"She's brighter than she lets on, and whether she admits it or not, she knows what happens when your looks go or a man's interest wanes. Having been raised to believe that only sugar feeds hunger, she's now faced with the realization that such advice referred to a superficial hunger. She's beginning to understand that if she wants to avoid relentless heartbreak, if she wants more in her future than her mother had to look forward to had she lived, what most of the girls she grew up with have to look forward to, she has to face reality. That's frightening to her, and that," Eve said, gesturing toward the girl's room, "is a major part of why she's behaving as she is."

"Have you avoided the heartbreak?"

Eve ran her finger around the rim of her glass. "You cannot keep your itchy mind off of my love life, can you?"

"You said you wanted honesty."

"Must yours always revolve around sex?"

"I didn't promise not to bring up the subject."

"But we agreed that an affair wasn't a good idea for us."

True. However, tonight…tonight he wanted a reprieve from his job, maybe even from himself. Nothing would do that faster than focusing on a desirable woman. The problem was, not just any woman would do. With each year, he was becoming more and more particular. Now things were worse—he only wanted Eve.

"Okay, let's make this fair," she said, breaking into his thoughts. "We'll take turns."

He must have missed something. "Doing what?"

"If you get to ask probing personal questions, then so do I."

"Only if I get to go first."

"You already did. You asked about heartbreak."

"Forget that. I've thought of a better one." He might as well find out straight off if she meant what she'd said. "Did you run around with your blouse unbuttoned to your navel when Sumner was alive?"

She glanced down, but remained surprisingly unruffled by his pointed look. "It's not, it's hot, and I'm sitting, which leaves me perfectly decent."

"Not from this vantage point, which for the record seems too damn far away, though close enough to be reminded that you're not as small as you claimed."

This time her only reply was to point to the seat directly opposite her.

He eyed it and then offered her a benign smile. "Was I complaining?"

"I think it's my turn now."

He chuckled and sipped his drink, wondering what she would hit him with.

"Why don't you wear your gun?"

The song upstairs ended and an equally maudlin one began. Ben almost wished for another dose of rap. "That's hardly provocative."

"*Provocative* is your word. I said *personal* and *probing.*"

"Well, who told you to ask me that one in particular? Rae? Mama Lulu?"

"Neither, why?"

"Your timing is eerie."

"How so?"

"The gun was my father's...and I was at the cemetery prior to coming here."

"I'd heard he was killed on the job."

He knew his intended grimace came out closer to a smirk. "It was more like inviting a guy to shoot him, and the son of a bitch did."

For only the second time since he'd met her, Eve appeared at a loss for words. "That's terrible."

"Yeah." He drew a deep breath, accepting that he might as well tell her the whole story, although it would likely mean leaving sooner instead of later. She sure knew how to ruin a party.

"After my mother died, there were women," he began. "Plenty of them. But none the old man ever got serious over. You could say I learned most of my bad habits from him."

"Some people would say many of the good ones, too."

Not as many as thought so before the scandal. "The point is, in my senior year in high school, something changed. I couldn't put my finger on it at first, except to note that he was away from home at odder hours than usual, and sometimes not even his men knew where to find him. When he was around, he acted preoccupied. Looking back, I suppose I knew what was up, but at the same time I didn't want to know."

"She was married."

"Bingo."

"The wife of an important town official?"

"Worse. Do you know Alice Potter?"

Eve frowned. "I suppose I should if she's local, but—"

"The widow of the Reverend Ira Potter."

Her eyes went wide. "*That* Potter? He had an affair with a preacher's wife? How on earth did they keep that a secret in this town?"

"They would meet elsewhere or use his car, I guess. All I remember is that she smelled of roses, and whenever my father came home after having been with her, I sneezed. Then one day I was in the supermarket picking up a few things we needed, and I bumped my cart into her, making her drop some stuff. When I helped her pick up everything, I started sneezing, just as I did at home. Guess I must have turned as red as those hibiscus over on that railing," he said, nodding to the opulent blossoms.

"Did you tell your father that you'd figured it out?"

"It was the night we had the biggest fight of our lives."

"Because you were ashamed of him?"

"Hell, no. Well, not exactly. I mean, who was I to criticize him when I was chasing any skirt I could get my hands on. But it was *who* that mattered to me."

"Ben Rader! You were a snob?"

How did he explain? "If you'd met my father, you would have understood. He was bigger than life. You think Sumner was something? Even he called my father a walking legend."

"Like you."

He wanted to be flattered, but knew there was no comparison. "Different man. Different era."

"If you say so. What about this Potter woman?"

"She was...she was the plainest, dried-up little thing you could ever imagine. The idea of the two of them together was laughable. The old man back-handed me for saying that. I remember the force of the blow knocked me clear across the room."

"Oh dear. Never try to reason with a man who thinks he's in love."

It might be ancient history, but Ben needed a sip of his bourbon as he pictured those days again. "Nothing was the same after that. After graduation I went straight into the service and worked toward my degree. I wouldn't let him put me through school."

"Because he continued the affair?"

"For several more years, and as a result I don't think we spoke a half-dozen times. I figure it must've been the biggest secret in town. Maybe in the county."

"Until her husband found out?"

"Something like that. The last time we spoke, my father told me he wanted to marry her. He said he couldn't stand living a lie anymore and intended to confront Potter to ask him to give her a divorce. The next day he found Potter outside his church. It was reported that they exchanged a few words and the reverend started crying like a baby. Then he grew really agitated...until my father handed over his gun."

"Dear God."

"Crazy, huh? Even after eight years I can't believe it happened."

"What about the reverend?"

"After he shot my father, he turned the gun on

himself." Ben listened as the tree frogs began to sing. Some Greek chorus, he mused.

"And Mrs. Potter?"

"She buried her husband."

"Poor woman."

That snapped Ben out of his private brooding. "Excuse me?"

"She must have loved your father very much. At the same time, she had to have felt a huge responsibility to her husband. In the end she lost. Everything."

"You're incredible."

"It's a sad story, Ben."

"It's a stupid one, a stupid waste! And for what?"

"Love."

He didn't like what happened inside him whenever he heard that word. "Bullshit. He didn't believe in it. Sex, sure. Love—"

"How do you know?" Eve sat up. "You're basing your reasoning on hurt and disappointment without any thought for the emotions that were obviously very real between your father and Alice."

Ben glared hard into his drink.

After several seconds, Eve said more gently, "The gun, it's your father's, isn't it? That's why you don't wear it."

"Well, could you?"

She remained silent, as though to contemplate the dilemma, but ended up unable to decide. Frowning, she asked, "Why did you go to the cemetery just now if you haven't forgiven him? What happened there? Something did, it's still written all over your face.

That's why you came to me...behaved the way you did, almost daring me to throw you out."

So much for thinking he could simply spend some time with a desirable woman, drool a bit, drink more and go home to crash until morning. "I'd heard someone was putting flowers on his grave. I had to see for myself."

"Of course...she's still in Parish."

"How did you guess?"

"I told you, she loved him."

Old anger stirred in his belly like a twisting knife. "If she'd had a decent bone in her body she would have left Parish."

"I don't see how she could have."

Tempted to toss his sweating glass across the porch, he switched hands and rubbed his wet palm into his thigh. "That's what she said. And she looked at me with those calf eyes...stood there and looked as though I was supposed to know what she wanted."

"Forgiveness for taking your father away from you."

"Well, she's got a long wait before that happens."

"Ben, I'm not condoning what they did behind her husband's back, but it's not their fault that they fell in love."

"Look, that's garbage, okay?"

"Just because you've never felt those emotions—"

"Have you?"

"No, for which I think I'm greatly relieved. It must be scary to feel that intensely about another human being."

"And I think you don't know what you're talking about, so let's change the subject."

With that, Ben swallowed the rest of his drink and made himself another. He wasn't sorry he'd told her the whole story, but he would have preferred telling off old Alice Potter more, upsetting her so much that she wouldn't dare cross his path again. But he had a feeling they were destined to repeat the evening's scene. The woman probably wouldn't be happy until she drove him nuts.

When he realized Eve continued to sit there and watch him, his agitation grew. "It's my turn," he muttered. "So tell me something."

"Like what?" she asked, all innocence herself.

"Hell, I don't know. Tell me something about you that I'm not expecting. Tell me something that'll make my jaw hit the glass top on this table. Tell me—"

"Sumner liked to watch me bathe."

Ben's intention to do something about his sexual needs had been pushed aside out of necessity, and he knew he'd been inviting trouble by tempting Eve. But he hadn't expected her to be this successful. Or, he thought as she touched her glass to her throat then slowly eased it down the open V of her shirt, to enjoy it this much.

"Go on. Tub or shower?"

"Oh, tub. He was a traditionalist in many ways, and quite the romantic. He would order all kinds of French soaps and lotions and sponges for me, then conducted quite an elegant, tantalizing ceremony as he presented the packages to me. Maybe that's why I was never really shocked."

"You enjoyed it?"

"It's not against the Rader law of order to like presents, is it?"

"Of course not, but I thought you said..." Ben frowned, not at all pleased with what he was thinking.

"That ours was strictly a business arrangement? That was true enough. But there were times when he had to deal with a real fear about his pending death. Lord knows I'd seen enough illness in my work to understand what it can do to the strongest people. What a deep loneliness it breeds."

She scooped up her hair and lifted it over the back of her chair. Ben paid close attention to what the silk did to her nipples.

"Nothing like putting a new spin on the Florence Nightingale image," he drawled.

"Actually it had more to do with being a human being than being a nurse. More especially with being a woman. Is it my turn now?"

"No, this is a multipart question. Tell me about this...ceremony."

"You're bad." But the liquor Eve had drunk was mellowing her considerably, too. "Well, it would begin with him asking for a pitcher of dry martinis, which I was to bring to the master bathroom. He always did it around this time in the evening. I suppose that's what reminded me."

As if she was likely to forget something like that. Envy churned in Ben's stomach. "He liked to watch you undress."

"Sumner never apologized for adoring women."

"Dirty old lecher probably thought he had a right to you, all things considered."

"No, he always made it clear that I could decline

at any point. But there was something sweet about all those candles and scents. Something quite erotic, too."

Ben narrowed his eyes. "Made him a happy man, did you?"

"I tried my best. Now, are you over feeling sorry for yourself?"

"No. Did you let him touch you?"

She sipped her drink, and her eyes appeared almost catlike over the crystal rim. "I think I'll let you use your imagination about the rest."

Ben fought the battle between admiration and sharp jealousy and lost. "Does Ashworth let you jerk his chain this way?"

Her animated face betrayed her shock and hurt. But quickly recovering, she put down her glass and rose. "I see that not only did I overrate your ability to be kind, I underestimated your cruelty."

She headed for the screen door, but closer, Ben not only kept her from opening it, he trapped her between the steel frame and himself.

"Wait," he said against her hair, drawing her scent deep. The luscious, clean fragrance of her soap and shampoo got to him as effectively and thoroughly as the bourbon had. "I apologize."

"Not interested," she said to the door.

"Hear me out anyway." An urgency rose in him, a need for clarity. "This—whatever it is that's happening between us—doesn't altogether thrill me."

"Old news, Rader. Let go."

Instead, and because he needed to touch her, he took hold of her wrists and directed her hands around his neck. He could feel her pulse quicken, her body tense, back against his.

"Ben, I don't react well to the push-pull technique."

"I'm not proud of it myself outside of an interrogation room."

Simultaneously pushing aside her hair with his nose and pressing his mouth to the side of her neck, he slid his hands into her shirt to cover her breasts. Her gasp was as sharp as the pleasure and hunger that speared through him. He'd never touched a woman so sleek, firm and instantly hot; she radiated a sensuality he wanted to immerse himself in as deeply as he wanted to thrust himself into her body.

"Justin or Bree might come downstairs."

Although he knew she was right, it annoyed him that she could stay logical when all he could think of was putting his mouth where his hands were and discovering what kind of sounds she made when driven to her own sweet madness. But knowing she would start resisting if he didn't do something, he spun her around and pressed her against the wood siding and out of immediate sight of anyone inside. He'd wanted her facing him anyway, so he could get at her mouth.

Kissing her again was like suddenly finding a stream of sweet oxygen after holding your breath for an interminable length of time. He couldn't get at her fast enough. And when their tongues met, it was as powerful as when lightning struck his rental home in Jackson and melted the adapter on his answering machine. All he could do was sink his hands into the silk of her fragrant hair and hope to heaven he didn't suffer a nuclear meltdown.

He admired a woman who wasn't shy about taking what she wanted, and Eve didn't disappoint. Once she accepted the idea that this was going to happen, she wrapped her arms around his neck and met him halfway. That allowed him to explore more of her curves and hollows, and made it easier to shift his hands to her bottom and move her against his aroused body.

"Come to the cabin with me," he murmured against her mouth.

"I can't."

"Bree won't know you're not down here."

"It's not that."

"What then?" he asked, finding a slow, tantalizing rhythm to torment both of them. "It can't be because we haven't known each other long enough."

"That should matter, but I'm not hypocrite enough to use it as an excuse."

Despite what he'd accused her of earlier, she was proving to be one of the most honest women he'd ever met, and somehow that made the attraction all the stronger. "Then why?"

"I've never lost my head over a man, Ben, and I don't want to start with you. Before we go any further, I want to be sure I can handle it when it's over."

The confession pleased him. "Hell, let it start first," he drawled.

"I'm serious."

He leaned back to study her expression, which was getting harder to do with only a soft light filtering through the screen door, but there was enough to determine she wasn't playing hard to get. She did feel strongly about what she was saying.

He stroked her lower lip with his thumb. "I don't like it much, but I respect your reasoning."

Eve's idea of saying thank-you was to bite gently on his finger; however, it was the brief caress of her tongue that nearly had him changing his mind. "Damn...if I thought it would work, I'd beg you to wrap your legs around me. I'd be quick, I swear."

"See, you still don't get it. I don't want our first time to be quick."

Sweet heaven. They might not have much of a choice, he thought, lowering his head for a final kiss. "Okay, you win again, Red. Only this is it. The next time I get this close, you'd better have come to terms with things."

12

Maybe he shouldn't have been doing this, but for several days Justin had honored Lacey's plea to keep away, and here it was the Wednesday after the Fourth of July, and he couldn't stand it any longer. He had to know if she was all right. So now that Eve and Mama Lulu had left for town to run errands, and Bree had taken advantage and split, he was heading for the lake.

Although he took his sketch pad, he didn't bother with much else, no water, food or anything. Not only didn't he want to waste time with preparations, he had no idea if he would be able to stay, or for how long.

The closer he got to the lake the greater his excitement. Just seeing Lacey for a minute would be great. God, he hoped she was all right. For hours every night he'd lain in bed worrying. If she had new bruises, he didn't know what he would do.

It had rained last night, but the ground was drying quickly thanks to the brilliant sun rising fast behind him. Eager to get to his usual spot, he came out of the woods fast and almost missed the fisherman casting near where he usually sat. It took a frustrating fifteen minutes of hiding behind a thicket of wild roses before the guy let his boat drift toward the Ashworth side of the lake. As Justin watched, he thought about Lem and how weird it would be if the fisherman snagged something that would shed new information on his death. Just yesterday he'd come into the kitchen to see Eve consoling a weeping Mama Lulu. Eve explained to him later that Chief Rader had brought news after finally interviewing the coroner. It seemed that old Doc Tinney had forgotten to add a little fact to his report that came up during his conversation with Ben Rader. Apparently, Lem's clothes had been wet and soiled on *both* sides; that, Ben said, offered strong proof that he had been rolled over and subsequently drowned.

Goose bumps grew on Justin's arms despite the temperature. Rolled over...drowned on purpose in the nasty, larvae-filled water on the bank. Who could be so cold-blooded? The chief said once word got out, people around here would really be looking at each other differently than before.

Well, Lacey was one person who would be exempt from that kind of scrutiny and suspicion. And on a happier note, he had a surprise for her. The other day he'd gone to the high school and convinced them to lend him one of the few books on signing they'd had in the library. He'd been studying ever since and hoped he'd learned enough to make communication easier.

He found her weeding her garden. Once he determined that the pickup truck wasn't there, he found a golf ball–size stone and threw it in her direction to get her attention.

When she spotted him, he could feel her hesitation.

"Please." He not only said the word, he held his right hand flat against his chest and made a circle. Then added the rest. "Don't run away."

Once she'd cast a wary look around her, she approached him. Although barefoot as usual, she moved normally today; and once again she had on the worn dress he'd seen her in the other times.

When she reached him, he set down his pad and the book he'd brought, and placed his hands, knuckle to knuckle, at this chest to begin signing the question "How are you?"

To his dismay she stared as if he'd dropped out of the sky.

"I'm signing," he enunciated so she could read his lips.

She shook her head.

Confused, he frowned, his signing vocabulary not going that far. "I don't understand. Are you saying I didn't do it right?"

She shrugged.

Maybe there was more than one technique? He hadn't considered that. "How did you learn to communicate?"

Once again she shook her head, only this time she ended by touching her chest.

"Great," he muttered to himself. "I should have guessed. You taught yourself whatever you know." The implications of that suggestion disturbed him. She could read a bit, too, which meant she'd had some tutoring of one kind or another, but she couldn't sign in the standard way, and that meant what?

He leaned over, extending his hand to indicate height—hers as a little girl. Then he touched his ear.

She nodded, and quickly began gesturing. Most of it was Greek to him, but he thought he got the gist of it.

"Fever or something. Didn't they get you to a doctor or hospital in time?"

As she studied his lips, her dejected look told him that maybe she never got there at all.

"Why about this?" He touched his lips. "All at the same time?"

She didn't seem to be following that, and Justin had so much more to ask. He decided to let that go for now.

He sat down on a dry patch of warm, sunny grass and patted the ground beside him. After the slightest hesitation, she sunk to her knees and watched him flip through pages of his sketch pad.

"Look," he said, wanting to share the drawings he'd made of her during their time apart. "These are you. This is how much I've been thinking of you."

He'd worked hard and diligently, sketching her from memory, how she'd looked at the door of the house, in her garden, hanging the wash. In each drawing he'd added how nature was as attracted to her as he was—a bird on the wash line she was hanging clothes from, a butterfly hovering on the blooming chives near where she weeded...And always he captured her sweet but sad expression, her soft mouth, eyes at once young as well as a bit melancholy, all framed by an abundance of wavy hair.

As before, she stared at the drawings, but this time there was wonder and appreciation, and soon she was flipping through the pages herself. Her small hands, the bitten or ripped nails grimy from work, traced the way he made her hair look, as if it danced in the wind. All of his drawings depicted part fairy and part woman.

"So sue me, that's how I see you," he told her sheepishly when she gave him a look of mild skepticism. "Fragile like a sparrow, but magical like a wood nymph."

Eager to show her something else, he flipped to the back where he'd written her name and each letter was formed from a garden of flowers, birds and playful insects. "Can you tell that spells Lacey?"

After a first gasp, she bent close to the paper, studying each tiny blossom and creature and uttering the softest cooing sounds.

Thrilled that things were going so much better than he'd hoped, Justin ripped the page from the pad. But when he tried to give it to her, she pushed it back at him.

"It's all right. I did it for you. It's a gift. Why can't you take it?" He didn't mean to press, but she'd refused it a third time. "Is it because of him?" He quickly sketched the stocky bearded man he'd seen from afar.

Lacey stared at the spare few lines that captured the man all too well.

"Is he your husband?"

When he ducked his head and repeated the question so she could see his mouth, she shook her head adamantly.

Thank God. "Your brother?"

She began to shake her head again, only to sigh with exasperation. Suddenly she stuck out her hand and sliced her other hand across it.

Now what did that mean? "Half brother? Maybe stepbrother? Well, whichever he is, he's a lousy slug to use you as his punching bag the way he does. Why do you stay?"

Too late, Justin thought of the old man he hadn't seen since they'd moved in. "Is it the other man?"

Lacey had trouble following him, but slowly nodded.

"Is he your father?"

She shook her head and pretended to stroke a beard.

"Grandfather!"

That prompted her to signal that the old guy had experienced some problems with his heart. It figured. He would have to be that sick not to do something to protect her from the big lummox that was abusing her.

Ever so carefully, he turned to the matter of her half brother or stepbrother again. "Why does he hit you? What makes him so angry?"

She looked away.

Justin knew he was in danger of losing any ground he'd gained, and decided to back off before he frightened her off permanently. With the utmost care, he touched her arm. "Look, I won't ask any more questions for now, okay? If there's something you want to tell me, I'll listen. Whenever you're ready. Deal?"

When she gave him a slight nod, he began to sketch her again. She didn't seem happy about that and pointed to the water where the lilies hugged the bank. If she could have heard him, he would have asked what she thought the flowers had over her, but the scene did give him an idea, and he quickly drew a scene where a frog stood on one of the wide leaves offering a morsel of bread to a fish peering up at him.

Lacey shifted closer to watch him do more. Their closeness caused her bare arm to brush against his, her hair to tangle around his pencil and his fingers. The innocent contact did incredible things to his heart. So moved was he that he had to close his eyes against the rush of emotion that was all too new to him. He didn't expect her to touch him, not voluntarily, and the shock of her fingers on his cheek had him jerking back.

"Sorry."

She pointed to his eyes.

"It's only…ah, heck. I have to ask. Lacey…*did* you miss me? Even a little?"

She smiled and touched his chin.

"I see, you only care about my looks," he teased.

She shook her head and pointed at him, herself, then drew something around and over his head.

"What…?" Realizing what she meant, he felt heat flood his face. "Believe me, I'm no angel. Especially not when I think of you. Lacey—" he cleared his throat "—will you let me help you? I can't stand thinking of you having to go through heaven only knows what. You can trust me. Honest."

Although she'd watched his lips and he sensed she'd grasped the majority of what he'd said, she made no immediate reply. Then he saw the swell of tears in her eyes.

She pointed to the tablet again. Guessing she wanted to write something, he offered her the pencil, but she brushed it away and motioned for him to use it.

He understood now. She didn't want him to talk about anything serious.

Dejected, but by no means defeated, he sighed. "All right. I guess I just have to prove to you that I'm trustworthy."

And he would, he promised himself. He would.

"At least walk with me a ways," Fred Varnell said to Ben. "How else can I impress upon you that when given a chance, when we pull together, this is a fine little town?"

Ben began strolling up Main Street with the mayor, but only because he wanted to find out what the guy was up to now. He had no interest in the group converging at the other end of the block, where the lawyer would soon be officiating in the land dedication for the new library, and had no intention of wasting his time observing it.

"Right, Fred. Now all we have to do is hold a mirror up to the hypocrites, issue the bigots a conscience and remind a few individuals that white-collar crime is as serious as any other variety."

Behind wire-rimmed glasses, Fred's eyes grew wide. "I know we've earned a black eye or two lately, but surely you aren't suggesting we have more than our share of, er, unethical business practices going on in this community?"

He nodded toward Trevor Hughes's limousine-length pickup truck as the businessman drove toward the same destination they were heading. "There's a prime suspect right now. How else do you explain his success? There hasn't been the kind of growth in Parish to justify his building his store to double its original size. I'll bet he's involved in money laundering or something equally slick.''

"Nonsense. You haven't taken into consideration that the next nearest lumberyard of any size is in Greenville, so he's servicing several small pockets of population in the outlying areas. Also, don't forget Perry Ashworth used Trev exclusively to rebuild and expand his stables after that tragic fire.'' Warming to his subject, Fred beamed. "And now we're about to get a new library, the construction of which I'm sure Trevor will be directly associated with.''

Ben censured that with a grunt. "You're planting a sign that says Future Home of. If it stands there as long as the one for Gentry's Funeral Home, those kids the library was intended for will have rug rats of their own before another shovel of dirt is moved.''

"Not the best example.'' The mayor held up his right index finger as though arguing a point of law, a common stance for the practicing lawyer. "The Gentrys had some, er, domestic difficulties.''

"Yeah. Sally's having trouble dealing with the fact that Monroe prefers fondling corpses to her.''

The somewhat straitlaced attorney grimaced. "Ben, that's a sick rumor...and total hearsay!''

"Sure, sure. So why is she still drinking cheap wine and sneaking out before dawn to hide the bottles in the trash on garbage-pickup days? My men can set their watches by her.'' Town gossip was still something he could count on from his men, although Sally's pitiful problem was hardly something he wanted to hear about. She'd been a fun girl back when they'd dated.

Fred cleared his throat. "Sounds as if the communication level is improving in your department. I'm glad to hear it because that's what I wanted to talk to you about.''

Here we go, Ben thought. ''I am not going to speak to the D.A. on behalf of Jack Haygood. Shit, Fred, I can't believe you're going to ask me again.''

''Do I have a choice? You know his father-in-law sits on the city council, and that Jack's mistake inevitably reflects on the entire family.''

''Mistake. That's a good one.''

''Jeb's practically on his knees begging I do something for his little girl.''

''Then offer your services to Jerri Lynn so she can get a quick, cheap divorce.''

The mayor didn't look pleased with the suggestion. But he was nothing if not tenacious. ''Jeb's offered to write a check to the Cobb family for the two thousand dollars if they'll let the matter drop. He might even go a bit higher, but that's off the record.''

''Let him ask the family,'' Ben replied, personally disgusted with Jeb Whitehead for suggesting the idea, and Fred for agreeing to voice it. ''I doubt they'll be interested.''

''I was hoping you'd do that. As a favor to me? You could explain to them that it's a fair deal. After all, there's no real harm done, right? It's not as though Haygood's going to get his job back.''

So he said, but that was probably somewhere on Fred's list of possibilities, as well. ''After what Dr. Tinney passed on to me? You want me to excuse the theft of a *murdered* man's money?''

It was news that had officially reopened the case. Once he'd pressed old man Tinney to sit down and

review the file with him, the coroner had admitted
he'd overlooked the condition of Lem's clothes—
other than not having found any bullet or knife holes.
But upon studying the photographs once again, he'd
said, with no small embarrassment, that he hadn't noticed how odd it was that Lem's clothes were soiled
on both sides, and had been when Tinney had come
upon the supposedly uncontaminated scene—a physical impossibility, given the way Lem had fallen. Ever
since, the news that they were indeed dealing with an
unsolved murder had many of the town's residents
behaving as though Jack the Ripper was back in business.

Fred slowed, his expression pained. "It sounds
even worse when you say it."

"Good. Then maybe you won't bring up Haygood
again. I thought you asked me back here to put this
mess to rest?"

"As an *accident*. I'd hoped you could dispel rumors, resolve allegations. Prove me wrong!"

"You politicians, you're all alike. What this town
needs is a heavy dose of the truth." Ben patted his
pocket, and remembered he'd left his cigarettes in the
glove compartment in place of the gun now on his
hip. Tinney's news had changed things for him, too.

Fred sighed. "Any suspects?"

"I told you before—everyone in Parish, including
you."

"I'm beginning to hate this job. By the way, the
city council isn't thrilled with you asking for more
money for the new guy you're hiring, either."

"What makes you think I'm bringing in a male
replacement for Haygood?"

That almost caused the mayor to walk into a concrete planter. "You're hiring a *woman?*"

Across the street Ben saw Eve being escorted to the event by Perry Ashworth. He could have done without seeing the guy's arm around her waist. "Thought I might give the male population another reason besides heat rash for all that scratching." The couple stepped onto the uneven ground of the empty field, and Ben narrowed his eyes as Eve gave Ashworth a smile that suggested she liked his hand where it was. "Hear this, Fred. I take full blame for being stupid enough to accept this job. But believe me, I will solve the Cobb case, and I'm going to hire whomever I think best suited for the job. If any of that presents a problem for you, you can take this badge and gun and—"

"I get the picture. But no feminists," Fred pleaded. "It's just not...Parish."

"Who do you think is getting you your library?"

As they started to cross the street, Ashworth laughed at something Eve said and leaned over to kiss her on the cheek.

"Ah! Well, I'll admit Eve Maitland and I have our disagreements from time to time," Fred replied, smiling at the scene before him, "but she's quite the diplomat when she wants to be, as you can see for yourself."

Staring hard at Perry, Ben asked, "Why does Ashworth have so much night traffic at his place?"

Fred's reaction reflected sheer befuddlement. "Pardon?"

"An eighteen-wheeler almost ran me off the road the other night, peeling out of there. And a couple of nights ago I heard one at two or three in the morning.''

"I don't know anything about that, but it makes sense. If you had to deal with the high-strung animals he raises, you wouldn't want them to suffer traveling during the heat of the day, either.''

"The rig that almost got me wasn't a stock trailer.''

"Really? I'm fairly certain Perry buys feed and whatnot in pretty large quantities, probably for the price break as much as anything else. He's turned into quite a shrewd businessman.'' Approaching the group gathered for the dedication, he called, "Perry! The chief here is complaining that you're disturbing the peace.''

Ben could have kicked Fred clear into next weekend for opening his big mouth, but he kept his expression impassive as Ashworth extended his hand to the mayor.

"Am I? In what way, Ben?'' Perry only issued him a cocky smile.

"Those late deliveries at Bellemere.''

"Interfering with your beauty sleep, I see. Sorry, but I don't dictate the freight lines' schedules, even though those big jobs occasionally wake me, too. I hope you haven't been disturbed, Eve?''

She looked from one of them to the other, her welcoming smile to Ben turning into a frown of confusion. "No, this is the first I've heard about it.''

"Good. Because for you I'd be obliged to raise hell.''

Before she could respond, Ben muttered, "Just tell them to stop at the end of your driveway before turning onto the county road. I'd like to skip ending up as someone's hood ornament if at all possible.''

"Absolutely. You certainly are putting in long hours, Benjamin Tyrell.''

The son of a bitch knew he hated being called that, even though the names were from both of his grandfathers who'd died before he was born. "Maybe, but it would raise more eyebrows if I slept while a murderer walked the woods, or maybe these streets, a free man. Besides—'' he slid his gaze to Eve ''—it's too hot to sleep.'' He let his eyes tell her who was making the nights feel even hotter.

She looked like a blueberry confection in her navy silk sheath and white accessories, properly demure for the widow of the town's most famous and influential citizen. Tantalizing, too, because whether she thought so or not, her feminine body challenged any outfit to hide that she was all woman. Today her hair was swept up in a classy chignon that exposed her graceful, long neck. Without wanting to, Ben remembered how marble-smooth her skin was there. As smooth as her breasts...

"Hello, Ben,'' she said. "I'm glad you could come.''

A part of him was too willing to lap up the warmth in her eyes. He had to brutally remind himself that she was here with Ashworth, and that she had put *his* feelings, *their* attraction, on her timetable.

"I'm not staying,'' he replied, disgusted with himself. "If I can't arrest anyone for polluting the air with empty rhetoric, I don't want to listen, either.''

"Ever the sweet-tongued devil,'' Perry murmured.

Ben studied the man in the expensive white suit

that had probably cost more than he made in a month. Distrust mixed with his jealousy and dislike, and tempted him to put Ashworth in his place once and for all.

"I saw that Bree got another speeding ticket," he said to Eve. "Did she tell you?"

Her pained expression gave him his answer. "How bad this time?"

"Ron only wrote her up for twenty miles over the limit, and it was after business hours, but he said she was going considerably faster. Have another talk with her. If she doesn't care what these things do to her insurance premiums, remind her that she could kill herself or someone else driving that fast."

"For all the good it will do, but, yes. Of course, I will."

He knew it was getting more and more difficult to deal with the girl. The few times they'd talked since that night on the porch, their conversations had been mostly about Bree's increasing wildness, his frustrations with digging up more on Lem's death and the continued headaches the Cobbs were having. The reminder of their mutual friends would sour the rest of his morning.

"I'd better move. I have to get over to the market." Business had picked up somewhat since his friends had reopened the store, but not everything was going smoothly. "Someone threw a brick through the Cobbs' front door last night."

"No! Those poor people," Eve said as several others made sympathetic sounds. "Ben, you should have called me so I could bring Mama Lulu."

"Luther's concerned what all this stress is doing to

her. He and Rae said they're all right for the moment.''

"She won't like that much. Do you have any idea who on earth—"

"This isn't the time." His look admonished, but his tone wasn't unkind when he added, "For Mama Lulu's sake, hold off saying anything to her. I'd like to be there when you do. Can I stop by later this afternoon, or early evening?"

"Whenever you can manage it."

Perry cleared his throat.

"Oh, dear." Eve murmured a quick apology. "Perry and I have a—"

"Let me know when there's room on your social calendar. I have work to do." With a nod to Fred, Ben walked away.

It was Ashworth's smug expression that had provoked him. Now he would get to spend the rest of the day thinking of her being with that snake. He needed that eating at him about as much as he'd needed learning who'd been seen driving away from the Cobbs' last night.

They had been lying in the tall grass for several minutes pointing out intriguing or amusing clouds to each other. Justin had played similar games with Bree countless times when they were kids, but those childlike moments had been nothing like this.

Every time Lacey pointed out a new puff of white to him and signed what it reminded her of, he would draw a more comical rendition for her. Often, that had her making soft, delighted sounds and she would roll into his side, burying her face against his shoulder. It made him feel... There were no words.

A loner, he didn't have any close friends, nor had he ever held a girl like this. Painfully shy, he had even passed on his senior prom, intimidated by the idea of having to make small talk with sophisticated girls he didn't begin to understand.

Lacey was different. They were alike in some ways. Both of them were damaged people in a way, only her wounds were deeper, he guessed, and more evident.

Over the last week or so, in the stolen minutes and hours they'd spent together, he'd grown used to avoiding any subject that would upset her, and she'd been sweet and patient with his bouts of awkward chatter that she couldn't possibly follow, then his stretches of brooding silence. They'd become friends. And more than friends, at least as far as he was concerned. He was falling in love.

"You know what?" he murmured. "As much as I like the clouds, I like the blue sky best. Look at it. Do you know what that color makes me think of? Freedom." He lifted his hand toward the riveting blue. "You can't see the end of it, it just goes on forever, out and out and out... Sometimes I think I'd like to be on a rocket that would take me there. It's so big compared to here. Sometimes it feels too crowded on Earth. Do you ever feel as though there's not enough air for you to breathe?"

He felt Lacey's gentle touch on his lips and turned his head to see her raised on one elbow watching him, a worried expression on her face. She shifted her hand to her chest and clenched it into a fist.

"Aw, no. Not real pain. A loneliness sometimes that I can't explain. I have a sister. Bree's my twin, and they say twins are closer than any siblings can be, but those moments have always been rare for us, so I'm left feeling...feeling as if God forgot to give me the other side of myself."

Lacey stroked his cheek with the back of her hand. Because Justin was certain she understood only a fragment of what he was saying, he gave her an apologetic smile.

"I'm not really sad. Being here with you is the best part of my day. Only it makes me miserable to know I have to go home and you have to go back down there."

To his amazement, this time she silenced him with her lips. As softly as a sigh, her hair cocooned them, her warmth enveloped them, and the absolute sweetness and goodness of the moment prompted a sudden stinging in his eyes. Embarrassed and yet indescribably happy, he closed them. It would kill him if she saw and thought him weak, or worse yet, a fool. Memories of his father's mockery held fast, haunted him.

When he felt her withdraw and heard her sit up, he forced himself to look. Better to know right away, to have the knife slaughtering what was left of his innocence slide through him quick and be over with it. But to his amazement, she eased her dress strap off her left shoulder, slowly, ever so slowly...and then her right. He didn't understand how her hand could be so steady as she took hold of his; his shook like the paintings and photographs on the wall over his desk when Bree stormed out of his room and slammed the door behind her. Even more than after a berating from his father. She brought that despised limb to her lips for a kiss, to her throat, where he learned her pulse was as rapid as his, and down...down...

He became her third hand, lowering the faded cotton, exposing pale, apple-size breasts. Nipples, rosy, and as taut as the Nubian statuette he'd seen in a museum catalog, were within reach, but all he could do was lie there, caught in limbo between terror and desire.

His mouth drier than ashes, he whispered, "Y-you don't have to do that."

Trusting, luminous brown eyes held his gaze as she nodded, and when she moistened her lips and swallowed hard, he realized that this wasn't easy for her, either. But her courage tripled, quadrupled his, for she brought his hand from her lap to her breast.

That first wing stroke against her delicate nub brought a strangled sob from her. Horrified, Justin recoiled, scrambled to a sitting position.

"I'm sorry!" he rasped, certain he'd hurt her.

To his amazement, she shook her head and signed frantically. At first he didn't understand. When he finally did, he wished he hadn't.

"He hurts you there. *Him?*" His mind didn't want to accept the possibilities. He'd read about cases in the paper, saw them on TV, but it was bad enough to deal with the knowledge that she'd been subjected to physical abuse, to learn it went further was too much.

It couldn't have been more than a few seconds that he sat there in dumb horror, but it must have seemed longer to Lacey. With a sharp gasp, she spun away from him and tried to cover herself.

"No!" He reached for her, and careful not to upset her any more than he already had, he urged her to face him again. But how did he make her understand what he meant, what he felt? "I hurt...for you. I'm angry...for you."

Reading his lips as well as the signing that came more slowly because they were still so new at it, Lacey nodded, and eyeing him from beneath her lashes gestured from herself to him.

"Wh—? No, you can't give yourself to me. That's not a reason, just because...because I don't hurt you."

She repeated the motion, but this time added the message that was almost too much for him to deal with.

"'It doesn't hurt when I touch you.' Oh, sweet Lacey." He leaned forward and pressed a kiss to her forehead, cupped the back of her head and urged her to rest against his shoulder. His heart was trying to burst through his chest, his mind was unraveling. Around them the world continued as before, bright, hot, clear. But in this tiny spot that was their universe, everything had changed.

"I'm sorry. I'm so sorry."

Question after question raced through his mind. How long had this been going on? How could she stay? Of course, there was her grandfather, but he wouldn't have asked her to endure this. He would understand the need to protect, to save her.

Justin couldn't let her go back, not now that he knew. When he told her as much, she shook her head and, as expected, signaled "Grandfather." Then her expression changed. She took hold of his head and gently urged him toward her again.

This time he understood. She wanted to know a tender mouth on her breasts, hands that caressed instead of bruised, she wanted a memory to make the rest bearable. His body stirred with new hungers, but his heart and mind protested. This wouldn't resolve anything, and she couldn't have asked a more unqualified person. He knew nothing about pleasing a woman, had no finesse or experience to draw on.

"Lacey," he groaned, brushing his cheek against her. Surely she had to have some idea of what she was doing to him?

The sound she made reminded him of the whisper of the sea in a shell. Heaven forgive me, he thought. But if the desire to protect and assuage had any value...

He turned his head and brushed his feverish lips against her turgid nipple, and her subsequent shiver, though brief, nearly had him recoiling and apologizing again. But when she didn't pull away, didn't strike at his shoulders, he did it again, and again. He wet her and suckled, until, overwhelmed with her generosity and his joy, he nuzzled her with his entire face like a grateful pet. It didn't matter that it made him seem inexperienced and overeager, he cared only about pleasing her. Impulse and instinct were his guides. He didn't know if that was enough for her, but they were enough to send his heart soaring to where the air was thin.

When she eased backward onto the grass, she drew him with her, and the sensation was like that of floating. When she began unbuttoning his shirt and finally slipped her slender, strong hands into his jeans, he almost cried out in ecstasy.

She did, but how could she? She wanted him!

Somehow, he vowed, easing himself over her, he would make himself worthy.

"No more. We have to stop." Once again Eve checked her watch, hoping she'd made a mistake the first time. "Perry, I'm sorry, but I had no idea we'd been at this so long."

He let the bottle of champagne he'd taken from the ice bucket hover above the glass for a second or two despite the water dripping on the linen-covered table, and gave her one of his endearing boyish looks. "Do you hear me complaining? Stay a bit longer. This has been such a treat for me."

"You should be knighted for your patience." Eve had to shake her head. "How can you be so nice after I nitpicked over almost every idea you showed me for the library?"

"What do you mean almost?"

She laughed. "Good. You're still a little human." Closing the notebook she'd been writing in, she sighed. "Seriously, I am grateful that you were such a good sport about this, not to mention so giving with your time." This had been their first opportunity to go over the ideas each of them had come up with since he'd agreed to cosponsor the library with her.

"Let me open another bottle of wine and I'll consider forgiving you."

"You'd also have to drive me home."

"It would be my pleasure. Then again, you could

make Herv happy and crash in one of the guest rooms tonight so he doesn't feel he's wasting his time dusting this place.''

"Wouldn't that raise eyebrows, considering that I'm not that far from home. Besides, Mama Lulu would have a fit if I left her at the mercy of Bree.'' She stuck the rest of her papers and folders into her briefcase. "We have more than a good start here.''

"When do you want to meet again?''

"Well, I'll start phoning these contractors you suggested in the morning. Hopefully, we'll have some bids within the next few weeks.''

"That long?''

"You said yourself that there'll be an awful lot of details they'll have to work out before they can come up with a reliable estimate.''

His wry expression suggested that she'd misunderstood him. "I meant, why should I be punished with your absence because they're slow?''

"Gee, you're good for my ego.'' Eve swept up the briefcase and her purse, and headed for the French doors. She really did want to get out of there. Things were getting entirely too personal.

Perry stepped into her way. "And you're rough on mine.''

Even when he wasn't smiling, he possessed a charisma that demanded attention. He was aristocratic and sexy in a cultured sort of way, and she would have felt gauche in his company if she had been a weaker, less grounded person.

"Somehow I doubt that.'' She'd never noticed much getting to him, save the loss of his father—and virtually nothing since. Why, they'd spent the entire afternoon sitting on this back terrace, and even though they'd been adequately protected by a lattice canopy heavy with wisteria vines, the air remained blistering hot. And yet, except for removing his jacket, he'd remained formally dressed. He hadn't even loosened his tie, while she could have cheerfully murdered the inventor of panty hose and bras. "Admit it, Perry dear, the only female likely to get under your skin is the little lady who'll win at least one leg of a Triple Crown race for you. Now please be good and open that door so I can get home before Mama Lulu accuses me of abandoning her."

He looked as though he was about to do just that, and then to her surprise he bent to kiss her. It wasn't intended as one of those friendly, on-the-cheek kisses, either, but luckily she turned her head in the last minute.

He sighed after his lips grazed her jaw. "Eve."

"What are you doing?"

"If you'd give me half a chance, I'd show you."

13

Eve didn't know what to say. "And risk our friendship?"

"*Low* risk...and high yield," Perry replied, his tone hardly bankerish. "Something two veteran realists like us would appreciate and find quite a turn-on."

She had never heard him speak this way before. "How romantic."

"Darling, I was romancing you all afternoon. I've been romancing you since they put Sumner underground. It's not getting me anywhere."

"Because there's nowhere to get. Perry, I thought I made it clear by now about Maitland Hall. It's in trust for Sumner's heirs."

"And I thought I'd made it clear that there's more to life than Maitland Hall."

She was glad to hear she'd been wrong. "Then let's put it this way. You're not in love with me."

"But I like you...very much. And—" he touched her cheek "—I want you. We could have something. I've watched you for a long time, Eve. There's spirit and passion in you, and not all of it is consumed by Maitland interests. Am I being too crude?"

"Of course not. But your timing leaves a great deal

to be desired. You know better than most about what I'm dealing with at home and in this town."

"All the more reason for me to argue my case. Maybe you need to lean on someone for a change."

"Perry, I've never leaned on anyone in my life! I wouldn't know how."

"This is where you could find me a tender and attentive teacher."

Yes, it was definitely time to get out of there. She touched his chest. "I am flattered. But I really can't think of anything like that right now."

He studied her face. "Is there someone else? It's Rader, isn't it?"

"I'm not having an affair with *anyone*."

"That's not exactly what I asked, and I've seen the way he looks at you."

"You men. Must everything be a contest with you? I think we should all be concerned with Lem's case instead of who's getting the upper hand with the Widow Maitland."

"I am. If there is a murderer on the loose—and frankly, despite what Rader says, I have my doubts—I want to be as close as possible to you."

His skepticism came as no surprise. Everyone was talking about Ben reopening the case, and rumors were running rampant regarding all the evidence he did and didn't have.

"That's sweet," Eve replied. "But I think like you, we're relatively safe at the house, what with all the people we have around the place. Speaking of which, I heard you lost a few hands due to Ben's intense questioning."

Perry grimaced. "I know that not everyone who

comes to Bellemere flashing a green card is here legitimately, and that our business occasionally attracts someone with problems in their past, but if they're good workers, I let them earn a fair wage. Ben seems to think once a con always a con."

"I suppose he's seen too much of the other side of people."

"Yeah, well, I'm just glad that if Lem did have to buy it, that it happened where it did."

"Good grief! How can you say that?"

"Easy. I don't know if Mama Lulu could stand seeing Rader bullying and tearing into people at Maitland Hall the way he does here."

Surely he was only doing his job? Eve didn't know what to say, especially when her feelings regarding Ben were complicated enough without that criticism. "I really have to go," she said again.

This time Perry acquiesced.

He escorted her through the cool elegant house where huge dark furnishings, somber portraits and landscape paintings offered a dramatic contrast against high white textured walls. The polished hardwood floors made those at Maitland Hall seem dull in comparison, and it was the same story in every room. She'd been given the grand tour months ago, so she knew. That was also how she'd found out that Perry was an avid collector of expensive things—art, guns and, of course, horses. The reminder had her wondering. Surely he didn't see her as something to be won or possessed?

"Are you upset with me?" he asked as she placed her things in the sedan and turned back to say goodbye.

"Of course not."

"And you won't make excuses not to talk to me when I call the house?"

She might not see them as lovers, but he had been good to her when others had acted suspicious and standoffish. She considered him a friend. "Only if I'm not home."

"Then may I be allowed to kiss you goodbye?" At her droll look, he added a formal bow. "Properly, of course." Then he quickly leaned over and kissed her cheek. "I hope you don't have any trouble with Bree again tonight. Call me if you need help."

Although she assured him that she would, it was a relief to drive away, and that made Eve feel guilty. She really did like Perry, but his remarks and admission were troubling. And what if Bree found out how he felt? Regardless of whether or not she disapproved of the girl's fixation on him, Eve didn't want her stepdaughter to have more reason to reject her.

She was deep in thought when she arrived at the house and saw Ben's truck. Worried that he'd been waiting long, she hurried inside and nearly crashed into Bree.

"Hang on, kiddo. Where do you think you're going, especially in that outfit?"

The teen was wearing the shortest sundress and highest heels Eve had ever seen. Eve wasn't about to let her leave the house looking like the main entertainment at a bachelor party.

"I have a dinner date."

"Sounds nice. With whom and where?"

"I'm eighteen, Eve. You don't have a right to know everything."

True, but Bree had given her no reason to be trusted, despite several stiff punishments for past incidents. "How about a more polite response, and maybe I wouldn't be so suspicious or concerned?"

"How about getting off my back? I'm sick and tired of your holier-than-thou attitude."

Pushing past her, Bree tried to make it to the door. Eve dropped her purse and briefcase and attempted to block the girl's exit.

"Bree, something doesn't feel right about this, and I'd like to talk it out. At the very least, I think we should discuss the ticket Chief Rader says you received for speeding in town again."

"Well, I wouldn't!" With a mighty shove, Bree flew out the front door.

If Eve hadn't been wearing heels herself, or such a narrow skirt, she might have managed to regain her balance, but momentum won out, and she flew into the curio cabinet that displayed Marcine's fan collection. One pane shattered at impact, and she cried out as sharp glass drove into her palm.

Either Bree didn't hear her, or else she didn't care. Seconds later the sports car screeched at the girl's rough handling and it sped down the driveway. At the same time, Ben and Mama Lulu appeared at the kitchen door.

Mama Lulu gasped when she spotted her. "Eve!"

Ben reached her first and crouched to help her as she tried to sit up without cutting herself more on the sharp glass. "What happened?"

She pulled a triangular shard from the fleshier part of her left palm before trusting herself to answer.

"Just being my usual brilliant self, and this is what I get for trying to keep Bree from going out tonight."

"I knew it!" Mama Lulu ripped off her apron and passed it over. "If grief's involved, that girl's got a hand in it. Lord, that cut's flowin' like a busted faucet." As usual, she either ignored or forgot that Eve was experienced in first aid and instructed her how she should fold the cloth around her hand.

"Do you want to go to the hospital?"

It was too tempting to enjoy Ben's warm breath caressing her temple as he spoke, and his arm felt too good supporting her back. She shook her head. "I'd rather not have to deal with all the speculation that would spawn. Besides, I don't think this is as bad as it looks. If you'll just help me up so I can get to the kitchen..."

He not only did that, he had her down the hall and at the sink before she could say anything else.

"Okay?" he murmured, staying close.

She might be, once her head stopped spinning. Thank goodness Mama Lulu nudged him aside with a "Let me see to her," and swiped the stained apron from Eve. Turning on the cold-water tap full blast, she forced Eve's hand under the fierce spray.

Eve gritted her teeth together. "I really could do this myself," she ground out.

Ignoring her, Mama Lulu bent forward to inspect the incision. Eve kept herself from swearing by watching how the woman's large breasts nearly filled one of the double sinks.

"Ain't as bad as I feared. It'll hurt for a spell, but you'll live."

"Thank you, Doctor. Now, would you do me a real

favor and dig out a big bandage from that voodoo box of yours?'' Behind her back she noticed Ben rubbing the back of his neck and checking his watch. She mouthed to him, *''Did you tell her?''*

He shook his head.

It could be that he'd only arrived himself and hadn't had time. Maybe he was waiting for *her* to break the news about the latest at the market. Whatever the reason, between that and the way the rest of her day had gone, she wished she could go upstairs and soothe her frayed nerves in a long, long shower.

''Say the word, I'll have her picked up.''

''Huh? Oh.'' She'd been slow to catch on because he'd spoken quietly, even though Mama Lulu was in the walk-in pantry. ''No, that would only make things worse.''

''So will pacing the floor all night.''

''Ben...''

''Okay, let's try this route—how was your meeting?''

God, his mood was no better than hers. ''We got quite a bit accomplished, thank you.''

''I don't doubt it.''

There was no missing his snide tone. ''Perry has a number of good ideas.''

''How many of them are repeatable?''

She told herself that she had no reason to feel guilty, but she couldn't look at him. It was a relief when Mama Lulu reappeared; however, not for long. Either the older woman had been listening or else the electricity in the room was crackling more than Eve guessed. She looked from one of them to the other.

''You want me t'git?''

"No," Eve and Ben said in unison.

The housekeeper's snort made it clear she didn't believe them. "No sense in me hangin' around a place where nobody's eatin' anyways."

"What do you mean nobody?" Eve asked. "Justin will."

"He's upstairs locked in his room. Said he ain't hungry. And I'll consider myself lucky to get a cup of my tea in you before *you* crawl into bed."

Frowning, Eve took the tube of medicated ointment Mama Lulu handed her and put some on her cut. By the time she was through, the housekeeper had a bandage ready. It gave Eve the time she needed to regroup. She knew what she needed to do next.

She gave Ben a meaningful look. "Tell her now."

Mama Lulu caught on quick. "Tell me what? What's goin' on?" she demanded of Ben.

"There's been another incident at the store."

She reached for the silver cross she wore deep inside the bodice of her dress. "How bad? Who's hurt?"

"Everyone's fine," Ben replied. "It happened after-hours again, and in a way it wasn't as bad as the other incidents. A brick was thrown through the front door."

A brief, mournful sound broke from her lips, and she began rocking. "Nasty folks fillin' this world, ain't no soul can deny it. How come you didn't say somethin' sooner?"

"Luther and Rae made me swear I wouldn't tell you until they knew you'd stay put. They send their love and want you to know they're all right. It's true. I've been keeping tabs on them."

Mama Lulu's dark eyes fired with challenge. "Think I'd like to see for myself."

Ben began to argue with her. Eve didn't bother. When he finally gave up, she told Lulu that she would drive her as soon as she was packed. Once the housekeeper went to collect a few things, Eve motioned that she would walk Ben to his truck.

"Hell, let me take her over there," he muttered, halting at the base of the stairs. "You're in no shape to be driving around."

She stayed on the veranda; it was safer that way. "I'm fine. Besides, she's annoyed with you and in the mood to lecture."

"And you're hurting. Even an insensitive redneck like me can see that."

She shook her head and averted her gaze. "Don't be nice to me, Ben. I'm not in the right frame of mind to handle kindness."

That had him retracing his steps, then he was lifting her chin to study her face. "Something happened over at Ashworth's, didn't it? No, don't deny it. He said something. Tell me."

"He just proved you right and me wrong, that's all."

His features hardened. "He wants you."

"So he says."

"What did you say?"

"You have no right to ask me that."

"The hell I don't. You asked me for time, and that gives me the right to know if you plan to lead us both around by the balls until you decide?"

Eve wrapped her arms around herself, tucking her injured hand close. She wouldn't answer, because if she did, she knew there would be no finding their way back from the hurt and ugliness. "Thanks for making it clear that your self-interest runs so much deeper than your compassion."

As she turned to go back inside, Ben stayed her. "Wait. Red, for..."

She waited, calling herself a fool for doing so, especially when he let her go as quickly as he'd grabbed her.

"Why the devil can't this stay uncomplicated?"

Eve knew the question was rhetorical and that he wanted no answer. She also sensed he'd been keeping something from her, and she closed her eyes and steeled herself for the worst.

After a sigh, he added, "What I didn't tell you or Mama Lulu was that someone else was near the Cobbs' last night. The person saw a vehicle leaving the area. Eve...they described Bree's car."

Two hours later Eve was driving home from the Cobbs'. As expected, once she passed on the rest of Ben's news, Mama Lulu not only had *wanted* to go to her family's, she'd *insisted* on it. Under the circumstances, Eve had felt it necessary to accompany her inside the Cobb home and apologize to Luther and Rae, too.

Shame was having a strange effect on her. She and Bree shared no blood, and yet the girl's actions stung as if a child from her own womb had committed the malicious act. Not even the Cobbs' graciousness and reserve had relieved her sense of personal disgrace. She was, she realized, dealing with new lessons about the South and its strong ties to history.

When she finally parked before Maitland Hall again, she sat in the last light of day and wondered how a morning that had begun with such hope could turn into this depressing evening.

"Recklessness," she murmured, eyeing the tree at the turn in the driveway. It carried the scar from another of Bree's impulsive moments. She'd been barely nine then, and at least that time the girl hadn't hurt anything except the tree.

From upstairs came the sweeping refrains of an orchestral piece Eve didn't recognize. Only when Bree went out did Justin play his classical favorites without using his earphones. How sad that in order to be himself, she had to be gone.

The beautiful, soulful music made her feel sadder, so did the thought of going inside and ruining his peace. On impulse she plucked the pins from her hair, dropped them into her bag and stuck her purse under the seat along with the car keys.

She needed something else, she decided, setting off down the road, and it wasn't to dump more bad news on her stepson. Let Justin feel the house was his for a while longer.

Strolling along the dirt road, she breathed in the moist scents of the earth and watched the first stars hint of the brilliance in the coming night. In the distance she heard a different music, the twangy rhythm of country-western. Dewitt Nellis was probably watching the Nashville channel again on TV. Their foreman drank beer until he fell asleep to that station, virtually every night, and had been doing that since his wife up and left just after Christmas.

What a lot they made. It seemed they were all misfits of one kind or other.

Lost in her thoughts, she came upon Ben's cottage sooner than she expected. What had her stopping, though, was discovering that he was there. You couldn't tell by the dark windows or the lack of any lamplight, but on closer inspection she saw the back end of the Blazer jutting out at the far end of the house. She and Ben didn't need any more contact tonight. She had only to close her eyes to remember his parting look. Accusation, desire, challenge…they were too much to deal with in her present emotional state. And yet she needed to ask him inevitable questions.

She started toward him, but it was as though someone was pushing her at the small of her back. When she saw the faint line of his long legs resting on the porch railing, she understood that he'd spotted her a long time ago and had been waiting to see if she would come to him, or run like Bree had run.

"Trying to finish off the evening by breaking your neck?" he asked when she stopped in front of the porch.

She glanced down at her high heels. Since she'd been walking slowly they hadn't given her much trouble, but in truth she also hadn't given sensible footwear any thought.

"Must be." Compared to the other blunders she must have made in his eyes, what could this matter?

Now that she was closer, she could make out that he had stripped down to jeans. Even his feet were bare, and his slicked-back hair suggested he'd stepped out of the shower only minutes ago. She envied him that, especially since the evening air was growing more sultry by the second.

"The Cobbs all settled and safe at their home?"

"Yes. What about you? I'd thought you would be out hunting Bree." He'd said earlier that he would have to track her down for questioning.

"Have been. As usual she's laying low somewhere. I may try again later. Want to help me kill time with one of these?" he asked, indicating the can of beer he held.

"No thanks."

"Guess it would be a letdown after vintage wine."

She refused to let the mild taunt get to her. "Actually, it's been hours since lunch, and I never finished my second glass. Besides, I want to take something for this cut," she said, holding up her injured hand, "in which case more alcohol wouldn't be wise."

"What would?"

"I'd hoped the fresh air and some quiet might."

"Is that the only reason you're out here?"

He was still itching for a fight. Maybe now more than ever, thanks to her stepdaughter. But she couldn't bear the thought of any more of that. "I didn't know you'd be here."

"I'm surprised you're not over at Ashworth's looking for sympathy from him."

Perry again. "Do you realize you're angrier at him than you are with Bree?"

"You spent the *day* with him."

"Ah...translated to mean I had time to sleep with him."

"Let me put it this way, if you spent that much

time with me, we wouldn't have been talking about any library."

Eve wanted to knock his feet off the railing. "How many times do I have to say it? I like him, but I'm not sexually attracted to him!"

"Well, that presents a problem, because the man who would be king won't make you his queen if he can't get under your skirt."

"Stop it! If you want to be angry with me for refusing to jump into bed with you at the first sign of a little chemistry, go ahead. But don't you dare medicate your wounded ego by turning me into a tramp. I'm not going to be defined by you just so you can avoid dealing with your own flaws."

"My what?"

"Your inability to deal with any woman past puberty or short of menopause on anything above a sexual level. It's obvious you resent females because of what happened with your father. Yet you can't bring yourself to blame him. Not Superdad, who you were all set to emulate. No, it's so much easier to blame an entire gender!"

Ben rose and set the can on the railing with a thud, which sent the remains of the beer shooting through the opening like a fountain. "I have one damn requirement when *dealing* with a woman," he said, his voice growing dangerously soft. "If she's responding to me sexually, she better not be flirting with the idea of getting it on with someone else, too. I don't share."

"I wasn't! And you're making it pretty clear that I'd have to be out of my mind to sleep with you!"

Ben came to the top of the stairs. Even in the near darkness she could see temper burning inside him.

"Try again. You usually wear your honesty like a purple robe. Where is it now?"

He was turning her world upside down. "Don't do this. Not tonight."

"And you call me dishonest. Lady, you're a coward."

"Damn you!" As he walked away from her, she launched herself after him, furious with his either-or attitude.

He started opening the screen door, and she slammed it shut with her uninjured hand. With a curse, he spun around and hauled her into his arms. With another, he crushed his mouth against hers.

At first their kiss was all energy and emotion, a dizzying combination that burned up the oxygen in Eve's lungs faster than a runaway fire devouring a paper warehouse. But even as she struggled for some much-needed air, she had to acknowledge an underlying relief, too, that the long days and longer nights of temptation were about to be over.

The arms she wrapped around his neck had never felt stronger, her lips had never matched another's passion so well. From day one they had been circling each other as if wary of what they might set off. Now they knew, and they were both beginning to tremble from the energy of it.

Before they'd satisfied that first sharp edge of mutual hunger, their bodies were radiating enough heat to send up steam. Ben abruptly tore his mouth from hers, only to tighten the strong arms already crushing her against him.

With his feverish forehead against hers, and his hot

breath searing her lips, he gazed deep into her eyes. "Say yes."

"We'll just be complicating things." She felt the need to warn him one last time—or maybe she was warning herself.

He slipped his hands to her hips and held her more firmly against his fiercely aroused flesh. "I'd say things are about as complicated as they can get."

Desire uncoiled deep in her womb and spread. She accepted that she could sputter all the logic she'd collected over the years, the bottom line wouldn't change. The only reason she would want him to let her go would be to lead her inside.

"I have to ask, do you have something to protect us?" They couldn't consider continuing if he didn't. She certainly hadn't come prepared.

"I have what we need."

But that wasn't all she was asking. When he realized that, Ben made a face.

"Ain't life grand? The brutal side of today's reality sure has taken the romance out of things. But to answer your delicately phrased question, I'm healthy."

"Thank you for not turning that into more of a production than necessary."

"Anything else?"

"No. Yes." She didn't like that her heart pounded harder than it ever had. "You don't have to pretend this has anything to do with romance. I may find abject crudity a turnoff, but you needn't—"

Ben touched his thumb to her lips. "Sometimes you talk too much."

It was just as well, she thought as he replaced the finger with his mouth and raced her to another stunning reunion with her long-neglected sensuality. She craved a few hours' escape from her responsibilities, ached for a physical release that would require little analysis and even fewer strings. And so when he opened the door and gave her a questioning look, she entered without another moment's hesitation. Following, he set the hook latch, but left the inner door open.

"We'll need the air," he said at her backward glance.

Too true. Already her clothes were clinging to her like a second skin, and with every intimate glance from him, her heart beat faster and harder, making matters worse. She considered their spartan surroundings. "Where do you want me?"

"All over me. The rest is negotiable."

As he reached for her again, he proved it. With him barefoot and her in heels, they were closer to being on equal ground, and she found that wonderfully satisfying. No uncomfortable stooping for him or awkward straining for her, their lips could hover and tease or lock together for a deep, tongue-tangling kiss, leaving their arms and hands to better service. In fact, after several moments of bold experimentation, Eve didn't care where he ultimately took her, only that he did—and soon.

"Do you know I made a bet with myself the first day we met that your mouth would be good at more than cutting me down to size," Ben murmured as he skimmed his lips along her cheek to nuzzle her diamond-studded ear.

"Gambling with yourself doesn't sound very profitable."

"It is when you're playing Mississippi Mud." He eased down the zipper from her nape to her waist.

"Explanation, please. I'm still learning my colloquialisms."

"Bluff poker. Nothing's wild, but there are no rules. The winner takes all."

"How friendly."

"It can be." Ben bared one of her shoulders to the humid air and a steamy kiss, then repeated it with the other shoulder. "Extremely...satisfying. See...regardless of my strategy...even if I lose...I win."

"Chief Rader, is this where you tell me you wouldn't mind being tied to a four-poster bed?"

As he chuckled, his breath tickled the newly exposed skin at her breasts. "Let's leave that as a contingency. Right now I need my hands...and will for some time to come."

The sensation of her sheath skimming down her body was a prelude to yet another series of skillful caresses. Eve wondered how a man with such large, work-rough hands could explore and coerce with such finesse. Then he was backing her farther into the room in the slowest of dances, and all that mattered was that he wouldn't stop.

She lost her bra in a doorway. His bedroom, she realized as he pressed her against the doorjamb.

"I used to buy into the theory of bigger is better, but you've just converted me into being a connoisseur of...finer things."

He was staring at her nipples, which were fair and almost painfully taut just from his unabashed inspection. When he brushed the backs of his fingers against one, she closed her eyes at the exquisite sensations.

"Look at you. Thanks to your sexy lingerie and your sexier preference not to wear any, these have nearly been my undoing on several occasions. Do you know what it does to learn you're that responsive to me?"

She splayed her fingers into the dark hair covering his chest. "Tell me."

He showed her instead by covering her with his mouth. It was like suddenly finding herself on the wrong end of a blowtorch. When he sucked harder, she wondered if she might really go up in flames.

"Ben..." She endured the dark, wicked assault as long as she could, then directed his mouth back to hers, because she wanted to slide her hands into the waistband of his jeans...because she wanted to urge him closer to where she burned most.

The message worked. After a deep-throated groan, as well as a few wild moments of wrestling to imprint themselves on each other, Ben resumed their journey toward his bed with increased urgency.

She stepped out of her shoes somewhere along the way. Just as she felt the mattress with the backs of her legs, she lost her half slip.

The bed was unmade, barely covered with a fitted white sheet, but it was cool against her skin. A welcome sensation, especially when Ben pressed her deeper into the bedding with his powerful body. As he slid a muscular leg between hers, she closed her thighs around him.

"Would this be a good time to tell you that I'm not married to the idea of prolonged foreplay?" she murmured, loving the whisper of denim against nylon as much as the friction.

"Me, neither. Problem is...I keep finding another part of you that begs touching, and I change my mind."

Having prepared herself for a night of unapologetic, vigorous sex, he was captivating her with romantic considerations. Eve didn't know whether to kiss him or run for her life. Had she said this would complicate things? Everything, *everything* between them would change after this.

"What?" he asked when she remained silent for too long.

"I just realized that you're easier to understand when you're angry with me."

"Red, I may have been ticked, and I may have been riled, but I have *never* been angry with you."

She couldn't help smiling. "Really? Somehow the difference has escaped me."

He studied her for several seconds, his gaze moving over her face like a restless wind. "Try looking at another man the way you're looking at me right now, and you'll find out so fast you'll get whiplash."

"You aren't serious. That again?"

He swept his gifted hands over her, branded her through her lacy designer panty hose, returning repeatedly to her damp heat, until she was barely able to keep from surrendering to quick relief.

"Yeah, that again," he said in that voice even dimwitted Red Riding Hood could have identified.

They fought a war of wills, and Eve found herself wishing she possessed some real power to make him more than hungry, beyond jealous. Sure, she'd received her share of male attention—women who enjoyed sex always gave off some signal that was unfailingly picked up by men—but not one of the few she'd taken as a lover had ever breached more than the outer shell of her, or understood her secret self. Most of the time she considered herself lucky, when she wasn't worrying that she lacked something vital in her emotional makeup. But occasionally, like now, she wished there was someone…someone who only knew he could breathe, eat…*exist*, because she walked on this planet, too.

A sentimental thought. A foolish one. Determined to vanquish it, she shoved his jeans over his hips. "Come inside me now."

But he had his own agenda. With every stroke, every kiss, he brought home the reminder of how long it had been for her. He wasn't an easy man; maybe he would yet prove a cruel or dangerous one, but his unexpected sensitivity as he finished undressing her, kissing and caressing every new inch he uncovered, got behind her defenses with breathtaking ease, and shattered every preconceived notion she had about him—or herself. By the time he rose from the bed to kick off his jeans and get their protection, she knew she might have agreed to this regardless of whether she'd been committed to another or not.

Before the shock of that revelation stopped reverberating through her, the mattress yielded under his weight.

"Having second thoughts?"

Plenty, only they'd come too late. She could no more stop this than she could stop feeling. But before he could question her more about her hesitation, she pushed him onto his back and straddled him.

Sweeping back her hair, she said, ''I was remembering something you said about wanting me all over you.''

If this was to be their blip in time, she wouldn't waste it brooding. She wanted a perfect memory to warm her through the winter of her life when even the gulf wind failed to soothe the chill that loneliness would settle in her bones. As she took him inside her, as he stretched and filled her, she watched, fascinated with the beauty of their joined bodies, how every muscle in his torso and face tightened, and how his eyes grew feral in the twilight. She memorized it, all the while absorbing the elemental sensations swelling, building inside her, as he was.

So good. So very good.

She rode. He drove. Neither spoke. The only dialogue came as their eyes met and clung; the only sound was their accelerated panting as he found more sensitive spots to coax and incite, and the whisper of their sweat-slick bodies moving against each other.

About to tell him that she wanted no more, that she needed it to end, he muttered a harsh expletive and rolled her over, gripped her hips and impaled her anew.

The tremors started immediately and in unison, something written about often and so rare in real life. She opened her mouth to cry out, but he crushed his mouth to hers and took her that way, as well.

And taught her she'd known nothing about pleasure.

14

Ben wanted to keep touching her. For minutes afterward, with silence underscoring the throbbing within and around them, he fought the urge to stroke her silky hair, her translucent, sleek skin, and the subtle swells and hollows of a body he was in danger of developing an obsession for. The logical side of his mind warned him to keep some distance; the lonely, hungry side yearned for the longest eclipse in the history of astronomy, anything to hold off dawn.

In the end, however, she was the one to attempt a withdrawal. That decided him and he slipped an arm around her waist and held her beside him.

"Where's the fire?"

"I should get home."

He had no idea what time it was, but he did know it was too soon to say goodbye. "Already sorry this happened?"

"It's a matter of Justin often coming downstairs to say good-night before he turns in. If he sees my car out front but no sign of me, he's liable to get worried."

"Give me another hour."

He couldn't remember ever asking for that or having a more fervent need to keep a woman in his bed.

From the way Eve rose on one elbow and stared at him, he gathered she was surprised, as well. He knew it for sure when she reached over him for his lighter on the pack of cigarettes on the nightstand. As she lit the stub of a candle there, Ben wondered when she'd had time to notice them. For his part, a tornado could have ripped the roof off the place; his only thought had been to get her here and to bury himself inside her.

"It's a female thing," she said when she saw his bemusement. "Do you think I'd miss something as unusual as a candle by a man's bed?"

"The explanation's anything but romantic. The lamp bulb burned out and there aren't any extras. And now that I see the benefits," he added, noting the enticing picture she made, "I may not bother buying replacements, after all."

"What a gallant recovery."

"Yeah, well, I may be unmistakably human, but I have my moments."

She looked down the length of his body. "I would say you're somewhat more than...human."

What could he do? He was becoming aroused again. As with the rest, that, too, was one for the record books. "I'd tell you that it's been a while for me, but I doubt you'd believe me."

"If it's the truth, why shouldn't I?"

He didn't want her to know how true. "So, will you give me that hour?"

She didn't rush her answer. "I warned you that this would complicate things."

"You can say one 'I told you so.'"

"I'd rather feed my ego this way..."

She planted a kiss on his chest, then another and another—feathery caresses, tender nibbles and licks, until he ached and blood began to pound in his head and groin. And with every move, her hair acted like thousands of fingers tantalizing and inciting. Ben couldn't keep his hands out of it.

"Glorious," he murmured. "You know, I'd almost convinced myself this came from a bottle."

"With my coloring?"

"Guess I'm in denial because you represented, *represent,* a problem for me, prompting me to look for cracks and flaws."

"They're not hard to find."

"The point is, they don't make any difference. Maybe it'll be a good thing if I'm gone soon."

Eve sat up. "Gone...? You're leaving?"

"It could happen, mostly because I've found a replacement for Jack Haygood. He's an ex-local who's wanting to transfer from Greenville to be closer to his parents. His father suffered a heart attack a few months ago and he's needed here."

"What's the problem with that?"

"He's black."

"Is he the man you wanted?"

"We'd be fortunate to have him."

Eve smiled. "Good for you...and I also see your problem. Fred Varnell and the city council will hemorrhage. But you won't back off your choice, will you?"

"Nope. Add to that the slow progress I'm making with the Cobb case, there's every reason to expect the powers that be to consider cutting their losses, as far as my contract with them is concerned."

"But what else could you do about Lem's case that you aren't doing now, except to maybe work on it twenty-four hours a day and ignore that you have a town to oversee, as well...."

He hadn't meant to get into this, and as her voice drifted off as she glanced away, he knew she was thinking about her role in things. About Bree. She might even be remembering that one of the few solid items of evidence he'd come up with implicated someone with financial means, which, as far as he was concerned, meant keeping his focus on Bellemere. That's not what she or anyone in town wanted to hear, either.

"Look, something may work out," he said, certain he'd killed the mood between them. "I just didn't want you to think I was leading you on."

She dismissed that with a shake of her head. "You've been nothing if not blunt about what I could and shouldn't expect from you."

Sweet sanity, she was something. Something to look at, and some kind of lady. If he had a decent bone in his body, he would let her go now before he brought her more headaches than she already had. Only, his nobleness didn't come close to outreaching his hunger for her.

"How's the hand holding up?" he asked abruptly.

"Wh—? Fine."

"Good. Then if you've become such a fan of my directness," he drawled, pulling her to him, "why don't you crawl back on top of me again, and I'll see what I can do about really impressing you?"

With a soft throaty laugh, she did, and although he enjoyed the husky sound, he stopped it with a kiss.

Not one of the greedy kisses like before, but one that left no question that the time for talking—at least talk about work and problems—was over. It had to be; what if this never happened again? Come morning, if she was smart, she would have the clear mind to promise hereafter to keep her distance. With that possibility hanging over his head, he wasn't about to let anything else come between them, except some well-earned sweat.

"Someday I want to see you in a bubble bath," he said, letting his hands roam at will. "Sumner was right. With your hair piled high, your breasts lifting out of the milky water and your hands…"

A deep rumble came in through the screened window. Annoyed, Ben listened. It was one of those damned trucks again. This would be a perfect opportunity to get an answer to his unanswered questions about the goings-on at Bellemere. But he'd already put in a fourteen-hour day, and he'd stopped counting the total for the week. About to curse Ashworth out loud, he felt Eve's fingers close around him.

"What about my hands?" she whispered against his lips.

To hell with the trucks, he thought, thrusting his hips to encourage her. To hell with all of it…at least for another hour or so. "They're great where they are. Perfect."

And with a groan, he lifted her so he could get at her breasts again…sink into her slick heat. Then he took what he wanted…gave her what she wanted. As before, pleasure grew quickly, pushed aside every question and concern—even sound, except for the sighs and murmurings of encouragement each of them made.

It was all the reality Ben cared to know about for a long, long time.

Eve returned to the big, silent house convinced there would be no sleep that night, not when the greatest part of her mind remained with the man who'd surprised her by insisting on walking her home. She tried to remind herself that what they'd shared was just sex, and that his attentiveness was primarily about a possible murderer in their midst. But her body was still humming with the lingering sensations…and his caution was wise. Still, it was a relief to say good-night and head for the solitude of a long shower.

Afterward, she slipped on a white cotton robe, tailored and sensible, and went down the hall to knock on Justin's door. Upon his murmured invitation to enter, she did.

"How's it going?" she asked, inwardly sighing when she spotted him hunched over his drawing desk. He'd been in much the same position when she'd last checked on him before taking Mama Lulu to the Cobbs'.

"Okay." He blinked as if struggling to rise out of some trance. "What time is it?"

"Close to midnight."

"I guess Bree's not home yet."

"Uh-uh. Listen, my friend, aren't your eyes begging for a reprieve?"

"Now that you mention it, they are burning. But I had so much I wanted to get done."

He looked back at his tablet and dragged his teeth over his lower lip. Eve sensed he was debating whether or not to show her something. She hoped he would. She wanted to finally see what, or who, he'd become obsessed with, but it was his decision to make.

"I'm impressed," she told him. "You've been going like a machine for days. I hope it's been worth it."

"I hope. I've been learning some hard lessons about taking inspiration when it comes." His shrug turned into a shoulder roll to ease tired muscles. "Up until recently, it was an empty cliché to me."

"I suspect some people never figure out that much. Are you pleased with the results?"

"At times. At least I think I'm getting close to what I'm reaching for. Not often enough, though, to do her credit." He scratched his head, his fine blond hair looking as if he'd done that a number of times tonight. "I, um, met someone."

Eve nodded and smiled against the odd little twinge in her heart. "So I gathered. Are you okay? Happy?"

"Yes. No. I mean I am, but... She's different, Eve."

Once again she was getting a crash course at what being a parent was all about. No sooner had one fear been relieved than another took its place, and of immediate concern were all the variables that vague word *different* could cover. In a small town like Parish, let alone among the rest of the society that included the Maitlands so warmly, that could present problems she hadn't considered, and personally didn't care about.

"Are you saying she's from a different ethnic background?" she asked gently.

"No. She's hearing- and speaking-impaired."

Eve nodded, somehow not surprised that the boy had found a wren with a broken wing. "Do you know if this was a condition from birth?"

"I'm not sure." He brightened. "She can read my lips sometimes."

"That's terrific. Does she try to speak? How else do you communicate?"

He blushed and turned away. Not out of embarrassment, she realized a moment later as he stretched for a book on the next table.

"I'm learning to sign. We both are, I guess. She doesn't seem to have had a lot of schooling. As for talking, she'll mouth words sometimes, but I haven't actually heard her make any noise except a kind of breathy laugh once or twice. She's not a happy person. Usually, I'm lucky to get her to smile."

Eve could only imagine what he wasn't telling her. "When did all this happen? I haven't noticed you taking out your van much." Before his death, Sumner had bought both kids the vehicles of their choice as early graduation presents. Justin had chosen a blue minivan, explaining it would transport his canvases and supplies best, but more often than not it sat in the garage. Eve had a hunch it would need a new battery before it got enough mileage on it for its first oil change.

"I haven't needed to drive anywhere," he replied, a note of reluctance entering his voice. "Besides, the easiest way to reach Lacey is to walk. She lives on the other side of the lake."

That explained a good deal, but spawned yet another wave of concern. He knew how she felt about anyone being near the lake these days, especially alone. "Not great news, but obviously you had your reasons for going over there without telling anyone."

"Only that I knew you'd worry." Justin stroked at the peach fuzz that might one day evolve into an attractive mustache. "And I guess you're already remembering there are only a few rent houses over on the northwest side...?"

"So her family is poor."

"Not merely poor, they're...they're a little strange."

Eve was beginning to wish she hadn't begun this conversation.

"To be blunt, I'm worried for her. I think—no, I'm pretty certain she's being abused. But when I try to talk to her about it, she either runs away or changes the subject."

Eve stared at the papers strewn on the carpet around his chair, but she wasn't really seeing the uncharacteristic mess. Her mind was racing. "Have you seen anything to substantiate your intuition?"

Once again he gnawed at his lip. "Some. Bruises. I think her stepbrother, or whoever he is, has a temper and takes things out on her."

No matter how often she heard such things, it never ceased to stir some unspeakable outrage in Eve. But she also knew that what Justin needed from her at the moment was clear, rational thinking. "Could you be more specific? Do you have an idea how bad it gets?"

He closed his eyes, his patrician features tightening. At that instant, he'd never resembled his mother more, Eve thought, remembering the photo album down in the library that she'd once studied to try to get to know her family better.

"I can't answer that. To be honest, I've been trying not to think about it. Then again, I can't help but do that, what with only the three of them in the house, and her grandfather being bedridden."

"Is he disabled?"

"He had a stroke or something."

The life-style he was describing didn't improve the scenario Eve was imagining. "How old is your friend?"

"I'm not sure."

"Give me your best guess. If she's a minor, we can get someone out there to investigate based on what you've seen. If she's over eighteen, things get much more complicated."

"What do you mean?" As expected, Justin looked distressed by that unpleasant, and anything but fair, news.

"If she's older, the court has to respect that she might not want out of the relationship with the step-brother, whatever it is."

"No! What choice does she have? She's responsible for the old man, and she probably didn't think she had anywhere else to go!"

Everything he said made sense. But Eve had to make him understand a few tough truths. "On the other hand, this might be the only behavior she's known and she might think it's normal. She might have endured it for so long, she's begun to believe she deserves to be treated the way she is. It's complicated, but what happens is she becomes a codependent, a person who gets her sense of identity from this brother figure, even as she despises him for it.''

Justin's face grew flushed. "She doesn't want what's happening to her!"

"I believe you, but there are times when the mind does strange things to protect itself.''

"Not Lacey. She hates him, I can see it!" But no sooner had he made that impassioned declaration, than Justin looked devastated. "But she's terrified of him, too.''

"All right, taking that position, what do you think you want to do about the situation?''

"I guess I need to talk to her again. Get her to tell me more.''

"That's wisest. And I will help you in any way I can.''

He sighed with relief. "I was afraid to ask, what with Bree giving you such a hard time.''

"Don't you worry about that. It sounds as though you have enough on your plate without taking on your sister's problems." She added a wink, wishing he was younger so she could hug him. "I'll be downstairs if you need me. Don't work yourself past exhaustion, please. Your friend is lucky to have you, and she'll need you strong and healthy to help her get through this.''

Justin nodded. "Thanks a million, Eve. I feel better with you knowing.''

"I'm glad you had enough confidence in me to tell me.''

But her pleasure in that sharing didn't last. By the time she made it to the base of the stairs, Justin's news had her rubbing her forehead.

How fitting that her wandering through the house to check on doors and windows would bring her to the formal living room where the portrait of the last patriarch of the family hung over the fireplace. "Well, Sumner," she murmured, gazing up at the distinguished, arrogant smile of her late husband. "And you thought you had problems...."

There were no earth tremors, so she doubted he was reeling in his mausoleum over in Vicksburg beside Marcine and the rest of the Maitland clan. That's where the family had established itself after leaving the colonies, and where some had died of starvation during the Civil War battle fought there. Since her agreement to fill his shoes, Eve had made a point to learn what else she could of the family tree in order to pass it on to Justin and Bree, and the results were colorful, to say the least. Along with the successes, there seemed to be as many fools and miscreants in the Maitlands' lineage as in the Hudsons'. The difference was, the Maitlands seemed to enjoy making their insanity sound like high theater.

Cynical thoughts. It would almost be easier to think of Ben.

Touching her fingers to her lips, she remembered their passion and how she'd wanted their time together to last. She shook her head at Sumner's portrait. "You told me it would happen one day. Did you ever guess it would be someone like Ben Rader?"

The shrewd businessman had warned her, "One day you'll meet your match, Evie. If I had ten years left in me, I'd make sure it was me. But it's going to be someone else, and when he comes, don't you disappoint my expectations of you. You give him the same kiss-my-ass sass you gave me. Make him earn what you've got to give. Hell, bring him to his knees and then convince him he likes the view from there. If not for yourself, then for God's sake remember you're a Maitland now, as much as any of us.''

As she remembered, Eve shook her head. ''You old alligator,'' she murmured to the portrait. ''You knew how to dare me into accepting the challenge.'' If only he hadn't lied about the size of mess he would be leaving behind.

With a sigh, she headed toward the kitchen and the coffee she would need if she planned to stay alert tonight.

Bree paced back and forth in the tiny efficiency apartment, as she had been for what seemed like hours. She was bored, pissed and getting claustrophobic. This business about staying out of sight was for the birds, and she'd about had her fill of it. What was going on? Was he embarrassed about her or what? The least he could have done was leave her something to do. So far, all he'd done was dictate: don't go outside, don't play the TV too loud, ditto the stereo... What a comedian. The only station that came in decently on the tube was an evangelical one, and the stereo wasn't much better with its hillbilly caterwauling. Monks lived better than this. If it wasn't for the well-stocked refrigerator, she would have left by now; on the other hand, how often could she switch from beer to wine, to beer, and so on?

''Son of a bitch promised to take me dancing,'' she

muttered to her reflection as she paused in the doorway to the bathroom.

If she'd known she would end up humming to
corny songs as she made up her own line-dancing
steps, she would never have agreed to stay put. She
was Gabrielle Maitland, of legal age, stinking rich and
damned fine to look at! No one wasted her time like
this!

"Shit." And she'd believed dating an older man
would be romantic and exciting. She'd saved herself,
played hard to get, for this? She was getting depressed, and she didn't like being depressed, unlike
Justin who approached melancholia like the rest of
his stupid *art.* "Come on!" she cried, retracing her
steps for the beer she'd left on the kitchen counter.

The can was empty.

"Oh, hell. Enough's enough."

Flinging the aluminum container across the room,
she stumbled around until she located one of her
strappy high heels. It took a considerable amount of
time to secure it, and even more locating the other
one and getting it on. Finally done, she found her
purse and wobbled out into the night.

Now, where'd I leave the fucking car...?

To her right she heard a truck rumbling away and
the abrupt bark of male laughter. "Work, my foot."

The assholes were having fun without her. Well,
let them. Maybe she had arrived unannounced, but
he'd asked her to stay. If this was how he treated
someone he claimed to respect and wanted to get to
know better—

"Where're you going, baby doll?"

He'd come out of nowhere, grabbing her from behind, and he'd scared the crap out of her. Even if she did like his warm breath tickling her ear and the way his big hands nearly spanned her waist, he needed to learn a lesson.

"Let go," she muttered, slapping at him. "Go find yourself another groupie. From now on I'm only interested in a man who's interested in *me*."

"I'm interested." As if her sharp smacks meant nothing, he slipped one hand into the low-cut neckline of her dress and fondled her breast. "How long have you been wandering around out here?"

"Wouldn't you like to know."

"Come back inside. We're through with work for tonight. You and I can have a drink."

That's all she needed, another drink; as it was, she didn't know if she could find her car back behind the building where he'd told her to park it. But what kept her focused was her annoyance with him.

"What if I promise to open a bottle of champagne, pour it all over you and lick it off."

His provocative suggestion, along with the shocking things he was doing as his other hand made its way under her skirt, had her shivering in luscious anticipation. There would be no such thing as a quickie, no selfish boy's clumsy groping just so he could announce he'd screwed Bree Maitland.

"You really want me." She voiced the thought more to cut through the haze brought on by alcohol than to verify it with him. "It's not just my money or a way of getting closer to Eve."

"Eve who?"

She giggled, delighted at his irreverent humor. Maybe they didn't have much in common, and so what if he wasn't her first choice as a lover? He spoke to something primitive inside her; she liked his hands on her. She would not be in control with him, but that appealed to the gambler in her.

"Come on inside, sweetness. I've got something really good for you to try."

God, if she took anything from his stash, she would fall flat on her face and miss her own "deflowering." "Convince me," she murmured, twisting around to offer him the temptation of her pouty lips.

His grin was a slash of white in the darkness. "With pleasure, baby doll. With pleasure."

Minutes before five o'clock in the morning, Eve woke on the couch in Sumner's office from the sound of a car coming up the driveway. Bree never drove that slow. What if it was the police coming to tell her there'd been an accident?

No, she wouldn't let herself think that.

As she rose, Marcine's journal slipped off her lap and onto the floor. She'd been reading it in her continued attempt to better understand her stepdaughter through her parent, but the only thing she'd come away with before falling asleep was that Bree's mother had been as impulsive and obstinate about having her own way as her daughter was. With a breathless curse, she swept up the leather-bound book, tossed it onto the couch and hurried into the foyer. Bree was fumbling with her keys as Eve unlocked and opened the door from the inside.

"Good God, Bree..." Even in the dimmest light from the chandelier, Eve could see that the teenager had experienced quite a night. "Are you all right?"

She looked like hell, her makeup smeared or worn off, her face puffy from lack of sleep, too much alcohol and who knew what else, and her hair resembling a bad wig. The thing that frightened Eve, however, was that beneath the embarrassment and resentment, the girl looked hurt.

"Hey..." Bree barely survived keeping a hiccup from becoming a burp. "If it isn't the dragon lady."

"And what are you supposed to be, the poster child for the local moonshiner?" She stank, too, and Eve didn't want to think who she'd been with, let alone if there'd been only one. "At least tell me that you were smart and practiced safe sex?"

"What's the matter? Afraid I'll make a granny out of you?"

"No, my nightmare is picturing you as a mother. In fact, when you get upstairs, take two seconds to look in a mirror and imagine yourself holding a little bundle of joy. Consider how you would feel if your baby had been exposed to some disease or addicted to a drug you'd indiscriminately put into your body. Do any of those horrible images get through that fluffy head of yours?"

"It's always a pleasure to come home to you, too."

Eve let the girl brush by her, climb three stairs before she decided she would lose nothing by pushing a bit harder. "By the way, just so you don't think you fooled anyone the other night... There was a witness."

The teenager paused. Wobbled. "Are you talking to me?"

"Gotcha," Eve whispered.

Bree turned slowly. "Got what? I haven't the v-vaguest idea what you're blabbering about."

"I think you do."

But the girl had trouble standing, let alone thinking, and lowered herself to sit on the stair above her. "A witness to what?"

"The brick through the window at Cobb's Market. Your car was identified by someone at the scene."

Beneath her tan, Bree's face grew pale. "Wh—? You're nuts."

"I almost wish I was."

"Yeah, well, *I* wasn't there!"

"Is that why you charged out of here yesterday evening when Chief Rader came over?"

The girl didn't seem to remember that event much better than she did anything else. She did, however, eye the fresh bandage on Eve's hand, but she didn't go so far as to ask how it felt, or to apologize.

"Would you like to know what it was like to pass on the cheerful news to Mama Lulu?"

"No. Who said it was me?"

The question was both an obvious and fair one. What embarrassed Eve was that she hadn't asked Ben herself until later—until *after* she'd slept with the man and he'd walked her home....

"About Bree...are you sure?"

"I wouldn't have dumped that kind of news on you if I wasn't."

"Who is the witness?"

"Don't ask that."

"Excuse me, but why not? Especially now?"

"Did you have sex with me because you thought I'd spill my guts to you?"

"Of course not."

"Then consider the witness and how safe he would feel if the guy with Bree found out who that person was."

Remembering that, Eve shook her head at her stepdaughter's terse question. "I don't know. Chief Rader won't say, for legitimate reasons, I might add."

"You would, but it's my neck." Bree hauled herself to her feet, suddenly as sober as Eve had ever seen her. "I'm going to bed."

"This isn't going away, Bree. Chief Rader will be here, within hours, for all I know, to question you. I'd like to know if I need to call for our attorney to be present."

"I don't know!" her stepdaughter screamed back at her. Angry tears filled her eyes. "God, you are one— I never liked you, but I *despise* you for taking a stranger's word over mine!"

She ran up the stairs, stumbling at the top, then disappeared down the hall. Seconds later, Eve heard Bree's bedroom door slam shut behind her.

With a sigh, Eve sunk onto the bottom stair and buried her face in her hands. She'd never felt more uncertain, and alone.

15

Ben gripped the telephone receiver tighter. "Say that again?"

"I'm sorry, Chief, I really am. You have every right to be upset," Dr. George Tinney replied, although his tone reflected more confusion than sympathy.

"How the hell could the state lose something as unique and large as a varmint trap?"

"Well, that's the thing. I warned you about the forensics people down in Jackson being overloaded with work and understaffed. They had an opportunity to send it to Memphis, but now Memphis insists they don't know anything about it."

Christ. This could not be happening. Ben wondered what else was going to go wrong with this case. He'd sent off the thing for analysis right after finding the cigarette butt. At least he had the manufacturer's name and witnesses who would testify having seen the piece. But he wasn't about to let Tinney or those lab jockeys get away with anything.

"You tell them to find that trap, George, or so help me, I'll go up there and turn that fucking place inside out!"

He slammed down the phone and dropped his head

onto his forearms. About to curse more creatively to assuage his molten temper, he heard a crash outside his office.

"Are you shittin' me?"

Dewey Pearl's ear-piercing squeak told Ben that what he'd been waiting for was over. The new guy had obviously arrived.

Pushing his problems with Tinney aside for the moment, he went to the door of his office to see Pearl picking his chair up off the floor as he gaped at the tall, trim man wearing the uniform of Parish's finest. "Is there a problem?"

Dewey cleared his throat. "Uh…well, sir, I don't exactly— Is he for real?" he asked, indicating the newcomer with his thumb.

The man observing him remained calm and waited for Ben to answer. "Anton Lasalle Jones, meet our dispatcher, Dewey Pearl. You'll find that he's not usually so…tongue-tied. His preference is sticking his foot entirely into his mouth."

"Guess I've done that a few times myself." The young cop inclined his head and held out his hand to Dewey. "Call me Al. Or Jones. What about you?"

"Just Pearl, I s'pose." Dewey couldn't stop staring and barely recovered in time to shake the man's hand. "Where're you from?"

"I was on the Greenville force for six years. Got family here, though."

Ben decided they could work through the rest of their first-day awkwardness later. "Jones, grab yourself a cup of coffee and come in here. We'll get the rest of your paperwork out of the way so you can get started."

A short time later, Al Jones closed the office door and settled in the chair Ben pointed to with his pen. The younger cop had a military bearing, but a pleasant smile-prone face to complement his proud features. His intelligent brown eyes met Ben's gaze without wavering when he said, "You didn't warn them."

"That you're black? Nope. I didn't tell them that you're overqualified, either, and that's the only thing they should be concerned with."

It was true. At thirty, Jones had twice the education of anyone in the department, nearly matching Ben's, and there were two citations on his résumé. He could also converse adequately in Spanish, had been active in community volunteer programs and liked to rebuild vintage cars in his free time. None of that would have gone over well with his new workmates, who would consider all that showing off, so any personal information Jones wanted to share was his business.

"I gotta admit," Al said, tugging at his earlobe, "for a minute I thought I'd stepped back in time, even for Mississippi."

Ben nodded, his mood grim despite his hope that things would work out well for the guy. "Oh, you'll still feel it now and again—small towns are slower to change, as your family already knows. Just remember, you're here because the dynamics of this community *are* changing. So far, it's been an uphill battle, and no doubt your presence might instigate a few heels digging in. But I did warn you that it wouldn't be a cakewalk."

"As long as I don't wake one night to find a bunch of guys in white hoods on my folks' front yard."

"If you do, you call me and I'll be right over to

help you knock some heads together and haul some butts to jail.''

Jones relaxed somewhat. "That's what ultimately convinced me to take the job. My mother pretty much keeps up with what goes on in town and she said you were as hard on the digestion as chicory coffee, but that you're honest and fair.''

"We'll see if you agree. No doubt your family's already pointed out that we also have an element of crime bleeding into our community. Add your home-grown prejudice to that, and you'll see how things might get touchy now and then. I'm not proud to have to say this, but a degree of that trouble may come from the other cops in the department. It's up to you whether it gets better or worse. If you walk around with a chip on your shoulder, I guarantee you that they'll work overtime to knock it off.''

"That's not my way.''

"You wouldn't be here if I thought it was.''

"It's important for me to make this work.''

Ben thought of what he'd learned through their interview. Al Jones's father's second heart attack had left the man weakened. Perhaps permanently dependent. As an only son, Al felt it his responsibility to be close and help out.

"It's important to me, too,'' he told him. "Why do you think I did everything but beg your former captain to release you from having to give two weeks' notice? Inevitably, word would've gotten out that you were coming, and that would have given everyone too much time to gossip and insulate their prejudices.''

"I appreciate that.'' Al's look bespoke respect.

"I have another reason.'' This was as good a time

as any to explain it. He hadn't earlier, not wanting to overwhelm the man. "The Cobbs are a local family who operate one of the two markets in town, and they're being harassed and not so slowly driven toward bankruptcy. Maybe your folks know them. They're friends of mine, and I came back to Parish because Luther Cobb's youngest brother was found dead over near Moss Lake under odd circumstances."

"I heard about that."

"You be careful if anything comes up that takes you out there."

"You think one situation has anything to do with the other? My folks have been talking about the rumors of drug problems in the area."

"They're not rumors."

"We have a similar problem in Greenville. Our location between New Orleans and Memphis make us a fair relay point for traffickers. Vehicles get switched, money gets laundered, and local kids get targeted as a source of added revenue. But Greenville's large enough to hide the guilty parties. It's got to be tougher to pull off here."

"Oh, I have my hunches about who the power players are, but so far I haven't had much luck getting any real evidence on them; they raise the level of fear around them just because we are a small community. And they're keeping us busy by stirring up trouble in other arenas."

Al nodded. "I'm following. Terrorism on a small scale. I'll feel out my family's friends and neighbors. They'll talk to me before they talk to you."

That's what Ben had been hoping to hear. He'd barely gotten Lem's girlfriend, Tilly, to open the door to him, let alone listen to what he had to say. "As I said, whatever you do, watch your back. Country living isn't the same as it used to be."

"What is, sir?"

Amen to that, Ben thought, reaching across his desk to offer his hand. "Welcome aboard."

After he gave Al several personnel forms that needed filling out for payroll and medical coverage, Ben directed him to Haygood's old desk. By then Buck Preston had arrived and his reaction wasn't that dissimilar to Dewey's, so Ben hung around to make sure things settled down.

When he returned to his desk, the phone rang again. He wondered if the gossip mill had already kicked in to full gear about Al, and if this was his first protest call. He was delighted to hear Eve's voice.

"Is this a bad time?"

If she only knew. But he'd barely slept last night, her effect on him had been so powerful. Just hearing her low, sexy voice had him remembering how it had been between them, stirring his body into an immediate craving for another, longer night with her. "No, I was about to call you. How's it going?"

"Generally or personally?"

She sounded as tired as he felt, and that made him doubly pleased to hear the hint of flirtation in her voice. "If you have to ask, I didn't make half the impression I thought I did last night."

"I still can't believe it happened."

"You're not too sore or bruised or anything, are you?" Desire had made him demanding.

"Not where it shows."

"You'll have to let me see later, and I'll kiss it and make it better."

After a faint, indescribable sound, she sighed. "Ben, this is insane. We can't talk about us when there are so many critical things to deal with."

She was right, but he didn't have to like it. "Did Trouble make it home?"

"Barely. I half wish one of your people had stopped and arrested her."

"Was she in any shape for you to tell her the news?"

"Probably not, but I did it anyway because I didn't know when we'd be hearing from you. Needless to say, she's denying it. Do you want us to come down there so you can take her formal statement, or can you come out here?"

If he asked Eve and Bree Maitland to report to the station, the town might never recover. "I'll come there."

"Fine, but Ben...I'm not going to call our attorney. I'd like to know that I'm not wrong in making that decision. You'd tell me if I was, wouldn't you?"

The question jarred him when it shouldn't have, a strong reminder that the lady was keeping her priorities straight with much better success than he was. "Don't doubt it," he replied, ignoring a heaviness in his chest. "What's a good time for you?"

"Be ready at ten."

Justin listened to Eve leave Bree's room and head back downstairs. He waited until he couldn't hear her footsteps, before stepping across the hall. Tapping softly, he let himself in.

Under the tangled sheet lay a lump that didn't move. "It's only me," he whispered, carefully closing the door behind him.

First the pillow covering her head moved, then she uncoiled from the tortured knot she'd twisted her body into. "Come to gloat, too?"

"You should know me better than that." The floor resembled the final resting place for flotsam. Justin maneuvered carefully around the mess, and settled on the edge of the bed. "What time did you get in?"

"As if you don't know," she mumbled from beneath the encased duck down.

"I'd worked late. You know how I am for the first hour or so after I fall asleep. You could tie me to a bungee cord and drop me off the roof and I wouldn't know it."

Bree sat up, tucking the sheet under her armpits, and swept her blond mane back with her entire forearm. "Okay, okay, spare me. Sheesh, my mouth tastes as vile as ditch water. I'd kill for a glass of champagne."

Justin reached into his shirt pocket for a plastic container of breath mints. "These might be wiser than alcohol before breakfast. Fewer calories, too."

She glared at him, her eyes ringed like a raccoon's with yesterday's makeup. "Up yours."

"I'm only trying to help. You might consider losing the habit of sleeping on your face, too. You look as though you gained five pounds overnight."

"How sweet of you to share that insight," she sneered. Shoving away his offered candy, she snatched her purse off the night table and began digging inside it. "What's with the vanity sanity, anyway? The closest *your* mouth is apt to get to another human being is the dentist, but our next cleaning isn't until after Thanksgiving.''

Justin had no intention of responding to that. He knew better than to load a weapon for her to use on him. Instead, he thought about what he'd heard Eve say. ''What's happening at ten?''

For a moment, Bree's confidence slipped. ''Ben Rader's coming over.'' The squashed cigarette she lifted to her lips and lit with a hot-pink lighter shook in her hands. ''In his *official* capacity, from what I hear.''

Although her words were as disturbing as her unsteady hands, what had Justin doing a double take was the cigarette. ''Is that— Bree, that's grass!''

''Quiet!'' Bree pointed to the open French doors and windows, reminding him that Eve could be below on the porch.

''Where'd you get that?'' he demanded in a loud whisper.

''Wouldn't you like to know. I figure if I'm going to jail, I might as well be guilty of something.''

''They don't jail people for stupidity.'' Justin didn't know what was more outrageous, the silly-looking joint or her attempt to sound worldly, though for all he knew, she might be smoking the thing properly. Either way, she didn't seem to be enjoying the thing much. ''You look like a dog sniffing a skunk through a screen door.''

''Go to hell, Your Flatulence.''

Justin rose and put several feet between him and the green-gray smoke surrounding the bed like mosquito netting. "What about Ben Rader? Why's he coming after you?"

"They're going to try and pin the problems the Cobbs are having on me. Can you believe it? Jesus H. Christ, Eve protects those people more than she does us! If I knew someone in the KKK, I'd sic 'em on her."

"Bree!" More often than not, it had been Mama Lulu's breast that had pillowed them when they were young; Mama Lulu who had wiped their noses and seen that they had Easter eggs to hunt and cookies to leave for Santa. His sister's behavior made him sick. "Just tell me one thing, is this about the vandalism and stuff at the market that has Mama Lulu and Eve so upset?"

"Duh, hello…where have you been? Go ask Eve your inane questions," she muttered, crushing out the joint. "I've gotta go get cleaned up so I can find out who this witness is that supposedly saw my car. Bet it's Connie Craig. She must've heard I'm the reason Donny broke up with her, and wants to get at me."

"Donny! I don't care if he did graduate with us, he's too young for you."

"No shit, and I only went out with him once, but she hasn't figured that out. I hope she swallows her stupid retainer."

Justin had stopped listening, instead brooding over this latest mess she'd gotten herself into. "So you're saying that wasn't you?"

"Oh, crap, I don't know."

"How can you not know? You either were there or you weren't!"

"It's not that simple. We were partying."

And she didn't look entirely repentant about it. Justin wanted to ask who "we" meant, but knew she would never tell him. In any case, his twin was in way over her head, and he felt a need to try to talk some sense into her before she went completely out of control.

"Why would you want to do that to yourself? Don't you listen to the news, read the papers? Do you want to die?"

"Please. I'm not going to die."

"I'll bet that's what Cassy Ann Wheats said."

"She got careless."

"Says who?"

Bree narrowed her eyes. "What's this? Did Eve draft you to try to fish information out of me? Forget it. Stay out of my business, and I'll stay out of yours."

She wrapped the sheet around her and squirmed off the bed. At least she tried. A spasm of pain distorted her pretty face, and she had to grip one of the bedposts to stay on her feet.

Justin stepped forward. "What's wrong?"

"Nothing."

But when she passed him on her way to the bathroom, Justin saw the smear of reddish brown on the white sheet. "Bree! You're bleeding!"

She glanced back, saw the stain and swore. Half stumbling, half running, she made it to the bathroom and slammed the door shut behind her.

"Bree? Are you okay?" he called at the door.

"Son of a bitch, will you get out!"

Still shocked by what he'd seen, Justin stood there, unsure what to do. Did women bleed that much?

What about the pain? He'd never seen Bree almost brought to her knees by menstrual cramps.

Troubled, he left the room. As he checked his watch, he saw it was nearly nine o'clock. "Blast." This put him in a quandary. Eve needed to know about Bree's condition, but he'd told Lacey to look for him by nine. He was as anxious to check on her as he was concerned for Bree. But if he wanted to be around for the inevitable brouhaha when Chief Rader arrived, he needed to make tracks.

When he got downstairs, he took it as a sign that Eve was on the phone in the study. He would tell her after he returned.

As he'd been hoping, Lacey was watching for him, and his heart soared at her beatific smile, and the way she ran to meet him by the big oak. She threw her arms around his neck and lifted her sweet face for a kiss, and the rush of joy sweeping through him almost left him too weak to balance them both.

"You don't know how good it was to see you smiling and running to me instead of running away," he whispered against her hair. It didn't matter that she couldn't hear him. With every meeting, they were growing closer, learning to communicate on another level where words weren't always necessary.

Lacey leaned back and touched his face. She seemed to like to do that a great deal, and it would have embarrassed him, except that he liked to do the same thing to her. In fact, today she had a glow about her that he'd never seen before.

"You look so pretty," he murmured, adding a smile and nod as she gestured to her dress. At least two sizes too large for her, the pink cotton with the tiniest bit of crocheting at the collar wasn't new by any stretch of the imagination; however, Justin guessed it must be the one she kept for special occasions like church or going to town—if she ever got to do anything like that.

Thinking of her constraints reminded him of the old man inside. He asked, "Is your grandfather okay?"

She nodded and pressed her hands together and laid her cheek against them.

"Sleeping. Good. And you, how are you doing? No trouble from your stepbrother?"

Some of the light left her smile, but she didn't get as upset as she sometimes did. She shrugged, and took his hand and led him to the towel she'd spread for them in lieu of a blanket. He saw a plastic plate of vanilla wafers and a fruit jar of ice water. The spare snack left him with a lump in his throat and confirmed his hunch of how little she existed on.

"This is wonderful." He forced himself to take one of the bland-looking cookies. "Great," he murmured upon taking the smallest nibble. "Did you make them?"

She nodded and touched her chest then pointed to him.

Overwhelmed, he wanted to sweep her into his arms and run off with her. He wanted to tell her how desperately in love he was. But it wouldn't be fair to burden her yet with the full weight of his feelings. She was still such an innocent in so many ways. So he settled for drawing her into his arms and kissing her forehead to thank her.

"Listen, I have some wonderful news," he said,

unable to keep it to himself any longer. "I've told Eve about you."

Her smile wilted.

"No, no, it's all right. I told you how good she is. Besides, she'd already noticed a change in me, just like I see the change I've made in you."

She blushed at that, but then he knew he was probably doing the same.

"Eve said she would help you."

Although she'd been watching his lips, Lacey remained wary and confused.

"You could come to the house. You wouldn't have to put up with...with *that!*" He flung his arm toward the shack he loathed. "Don't you get it? You could be free of him!"

With her gaze avoiding his, she signed that her grandfather needed her.

Justin wanted to assure her that her grandfather was welcome, too, but that would be premature because he hadn't cleared the crucial detail with Eve. But surely she wouldn't mind.

Right. Like she doesn't have her hands full, as it is.

The touch of Lacey's lips on his cheek had him cursing himself for not being sure he had the right to speak up. "We'll get things straightened out. I *am* going to get you out of there," he vowed, grasping her shoulders.

With a sad smile he was coming to know all too well, she touched her fingers to his lips to signal she wanted him to stop talking, and gently pushed at his chest until he lay back against the towel.

"Oh, sweetheart, you know this isn't necessary. I mean, I really shouldn't…"

The sweep of her hair brushed across his chest and tickled his chin before she rose to touch her lips to his. As always when she got this close to him, he began to tremble inside and out. He had no way of proving it, but surely Lacey kissed like no one else. Part breeze, part butterfly, she seeped into him, filling him and filling him until he was intoxicated from her. Today, with the added temptation of sugar on their lips, she was irresistible.

"Lacey, Lacey…we shouldn't be doing this. There's so much to talk about. I don't want to take—"

She didn't let him finish. As she spread another series of kisses all over his face, she unbuttoned his shirt, allowing the sun to warm him as thoroughly as her tender lips did. Even if he hadn't had the memory of last time, she would have had a devastating effect on him. She was simply too sweet and too generous.

Gently cupping her head with his hand, he shut his eyes tight and struggled to find the willpower to stop her. But then her breath tickled the skin near his belt buckle, her fingers loosened leather.

Lost in the wonder of it, he was as shocked as Lacey by the feral roar that erupted behind them. When he opened his eyes simultaneous to her strangled gasp, he saw her being dragged up by her hair and flung across the grass by a wild man. Before he could do anything to help her, the lunatic kicked him in the side with a booted foot.

A cannonball of pain exploded within him. Gasping, Justin tried to roll away to protect himself, but the battering ram struck again and again, catching him on various parts of his body.

"Slimy bastard! Little prick! I knew there was something fishy going on. I'll show you...I'll show you!"

Again and again the blows came—to his ribs, his stomach, his back and his head. Although blinded by agony, he focused to one thought: getting Lacey to run before the maniac turned on her.

"I'll teach you to sniff around what ain't yours," the giant snarled, looming over him.

Justin lifted his head to plead for both of them. The words locked in his throat as an explosion ripped apart his groin.

"Welcome back, Mama Lulu. How's the family?"

Rae had just driven the older woman back to Maitland Hall, and put on a brave face to Eve; but as Eve followed Mama Lulu inside, she felt a need to get at the truth.

"Doin' the best they can, considerin' Mr. Hughes over at the hardware store said he can't give Luther no more credit for repairs after this, 'cause he ain't paid what he owed for the last time. Figure the Lord'll settle things in His own time."

Eve thought that was all well and good, but she wanted to do her share, as well. "You tell Luther and Rae that I'll sign for the repairs. I'll go call Trevor Hughes right now and tell him to give Luther whatever he needs."

Although Eve had responded to many crises in the same way, Mama Lulu looked taken aback. "How can you do that?"

"Easy, believe me. If it wasn't for me and my grand ideas, Luther and Rae wouldn't be suffering so. And under the circumstances..." She wondered if Mama Lulu knew about Bree's probable involvement yet.

"For your sake, I hope she ain't involved."

Eve pressed her fingers to her lips. Rae had given no hint that they'd known, but of course Ben would have told them. "Mama Lulu, I don't know what to say. I'm so sorry. Ben's going to be here in a few minutes to talk to her. You have every right to sit in if you'd like."

"Thank you. I would," she replied with quiet dignity. "Maybe it will help me understand why."

That would be refreshing.

Ben arrived not quite an hour later, and Eve found herself having to deal with guilt because of the rush of pleasure that swept through her. Not wanting him to notice too much, she slipped her damp hands into the pockets of the tailored slacks she'd changed into.

He reached the door just as she did. When their eyes met through the screen, she couldn't help remembering how he'd stood there only hours before and kissed her good-night.

"Wow," he murmured, his gaze sweeping over her.

She'd put on another of Sumner's gifts to her, a trouser and silk blouse ensemble in camel. The style was reminiscent of those in wonderful old forties movies.

"Hello yourself." She stepped aside as he opened the screen door and entered. "She hasn't come down yet."

"Good. Then there's time to tell you that you look good enough to eat—and that I'm starving."

"Not really. Mama Lulu's back, and planning on joining us."

He took his gaze off her only long enough to glance toward the kitchen. "Next you're going to sidestep telling me when I'm going to see you again. When we said good-night, you were damned vague."

"Well, at the moment, even the continuation of civilization as we know it is 'damned vague.' At least it is around here."

"I hear you, but what's that got to do with us?"

"Spoken like a man whose brains have gone deep-sea fishing."

Ben flashed her an unabashed grin. "Someone once wrote of us good ol' boys that we don't have problems, we have erections."

She had to clear her throat to keep from laughing. "At least you're honest about it." Before she could say more, though, she heard a door open upstairs.

Bree appeared and descended toward them, dressed in tight red jeans and an equally figure-molding red top. Intercepting the look Eve exchanged with Ben, she announced, "I thought if I was going to be forced to sit through this fiasco, I might as well dress for the role you've defined for me."

Any hope Eve had that they could resolve this problem without scarring each other more died as brutally as the cricket Bree crushed as she stepped off the last stair. At the crunch, the girl glanced down and kicked the poor thing toward the screen door.

"See what happens when you give the help too much time off?"

"God, Bree." If Eve hadn't seen the moment of fear in the girl's eyes, she would have given her a piece of her mind there and then. As it was, she barely managed a terse, "I suggest you think about the difference between being thought of as a fool and erasing all doubt, and keep silent until spoken to." Adding the same don't-push-my-buttons look she used to bestow on fresh young nurse graduates and more impudent interns, she led the way to the study.

"Can I offer you anything to drink, Chief Rader?" she asked, stopping at the door.

"I'm fine, thank you...Mrs. Maitland."

Bree brought up the rear. "I'll take some coffee," she said with her most feline smile. "You scheduled this so early, you didn't leave me time for breakfast. Two sugars and be generous with the cream, as always."

Eve ignored her and turned toward the kitchen, intending to notify Mama Lulu that they were going to begin, but their housekeeper must have heard them. "Okay?" Eve asked softly as the woman drew near.

"As best as I'm gonna get, I s'pose."

"Come sit here." Eve led her to one of the high-backed chairs.

Bree had circled her father's massive oak desk and flopped down on the wine red leather chair beneath his portrait. She stopped swiveling back and forth like a five-year-old visiting a parent's workplace the instant Mama Lulu settled across from her.

"Is this some kind of joke?"

Eve shook her head. "Mama Lulu is here on behalf of the Cobbs."

"I smell a setup. Where's our lawyer?" the teen demanded.

Ben posted himself at the door. "Relax. All you have to do is answer a few questions. With a little cooperation, this doesn't have to go to court."

"I'll bet. For your information, I'm not going there regardless, I don't care who said they saw my car—"

"My son did," Mama Lulu said, her head high.

Bree had begun to rise and dropped back onto the chair.

No less surprised, Eve looked from their house-keeper to Ben. *Luther?* All this time it was him, and Ben had refused to tell her? Not even Rae had wanted to give her a hint.

"Mama Lulu," she began, feeling sick to her stomach. "You should have said something."

"Didn't know till I talked to the children."

"Of course." Luther probably hadn't wanted to tell her then, either, but she'd undoubtedly bullied him into it. "I'm at a greater loss of words than ever."

"Hey!" Bree folded her arms across her chest. "What happened to 'innocent until proven guilty'? Why should I want to hurt Mama Lulu's family?"

Ben uttered a disdainful grunt. "Don't pretend you care. Your record so far reads like a sociopath in training, the way you never think that rules apply to you and your lack of consideration for others. You can't walk out the front door without getting into trouble."

"A few traffic tickets, a practical joke here and there among friends!"

"You don't seem to have any friends left, young lady," he said. "I've checked around. No one wanted to admit, let alone claim, a connection to you. It seems your drinking and other *habits* have surpassed anything the kids in your old circle want to be involved in. No one sounded sorry that you don't call anymore.''

''That's a lie! If I threw a party here tomorrow, they'd run each other down to get here.''

Ben cocked an eyebrow. ''Including the girl whose car hood was battered by that birdbath you threw?''

Bree's mouth fell open. ''How did you find out about that?''

Ignoring her, Ben told Eve, ''She paid for the repairs herself. She must get one helluva'n allowance.''

''It's not that generous,'' Eve shot back, afraid of what other bits of information he'd come up with. Then she added to Bree, ''When did this happen?''

The teen scowled and swung the chair around to gaze out the front window. ''After finals. The night I said I was going to sleep over at Marcy Varnell's. Everyone wanted to party, to relieve the pressure from cramming for weeks. Lem...well, Lem helped me get a couple of kegs and... Look, I wouldn't have tossed the thing at Jill's car if I hadn't found out that she'd stabbed me in the back and cost me the prom queen title.''

Eve didn't remember a Jill. And not only was she dismayed to hear that Bree was virtually friendless at this stage, but that no one around town had seen fit to tell her about her stepdaughter's outrageous behavior. ''Where on earth have you been getting the money?''

Bree ignored her and shot Ben a resentful look. ''What I want to know is what does any of that have

to do with what any idiot knows is a racially moti-
vated attack on the Cobbs?''

"Why don't we ask the guy you were with that
night?" Ben pushed away from the doorjamb and
strolled around the room. He smiled coldly at her
fearful stare. "Now, how do I know that? you're wondering. That's my secret. But I'll tell you this—he's
someone considerably older than you. The question
is, do you even know what he's doing to you, let
alone everyone else? Have you smartened up enough
to figure out that you're being used?"

For an instant Bree looked as if she was about to
blurt out something, only to clam up tight. Eve
thought the way the girl winced when she sat back in
the chair was equally disturbing.

"I don't know what you're talking about," Bree
said.

Ben approached the desk and rested his palms on
the top. "Then ask your boyfriend to explain it to
you, and tell him that his days are numbered. I'm onto
him, and what he's doing. Tell him the Cobbs never
got the money he left on Lem. Tell him that he's not
creating the diversions he thinks he is by getting attention off the drug situation. Tell him that his ass is
mine."

Eve was about to warn Ben he'd gone far enough
when the harsh sound of a blaring horn stopped her.
Everyone in the room started at the noise, but she was
first into the foyer, and arrived on the porch just as
Dewitt Nellis braked his truck behind Ben's Blazer.

"Ms. Maitland, come quick!" the foreman yelled.

Eve was already running because she'd spotted the
boy slumped in the passenger seat. "Dear God, Justin!"

16

No one could have beaten Eve to the truck, and she practically ripped the door open to get at Justin. "What happened?" she demanded of Dewitt.

"Found him crawling on the trail leading up from the lake," the foreman replied. The amount of blood on his own clothes testified as to how he'd worked to get Justin here. "Haven't been able to get him to say much. He mumbles a name, I think. Can't quite make it out, though, and if he tries to say more he starts coughing up blood."

It was hard to tell where all the blood was coming from, but Eve could see his lower lip was split wide and his nose was broken. With one eye swollen shut and another brutal laceration across his left cheekbone deforming him, Eve could barely recognize the boy except by the color of his hair.

"Oh, babe, hold on," she crooned. "Try to stay still." For the moment she left him slumped forward to protect him against suffocating on his own blood, and even though that meant she couldn't check for other bruises that would confirm her suspicion of internal injuries, his rapid but weak pulse, and his writhing, told her enough. "We'll get you to a hospital soon. Ben, can you—"

"Eee." The boy groped blindly for her arm, but missed. "Hep. Ha to—" He gagged and went into another violent coughing fit.

"Don't try to talk, sweetie."

"La…" He groaned.

Without turning away from the boy, she called, "Ben, can you call on your radio for an emergency helicopter? It's close to an hour's drive to Greenville and he's hurt too badly to risk that."

"You've got it!" he replied from behind her.

Bree moved to the other side of the door and peered through the open window. "He looks terrible. What do you suppose happened to him? Everybody likes Justin. They may think he's a bit stuck-up because he doesn't socialize much, but—"

"Quiet," Eve snapped, and accepted the apron Mama Lulu passed over her shoulder.

"Laz," Justin moaned again.

"He's trying to tell us something," Bree said with growing excitement. "What're you saying, Just? Eve, listen!"

She'd been busy folding the apron so that it would do the most good against the wounds until she could get some gauze pads. "What, Justin? What did you want to tell us?"

"Hep…Laze."

Dear God, his lip was so swollen he couldn't enunciate and she couldn't tell who he was— "Lacey! You're talking about the girl you mentioned yesterday? What about her, sweetheart? Was she with you?"

"Uh. He ha' her. *P'ease.*"

"Ben!" Eve cast an anxious look for him, for the

moment her concern and disappointment in the secrets he'd been keeping from her regarding the Cobbs irrelevant.

He waved from his truck and ran over. "What's up?"

"Justin was with a girl when this happened. She lives across the lake. There's a brother or stepbrother, I'm not sure which, who Justin's been worried about. I think we're dealing with abuse, Ben. Oh, dear Lord," she groaned as it sunk in. "I'd told him that I needed more information before we could do anything. I should have called you right away."

"Easy," Ben murmured, squeezing her shoulder. "Can you give me more specific directions?"

Eve leaned closer to Justin. "Which house, sweetie? Can you tell us something to help Ben? He's going to go help."

Justin raised an unsteady finger. "B-by dam." He broke for another series of coughs. "Hurry!" he gasped.

Eve turned to Ben. "She's hearing- and speaking-impaired. But she might be able to read your lips."

"I understand."

"And Ben, there's an old man. Her grandfather. I think he's bedridden. Bring them both here if they don't need... Well, if you can." *And be careful,* she said with her eyes. No matter what happened between them, Parish needed him.

Ben frowned as if not liking what he saw in her eyes, but when he spoke it was merely to murmur, "Done." Then he was running for his truck.

Eve didn't watch him drive away. Filled with concern as well as guilt, she focused wholly on Justin.

"Did you hear that? It's being taken care of, hon. Chief Rader's gone to get Lacey. Now let's focus on stopping that bleeding and getting you more comfortable."

Less than twenty minutes later, the helicopter arrived. By then, Eve and Dewitt had Justin on the cushioned chaise they'd carried from the veranda to a spot of shade near a recently plowed field where the chopper could land safely. Eve had directed Bree to collect more cushions to elevate Justin's head and shoulders, and Mama Lulu brought a bowl of water, clean towels and gauze pads. Through it all Justin drifted in and out of consciousness, rousing several times to cry out for Lacey.

When the EMS personnel rushed to them, Eve introduced herself and gave them a concise summary of Justin's status and his medical history. She knew she couldn't accompany Justin, so as soon as he was strapped onto the stretcher, she kissed the top of his head and assured him that she would see him as soon as she drove to the hospital.

As she backed away to join the rest of the group, Dewitt leaned close to her ear. "Maybe you best let me drive you, ma'am. You're in no shape to be dealing with traffic."

Eve could hardly bring herself to take her eyes off the helicopter until it was airborne. She'd been thinking she'd finally found out how difficult it was to remain levelheaded when the injured person was someone you felt a deep emotional connection to. Finally, she took a deep breath and hugged a startled Dewitt. "No, but thank you so much. You probably saved his life."

"I was just glad to find him, Ms. Maitland. But about driving..."

She patted his sinewy, strong back. "I appreciate the concern, but I'm fine. You'd help me more by staying here to be my eyes and ears. I don't know what Chief Rader will find down by the lake, and I'd like our people to be alert and offer their services if they're needed."

"I'll ride with you," Bree said quickly.

Eve had almost forgotten that the girl was around. Looking at Bree now, she could see sincere concern in her eyes, but it was Justin's well-being that they needed to be concerned with.

"That's not a good idea, either," she said, heading toward her car. "You stay put in case Dewitt needs to get a message to me. I'll keep in touch by the car phone."

"Mama Lulu can do that."

"Mama Lulu," Eve said, stopping by the car and exchanging speaking looks with the housekeeper, "is going to be quite busy getting two guest rooms ready in case Lacey and her grandfather arrive. You might offer a hand there to save her from running up and down the stairs so much."

"But he's my brother! My *twin!* I have a right to be with him!"

The day's heat and the stress was finally getting to her, and Eve wiped at her forehead with the back of her hand. "I'm not being insensitive, Bree, although I do find it odd that you're remembering your biological connection now. Where was all this concern and closeness before?"

"That's not fair. We're close, we're just... different."

"So respect that difference. Right now he needs peace and quiet, and plenty of rest."

"I know what's going on. You just want to make everyone think you're the only one who can do anything, the only one who cares about him," Bree sneered, clenching her hands. "Well, you don't fool me. I saw that look you gave Ben Rader. You're already working on him just as you worked on Perry!"

Eve couldn't believe the girl's audacity, or timing, for that matter. "That will be enough."

"You're the one who should have the shit knocked out of her, not him! You!"

As the girl stormed into the house, silence hung like a time bomb about to go off. When the screen door slammed behind her, Eve sighed and turned to apologize to Dewitt.

He held up his hand. "'Scuse me if I'm out of turn, ma'am, but I can't help thinking Mr. Sumner short-changed that girl a turn or two with a strong switch."

Until today, the only opinions Dewitt had ever offered were those regarding fertilizer ratios and crop rotation. It came as a relief, especially now, to find out he saw more than he let on. As she saw Mama Lulu's nod of agreement, she smiled. "If I wasn't concerned about rabies, I'd consider making up for that."

Dewitt's mouth twitched and he touched the brim of his hat. "Yes'm. Good luck to you, and y'all come home soon. We'll take care of things here until you do."

Never more grateful that he'd stayed on after his

problems with his wife, Eve thanked him again and watched as he drove away. "I'm a lucky woman to have you good people, Mama Lulu," she said, aware of her housekeeper's somber presence behind her.

"Don't you start talkin' as foolish as that girl. We're here 'cuz you get down and dirty right beside us. Now, before you take off, you come inside and change outta those things."

"But I promised Justin—"

Trading her majordomo tone for one far more tender, Mama Lulu took hold of Eve's arm. "Young Justin see you lookin' like that, you'll scare him all over again. Besides, whiles you're doin' that, I'll be packin' you an overnight bag just in case. C'mon, child. Maitland Hall needs a feisty Yankee now more'n ever."

Although Eve winced once she realized what she'd done to the lovely outfit, she was more concerned with what she could be heaping onto Mama Lulu's shoulders. "Oh, God. I didn't consider— How can I abandon you with Bree on a tirade?"

"Ain't nothin' to say about it. That's why they're emergencies. I'll take a broom to her backside if she don't quit. We'll be *fine*. And if that child and her papa come, they be fine, too. You just drive with your mind on the road, and get that boy home soon as you can. I'll be startin' some corn puddin' and broth that'll go down easy."

Afraid she was going to get emotional, Eve whispered, "Bless you, Mama Lulu," and hurried to change her things.

As an afterthought, Ben reached for the radio's mike again. "And no lights or sirens. For all we know, this could be a hostage situation. We don't want to provoke him into doing anything crazy.''

He was driving in from the west. Buck and Al were coming in from the east. He could see them up ahead, and also the house Justin had identified. It was a gloomy place, nothing more than a shack, and it gave him a bad feeling.

Noting that there was room around the back, he got on the radio again and told Al to cover the rear in case there was an escape attempt.

''What a dump,'' he murmured to himself as he came to a stop at the front and killed the truck's engine. He supposed he'd seen worse, not only in Jackson but when he'd been in the service traveling around the world; however, it was concern about what could be going on in there that made this place particularly ugly.

Buck parked about a dozen yards to his left and, like him, eased out of his vehicle, staying low behind the car, no doubt his gun already drawn, Ben thought, only now releasing the safety on his holster. Although he wore his gun all the time these days, it remained a hot poker against his thigh. Sometimes he told himself just to buy another and put his outrage about the past behind him once and for all. But as of yet, his bitterness hadn't allowed him to do that.

What tragedies were being written in the one-story house before them? Ben eyed the open windows where curtains—little more than rags—were drawn back, signaling there was no air-conditioning. In the midday heat the place had to be like a prison sweatbox, extra bad news if there was a senior citizen in there. Motioning to Buck, he approached the stairs.

He kept his back against the smooth board siding, its heat burning through his shirt. When he reached the last step, he knocked on the wooden part of the screen door. As was the case with most of the house, its wood was peeling and one side of the screen was ripped. Half the lake's population of flies and mosquitoes probably knew about that hole.

When he received no answer, Ben knocked again. "Police! Anyone in there?"

Suddenly a commotion erupted inside. Ben heard a sharp sound like a slap, a crash, and then footsteps. Ben motioned to Buck to let him know someone was coming.

The wild-haired, whiskered man who appeared at the door nearly filled every inch of screen. Huge as well as overweight, Ben compared him to slight, fine-boned Justin Maitland and understood the kid was lucky to be alive. The boy wouldn't have had a chance in hell against this version of King Kong.

"Whaddya want?" the burly man demanded.

"We have a report of a disturbance at this address. Would you step outside so we can discuss the matter?"

"Somebody's jerking your chain. Ain't no disturbance here. In fact, I was just trying to have me a nap before I go to work."

As he began to walk away, Ben called, "Hold it. Where's the girl?"

The man stepped back to the door and scowled at him. "Ain't no girl here. I said you got the wrong place."

But his eyes said otherwise, and when Ben saw him glance toward Buck, then over to the road as if gauging his options for escape, he knew they had the right guy.

About to warn their suspect not to do anything foolish, the man reached for the inner door and swung it shut. A second later Ben heard the back door burst open and Al Jones yelled, "Freeze!"

Ben was already yanking open the unlatched screen door, and thrust open the inner one in time to see the man throwing a chair at Al. More than Al, he realized, seeing the cowering figure his newest officer was trying to urge behind him.

The wooden chair clipped the young cop on the shin, sending him stumbling over the girl. Taking advantage of that, the giant roared and flung himself at them. "You get your hands off her, you—"

"Freeze, mister!" Ben shouted. "Freeze or so help me I'll drop you right here, right now."

The angry man came to a halt within arm's reach of Al, and slowly raised his hands.

"Now," Ben said, quickly shooting a glance behind the door and down the hall to make sure there were no other surprises waiting for them, "lock your hands behind your head and get facedown on the floor. Do it!"

The aging floorboards groaned as the man lowered himself to his knees, then rolled himself onto his side, and finally his belly. A difficult maneuver to achieve for someone of his bulk, and he didn't go down without comment.

Ignoring him, Ben glanced back as Buck entered. Ben nodded to indicate the prone man. "Cuff him and read him his rights. I'll look around. Jones? How is she?''

"Uh, I could use a sheet or blanket for her, Chief.''

There wasn't much left of the poor kid's dress, and only her long hair and her arms kept her from total humiliation.

"I'll bring you what I can find.''

He peered inside the first room that had a large unmade bed and little else, and moved on to the second and only other room. It was more like an oversize closet, and that's where Ben found the old man. The smell warned him first, followed by the incredible heat that the south-facing window made worse. The poor wretch was lying there staring at the ceiling, more skeleton than human being. He could see that the girl had tried to keep the place clean, but it was a losing battle. Ben was repulsed by the living conditions she and her grandfather had been forced to endure. Hell, there was no bathroom, and in the kitchen only some prehistoric excuse for a stove and refrigerator.

There was nothing he could do for the pitiful soul, except to call for an ambulance, so as soon as he spotted a folded sheet on a shelf at the foot of the bed, he snatched it up and returned to the others.

"Buck, better radio for the EMS people. Tell them we have a senior citizen suffering from heat prostration.'' He tipped his head to indicate their prisoner. "Has he said anything?''

"The usual bull. You'd better do something for the girl, though. I don't think she likes your new boy wonder any more than the rest of us do.''

"There'll be no more of that,'' he said quietly.

Then he went over to Al who was trying to talk to the girl now hunkered in the corner, shivering and weeping. "I think some of the reason you're having problems, Al, is that she can't hear you," he told the young cop. "She can't speak, either."

The other cop exhaled in relief. "I was really beginning to worry." He glanced across the room at Buck, but said nothing.

"I warned you it wouldn't be easy."

That seemed to bolster the somber man. "I'll be okay, Chief."

"Good. I'll take over here. You keep an eye on our friend, while Buck calls in our status."

As Al took over for Buck, Ben unfolded the sheet and eased it around the girl's shoulders. She stiffened at first, and Ben sensed that if it was possible, she would have vanished into the faded wallpaper. That had him checking his anger, kept him from dragging the worthless piece of crap behind him outside, into the lake, to squeeze the last breath from his lungs. Instead, he patted the girl's back and stroked her hair until she stopped sobbing and shaking enough to peek at him.

He saw haunted, terrified eyes, a split lip and a sweet, heart-shaped face. Hard-shelled as he was, his chest ached and his stomach rolled at the sight, but he hid it all and summoned a tender smile.

"Lacey?" Her subsequent blink had him guessing she understood. At least she started focusing on his mouth. "It's okay. You're safe now. Justin is safe."

The moment he said Justin, new tears flooded her eyes, and she began signing to him frantically. He tried to guess what it all meant.

"He's fine. Justin's alive. We're going to take you to his home. You're safe now."

Apparently he made some kind of impression. By the time medics arrived, Lacey had latched herself to his side and wouldn't let anyone come between them. In the end, he had to take the girl in his truck and follow the ambulance carrying her grandfather to Greenville.

Once there, she continued to balk at any sign of being separated from him. Knowing he couldn't be in the cubicle during her examination, he asked a nurse to find Eve. The results were as profound as rattling off the combination for the safe at Fort Knox. Within minutes, swing doors flew wide, and she swept through emergency like some fiery angel bent on setting order, a female intern, a female social worker and two nurses scurrying behind her to guarantee that.

She immediately focused on the young male doctor who'd wanted to examine Lacey, asking him for a private word.

When she returned, it was without said doctor. At her brief signal, her entourage stepped several respectful yards away from the cubicle, and she finally approached him.

"Let me guess," Ben drawled once she stopped before him. "The Maitlands are big donators here, as well?"

"Sumner wasn't pleased with where I had to wait during his chemo treatments, so he built them a new reception center. Since then we've been working on a few other things." Lowering her voice, she added, "I'm so relieved to see you. Both of you."

He understood the slip. He was feeling a little light-headed himself, and he was all but devouring her with his eyes. It was a strange reaction since they hadn't been separated all that long, and when they'd parted, she'd been disappointed, maybe even annoyed with him for his secretiveness about the Cobb case.

"We're okay," he murmured. "It wasn't a picnic for Lacey, but I think she understands that things would have been far uglier if we hadn't gotten her out when we did."

Eve smiled gently at the wide-eyed, anxious girl, but when she spoke it was to him. "Yes, I've been hearing that you've made quite a conquest."

"You win some, you lose some."

She let that one pass and replied, "What about the grandfather?"

"He's across the hall. His condition is as bad as you'd guessed. I doubt he ever had a clue as to what was going on, and he sure as hell wasn't able to be of any help to the kid. By the way, the stepbrother's name is Roy. Roy Lindale. I have him in a holding cell at the station. Lacey—" he took Eve's arm and urged her closer to the trembling teenager "—this is Eve. Justin's stepmother."

Eve gave the girl another reassuring smile and quickly dug into her white leather purse for her wallet. When Lacey saw that what she was taking out was a photograph of Justin, her small face lit with joy. Eve gave it to her, and the teen crushed it to her chest, tears once again flooding her eyes.

"He must have been the only source of happiness in her life," Ben murmured, turning his head to keep

Lacey from reading his lips. "Wait'll you get a peek at good ol' Roy. It's a miracle she isn't in the vegetative state the old man is in."

"The people outside are experienced with treating abused women and children. They'll make the examination as quick and painless as possible."

"And Justin? How's he?"

"Resting. Also lucky to be here. He has two broken ribs, a broken nose, about twenty-six stitches and—how do I say this delicately?—that son of a bitch Lindale almost succeeded in nullifying a strategic part of his anatomy."

"Ah, hell. Poor kid."

Eve pretended to be deeply involved with refastening her purse, which allowed her to keep her head down. "I don't care what you have to do, Ben, but I don't want to hear that he made bail."

"He won't. I usually avoid making promises, but you have my word on that one. Is there going to be any permanent...a problem for Justin?"

"The doctors don't think so, but they've sedated him to give him a break from the pain. I know that once he wakes and hears that Lacey's safe, he'll improve even more quickly in order to get home."

Ben watched her observe the girl. He knew Eve had to be emotionally wiped out, but it was obvious her compassion was running on all cylinders. He could only imagine what plans were being spun in that stunning head.

"You want to take her home with you, don't you?"

"Not want. I *will* take her. If we find she's underage, you won't contest that, will you? She'll be more comfortable at Maitland Hall, as well as know at least one person, plus have the benefit of on-the-scene medical expertise. Besides, I think she and Justin will be excellent therapy for each other."

"Covered every base, have you?"

"Is that a yes or no?"

"If I say yes, will you forgive me for upsetting you earlier?"

Eve lowered her eyes. "We're keeping professionals from doing their job."

"That's what I was doing. Being a professional to those I'm paid to protect and serve."

"I had time to figure that out while driving here."

"Then I'll back you any way I can."

Clearing her throat at his sexy murmur, Eve gestured toward the exit. "Why don't you go find yourself some coffee while we make friends. The sooner we get this over with, the sooner I might be able to get her upstairs to see Justin."

Ben didn't get back to the station until late afternoon. He stayed at the hospital until Lacey's ordeal was over, and she seemed accepting of Eve's plans for her. When he did return to Parish, it was to the news that nearly a dozen people—from city-council members to business owners—had called about Al. Which was why he unceremoniously dropped the handful of pink papers into Dewey's trash can.

Otherwise, the office was surprisingly quiet. Buck was busy giving yet another play-by-play report about their "raid" to someone over the phone. "Careful," he said as he passed the man. "You'll have people thinking we waged the second gunfight at the O.K. Corral.''

Grinning, the cop covered the mouthpiece of the receiver. ''It's just my wife. I'm tryin' to impress her so I'll get me some noogies tonight.''

''But you gotta admit that Lindale's one big mother with an extra-bad temper,'' Dewey interjected, following Ben. The excitement in his voice bespoke a desire to be part of the group and taste the action, if only vicariously. ''We'll all have to be on our guard going in back.''

He was referring to their sorry excuse for a jail that consisted of two shoe box–size cells that traditionally remained empty except for New Year's Eve, Super Bowl Sunday and when Old Miss played a home game. Otherwise, drunks were chauffeured home, and the disorderly were given a stiff lecture, a threat or a kick in the butt, whichever best applied to the situation. Ben still had to be convinced the thing would hold a man bent on escape, let alone one of Roy Lindale's size. What he didn't tell his men was that he half hoped Lindale did attempt something. He wouldn't mind an excuse to put a bullet in some part of Big Roy's anatomy that would guarantee prolonged agony.

''Just don't go back there when there's no one to cover you,'' he said, aware Dewey would have forgotten most of anything he'd ever learned in school. ''Don't carry your keys, and for Christ's sake, *never* wear your gun.''

The dispatcher nodded vigorously as if listening to Moses delivering the Ten Commandments. ''You bet,

Chief. I'll pass that on to the others, too. By the way—" he checked his log "—a reporter from the county paper called and wants to interview him."

"No."

"Oh, and you, too, of course."

"Ditto the first response."

The former storm-window salesman followed him a few steps. "Why not, sir?"

Ben didn't feel like explaining. Reality was leaving a bitter taste in his mouth, but he also didn't want to go through these questions every few hours, and so he stopped and slowly turned around to impale the shorter man with his gaze. "There's a young girl out there who's been stripped of her childhood, and her dignity. She has to try to rebuild her life out of what Lindale didn't crush, shatter or soil. Do you really want to splash her picture and every graphic detail of her nightmare all over the county, maybe the state, just so you guys get your names in the paper?"

Dewey hung his head and looked guilty...too guilty. Ben narrowed his eyes.

"Now what?"

"The mayor wants to do something official."

"He can sign my paycheck." He turned to Buck, who'd ended his call and had joined them. "Maybe you'd better drive on out to the Lindale place and make sure everything is locked up and secure. Put tape across the doors. It might help keep away a percentage of the gawkers and vandals, as well as any reporters."

Ben barely settled in his office when a beaming Fred Varnell entered the station. He gave Dewey a jaunty salute, and slapped him on the back, before continuing through. *Grinning fool*, Ben thought.

"Well, you don't do anything small-time, do you, son? Congratulations. You've saved the community from a dangerous felon."

"No, Fred. Just a bully."

"Don't be modest. Why, for all we know, that animal's been attacking other girls in the area."

Ben had been rubbing his face and wishing for a long shower and a shave. Hearing Fred's little speech, he splayed his fingers to stare between them at the politician. "You'd like that, wouldn't you?"

"No—no! I simply meant... Well, it's a possibility, isn't it?"

"You're a sick man, Varnell. Listen closely...there isn't anyone else. This time. And thank the god that made you for that. Lindale's the type whose dick and brain combined wouldn't crowd a culture tube. He's that disgusting sediment of humanity that lives on the sidelines of life, and fucks whatever's handy."

The insult slipped over the mayor like oil on wet lettuce, and he settled in a chair, looking as if he'd just been made privy to exclusive information. "Uh-huh, uh-huh. Damn, that's scary. I want you to know the community is proud that you're diving right in there and cleaning out the scum." Sitting back in his chair, Fred then assumed a more statesmanlike pose. "There is one small matter that's come up that I feel obligated to talk to you about."

"Forget it." Ben flipped through the handful of phone messages that Dewey had set in here earlier. "Jones is staying."

"See, Ben? This is where you founder. You've done a grand thing today, a grand thing. Keep up the good work and by year's end you could be man of the year at the chamber of commerce's Christmas banquet."

"Don't nominate me, Fred. I won't come."

That one finally drove home. "Damn it, Ben, don't keep slamming doors in my face!"

"Say what you really came to say and then please go home to your dinner, meetings, or whatever. It's been a long day, and I still have a minimum of three hours of work that has to be done before I can kick off these boots."

The older man pointed his neatly manicured finger at him. "You want it without window dressing, I'll tell you plain. You shouldn't have hired that colored boy, Ben."

"He's not a boy, he's a man, and his name is Al Jones."

"Is he some kind of friend of yours that you owe a favor to or something?"

The question made Ben want to grab Fred by whatever was handy and throw him out. What stopped him was the reminder of the growing number of people counting on him to perform miracles. "You knew I was going to replace Haygood."

"But I thought you would choose from among our local boys!"

"Who would that be, Fred? Your older daughter's husband? How can I issue a weapon to Parish's only would-be golf pro? I don't care if he was a constable at one time, I wouldn't sleep nights knowing he was out there with a gun when everyone knows his moodiness has Barbara Rose swallowing Prozac just to get through a PTA meeting.''

Fred touched the knot on his tie. ''She and Jimmy Mack are in the hands of a good counselor, Ben. Besides, he wasn't the only candidate for the position.''

''You're right. There was Bum Poag's boy, but I don't think you'd okay the budget increase to pay for the custom-built chair we'd need for his wide ass.''

''Oh, all right, I know the pickings were lean,'' Fred replied. ''But you couldn't find a ni— Did you have to pick one so...dark?''

''You know what, Fred? Right now I wish he was so black that he'd look like a pair of eyeballs floating through the streets at night. The man is qualified, and he is staying. Get over it.''

He'd never seen Fred turn so red. For a moment, Ben wondered if he hadn't finally succeeded in giving the guy a stroke.

The mayor rose, his dignity barely intact. ''This may not be the last you'll hear on the matter.''

''It's your decision.''

The mayor left, and for the next twenty minutes or so Ben enjoyed the silence that had descended over the station. He managed to move enough paperwork to where he was ready to hear what Lindale had to say for himself. But no sooner did he circle his desk than the front door burst open and Buck ran in making more noise than Farley's ghost.

''Chief! Chief, I think you better have a look at this!''

The cop held up both sturdy hands like a fisherman

showing off the day's catch. Only he wasn't holding up fish on a trotline. Rather, in each hand was a varmint trap....

Varmint traps. Just like the one that had been around Lem Cobb's ankle.

17

"**I** got a right to make a phone call!"

Ben leaned against the dull gray wall opposite Roy Lindale's cell and continued his placid study of the man. He was pleased to know it made the creep very uncomfortable.

"You go deaf or something? I want a lawyer!"

"You haven't been charged with anything yet," Ben replied.

"Then let me outta here!"

"Cooperate."

The word, repeated three times already since he'd ventured back here, sent the man chasing from one end of the cell to the other, yelling obscenities and jerking at the bars like a rabid animal. Of course, that had been Ben's intent. He had no plans whatsoever of letting Lindale go. He did, however, want the guy to wear himself out, thus assuring the night shift a hassle-free duty. He also wanted to push the man's panic button so that when Ben did play his trump card, it would have the greatest impact.

He waited until Lindale came back to the middle of the cell and glared at him through the bars. A dark, dull-featured man, his lack of hygiene was beginning to make even the six feet between them inadequate.

But despite the offense to his olfactory cells, Ben stayed put, and he remained indifferent to the growling man's malevolent gaze. It was easy to do when he thought of what *could* be happening: Lacey enduring his perverted, disgusting attention day after day, night after night...

"Would you like to know how your grandfather's doing, or your stepsister?" he said, ready to taunt the man all over again.

"No."

"Guess that makes sense. Anyone who would let family live in the slop hole you subjected yours to couldn't be expected to have a conscience."

"Hey! They were lucky they had what they did. I didn't owe them shit. And did they care that I had to work two, sometimes three, jobs to support us? Hell, no!"

"You didn't have it so rough. You still found time to make your stepsister's life hell."

"I never touched her."

"Guess she gave herself that split lip."

"Damned straight. You never met a clumsier female."

"Are you going to tell me she ripped her own dress to shreds, too?"

"That punk did that! He would've raped her if I hadn't got home when I did. It's a miracle I was let off early."

"Justin Maitland told us that you attacked them."

"Well, he's a friggin' liar. I had to defend myself from him!"

Lindale raked the hair off his face with hands that resembled meat cleavers, making the comment a joke.

Ben smirked. "That should give the jury a good laugh when they see that poor skinny kid."

Roy's thick lips went slack. "What jury?"

"He's going to press charges. So is Lacey. A prosecutor couldn't ask for two sweeter kids to put on a stand and sell his case. Yup, they're going to have quite an impact on that jury."

"You son of a bitch! You get me a phone right now! I want a *lawyer!*"

Ben scratched at his whiskers, pretending confusion. "Are you sure? You just said you have a tough enough time making ends meet. How are you going to afford legal counsel of a quality to match what the Maitlands can afford? By the way, did I tell you that they're going to pay for Lacey's attorney, too?"

"I'll manage," Lindale sneered. "I'll pay for it by suing you for everything you've got, you lousy..."

As his prisoner ranted on and on, Ben counted the bars that ran the distance of the room and then those separating the two cells. When the guy finally paused for a breath, Ben drawled, "Well, you would have a fighting chance, I'll give you that. Even when we add abuse and rape to the assault charge, I can see where a slick lawyer could still help you walk. That's why I'm not taking any chances. I plan to add one more charge."

Lindale looked completely befuddled. "What other charge?"

Ben stepped over to the door that led back into the main part of the station and rapped twice. From the other side came a sound of shuffling and metal clanging together. When the door opened, Buck Preston filled the doorway, proudly holding up the traps he'd collected at the shack.

"Recognize these?" Ben asked, his tone conversational. "What a coincidence that they're the same kind of trap that was found clamped around Lem Cobb's leg. You remember Lem? He's the guy who died on the other side of the lake. His family's been convinced all along that there's been foul play involved with his death, and I've been following up on that theory since I've been back. Well, guess what? These traps are starting to convince me they're right. Sleep on it."

Roy Lindale screamed. He was still screaming obscenities and howling pleas when Ben left the station a half hour later.

When Lacey reached for her third brownie after dinner, Eve concluded neither the girl's lip nor today's trauma was giving her appetite any trouble. But enough was enough.

"Hon, maybe you'd better call it a day, or instead of worrying that you'll be up all night with nightmares, you'll be suffering from a tummy ache."

Observing from her usual spot at Eve's right elbow, Mama Lulu uttered an unconvinced grunt. "Ain't like she's a puppy. She'll know when she's full."

If she was an average American girl, Eve supposed that would be true; however, she'd already explained to Mama Lulu what kind of existence the teenager had been subjected to. She doubted Lacey had ever tasted anything close to the standing rib roast, spinach soufflé and stuffed baked potatoes they'd had for dinner, let alone Mama Lulu's scrumptious brownies.

"Well," she murmured, relenting, "it's not as though she can't afford to gain a few pounds."

"Sheesh. She'll thank you for that when she can't fit into all that stuff you bought her."

Bree's censure put an end to a hostile silence that had dragged on through most of dinner. She'd responded to a few of Lacey's signed questions, but had otherwise kept her eyes on her plate, forking her food into mush.

Eve put down her coffee cup, wondering if this was jealousy rearing its ugly head, not only of the few outfits Eve had purchased for Lacey on the way home, but the basic special attention being bestowed on the girl. She hoped not.

"You have a point. At her age, bad habits can set in rather quickly. We'll be more conscientious from here on out. Thank you, Bree."

"Don't patronize me."

"I wouldn't waste my time."

Bree shot her a quick glance, as if doubting her seriousness. Finally, she set down her fork and faced Eve. "What do you suppose it's like? I mean, being deaf and mute."

It was the first real interest Bree had shown in the girl since Eve had introduced them to each other. "Ask her," she said, nodding toward Lacey. "I told you, she's fairly skilled at reading lips, and I think she's more shy than uncomfortable with our questions. But she may prefer to have her condition described as hearing- and speaking-impaired."

"Oh, do let's be politically correct."

"What if we call it simple consideration? Not long

ago the term you used made people think mental re-
tardation.''

''Bummer.''

''You only have to be around Lacey for a few
minutes before you realize she has a fine head on her
shoulders. Granted, today scared her to death, and all
this change is overwhelming for her, but she's absorbing things quickly. She's studying you now.''

Bree swung around to look back at the girl. For a
moment they simply stared at each other, then Lacey
brought her fingers to her lips, flared them as she
made a circle around her face and returned to the
initial position.

''What does that mean?''

''Well, Justin told me that he doesn't think she's
had any formal training, that she's basically devised
her own language using the skills she had at nine or
ten when she became ill and lost her hearing. But I
have a hunch she just told you that she thinks you're
very pretty.''

''You said she lived like a hermit, she has no basis
of comparison.''

''Bree. Look at her. She's sincere, isn't that all that
matters?''

Although her stepdaughter appeared to have second
thoughts about making the glib remark, she also
pushed back her chair and rose. ''It's been a long day
in more ways than one. I'm going to go up to my
room.''

Eve had hoped the day's events, what had happened to Justin, would cause some core change in the
girl. She'd even fantasized on the drive home that her
stepdaughter would take Lacey under her wing, since

the girl's grandfather had been held over at the hospital, and doctors had agreed that he would be better off at a nursing home hereafter. What with Justin also having to stay under close medical supervision for a few days, the poor little thing had to be feeling more vulnerable than ever.

"Would you mind waiting a moment and taking Lacey up with you? No doubt she's ready to call it a day, herself."

"I'll give her an IOU. I have a headache and I need to lie down. Now."

Eve didn't know if that was the truth, but she definitely didn't want Lacey witnessing one of Bree's tantrums at this stage. "All right. I'll do it myself. Sleep well."

She watched Bree leave the room without offering another word to anyone, and wondered if things would ever improve. The teen had good reason to avoid Mama Lulu, whom she hadn't looked at once throughout dinner, but why reject the shy friendship offered by Lacey?

"Don't think I'll be on this planet long enough to understand that one." Mama Lulu circled the table to take away Bree's full plate.

"Well, if you ever do, fill me in," Eve murmured from behind her linen napkin.

Grunting her agreement, Mama Lulu headed for the kitchen, but before she got to the swinging door, there was a knock at the front.

"Anyone at home?"

Ben's voice was a welcome break to the gloom that had settled around them. "Come in!" Eve called back. "We're in the dining room!"

As she listened to his footsteps in the entryway, she mouthed, "Ben" to Lacey and made a circle above her left breast where he wore his badge. As expected, the girl's face transformed, pleasure lighting her face like moonlight on a night-blooming flower.

Ben paused in the doorway, removing his hat and smoothing his hair. It was the most self-conscious Eve had ever seen him.

"I don't mean to interrupt," he began, his concerned gaze scanning the room and settling on Lacey.

Before Eve could reply, Mama Lulu dismissed his apology with a flick of her hand. "Set yourself down and loosen that belt. I'm gonna fix you a plate. You gonna save me from fussin' t'myself the rest of the night for all that food settin' in the kitchen."

Ben winked at Lacey and placed his hat on the buffet, then he lowered his long length onto the chair that Bree had vacated. "You're sure there's enough? I've a powerful hunger."

Bursting into girlish giggles, Mama Lulu disappeared through the swinging door.

Ben smiled at Lacey again. "You look much better," he said with gruff tenderness, although the swelling from the two stitches in the girl's lip distorted her sweet mouth considerably, as did the black-and-blue bruises where she'd struck her forehead when she'd fallen.

She nodded and touched her heart and then pointed to Eve.

It had been quite an event getting the teen showered and her hair washed and dried, then woven into the neat French braid. But Lacey seemed to like the results only second to her new yellow silk blouse and sunflower-print skirt.

Ben turned to Eve, his gaze changing. Within heart-beats he had her feeling as if she'd swallowed one of Mama Lulu's pickled peppers whole.

"Congratulations," he murmured. "It appears as though the Yankees have triumphed again."

She appreciated his approval as much as his ability to retain any sense of humor at this point. "It wasn't a complete victory. Some of the Rebels have retreated and sworn not to be taken prisoner."

"We can be a stubborn lot. You'll just have to be more stubborn." He glanced around and spotted the bar in the armoire. "Would you mind if I poured myself a drink?"

Eve blinked, his riveting gaze and the loss of it sending her momentarily adrift. "Sorry? Oh!"

As she began to rise, Ben motioned for her to stay put. "I don't mind getting my own bourbon. Be-sides," he added, once his back was to her, "our little friend is giving herself whiplash watching us, and I don't think she needs to see me salivating as I watch you crossing the room."

Eve's throat had gone too dry to reply, but once she realized he was right about Lacey, she kept her eyes downcast as she reached for her wineglass and took a necessary swallow.

"Seriously, though," she said, in control again, "how are you? How did things go when you got back to the station?"

"I am 'seriously' somewhere between bone-assed tired and euphoric. I'll tell you why when we're alone."

He had to be kidding; she had to wait? Bad enough to hear him say "alone." She almost had to press her thighs together against the heat and dampness the sexy murmur spawned. She was relieved when the kitchen door swung open.

"Here we go," Mama Lulu sang, breezing into the room with a tray filled with enough for two men his size. "Gotcha double the biscuits, 'cuz I know how you like 'em."

Ben whistled as he returned to his seat and admired the plate she'd prepared for him. "Do you know how long it's been since I had prime rib?"

"Figured as much. I'm gonna fix you a plate to take home, too. You may wake up hungry again."

For the next fifteen, closer to twenty, minutes, the three women watched in varying degrees of rapt attention as Ben proved his healthy appetite, along with his ability to wrap *them* around his finger. By the time he pushed back from an empty plate, Eve worried that maybe he'd succeeded too well. Having always been wary of, or at least unreceptive to, the idea of infatuation, she didn't want Ben challenging, let alone tempting, her emotions on such a level, and she was somewhat relieved when Lacey broke the spell by covering a yawn with her hand.

"About time," Mama Lulu said, patting Lacey's back and signaling the girl. "Let's go upstairs, baby."

Lacey said good-night, hugging Eve and Ben with a sweet desperation that had Eve's throat aching. "It's so sad," she said to him as they watched the girl leave, holding Mama Lulu's hand.

She told him how after he'd left, they'd finally determined that Lacey was in fact eighteen, but that her formal schooling had been limited to what her grandfather had been able to teach her before he became ill. "Apparently, her mother died when she was thirteen, and it wasn't much after that when her grandfather suffered his first stroke. I think Roy's abuse began shortly thereafter. Can you imagine? A child still having to deal with deafness brought on by an illness is suddenly attacked by the last healthy relative she has left. Where does she turn? Who can she trust? My God, it's possible that she's been enduring that bastard for five years! How has she survived? I've seen people carried away in straitjackets after experiencing less."

"You'll drive yourself crazy if you dwell on that."

But Eve wasn't finished. "One specialist said there's a chance that she could speak before, Ben. That she may have stopped because of the abuse. Just willed herself silent to keep from screaming."

"The important thing now is that he's locked away. Also that she's still young, and has good people around her who want to help."

Eve knew she was letting her emotions take too much control, but dear God, she hadn't inured herself to where she could keep an emotional distance, not to something like this. What good was having skills, and strength, and the ability to make a difference if you didn't use *all* of those things to effect a positive change?

Ben glanced at all the doors. "Can we go somewhere less...accessible?"

"You don't have to lecture that I'm my own worst enemy."

"Hey, I'll give you my opinion whether you like

it or not, but I won't lecture. What I do need to do is talk to you.''

Something was up. Eve told herself that she should have noticed it before. Without wasting another moment, she led the way to the study.

It was all she could do to wait until the door was shut before asking, ''What's wrong?''

''Plenty.''

Before she could ask for specifics, he had an arm around her waist, a hand buried in her hair, and he was angling his mouth over hers. She barely managed a glimpse of the depth of hunger in his opaque eyes, before he was surrounding her, invading her with it. Before her mind had a chance to accept *that*, he reduced her to a creature of sensation, and she could only wrap her arms around his neck and let him.

So you need this, she told herself. The pressures of the day, the past few weeks, had left her oversensitive in some ways, surprisingly hollow in others. What she wasn't prepared for was how, when he slid his mouth to the side of her neck and bit not quite tenderly, she gasped and almost climaxed there and then.

He muttered a brief apology.

''It's...okay,'' she whispered back shakily. ''It's the same for me.''

''Yeah?''

''Yeah.''

That unleashed something else in him. His hands began to roam with more intent, every kiss was a prologue to the next.

''Ben...''

''That's for smiling the way you did through dinner so that I could hardly swallow.''

"You did okay."

"Did I?" He slid his hands to her hips and pulled her closer, lifted and rubbed her against an arousal that proved otherwise. "And that's for having an answer to everything."

Finally, he tore at the tie at her waist, opened the wraparound copper and green satin lounge gown she'd changed into after getting Lacey cleaned up. Brushing it aside, he closed his mouth over her chemise-covered breast. "And that's for telling me you won't see me tonight."

Eve filled her hands with his hair and forced his head up so she could see his face. "When did I say that?"

"You didn't. But you will."

This time he took her mouth and drove his tongue deep, crushed her body against his. Soon every muscle in her arms ached from answering this burst of passion and from challenging with her own; soon every nerve in her body pulsated from excitement and a need for more.

"*Yes.*" The word became a hiss as he exhaled. "More. Stay with me. Do it with your tongue. Show me how you'd want it—fast, like this...? Or slow, like...?"

Both ways. Every way. She did everything but climb him like a tree, and would have done that, she realized, if he asked her to.

Then, abruptly, he moaned, "Enough," and burying his face in her hair, he rocked her back and forth, back and forth. His hold had never been so fierce, so desperate. "Ah, hell. I'm sorry."

She couldn't breathe, let alone think. "You have a mean streak in you, Rader."

."It's your fault, Red. You shouldn't show up in my mind every few minutes like a flash of sheet lightning."

"I'll turn over a new leaf immediately."

"Sure. Go ruin what little fun I have in life."

She chuckled, rubbed her face against his shoulder, his neck, the whiskers he'd been rubbing against her breasts as if he wanted some part of him to stay with her after he was sent home. "I'm too wrung-out to keep up with you, with this, tonight."

"Me, too. That's the hell of it. I'm beat. And I'm angry at half of the world. But my friend south of the border hears your voice and warns me that I'm going to have to make like a damned centipede to get out of here with my dignity intact."

If this was what his father had been like, no wonder even married women had risked everything for a Rader. "If you'd let go, I'd get you a cup of coffee, and by the time Mama Lulu comes down from tucking in Lacey, you and your...pal, wouldn't make a wake on a Petri dish."

"Smart-ass." He ran his hands from her hair to her hips again. "I have a better idea."

"We can't."

"Lock the door."

"That's assuming you could be fast."

"Red, you can't imagine how fast I could be."

"But then what about me?"

"Lock the door. You won't regret it."

"You might if Mama Lulu returns, checks the door and finds it locked, but we don't answer, so she circles out back to peer in the window, only to discover you turned that birthmark on your butt into a cute tattoo of a pair of lips.''

He crushed her against him as his body shook, not from uncontrollable passion, she knew, grinning, but from unrestrained laughter. She liked that, to be able to make him feel positive emotions and give him a few moments of something other than the grimness he'd been dealing with.

''Well, hell,'' he groaned at last. ''I thought it was dark enough the other night that I wouldn't have to own up to that.''

''If I didn't miss the candle, you can't think I'd miss the ultimate kiss-my-ass insignia? I've been wanting to ask you why?''

''A souvenir from my days in the service. Never start a drinking contest with sailors.''

''It's high up there on my list of don'ts.''

Although he smiled, Ben's eyes were serious as he slid his hands into her hair again and tilted her face up to his. ''After a day like today, how is it possible to laugh?''

''We're too big to cry.''

He stroked her cheeks with his thumbs. ''I want you. I know it's not going to happen tonight—''

''I can't allow myself to think about me right now.''

''Fortunately, I have the capacity to be selfish for both of us.''

He said that so seriously, she could barely keep a straight face. ''That's taking martyrdom to a new realm.''

''It would be worth it.'' Ben's gaze roamed over

her from head to breast. "Worth it to see you stretched across my bed again. I want to feel you wrapped around me. You were so tight, so hot... Look at you. All I have to do is remind you how it was and your nipples respond as if I've already made them wet. Are you wet here, too?" he murmured, dexterous fingers exploring beyond lace and silk.

Eve gasped. "Ben!"

One second he looked as though he might back her onto the couch—with force if necessary—and the next he was spinning away to lean heavily on Sumner's desk. Every breath tightened his shirt over his broad shoulders, and Eve could feel his tension radiate across the room at her.

"That was too close."

"Ben, I'm sorry."

"Don't be. I shouldn't have assumed I could..."

She watched his Adam's apple rise and fall as he struggled for control; watched as physical misery played out on every feature. His torment matched her own, and had her wondering about what they were doing. It could be that they were letting things get too deep, too fast?

"The hell of it is, I didn't come here to jump your bones. Admire them, definitely," he amended with a wicked sidelong glance. Then he grew serious again. "But I have news." Taking a deep breath, he crossed back to her. "We've had a development. It's Lindale."

He spent the next minute telling her about sending Buck Preston to the Lindale home, and what had been found there. The news proved both elating and troubling to Eve.

"Oh, Ben, that's wonderful! Did he admit the traps were his? Was he there the night—the night it happened?"

"I haven't gotten him to that point yet. For all his recklessness, he's pretty careful when it comes to talking. I've had to play him like a game fish, reeling him in a bit, then giving him some slack. I think I'll have what I want by tomorrow."

"His lawyer can't be happy about that."

"He doesn't have one. Yet." Ben shrugged at her doleful look. "So I'm pushing the rules. I'm still within the parameters of the law."

"Whose?"

"Just let me worry about that."

Eve didn't care for being dismissed, but she was already moving on to more important issues. "Has he said anything about the Cobbs? Do you think...don't tell me that Bree was involved with a—a pig like— Please. Not Roy Lindale?"

"I'll be able to tell you more by tomorrow."

To think it could all be over soon. Finally. "Do I say anything to her? To Mama Lulu?"

"Absolutely not. I know that sets you up for a sleepless night, but it can't be helped."

"Why should things change now?"

His look said he wanted to touch her again, but he kept his distance. "Where will you be tomorrow? Back in Greenville?"

She nodded, too aware of how alone she felt without his arms around her. "I know I'm asking for too much to hope Justin's doctors will release him in another day or two, but I think he'll recuperate faster here where he can also see Lacey. And I need to look into nursing homes for her grandfather. Then there may also be power-of-attorney matters that need attention. The family attorney—I don't know if you ever met Glenn Sawyer in the old days?—will be here later in the day to discuss that and Lacey's situation in general, also the Cobb matter, and Bree.''

"There's something you'd better consider. If Bree needs legal counsel, there may be a conflict of interest for him to represent Lacey and her grandfather.''

"You mean it's rather like the mistress of Maitland Hall sleeping with the cop who might put her step-daughter in jail?''

Ben's expression remained impassive. "Exactly like that. Only more public.''

"I'll lay it out for him and see what he says.''

"You're going to be busier than ever.''

"Don't remind me.''

"And I'll be alone with my fantasies.''

She met his intimate gaze, such a contradiction to his sardonic tone, and her body caught fire all over again. "Maybe that's not an entirely bad thing. What's the old saying about starving a fever?''

He didn't give her an answer, at least not a verbal one. What he did do was to close the distance between them, slip a hand behind her neck and draw her close for a kiss that within seconds had her melting against him.

When he finally let her go, his breathing wasn't any steadier than hers. There was also a glint of anger in his eyes.

"Don't shut us down. Not yet.''

He was crediting her with too much discipline, but

she was going to try to convince herself that it was possible. She had to.

Ben swore under his breath and reached for the doorknob.

As she listened to him retrieve his hat and storm out of the house, Eve wandered out to the foyer, but had to lower herself onto the velvet bench, she felt so weak. What she'd done needed doing. One of them had to be sensible. But dear heaven, the wildness in him called to something kindred in her.

How much easier life had been when she hadn't known that.

If she had been sleeping, Bree doubted she would have heard the soft keening.

For a few moments she lay in bed, certain of where the sound came from but reluctant to investigate. It wasn't her job to baby-sit Justin's sweetie, and she still wasn't feeling great herself. Hell, one champion of lost causes in the family was enough.

But the crying didn't stop, and the longer she listened, the more it pricked at her conscience.

Finally accepting that she wouldn't get *any* sleep without doing something, she rose and unlocked the connecting door between their rooms. It was fairly light in Lacey's bedroom due to the night-light Eve or Mama Lulu had put in there for her, and Bree could see the girl wrapped in a tight ball in the corner behind the rocking chair.

Brushing her hair behind her ears, Bree cautiously approached her, hoping she didn't startle the kid. The last thing she wanted was for Eve to charge in and accuse her of trying something.

Moving the chair out of the way, she crouched before the girl, her sleep shirt, which she wore instead of a bathrobe, slipping off one shoulder. Lacey was wearing a lawn gown that made her look as if she'd stepped straight out of *Gone With the Wind*. Bree wouldn't be caught dead in something so old-fashioned, but considering what they'd said happened to the poor thing, maybe the kid needed a sense of being covered.

"Hey," she whispered. "What's up? Some people like to sleep at this hour." It was probably too dark for the girl to read her lips, but she'd spoken as much for herself as Lacey because she couldn't stand hearing people cry, and had never known what to do around those who became emotional.

She squeezed the girl's shoulder to get her attention, and asked, "Bad dreams?"

Lacey leaned a bit closer, peered at her before slowly nodding.

Certain she was having a problem understanding her, Bree went to switch on the nightstand lamp. "It's all right now," she said, returning to the upset girl. "You're safe here."

The girl sighed and offered a halfhearted shrug.

"So don't believe me. Why should you be different than anyone else?" As soon as she said that, Bree grimaced. "I didn't mean to be a bitch. It's just that I have some problems of my own, and I guess I was feeling a little sorry for myself. Okay, a lot sorry for myself."

Tapping her chest and spreading her arms to encompass the room, Lacey then touched her finger to her forehead and shrugged.

"What do you mean, why? Oh, why when I have everything?" Bree eyed the room. "I hate to break this to you, kiddo, but this is nothing compared to what's out there, and I want my share of it. Maybe I've made some bad choices," she added softly, more for her own benefit than the girl watching her so attentively. She bit her lower lip as she thought of her biggest mistake last night, and how there could be long-term ramifications she was only beginning to consider. "But the bottom line is that I wouldn't be happy to have a pretty little house where you could raise flowers and bake bread for some guy day in day out."

When Lacey made a bird-flying signal with her hands, Bree chuckled.

"No, goose. I'm going to have my own personal jet, and visit a different country every week. But—" she made a face "—Eve will make sure I have a degree tucked under each arm before I get to do that."

At the mention of Eve, Lacey touched Bree's lips and shook her head.

"That's about right, you would think she walks on water. Wait until Justin gets home. You'll want to sit with him, but she'll decide you need to do lessons. Jeez...I can't believe anyone as innocent as you exists."

Lacey formed a *J* with her index finger and thumb.

"Yeah, Justin. He's my twin, you know. Did he tell you? No...I guess he thought of more interesting things to talk about." She watched the girl pretend to draw. "He sketched you. Yeah, I've been in his room and seen his work. That boy's got one big crush on you."

When Lacey frowned and shrugged, Bree gave her a lopsided smile. "You don't know what crush means?" She made the *J* sign and then put both hands over her heart and sighed like a starlet in an old silent film then pointed at her.

Even with soft pink lighting, she could tell Lacey blushed.

"Listen, my a— It's damned uncomfortable on this hardwood floor. C'mon up on the bed and I'll sit with you until you feel sleepy, okay?"

Once settled on the queen-size bed, she told the girl about growing up here, about how much she loved riding and how she wouldn't mind helping her do something with her hair and face. "You really could be cute in a cuddly, comfortable sort of way, and that's not a putdown, okay? Sheesh, if I said that to one of the girls I went to school with, they'd scratch my eyes out. Girls are so thin-skinned around here. You don't know this, but you've probably been better off not having any friends."

Lacey focused on the hair idea and scrambled off the bed to get a brush and comb that Eve had given her earlier.

Bree unwrapped the braid and showed her how she would look with it coiled up on her head for a party, and in a ponytail, and in a more elaborate French braid. Lacey liked the latter best and once again insisted on keeping it that way.

"Okay, but if you wake up with sore hair in the morning, don't blame me," Bree told her.

She had begun doing the other girl's nails when the door opened and Eve stuck her head in.

"Bree." For once she seemed at a loss for words.

"I was on my way to bed and saw the light under the door. Is everything okay?"

"Don't worry, I'm not torturing or corrupting her," Bree shot back. But one look at Eve's weary expression had her regretting her immediate attack. "She had a nightmare," she added matter-of-factly. "I thought I'd hang around a while and keep her mind off it."

"That's...nice of you, Bree."

"Don't blow it out of proportion. It's not a big deal."

"Right. Wouldn't think of it. Is there anything you two need?"

"We're fine."

"Then I'm going to turn in. Good night."

After she shut the door, Bree turned back to Lacey and made a comical face.

"Did you figure out yet that we're not best friends?"

Lacey pointed to the door and then made a big heart with her fingers.

"'All heart,' huh? Well, let me give you a crash course about life—it's easy to be generous when you're spending someone else's money."

Naturally, her wide-eyed companion didn't follow much of her muttering, and Bree decided that was all right, too. Justin wouldn't thank her for dragging his sweetie into her head-butting contests with Eve.

She didn't know how long she sat there thinking about things, but when she glanced down again, Lacey had curled amid the mountain of pillows Mama Lulu had set out for her like some fairy-tale princess and was drifting off to sleep. It left Bree with ambivalent feelings. This was the stepdaughter Eve should have gotten for her fantasy family. Gentle Justin definitely deserved her. Lacey Lindale was like him—a nice kid. About as exciting as oatmeal, and damaged, but probably not beyond repair.

Almost envious, Bree drew the sheet over the sleeping girl, turned out the bedstand light and returned to her room. She didn't close the door entirely, in case Lacey suffered another bad dream; but she didn't go to bed, either. Still restless, she went to the window seat, curling up there to watch the stars creeping across the sky.

Yes, Lacey belonged here, but she didn't. No telling where she belonged out there, either; she only knew she was getting desperate to find out and to put her history in Parish behind her.

Bree bit on her thumbnail, shadows of memories, snatches of conversations haunting her. Were they real?

Oh, God, oh, God, oh, God. What if I was there? What if I am guilty of what they say?

18

The scene she'd glimpsed in Lacey's room preoccupied Eve's mind quite a bit over the next few days, but that wasn't to say her mind and her time didn't stay challenged. Every day was full, with plenty going on to hurry sundown—always before she was ready. So much so that sometimes she wondered if she might finally run out of energy before their lives returned to some semblance of normality. Life at Maitland Hall had always been demanding, but it hadn't been this hectic since those first days after Sumner passed, and she yearned for the days when she could spend a morning weeding the flower beds. That last morning almost five weeks back now seemed more like a year ago.

A fever kept Justin in the hospital an extra few days. Although worried, Eve had meetings with lawyers that kept her from driving the hospital staff to distraction. There were also the trips to the nursing home she and Lacey had chosen for Lacey's grandfather, and taking care of all the legalities that entailed. Most stressful were the sessions Lacey had with the hospital-recommended psychiatrist; the teen always came out of those needing extra hugs, and a little quiet time.

The good news was the suggestion that the sooner Lacey was encouraged to assimilate into her new social surroundings, the faster she would put past trauma behind her. That had Eve locating a teacher in Greenville who provided the girl with books and videos to polish and mainstream her signing skills. Eve made a point of joining her as much as possible, discovering that the unique communication technique was an art form all its own.

"Eve," her stepson said Wednesday morning after enjoying his first breakfast at home. He'd touched her hand to stay her as she came to remove his tray. "How do I thank you for all you're doing?"

She kissed one of the few spots on his dear face that didn't resemble a hand-painted Easter egg. "You don't. You simply concentrate on getting well so you can help keep up with that little whirlwind downstairs in the kitchen. She has a bad habit of reminding me that I'm not eighteen anymore."

"It's a deal." But his smile soon yielded to a frown of concern. "What's the latest on Roy? Has Chief Rader called with anything new?"

He'd asked every time the phone rang yesterday. She was glad that she could update him now with the information that her attorney, Glenn Sawyer, had filed assault charges on Lindale on behalf of Justin, while at the same time Glenn's associate, Beau Chandler, had filed for Lacey's years of abuse. She added that Ben had stopped by last night with news that due to his pending arraignment, Roy Lindale was being transferred to the county jail today. Those charges alone could put him behind bars for some time, but they were hardly enough to satisfy Eve's desire for justice. She hoped Ben would soon slap him with manslaughter charges, as well. She hadn't shared the news about the traps with Justin or Lacey, wanting to wait until they were stronger. As for Ben, he was holding back on the last charge, insisting they needed that missing trap to perfect their case.

Alone with Ben in the study yesterday evening, Eve had argued about that. "Surely a jury would realize the missing trap and those you found are all his. You said he'd admitted to having hunted in the area in the past. Isn't circumstantial evidence enough?"

"If he was still walking free, and I was desperate, with no other way to get him behind bars, sure. But we have him where we want him."

"What if he posts bond and runs?"

"If the judge allowed it—and your attorney pals assure me that they'll argue strongly against that due to the threats Lindale made to the kids—he would need considerable financial help. That means someone would have to come forward to get him out, and *that* would be exposure nobody's likely to risk."

"Not if it was handled through an attorney. Client-attorney privilege? We might not ever find out who posted bond."

Ben admitted that was a possibility, but he was betting against its happening. "Old Roy is acting trapped and rattled. That suggests he doesn't have a big support group to encourage his silence. So, next, I'm going to show him the cigarette butt. It's not his, he's a chewer, but I think he knows who did drop it that night."

Although she'd shared the Cobb family's doubts about the coroner's reports and had been encouraged when Ben found that disturbing piece of evidence, the picture that was evolving in Eve's mind was leaving her shaken.

"Why? It always comes back to why?" she'd whispered. "Lem was...Lem. But I can't see him having anything to do with trash like Roy Lindale."

"There was money involved, that's reason enough. We'll find out the rest sooner or later," Ben had promised. "Have patience."

Eve had patience...and gratitude, because Ben was giving her the space she'd asked him for. But she also had Bree.

Her stepdaughter's good behavior lasted less than forty-eight hours after Justin returned home. On the first of August, the morning Justin was to return to Greenville to have his stitches removed, Eve rose early, as planned, and knocked on Bree's door to ask if she wanted to come along and make a day of it. When there was no answer, she'd peeked inside and found the bed hadn't even been slept in. What's more, Bree was just sneaking in, having climbed up a trellis—a near-miraculous feat considering her condition.

There was no point in arguing. Once it was evident that the girl was high enough to have never known if she'd slipped and broken her neck, Eve backed out of the room and shut the door.

Justin was told none of this. Eve wouldn't risk destroying the fragile threads of affection that were being rewoven between the twins since he'd learned how good Bree had been to Lacey. However, upon arriving home late that afternoon and finding Bree still passed out, she swallowed her pride and phoned Ben for advice.

"I don't know what else to do," she told him from Sumner's study. "I take her keys, she comes up with another set, or she takes someone else's vehicle. I can't lock her in her room, and short of posting a guard outside twenty-four hours a day, I can't put her under house arrest. I'm afraid putting her in a clinic is my only option. You know, the tough-love routine."

"And then what? So she dries out for a few weeks. You know what'll happen the minute she gets back?"

"Whoever is supplying her will pull her right back into her addiction."

"Right. What's more, she'll hate you for interfering."

"Hello? She already hates me."

"I don't know." Ben sounded philosophical. "She's angry and resentful, but on some level I think she admires you. So do I," he said, a different tone entering his voice. "And even if this is bad timing, I have to say it. I miss you."

Eve closed her eyes. "I miss you, too."

"Enough to be with me again?"

Not really...except every time she heard his name, his voice, read about him in the paper. But even as Eve thrilled at hearing his flattering admission, she was troubled, too. He was no Boy Scout and she was no ingenue. The desire he stirred in her was as mature as it was overwhelming, and if allowed too free a rein... Neither of them had room in their lives for such a reckless affair.

"That's a speaking silence, Red."

Eve groaned softly, resting her head in her hand as she sat at the desk. "I'm torn enough as it is. I'm living under a roof with three sexually active teenagers, one of whom is clearly taking terrifying risks. Sneaking off to meet you would be setting the worst of examples. It is an all-out affair you're driving at, isn't it?''

''To commence the sooner the better.'' When she didn't reply, his sigh reflected sheer frustration. ''It beats me why the two people who have a legitimate right to do it, can't. Will you at least— Oh, hell,'' he said, suddenly lowering his voice. ''Someone's coming in. *We need to resolve this. Call me, Red.*''

When Eve heard the click that told her he'd hung up, she was more relieved than upset.

''Call me, Red.''

The way things were going, if Bree didn't drive her to drink, Ben would.

The next afternoon, Eve got word that the contractor had come to finally bulldoze the old Rader homestead. The news brought a surprisingly strong wave of empathy, and the thought that she should call Ben and ask him if he wanted one last look at the place. Only the escalating tension between them, as well as the time constraints on the demolition crew, had her resisting.

She let Dewitt drive her over to the site in his truck. She'd wanted a word with the crew's supervisor to ensure certain trees would be saved.

''Ignore me and do what you have to do,'' she told her foreman after the matter was settled. ''I'll watch for a few minutes and walk back to the house. I've been holed up in waiting rooms and meetings so much, the exercise will be welcome.''

As the bulldozer began crushing the local love nest, she wondered if Bree had been meeting her lover here. She hoped not. She prayed that whoever the girl had been giving herself to had respected her enough to provide her with clean sheets. And used protection.

"Masochist," she muttered, pressing the heels of her hands against her eyes. For a moment, the pounding in her ears had her wondering if she was developing a migraine. Then it sunk in that the sound was coming from behind her. Glancing over her shoulder, she saw Perry emerging from Bellemere.

How debonair he looked on his favorite mount, Lancer. Under the circumstances, Eve couldn't help but have second thoughts about Bree's previous attraction to him. He might have been good for her, and the difference in their ages and levels of sophistication had been proven of less consequence, considering the indifferent wretch the teenager was obviously involved with now. Unfortunately, even if she tried to let Bree know she'd changed her mind, Perry had a choice in the matter, and he'd made it clear who he was interested in.

He brought his stallion to a halt before her. "Hey, stranger."

His smile was wry, his gaze admiring. Heaven knew why, she thought with self-deprecation. True, she was wearing a cool green sheath that complemented her coloring, but she'd traded her heels and hose for floppy sandals for this expedition; what's more, she'd been so preoccupied, she'd neglected to replace her lipstick after lunch.

"Hello. Did all the noise make you curious?"

"That and the phone call I didn't get."

"The...? Perry!" She clapped her hand over her mouth, belatedly remembering. "I promised to call you today!"

"Story of my life—out of sight, out of mind."

It was good of him to be gallant about her blunder, even when she didn't want the personal attention. And he'd already been extremely kind to her and the family. Upon hearing the news about Justin, he'd phoned to offer his support and assistance, and when she'd assured him that they had everything under control, he'd sent over the loveliest basket of flowers for Lacey, and another of hard-to-find art films for Justin. During her thank-you call, he'd asked to come over for the folder on the library plans, in order to pick up where they'd left off to locate a contractor. She'd put him off until today, but had forgotten to get back to him about a time.

"I'm so sorry," she began.

"Forgiven. It wasn't a locked-in appointment. But I am getting upset with you for another reason." He nodded at the half-toppled building that had been the Rader homestead. "Don't you have enough on your plate without taking on this?"

"This was when they could fit us in."

Perry gave her one of his infamous arched-eyebrow looks. "Since when does a Maitland get 'fit in'?"

"When she doesn't feel it serves anyone well to wield her clout."

He considered that and nodded his approval. "And you wonder why I'm your biggest fan. But damn it all, Eve—"

"Please don't lecture, Perry. I need a friend, not another conscience."

"You've got him, love. How's the ever-extending family?"

"We have our good moments, and those that would get us in the Dysfunctional Family Hall of Fame. Thank you for asking."

"You know I want to do more."

He wasn't simply flirting now to cheer her up; his eyes spoke of serious invitation, as they had that afternoon on his terrace. She told herself that she had to be certifiable not to be panting over him. Good grief, he *did* resemble a hero out of a Jane Austen novel, as some socialite had described him at an event they'd all attended in Oxford. He even looked the part today, dressed in his silk shirt and dove-gray riding breeches. But as fate would have it, it was another man who sent her pulse skittering, and her body into hot flashes, and it didn't make any difference that he wasn't smooth or debonair or even polite at times.

"Dear Perry...at this stage I wouldn't inflict us on my worst enemy, let alone a friend." She searched her mind to think of a way to change the subject. "By the way, weren't you supposed to go to some prestigious horse auction this week?"

"I did. I'm back."

"Ah. The trucks should be rolling in any time now," she said, admiring the haughty toss of his stallion's head.

Perry frowned. "Pardon?"

"That was a joke. Remember Ben—Chief Rader complaining about your delivery trucks keeping him awake? I thought if you bought any new stock, you'd need new supplies and that would mean—" She waved away the comment. "Forget it. It's not worth explaining."

"No, no. I'd just forgotten. Is he still complaining about the noise?"

"Not that I know of."

He waited, as if wanting her to say more. When she didn't, he added, "And how is our patient?"

Now *there* was a question she didn't mind tackling. "Justin's going to be fine. Lacey will be, too. They were so lucky, and they're a delight to watch. They give and take a unique strength from each other that makes you think you're with a couple who've been together for...well, for years. I don't know whether to be proud, worried or envious." She shrugged, and a little self-conscious at the way he studied her as though she was a complicated dessert he didn't quite know how to handle, she wrapped her arms around her waist. "The trick now is to keep all the appointments that make up a good part of our schedule these days. Speaking of which, I apologize again about having to put our plans on hold, especially since I'm the one who promised the community a new library soon."

"They waited this long, they can wait a bit longer. I'm not sure I can, though." He leaned over and brushed a strand of hair away from her mouth that a light breeze had carried there. "Why don't you—"

He was cut off by the sound of an approaching vehicle, and when Eve began to look to her right to see who else was coming, Perry shifted his hand to the back of her neck and tugged her toward him. For an instant she had a horrible fear that the spirited horse would balk and step on her, then that was replaced by the not-quite-centered press of Perry's lips against hers.

It created quite a bang...or was that a door?

"Come for dinner," he murmured upon releasing her. "I insist you do this for you. Ah, Benjamin. As usual, your timing leaves something to be desired."

Once Eve had prided herself on the ability to maintain her focus, but at the sound of Ben's name, her palms grew instantly damp. Ben didn't like Perry being within one continent of her just on a matter of principle, and considering what Perry had pulled... She spun around only to be impaled by his riveting gaze.

"Sorry to interrupt."

His gaze shot past her to the rubble. What he was thinking was anyone's guess, but Eve found herself having to lick her lips to be able to speak. The delay allowed Perry to beat her to it.

"She's concerned you wouldn't take it well, but there wasn't time to inform you. Scheduling problems with the contractor and all that."

Ben ignored him. To her, he said, "I stopped at the house first."

Convinced he wouldn't do that unless he had either very good or bad news, she immediately suspected the worst. "What's wrong?"

"We have to talk." This time Ben did give Perry a pointed look. "Do you mind?"

"I do have to be going, now that there are plans to see to." Perry smiled at Eve. "See you later, love."

"Perry, really, I—"

He rode off before she could finish, leaving her

standing there with her mouth open. She hated being put in a position where she became ineffectual, and she liked the vibes generating from Ben even less.

"Get in the truck," he said, his voice barely more than a growl.

The rude command was exactly what she needed to get back in gear. "Excuse me. When did I lose the right to speak or to make my own decisions? I swear, between Perry and you—"

"You want to finish making a spectacle of yourself in front of all those boys," he shot back, nodding to the crew, "we can do that. But I suggest you get in the truck."

Almost tempted to call his bluff, she saw the tension in his jaw, the glint in his eyes, and decided her stand on principle would be better served in the Blazer; she definitely didn't need to stir up more gossip. She did, however, give him a sharp look as she followed his directive.

When he settled behind the steering wheel, she asked with exaggerated politeness, "Are we having a good time yet?"

"You looked as though you were."

"What on earth is wrong with you? I came up here with Dewitt to sign a release and to point out a few trees I wanted protected. Perry just showed up. I have no control over where he rides."

"You do about who kisses you."

"Would you have been happier if I'd wiped the back of my hand across my mouth and spit at the ground? He took me by surprise. I realize now what he was doing—which I'll take care of in my own way and time—but when did you get the right to act like a... What are you *doing?*"

He'd turned into the side gate and had started up the dirt road, passing his place only to brake hard. The lurching truck shot her forward and she had to grab at the dashboard to keep from flying into the windshield.

She stared in disbelief as he not only backed up, but parked the truck at the house and killed the engine. "Are you out of your mind?"

Ignoring her, he climbed out of the truck, came around to her side and jerked open the passenger door.

"You have to be kidding, I'm not going in there with you. What if someone sees? Ben!" She winced at the painful hold he took of her arm. *"Damn you..."*

She could have put up more of a struggle, not that he wouldn't still get his way in the end; but at least she would have had the satisfaction of knowing she'd made her point. But ever-respectful of the family's image, she decided if someone was watching, it would be better to make them think they had a business matter to discuss.

Once inside, though, she jerked free, ready to do battle. "If this is your idea of a seduction scene, you missed my mood by a long shot."

"You told me there was nothing between you two." He took a step toward her.

The purposeful look on his face had her taking a step back. "That kiss had less to do with me than Perry trying to get a reaction out of you." It was a sensible reminder; unfortunately, she ruined the effect by backing into the wall.

Ben placed his hands on either side of her head. "Whether we wanted it or not, we are lovers," he said with deceptive softness. "And you know it."

Heaven help her, he was pushing her onto a roller coaster she wasn't prepared to ride. "One night doesn't establish anything, you've made that clear yourself."

"One night and one afternoon does," he replied, diving for her mouth.

In the last second she turned her head aside, sending his hot lips and hotter breath searing across her cheek, and his kiss landing at the sensitive skin below her ear. Every nerve ending in the area sent frissons reverberating through her, and she stiffened, hoping to outlast their tempting messages. In self-defense she pushed against his chest and tried to twist her body free, but he simply grabbed her wrists, clamped them against the wall and held the rest of her body there with his. The move told her immediately that although his mind wanted to pick a fight, the rest of him had other ideas.

"Damn it, Red, kiss me," he demanded, seeking her mouth again.

"Right after I die my hair blond. Ben, for the love of— I have to get home. Your screen door isn't even latched! Have you lost your...?"

She didn't finish because he'd given up on the wrestling match for her mouth to slide his down her neck. He tortured its tender length, found her pulse, uttered a deep satisfied moan at the frantic flutter he read there.

"That's what I wanted to know. I make you as nuts as you make me."

"No! I'm only…I'm just…"

He didn't listen, but moved on…to her chest, her abdomen… His hands took a wider route, shaping swells and curves, and while his mouth lingered to heat her womb, he slipped his hands to the hem of her silk sheath and reversed the journey, this time his fingers caressing bare skin.

Eve pushed at his shoulders, achingly aware that if she didn't get away soon, she was going to make an awful fool of herself. She clasped his head between her hands. "Stop it! You can't…"

His nose nuzzled the center lace panel of her panties, his breath both tickled and tormented. But her protest did have him rising, only to take her dress with him on the journey. To Eve's dismay, it ended up just above her breasts, which he framed with his hands to bury his face in the lusher cleavage.

Mouth and thumbs stroked over the thin lace of her bra and then tugged it down to do it again to the softer skin it had been protecting. That was her undoing, that heat and moisture laving and seducing. Suddenly, instead of pushing him away she was trying to merge her body with his; instead of trying to avoid the electric contact with his strong legs and the blatant thrust of his hips against hers, she arched closer in an attempt to intensify the pressure. Finally, when he locked his mouth to hers again, she yielded to the wildness in her and tightened the arms she wrapped around his neck.

Later her conscience would taunt her. Much later she would call herself every kind of fool. It didn't change the truth. She had been wanting this again, dreaming about it and him…so much so that nothing else mattered.

As he feasted on her mouth and ran his hands over and over her body, she came more and more alive…an odd thing, when all this time she thought she already felt too much. But those talented hands proved how much else he had to show her as he delved deeper and stole her moans just as he was taking everything else he wanted.

Her reward was that she'd never been so aroused, and she didn't want it to end until she knew what it was like to have him filling her, and pulsating inside her while she went out of control.

Their hands bumped, their fingers tangled in the race to strip her and release him. By the time they'd succeeded, they were breathing like divers on their last seconds of oxygen. Then he was lifting and entering her. She wrapped her legs around him as mouth sought mouth, devouring cries and moans with the same relish they'd consumed kisses. It was as if they knew this mindless insanity, this fiercely choreographed bliss was doomed to be as brief as it was breathtaking. And when they found what they'd been seeking, it was as one, and they held each other tight against the bone-trembling assault of what had been invited…and what hadn't.

Ben waited for the inevitable weakness, the emptiness to return. It didn't come. What did was a new stirring.

So the last time hadn't been a fluke.

The throaty sound Eve made told him that she felt

it, too, and the soft, feathery kisses she skimmed all over his face told him that she was dealing with a similar, relentless appetite.

"Hold on," he muttered, and carried her to his room.

He had no idea how he managed to get to the bed without breaking both their necks. They shouldn't have made it. But as he lowered her to the mattress, neither of them was exhibiting any signs of triumph. In fact, he didn't like his reactions altogether, let alone care for the way she was looking at him. They might as well have been strangers meeting for the first time.

"What?" he demanded.

"You don't want to know."

Not if she intended to blow him out of the water and tell him that what they'd just shared wasn't as fantastic for her as it was for him. But he suspected what she had to say wasn't that. Still, he couldn't resist flicking open the front catch of her demi-bra and brushing aside the ivory lace with his nose and lips to make sure.

"Try me."

"I'm not sure I want to deal with it, either."

"Okay, so you're a little overwhelmed that we can't keep our hands off each other. It's the same way for me."

"Leave it alone, Ben. You're only seeing a claw. But attached to that is a whole monster, and there's no sense in both of us having to face what we're in for sooner than necessary. You'll like it even less than I do."

He didn't understand one damned thing she was

talking about and, wanting her to stop, he cupped her breasts, stroked the undersides and nuzzled her nipples, fascinated with how the subtlest caress changed them. "You want this," he murmured, wetting her.

She remained silent at first. It suited him fine if that's what she wanted, but the soft catch in her breathing gave her away, so did the way she tightened her legs around him.

"Yes," she finally whispered.

The resignation in her voice had him abandoning his current fixation to study her face. She had never looked lovelier to him with her hair in wild disarray, her face flushed from passion but otherwise almost free of makeup, her lips blushing and swollen from his kisses, and her eyes...always those marvelous, mysterious eyes withholding a secret or two. Just looking at her filled him with an odd combination of awe and possessiveness. But he wasn't comfortable with the underlying fragility he sensed in her.

Then it struck him. "Hell. I didn't protect you. That's it, isn't it?" It wasn't that it had slipped his mind, he simply hadn't been able to wait. "Eve..."

"Don't say it." She covered her face with her hands. "I refuse to even consider that can be a problem at this point. Not on top of everything else going on."

Ben shifted higher on one elbow. "Then what's wrong? All I did was force you to be honest about us."

"Honest." She let her hands fall beside her head. "You're not being honest, Ben. Neither am I, for that matter."

The expression in her eyes had him imagining the

click of a gun hammer being locked back. "Could you be a little clearer?"

"Who was it that was talking about the acorn not falling far from the tree?" With a humorless laugh, she looked away. "But then don't ask me what my excuse is. Alice Potter and I aren't related in the least."

That was the last name he wanted to hear, especially now. "Is that supposed to be some kind of joke? You're suggesting we're no different than *them?*" He surprised himself at the bitterness he'd injected into the last word.

Her gaze remained vague, turned inward. "It's poetic justice, really, your arrogance about your father's choices, and my conceited thinking that I was saving the world from itself and therefore deserved to be protected from and be above such petty annoyances like love. Don't you know someone somewhere is having the biggest laugh at our expense?"

"You can't compare this, us, with them. Instead of being straightforward with each other, they acted like victims who had no choice and were being driven by something bigger."

"You won't turn to a block of salt if you say it, although knowing you, you'll think the salt preferable. Maybe I do, too." Her smile was sad. "Love, Ben. You think your father invited it? You think Alice did?"

"Just because I lost it and dragged you in here, you think we're—" he couldn't say it "—repeating history?"

"I warned you to let it go."

Her calm conviction made him want to wrap his

hands around her neck and squeeze until she took the words back. He'd only let her get away with criticizing his logic that night on her porch because... because...

"Damn it all to hell! We share a fantastic sexual chemistry, end of story!"

She didn't so much as flinch. "I think they probably did, too."

"Stop it."

"And it added to your father's guilt."

"Well, that's where we differ," he muttered. His temper in his touch, he reached beneath her and unzipped her dress. Done, he dragged it and her bra over her head and tossed it behind him. "We don't have to waste time on guilt."

She didn't challenge him, she merely watched, her eyes growing heavy-lidded as he slid one hand down to where they were still joined. As he manipulated her, began pumping deeper and deeper again, he could hear her voice as if she was living inside his head and his heart: *Love...love...love...* He tried to ignore it, obliterate it by thrusting harder, faster. He ravaged her breasts until she was writhing beneath him. But he couldn't shut out her voice; he couldn't escape the truth in her all-seeing eyes.

With a growl that reminded him of that monster she'd mentioned, he pulled out of her and flipped her over as if she weighed no more than a pillow, positioned her on her knees and took her from behind. Her fingers clenched the rumpled sheet, she pressed her face against the mattress to muffle her moan. How many women had he taken this way, how often with minimal concern to their pleasure?

This woman with her exquisite skin, her incredible red hair and surprising strength...her wit, keen mind and generosity...she was different. Damn her, why did she make *this* different? Why was it impossible to get enough...enough...?

Desperate to find the end of it, of her, he bent over her, claiming a breast with one hand, and seeking the hot core of her with the other. He had to prove to both of them that there was an end. This was only passion. Nothing lay beyond it.

Satisfaction stayed just out of reach.

With a breathless curse, he drew them both upright onto their knees, dragged one of her hands down between her legs and directed her fingers with his. "Show me what you want. Give me your mouth."

He might as well have shouted the words: *Don't love me. Just want me...and give...give...this.*

She drew him in, and set him on fire, and he was falling, and falling. It reminded him of something she'd once said about making his head spin.

So she was right about yet another thing.

But this had to be enough. He would make it enough, even if it meant being cruel.

"I need a shower."

"And I need to get back to the station."

Eve sat up and began braiding her hair to keep it from getting wet. She didn't want to think of the evil eye Mama Lulu would give her if she arrived back at the house with it soaked. Beside her, Ben lay where he'd sprawled after their second climax. So far, he'd only budged to check his watch and now that arm covered his eyes. She knew he was hiding from her, and that it was more than a male thing. He was hiding from himself, as well.

What surprised her was how calm that made her. It wasn't difficult at all to ask conversationally, "Why did you come looking for me? You never did say."

He made a grunting sound as if only realizing that himself. "I was reminded that Lem's girlfriend, Tilly, lived a few houses down from the Lindale place." He shifted to his side, and with no small reluctance rose on one elbow. "I wanted Justin to ask Lacey if she or her stepbrother had any contact with the girl, or if they knew Lem."

"Wouldn't it have been easier to ask Tilly those things first?"

"Uh-huh."

She watched him stare at her breasts as she worked on her hair, and as usual her body responded immediately to him. So much so that she held her breath as he stroked her with the backs of his fingers, the sensations almost too intense.

"If I wanted our conversation spread all over the entire county. You forget Tilly's a talker. *Look at you...damn, I love seeing this.*"

It took considerable concentration not to lose track of the conversation, or to beg him to put his mouth on her again. "Gossip, right. Was Lacey able to help?"

"In a way. She told me it was rare for any of their neighbors to be home during the day, and she never met Tilly. I guess Roy made sure she kept to herself."

Coiling the braid on top of her head, Eve tucked in the end to secure it. "And even raped her during the day to ensure there wouldn't be any sounds of a struggle at night.'' She rubbed her arms as a sudden chill swept over her.

"Don't go there, Red.''

She nodded and began to slip off the bed, but Ben touched her arm. Although reluctant to do so, she glanced over her shoulder.

Brooding thoughts darkened his eyes. She knew what he wanted to say, and didn't want to hear it. As it was, right now her own feelings about their relationship were too new and demanding on the heart without having to deal with his denial.

"I don't want to hurt you,'' he began. "What I said before—''

She touched her fingers to his lips. "Doesn't change anything.''

Frowning, Ben took hold of her hand and studied the gold band she still wore on her left hand. "For a woman who just told me that we're supposed to be in love, you're incredibly...calm about the whole thing.''

She wanted to correct him and say there was nothing "supposed'' about it. But a new awareness told her that he had to find that out for himself. "Something tells me you don't go for the hysterical or whiny type,'' she replied instead. "And I'm not the kind of person to sit by a window for hours reading sad poetry so I can recognize that I'm in a blue mood. Your passion feeds me, Ben, and mine feeds you. We can try focusing on only that. I'll be with you whenever you want me.''

"Soon.''

"But discreetly. I have to put the kids first.''

"Understood. Will that be enough for you?''

Her wry smile came easily when she looked down at proof that he wasn't quite satisfied himself. "Maybe the question you should be asking is what's enough for *you?*"

This time she did make it off the bed. But she could feel his eyes on her every step of the way out of the room. Not even Sumner with his seasoned appreciation for the womanly form could make her feel more feminine and alluring; as a result, it came as no surprise that she barely had the water a comfortable tepid when Ben joined her, the tip of a foil packet between his teeth.

Looking at it, then meeting the unapologetic desire in his eyes, made it increasingly clear how he'd crept into her heart. "Ben, I really do have to go home."

"I know, damn it, I know." But his strong arms left no question as to whether he would let her leave him. "Just once more."

"If you get my hair wet—"

"I'll be quick...and careful."

"In more ways than one, eh?" She pushed the shower nozzle lower so that it only sprayed them from their shoulders down. Then, taking the tiny packet from him, she slipped her arms around his neck. "So how were you planning to kiss me with that in your mouth?"

19

"Thanks, Ms. Oakes." Luther held the door open for the elderly woman, and then helped her pull her two-wheeled cart out of the store. "There ya go. Be careful crossin' the street, and thanks again!"

He was about to close the door when Ben pulled up to the curb. "He's here," he called over to Rae. She was behind the counter restocking bags. They'd been expecting this visit ever since Ben's call about an hour ago. He had wanted to make sure they knew he was coming, since he was running late and wouldn't be there until right at closing.

Luther supposed he knew why his friend wanted to talk to them. So did Rae, and the glances they exchanged as she rose from the floor spoke of more questions than answers.

"Look out," Ben drawled as he entered. "Was that a paying customer I saw leave here?" He slapped Luther on the back.

"Yeah. Ninth one today. You hire a black cop and people suddenly think it's safe to shop where they want. What is he, an ex–Texas Ranger? Craziest thing I ever seen. I just hope we make some money before your boy gets run outta town."

Ben grunted. "If that happens, it'll mean they got

me first, and *that* means you forget the business, you collect the family and make tracks, old son.''

''Thanks for cheering me up.''

''You started it by not believing you turned a corner. Why worry about something that's not going to happen?'' Ben turned to kiss Rae's cheek as she joined them.

''Is it really going okay with Al?'' Rae asked, her expression hopeful.

Ben wagged both eyebrows. ''So it's Al already?''

''He came by to introduce himself.'' Luther shut the door a bit harder than necessary to get his friend's attention. ''He said that *you* told him to do it.''

''Maybe I did.''

Luther saw the laughter in Ben's eyes and relaxed. ''You sorry S.O.B. What's got you in such a good mood?''

''Luther, behave.'' Rae added to Ben, ''He does seem nice. Are things working out?''

''There's some tension.'' Ben shrugged. ''But that's to be expected. Yesterday he and Buck Preston got into a shoving match over a chocolate doughnut. This morning he and Scranton got into it because Ron left the patrol car on empty. As long as nobody draws their gun, I think things will resolve themselves.''

''I'd like to invite him over to dinner sometime,'' Rae said, seeming pleased with what she'd heard. ''To let him know he's welcome and appreciated. Do you have any reservations about that?''

''He may not, but I sure do!'' Luther had no problem scowling as he crossed his arms over his chest. ''That's one good-lookin' boy.''

But he and Ben broke into a laugh as Rae playfully

nudged him. Then Ben asked how business really was doing, and Luther was proud to be able to say that there was some small sign of improvement.

"Maybe all this trouble we've been havin' finally got people's backs up and put some fire in their bellies. I don't know, and I don't care s'long as that register there keeps ringin'," he said, pointing over to the counter. Deciding they'd had enough small talk, Luther got to the point. He just couldn't wait any longer. "Well? You find out what you wanted to know from the Lindale girl?"

Ben cleared his throat and tugged at the brim of his hat until it almost hid his eyes. "Yes and no. She doesn't know Tilly, but that doesn't mean Roy doesn't. It only means Roy made sure she kept to herself. He, on the other hand, could have known both Tilly and Lem. I have to be in court tomorrow for another case, so I think I'll stop by the county jail and ask him more about that. It's time to show him that cigarette butt, anyway. Push harder."

"You think you can make him tell you who it belonged to?"

Luther was glad Rae asked the question. There would probably have been too much fear in his voice if he'd spoken up. He could kid and joke around with anyone—at least he could pretend to—until they got to the subject of Lem's murder.

"Let's put it this way," Ben replied with a reassuring smile. "So far, Lindale's explanations have more cracks than those left by the New Madrid quakes. What's more, sitting in the county jail is making him more vulnerable than when he was here. I'd say he's getting nervous enough to talk, yeah. The reason I'm here, though, is because I had an idea and I want to get your permission to try it."

Luther's stomach felt oddly empty despite the double helping of greens and juicy pork chops Rae had cooked for them, and he wished she'd stop looking at him as if he had a big S on his chest. Back when he was a kid, it had taken no time at all to figure out that being the eldest was no big honor. And life had proved being on one's own didn't change that. He was beginning to wish he'd run like hell when Eve said on that crucial day, "You look like an ambitious man, Luther. I'll make you a proposition."

"Dreamin' can kill you."

"What?"

Realizing he'd spoken out loud, he wet his lips. "Nothin'. What's on your mind?"

"You know we didn't get anywhere with Bree. Part of that was because of timing and what happened to Justin."

"If you're suggestin'— No, Ben. Push where you gotta push, but we ain't filin' no charges on Eve Maitland's family."

"Hear me out. I don't want you to do it. I only want Bree to *think* you are. Since Lindale's arrest and Eve's preoccupation with Justin and Lacey, Bree's gone back to her old ways, thinking she's gotten away with everything. In fact, Eve's admitted she's getting worse. I want to scare the kid straight."

"Are you sure, Ben? Is Eve going to be warned? She's been like a godmother to us. It would be a slap in the face to turn on her family now."

"Yeah." For the first time in ages, Luther was grateful for his wife's close ties to their landlord and backer. "She might even think I'm lookin' for more money."

Ben shook his head. "You know better than that. Eve's protective of those kids, but it doesn't interfere with her view of what's right and wrong. I won't do anything more without including her on things."

Luther shuffled around and rubbed his damp hands against his apron. It hadn't slipped by him that his friend was being awfully supportive to Eve all of a sudden. That and the way he'd been acting since he'd come from there had Luther wondering. Eve was a show pony sure enough, but if she was getting into Ben's head in a bad way, *he* wanted to know about it.

"Supposin' you tell 'em. Then what?" Luther demanded. "Ain't there a chance we could become a bigger target? Bree may not go straight to her boyfriend or partner or whoever he is. She may have someone else do it and he may come after us."

Ben held his gaze for a long moment. "I won't lie to you. That's in the realm of possibilities. But that's why, once we begin, I'm going to put Jones at your house and I'll shift Norm Friedman to days and park him here. However, if you want my gut hunch, I don't think you'll be a target."

"Who will be?"

"Lindale first and foremost. He has knowledge, and an offer to cut a deal. That's not being kept secret."

"But that's not all," Rae whispered, gazing up at him. With a gasp, she wrapped her arms around her waist. "Lord have mercy...Bree? You can't!"

"I don't see that I have a choice," Ben replied.

"And she's proven she's no saint, Rae. She's also made it clear that either she's nuts about the guy we're trying to find, or terrified of him. I need to know which it is, *who* it is. I'm convinced I know where he is."

"Bellemere." Luther was coming to hate that name.

Ben met his grim gaze. "The trail always did seem to begin and end there, and I don't know that Perry Ashworth's the one pushing her buttons, but he's moving in on Eve fast and hard. Is that coincidence or intentional?"

"Ben." Rae reached out, almost grasping his arm, only to draw back. "Tell me this isn't about jealousy. You always did have something against Perry, and I think everyone except Eve knows that if he's interested in anyone, it's her. If you're of a mind to step in the middle of all that—"

"This is business, Rae," Ben replied flatly.

"Business where Bree gets used no matter what happens," Rae murmured, a distant look in her eyes.

Luther put his arm around his wife, knowing she was thinking of their boys being in this kind of mess. It would break her heart to know that one of her babies might have slipped as bad as Bree had. But it would kill her if someone she trusted used her child as a pawn for any reason.

"The point is," Ben said, "I need corroborating testimony to whatever Lindale leads me to. He's a con. A jury will automatically suspect he's lying to get a reduced term. If I can get Bree to back up his testimony by pointing out the same guilty party, I have a guaranteed conviction."

That made sense, but Luther still needed reassurance. "Does Eve know? It would make a difference if we knew you discussed this with her already."

"Not yet. I only came to the conclusion that this was the best way on my drive back to town. But she understands that Bree's in trouble one way or another."

Rae shook her head sadly. "Guessing is one thing, dealing with it is another. Eve doesn't need that after all she's been dealing with. Ben, she's the first lady of Parish, but she works harder than anyone, always going, doing, fixing and supporting...never letting on if she's got problems of her own. This idea of yours has a bad feel to it. Ben, I haven't had a feeling this powerful bad since your daddy died."

He didn't answer, but his jaw worked and his Adam's apple bobbed up and down once as if he'd tried to speak and failed.

What the hell? Luther wondered. He'd never seen such a look on his friend's face, and he couldn't have described it if he'd tried.

"You'd lose everything you have?" Ben asked. "See Lem's death go unresolved because of Bree Maitland's recklessness?"

"She's not reckless, she's needy."

Luther noted both he and Ben were surprised at Rae's comment.

"Eve and I have talked about it a few times," she said with a challenging lift of her chin. "You men, you think you know so much. But you don't raise a child to think she's perfect and can do anything, then deny her the tools and freedom to live up to her potential. Gabrielle has a good mind, but she doesn't know what to do with it. Sumner starved her ambition and at the same time rewarded her for being lazy. He got her so confused by those mixed signals, now she expects to be adored no matter what she does. It's a dirty trick too many fathers have played on daughters, and I'll tell you, what Sumner left Eve has made me glad I had boys.''

Luther barely followed any of that. Women had long been a mystery to him, and he'd always been grateful he'd married one who let him know exactly what she meant when she meant it. Eager to resolve this situation, he said to Ben, ''All I got to say is I'm protectin' my wife and boys first. Do what you have to do, Ben, but remember that.''

Ben was remembering a great number of things the next morning as he left the courthouse. It was earlier than he expected to get out, thanks to the case getting plea-bargained, canceling the need for his testimony. Relieved, he focused on his next priority.

At the jail, he used the extra time to poll the guards about Roy Lindale. Who, if anyone, had visited him? Did he make any phone calls? Did he seem agitated? Worried? Unfortunately, the answers were far less helpful than he'd hoped.

Except for his court-appointed attorney, Lindale had received no visitors and had made no phone calls. While he did seem edgy and often paced in his cell for hours at a time and was heard muttering to himself a good deal, there were no substantial leads to glean from that behavior.

Ben was left sorely disappointed, and that made

him all the more caustic when he and Lindale finally came face-to-face.

"Enjoying being cooped up here like an exiled chicken?"

The ponytailed man sneered back. "If I'd known it was you wanting to see me, I wouldn't have left my cell. What do you want?"

Ben sat on the edge of the flat metal table in the middle of the windowless room and glanced around. Except for the two steel chairs on either side of the table, the place was empty, the composition no more cheerful than Lindale's cell. "It's hotter'n hell outside, but I hear the largemouth bass over at the lake are biting like crazy by the dam. Guess it'll be a while before you get to fish again. They'll probably be using lasers for fishing rods by the time you get paroled."

"Kiss my—"

"Ah-ah-ah. If you want to find out why I'm here, you can't run off at the mouth like a ruptured sewer line."

Roy Lindale leaned as close as he could to Ben. "Here's a news flash, Ace. I don't give a shit why you're here."

"You should. I came to continue our game of show-and-tell."

That had the heavily whiskered man staring hard at him. "You ain't got nothing."

"Sure? I think I have something that belongs to your friend. He dropped it the night Lem Cobb *found* your trap."

Narrowing his eyes, Lindale muttered, "What?"

Ben decided against drawing out the moment. If

Roy was going to cooperate, it would be because of the evidence, not the subtleties of manipulation.

His insides churned as he reached into his pocket and got out the small plastic bag. As he held it up, Lindale squinted and edged closer. A yard away he stopped and snorted.

"You call that evidence?"

"Look more closely. True, there's not much left, but I do have a brand name that tells me this is a custom blend from New Orleans. Now, even if you did smoke, I know this stuff would be too pricey a habit for a scavenger like you. But I'm letting the newspaper over in Parish print that you know who can afford it, and that you two were together down by the lake the night Lem died. I'm also going to report that the D.A. is considering a plea bargain in return for your cooperation."

Roy turned as green as if he'd been asked to chew on the filter. "You can't do that."

"Who's going to stop me?"

"I'll call my lawyer and counter-sue! I'll sue the paper!" He rushed to the door and banged on it with his fist. "Guard! I want my lawyer! I'm being black-mailed!"

Ben watched the bag swinging between his thumb and index finger, letting Lindale rant on for another few moments. He knew no one would be opening the door unless he asked them to.

When sweat broke out over the man's forehead and upper lip, Ben drawled, "Yeah, you call your lawyer. Maybe he'll bring you a minister, because the minute word gets out that you turned rat, your life won't be worth the price of a .22 short."

Lindale ran a hand over his mouth. "It wasn't like you said."

"What was it like?"

"I wasn't part of it. I wasn't!" he cried when Ben shot him a scornful look. "Yeah, I was there, but if they'd have spotted me, I would be as dead as Cobb."

This wasn't what Ben had expected at all and he wasn't sure whether to believe Lindale or not. The guy sounded panicked enough to be telling the truth, but he could just be a good actor.

Ben decided to see where this admission led. "We have your traps."

"I was picking 'em up. Trapping was better over there."

"Why trap at all? Depending on what you caught, you were breaking a half-dozen laws for pelts that aren't worth a damn this time of year."

"Who cares about pelts? I had to put food on the table for those two parasites, and with work being a take-what-you-can-get situation, every little bit helped. I'd collected two of the three I'd set out when I heard them coming."

It never failed, Ben thought, watching the man in the white coveralls. Sooner or later a con always wanted to share how clever he was. "Them?"

"Cobb and the other two."

Two. "Go on."

"That's it." Lindale pointed ahead of him as if he was seeing it all over again. "Cobb was running like half of hell was after him, and that was crazy 'cuz he wasn't dressed to be out there like I was. Shoot, just the week before, I got me a moccasin near as big around as my arm. It almost bit through my boots."

"What about Lem Cobb?"

"He found that last trap for me." The swarthy-skinned prisoner scratched under his chin, his expression reflective. "Did you ever hear if that fatback was still there when it got him? I'd been trying to outsmart some critter for a good two weeks. Sure would like to have figured out what I was dealing with."

It...he'd made it sound like the trap was a living thing. The man definitely belonged under lock and key. "No. There was no evidence of your bait. What happened to Lem?"

"Hell, what do you think? He went down, and let me tell you, I did, too. I didn't know what his trouble was, and I wanted no part of it."

"You sorry bastard, you never considered helping him?"

Lindale stopped in the middle of the room, his laugh harsh. "Yeah, right. Take on two guys with hunting rifles?"

"You want me to believe you weren't carrying the twelve-gauge, or the .38, or any of the other goodies we found at your place—all of which were registered to other people, by the way."

"Hey. Don't you start accuse me of stealin' 'em."

"You? A guy with a yard-long arrest sheet? What could I have been thinking?"

"My stuff's legal! Somebody gets short on cash, I make a deal, I don't ask what's none of my business."

"So you have money for loans, but you don't have the cash to buy your family decent food."

"Get off my back."

"I'll bet Lem Cobb would have appreciated you

meddling. Too bad it had to be you in those woods and not somebody else.''

"Listen, he bought it as easy as anyone with his problem could. *I'd* have been the one gutted like a deer. All he did was smack into that tree and it was all over.''

"Wrong. He drowned.''

"After. He didn't know none of that. They rolled him off that stump and into the water. He was lucky they didn't wait until he came to.''

Ben's heart was pounding like mad now. The information the coroner had noted about the bruising on Lem's skull, and later remembered about the condition of Lem's clothes, had just been confirmed by Roy Lindale. Lem had, indeed, been rolled over!

He pocketed the plastic bag. "Who were they?''

Lindale wagged his finger at him. "Aw, no. That's not the way it works. You owe me now.''

"For what? Some ghoulish story with nothing I can verify?''

"You got the body, my trap...''

He'd had a trap. "I need more.''

"I told you everything I saw. I stayed until they were gone and then I got the hell out.''

"I want names.''

"Well, you ain't getting 'em from me. Not without a guarantee to my lawyer in writing. Hell—'' he began pacing again "—you don't know who you're dealing with here. If this gets out, I might as well stick my head in one of those traps myself.'' He pointed at the door. "You call the guard to put me back in my cell. I ain't saying another word until I know I'm protected, man. *Guard!*''

* * *

"How are we doing in here? Oops. Pretty well, I'd say."

Eve had come upstairs to pick up Justin's lunch tray and to see how he and Lacey were doing, only to discover they'd put aside the books they'd been studying and were lost in a kiss. That didn't shock her, but she was glad she'd chosen this moment to arrive and cool things down.

Justin looked much better and Lacey was as close to radiant as Eve had seen her to date. Of course, they both blushed at being caught, and while Eve thought that sweet, she knew it was time to put some distance between them.

Gently touching Lacey's shoulder, she pointed to the tray and both said and signed, "Bring that down to Mama Lulu in the kitchen? Thank you, dear."

Once she was gone, Justin sighed. "Slick move, coach."

"Flattery will get you everywhere, but we're still going to talk."

He fiddled with the books and with straightening the sheet over his lap. "I know you're worried, and you're thinking of your responsibility to Lacey while she's living with us."

"I wish you'd teach your sister to lecture herself so I wouldn't have to," Eve drawled.

Justin rolled his eyes. "Ask me to walk on water already. Look, I know Lacey is younger than me in all the ways that matter..."

"It's more than that, sweetheart. She needs time to heal, to find out who she is as a person, let alone as a woman."

"We're in love."

Eve couldn't help remembering yesterday with Ben. "There's nothing wrong with my vision."

"You're not going to try to talk us out of it, then?"

"If this is meant to last, I couldn't talk you out of it if I wanted to. But I am going to remind you that you're going to be attending college shortly."

"Sure. And I want to. As long as she's welcome to stay on here."

Eve lifted an eyebrow. "The ultimatum was unnecessary."

"I'm sorry. I just felt it important to say the words."

Everything was changing again. "Maybe you're right." She covered his hand with hers. "I hope you'll always feel comfortable enough to tell me whatever is on your mind."

"Next to being able to hug her without feeling I've been shot...it's Bree I've been worrying about."

"Ah, from sugar to spice. There's a topic switch." His twin was across the hall, still asleep although the day was nearly half over. Eve knew Justin hadn't entirely missed Bree's unapologetic and erratic arrivals and departures, since she now did them with an in-your-face attitude.

"What are you going to do?" he asked her.

The million-dollar question. "It's what she's going to do that matters."

"Can't we help her?"

"Believe it or not, we're trying to do more than help her, we're trying to save her."

"Your 'we' sounds different than mine. Is she..." He bit his lip. "I've been listening some when Chief

Rader comes by. Is she going to jail because of the drugs?"

"Right now all I care about is keeping her alive. So is Ben Rader."

"He's here quite a bit lately." Justin ducked his head, but glanced up at her from beneath his lashes. "He likes you."

Eve wished Ben's feelings were so simple to describe. "Isn't fate full of practical jokes? But don't start building that out of proportion. We only met a little over a month ago."

"So did Lacey and I. And a minute ago you all but agreed that when you know, you know."

Eve groaned inwardly. "It's not a simple case of knowing. When you're older and have more history and...baggage, there's the challenge of changing and making accommodations. Also, some people are better at watching other people fall in love than doing it themselves."

"Then there are people like Bree who don't know how to love anyone but themselves."

"Let's take one of her challenges at a time." As Eve added a reassuring pat to his hand, she heard activity downstairs. "I'd better go see what's going on."

It was Ben. Unexpected, looking wonderful Ben. He was trying to untangle himself from Lacey's enthusiastic hug and Mama Lulu was scolding him for not letting her know he would be here around lunchtime. When he spotted her coming down the stairs, the immediate electric connection and sexual pull had her tightening her grip on the tray, wishing it was the banister for the rest of the trip. His gaze swept over

her teal green jumpsuit, but she saw how he was remembering yesterday and her more accessible sheath.
Only after she got closer did she see the lines of
stress, and the shadow of...was that doubt or concern
darkening his eyes? Considering where she knew he'd
been today, the soberness had her tensing inside.

In the midst of the commotion, the phone rang.
Mama Lulu threw up her hands and walked over to
the extension on the side table outside the study.

"I see nothing's changed here," he said over Lacey's head as Eve reached them. "Things are still
going on all cylinders. Sorry for not calling to warn
you that I was on my way."

"You only warn people when you're bringing bad
news. Is that why you're here?"

"Things have been put into motion that can't be
stopped. Can you find something for sunshine here to
do?"

With a faint nod, Eve motioned upstairs. "Justin's
ready to go over your math homework now." She
groaned because she had to pantomime more than
sign, not yet remembering all the correct movements.
"Did I mess up badly?"

Lacey shook her head, her gestures making it clear
that she understood. Blowing Ben a kiss, she hurried
off.

"You're getting good at that," Ben murmured for
her ears alone. "And you look—"

"Eve." Mama Lulu placed her hand over the receiver's mouthpiece. "It's Perry Ashworth. He's
sayin' you two had a luncheon date."

Eve heard Ben suck in a sharp breath. Yesterday,

as he'd driven her back to the house, he'd been adamant about their neighbor...

"Stay away from him, Red. Stay away from Bellemere altogether. I can't give you the proof you want, but he's trouble."

"How many times do I have to tell you? I'm not sleeping with Perry."

"I don't just mean sex. I don't mean just you. Keep everyone away from him and Bellemere."

"Ben, please—"

"I can't say more."

"You mean you won't."

"That's right, too."

She shook her head both for his sake and to respond to Mama Lulu, then went to take the call. She didn't like being put in this position, but she also didn't like the way Perry was pushing these days. Men, she fumed.

"Perry. This is a little embarrassing."

"Don't tell me that you forgot me completely or you'll break my heart."

"Of course not. But I told you after I called yesterday that today wouldn't be any better."

"So I'll have everything wrapped up, and I'll bring it over to you."

Eve opened her mouth to reply only to discover that Ben had moved directly behind her. Close behind her. It was a relief to see that Mama Lulu had withdrawn to the kitchen for the moment; but Ben's breath was warming her cheek, his heart was beating powerfully at her back and his hips were brushing up against her bottom. He was making it virtually impossible to continue.

"Eve? Are you all right?"

"Yes, I— Perry, that's a tempting offer, but not this time. I...I have a meeting in a few minutes with our attorneys."

There was a slight hesitation. "You're seeing an awful lot of them lately."

"Well, Lacey and Justin's situation is complicated. I'm so sorry."

"You sound different, darling. Troubled. Isn't there anything I can do? Let me sit in on the meeting, add another viewpoint, or at the least support? Say the word and I'll be there in five minutes. I'm free until later this afternoon."

"No, really. Thanks for being a good friend," she added quickly as Ben's hand covered hers on the receiver. "Let me call you back in a day or two when I have a better grasp on what's going to happen."

She barely had time to murmur goodbye before Ben's hand urged hers to hang up. Furious, she whispered over her shoulder, "What do you think you're doing!"

They were so close it was impossible to focus, and her lips tingled as though bee-stung.

"Trying to keep you from making a fool of yourself."

"I'm only allowed to be one when you benefit, is that it?"

"Close enough." He added a biting kiss as potent as any bee sting. "Toughen up, Red. This is no time to develop a chink in your armor. I need you."

The sound of voices had him stepping away, a good thing, as far as she was concerned. Ben Rader saying he needed anyone or anything was heady stuff.

She took a deep, calming breath.

"Where's Bree?"

"Need you ask?"

"You have to get her down here."

One look at his grim face and Eve quietly excused herself and went straight upstairs. Not quite fifteen minutes later she descended, a very unhappy Bree trailing several steps behind.

"This had better be important," the girl muttered. Wearing a short terry-cloth robe, with her face scrubbed shiny, and her hair hastily brushed back into a ponytail, she looked as innocent as Lacey, except for her mutinous expression.

"The chief say he want you downstairs, you come," Mama Lulu said, standing beside Ben.

Eve concluded he must have gone to fetch Lulu while she'd been upstairs, and the ramifications of that had her worrying anew.

"Oh, goody," Bree intoned as Ben gestured for them to head for the study. "The interrogation room again."

Once they entered, Eve invited Mama Lulu into the chair she'd sat in last time. When she eyed Bree questioningly, the girl shook her head.

"I'd prefer to take this standing. So what now, Chief Rader? Did someone decide they saw me robbing a bank in Jackson with Elvis? Or maybe they saw me link up with a UFO in Tupelo!"

Ignoring her, Ben said, "I had two meetings in the last twenty-four hours. At first they might sound as though one has nothing to do with the other, but bear with me and I hope to tie it all together. First and foremost, I should tell you that there was a witness to Lem's death."

"Well, I was close," Bree muttered.

"Bree!" Eve snapped. *"Not another word."*

Ben paused another moment before continuing with, "Roy Lindale confessed to being in the woods the night Lem died." He went to Mama Lulu and crouched beside her.

"You mean, that awful man was involved?" she whispered.

"No. Just in the wrong place at the wrong time."

"Don't tell me he says it was an accident," Mama Lulu told Ben. "You're not gonna make me believe it. Why, that man ain't nothin' but a liar. A wicked liar."

Ben took hold of her hand. "No, I'm not. But it was fast for Lem. You can take some peace out of that. He did fall because of the trap. He was unconscious when they put him into the water."

As the old woman began sobbing quietly, Eve came to her other side to offer her comfort. "You're saying he can identify who did it?"

"He knows. He doesn't want to talk without a deal and protection, but he saw the two men."

"You make him!" Mama Lulu cried, clutching his hand with both of hers. "You put the fear of God in him, Ben. You make him do the right thing!"

"To think we're so close," Eve murmured.

Bree inched closer and took hold of the back of the other chair. "What's Roy Lindale have to do with me?"

He gave her a long look. "It's Luther, Bree. He's ready to file charges against you."

20

Bree felt naked. They were all staring at her—Ben, Eve, Mama Lulu. She saw the accusation, the disappointment, the dislike, and the realization that she was alone struck her hard.

"He can't." Sadly, her protest sounded weak and unconvincing even to her own ears.

"He most certainly can." Ben shrugged. "And who's going to blame him? He's angry and hurt. He wants retribution."

"But I didn't *do* anything!"

"Don't you call my son a liar," Mama Lulu seethed. "For eighteen years I been puttin' up with your spoiled ways, and your connivin'. You turnin' into a nasty girl and a cheat who don't have the decency to tell the truth, even after you been found out. I'm ashamed, you hear? I'm ashamed for your family and for all of us who tried to love you even when we knew you'd been doin' wrong. You let us down."

Bree could feel the tears building inside her. She ruthlessly pushed them down; even so, her chin trembled and her vision blurred. "I am telling you the truth this time. I've tried and tried to think back to that night, but…I barely remember yesterday!"

Eve shot Ben a look of entreaty. "Take a deep breath, Bree. Then tell us what you do recall."

It wasn't much of a reprieve, but Bree was grateful for the chance to be heard, and said eagerly, "I know I had a date that night."

"With whom?"

Who...oh, God. She'd spoken without thinking things through, assuming it would be enough to say she'd been doing something other than cruising. "I...I prefer not to say," she replied, glancing away.

"This is no time to play games," Ben said.

"I'm not. I just— You wouldn't approve," she said to Eve. "You want me to go out with babies, and he's more mature."

"Don't try to tell me it's Perry," Eve replied, "because I won't believe you."

At the same moment Eve looked confident, Ben acted annoyed with her statement. Good, she thought, having a hunch what that was all about. She hoped Mr. High-and-Mighty got his heart broken.

"No, it isn't Perry!" she snapped. "It's someone who appreciates me for who I am."

"By getting you drunk night after night? By giving you drugs? Is he the reason you're out until all hours and look like a used-up streetwalker or junkie when you drag in? Good grief, is that your idea of love?"

"I'm not a junkie!" she shouted back at her. And she hadn't said anything about love. It was...exciting to live life a little on the edge, that's all. "I get high because you people drive me *nuts!* But I can stop anytime I want, and I will!"

Oh, how right he'd been. He'd warned her that her family and others would make things sound ugly if they found out. Okay, so maybe she drank a bit too much when he got too tied up with business, and maybe she hadn't cared for everything he'd taught her about what people do in bed. He'd apologized and hadn't done it again. And he was thinking about setting her up in her own little bookmaking business once she went to college, so screw Moxie Larouche. Who needed him? As far as she was concerned, they made a good team. For now.

"Bree, I could have come here with a warrant for your arrest, but I wanted to give you a chance to avoid that," Ben said. "I wanted to give you a chance to save your family embarrassment from unwanted media attention."

"Sure you did. And wanting to get into her pants—" she nodded toward Eve "—had nothing to do with it. Do you people think I'm blind as well as stupid? Why not focus on the fact that somebody's playing a dirty trick on me? If you can't find the real guilty person, then I'll find out who it is myself!"

"Bree!"

Ignoring Eve, Bree raced out of the room and charged up the stairs, taking them in twos. Once inside her room she slammed the door and locked it. Breathless, she hurried to the phone. She knew she had to be quick in case someone figured out what she was doing and tried to stop her from using her own phone line.

The phone rang three, four, five times. "Come on," she whispered, her heart pounding from nerves as much as from the run. She knew he carried a phone with him most of the time, and prayed this wasn't one of those moments when he didn't have it around.

On the sixth ring, she heard him pick up. "It's me," she said immediately.

"Hold on."

Obviously he had to get out of earshot of someone. That was fine. It gave her a chance to take a few more deep breaths. It was going to be all right. He sounded so calm, so...

"What the hell do you think you're doing?"

The harsh demand threw her off balance again. "You said I could call."

"In case of an emergency," he growled.

"This is one! For your information, Ben Rader is here making all kinds of accusations."

He paused. "What kind of accusations?"

"About me. About us."

"You *told* them about *me* after I warned you not to? What the fuck was I doing, talking to dead air space?"

His vicious tone lashed as deeply as her father used to when he was in one of his moods. "No! But remember that problem with the Cobbs? Ben Rader is saying that Luther is filing charges!"

"On only you?"

She didn't understand his cautious relief. "Well, yeah. Unless I give him a name, but how can I do that if I don't remember being there, right?"

"Right. So he didn't name me? You didn't, either?"

"No."

"Then he's full of bull." The anger vanished from his voice. "You know what's going on, baby. He's looking to make a few bucks off your family. Your stepmama'll write him a check and he'll go away. Don't worry about it.''

He might as well have told her to start believing in Santa Claus again. "Don't talk to me as though I were a child. Eve will let him take me unless I give them a name.''

"How can you give them one if you don't remember that it happened?''

"But it did," Bree said softly. "I wanted to believe you before when you said it was all their fabrication, because I was afraid, but...we were there. You did it, didn't you?''

"Did I?''

"Help me.''

"How am I supposed to do that? Do I monitor every minute of your day? You're an ambitious, crazy doll who's known for doing weird shit. Maybe you pulled something one night after you left me." When she remained silent, he snickered. "You want to play grown-up, then act like one, baby. Otherwise, kiss off.''

Bree felt as if she was on an elevator that had just stripped its gears. She clung to the receiver for dear life. "You can't do this to me.''

He gave a short, humorless laugh. "You did it to yourself.''

Although her teeth were almost chattering from outright terror, she managed to say, "I don't think you should make the mistake of underestimating me.''

He grew very quiet for a moment. "What else is on your mind, kid?''

"Ben Rader had more to say. It turns out that the

creep who attacked my brother was in the woods when Lem died.''

"So?''

She closed her eyes. The careful, wary way he'd spoken confirmed her growing suspicions. She didn't need to hear Lindale name names. She knew who one of the men had been.

"Don't get any ideas, baby doll. You know why nobody's turned me in up until now? Because they're not stupid. You, on the other hand, are proving to be one dumb broad—and a dangerous one at that. It's a good thing I have insurance.''

Bree didn't like the sound of that. "What insurance?''

"The best kind. The reason you don't remember that field trip around town when Rader's pal saw you is because we'd been partying, and nobody parties as big as you. You inhaled and swallowed everything I gave you and asked for more. Now I have these great pictures to prove what a hot little number you are. And if I hear one more peep out of you, a set of those prints is going to every journalist in this state who's ever heard the name Maitland. Do we understand each other? You need me, girlie, and you need my stuff, so shut your trap and keep it shut.''

Bree dropped onto the edge of her bed and stayed there long after he'd disconnected. Humiliation burned like acid inside and out as she thought of the photos. She didn't remember them any more than she did Luther's accusation, but she believed now. Oh, yes, she believed it was all true.

She'd made it so easy for him. She'd thought she'd

been sharp, worldly…ready to live life on a sharper edge. What sheer crap!

What a terrifying mess.

She hung up and crawled against the pillows where she hugged her knees to her chest. For the first time in her life, she wished she'd never been born.

Shortly after Mama Lulu excused herself to locate a new supply of tissues, Ben stood in the middle of the study knowing it was time for him to go, too. He had to get back to the station, and to pray that Lindale came through soon, since it appeared that Bree sure as hell wouldn't. But he didn't want to leave Eve in what had to be her darkest hour to date.

"You don't have to stay," she said, standing at the window, looking out. "I don't need my hand held."

It was getting downright strange, how often she could read his mind; and no, he supposed she didn't need hand-holding. He wondered if she remembered what it felt like—or if she had ever really known. Her great-aunt had sure done a good job making her an independent and self-reliant woman. So damned if he knew why it felt as if he would be tearing off a limb to leave her.

"Things are changing," he murmured.

"They always are," she replied, her voice void of any emotion save fatigue. "Every dawn you hope you can find and maintain a corner of serenity, a slice of sanity, and every sundown…" She turned her back on the window and its scene of botanical utopia. "I'm not a fatalist, Ben, you of all people should know that by now. I'll fight this, fight like hell to pull us through it. And I do mean all of us."

Following a gut need, Ben crossed to her and drew her into his arms. "I know."

"Let me go. Please. I can't let you this close right now."

"It's only a hug. Calm down."

"Nothing is just anything. Everything costs, everyone pays. I can't deal with that right now. I said stop!"

She managed to wrench away from him, but Ben saw that her success surprised her. It did him, too. Once she put enough distance between them, she gestured like a bird with a broken wing.

"I'm sorry."

"For what?"

"I don't know, isn't that a laugh? I'm so tired of all this, I'm losing the ability to think."

"You'll have it when the time comes."

It was one of her gifts, he understood now. That's why people came to her for advice and help, why they admired her, and, yes, resented her. She made reasoning and decision making look easy, and her sense of responsibility and commitment to justice made it appear even simpler.

"What Luther and Rae must be thinking," she said, massaging her temples. "What a pompous jackass I must have sounded like, trying to— And *you*. You could have told me."

"I am telling you."

"You didn't trust me."

"I've never trusted another human being more." He hadn't planned to say that, either. Hell, he hadn't realized it was the truth until this moment.

"How can I expect Mama Lulu to stay on here?" Eve continued as if she hadn't heard him.

"She'll stay because she considers this family hers as much as she does her blood family. And Luther and Rae...they're hurt, sure, but don't think for one minute that they're blaming you."

She didn't look pleased to hear any of that. In fact, she looked damned angry.

"Since when do you have all the answers? You've spent nearly all of your adult life in denial of the truth. How dare you lecture me!"

He couldn't argue with that even if it did smart like a scorpion sting. "You're right. I'll go see if there's somewhere I can do some good."

"Ben!"

He got as far as the door before the anguish in her voice got to him. Turning in time to catch her, he crushed her close and found her mouth with a blind man's luck. Maybe this was the way he could show her that he was trying. Trying for what he wasn't sure, but something about her made him need to want and to give more.

And as usual, she surprised him. He expected her to want tenderness and comfort; she demanded his passion. All of it. Even once he realized what she was doing—blocking out the fear, reaching for hope—he admired her for it. Heaven help him, he thought in a flash of stunning clarity, he adored her.

Too soon she began withdrawing. "All right," she murmured, unwinding her arms. "I'm okay now."

"I'll let you know when you're okay." He continued kissing her, moving quickly to where he could feel her pulse. That was his current favorite place because he could gauge her vulnerability to him best there. But finally he did let her go, only he did it slowly, lingeringly, until just his forehead touched hers. "I wish…"

"I know."

"I need a name, Red. Will you help me?"

"It doesn't seem that I have a choice."

"You do. But it might save time this way…maybe a life, as well."

"I'll do what I can."

"And I'll be in constant contact."

"You'll be too busy."

"I will be in touch," he intoned. Grimacing, he added, "I feel like those animals who sense when there's going to be an earthquake. All hell is going to break loose, and I want to make sure you're okay."

"Thank you."

He narrowed his eyes. "No arguments? No I-am-woman lectures?"

"You're the expert when it comes to figuring out the criminal mind. I'll follow your advice."

"In that case, I'll go way out on a ledge and repeat myself. Stay away from Bellemere."

"Ben."

"Not simply because I'm accepting that I'm eaten up with jealousy over your friendship with Ashworth. Let me put it this way…if a couple of guys were in your woods chasing a man with rifles, would your people notice something was amiss?"

"I've been trying not to think about that."

He pressed a last kiss on her forehead. "Call me the second she gives you his name."

As Ben drove back to town and passed the Ashworth estate, he had the strongest urge to pull in and see if he could provoke Perry into taking a swing at him, just for the sheer pleasure of arresting him. But by the time he got back to the station, he had someplace else to direct his unused adrenaline. Apparently, Mama Lulu had phoned Luther to fill him in on what had happened, and not five minutes after Ben settled behind his desk, his old friend stormed into the office.

"I got only one question," he demanded, hands on his hips. "Why ain't she here?"

Ben put down the mug of rust-remover coffee he'd poured himself. "I'm assuming you mean Bree? First, you didn't want me to do this, now you're upset that she's not locked up?"

"Yeah, well, I'd like this to be over. How much stress d'you think we can take?"

"She hasn't given us what we need."

"I know. My mother called to tell me what happened. It was ugly."

"Words are still preferable to bloodshed." He, too, was disappointed that things hadn't worked out; what he refused to do was let it be a wedge between himself and his friend. "No one, except maybe Eve, is more sympathetic and concerned with what your family is going through than I am. But I'm going to continue conducting this investigation in a manner I feel is most responsible and effective."

Luther stiffened, his strong chin jutted out like an invitation. "I guess that tells me all I need to know."

Ben didn't like the threat underscoring that comment. "Meaning?"

"I can't take much more of this hangin' over our heads. If you can't get her to talk, I will."

"Whoa." Ben had to move fast to block the door before Luther could escape. "You can't say something like that and not expect me to react. Come on, man, what's gotten into you? If I didn't know better, I'd swear I was hearing reverse prejudice."

"Maybe that's 'cuz I'm thinkin' I'm hearin' some shit, too. You call yourself a friend, but when it comes to protectin' the most powerful white family in the county, friendship can take a seat at the back of the bus."

Ben couldn't believe what he was hearing, and he was acutely aware of every eye in the station on them. "You don't mean that," he said quietly.

"You got until I close business tonight to decide."

"Don't threaten me, Luther."

"I said what I came to say."

The afternoon dragged for Eve, although she supposed it felt that way for everyone in the house. She'd gone upstairs to talk to Bree, but the girl had locked her door and refused to answer regardless of how long she knocked and tried to coax her to open up. The commotion got Justin's and Lacey's attention, and so she detoured to fill them in on Ben's latest meeting with Roy, Luther's threat and what Bree's reaction had been to everything.

"No wonder," Justin replied as Lacey sat quietly trying to follow. "The crying was really strange."

Tears from Bree's room? The last time she'd cried was at her father's deathbed. Afterward, she hadn't spilled one drop, not at the service or the funeral. Realizing how deeply she must be hurt convinced Eve that the girl could still be reached. Encouraged, she tried the veranda, but Bree had locked the windows as well as the French doors, and had drawn the curtains as if not even wanting sunlight to touch her.

"You'll have to let her decide when she's ready to talk again," Justin said when she advised him of her failure. "No one has ever been able to coax her down from her euphoric highs or lift her from her near-suicidal lows."

He was right. It was shortly after the dinner that no one ate when she came downstairs to the kitchen where Eve was helping Mama Lulu put everything away. Mama Lulu spotted her first and grunted before turning her back to the girl.

Eve glanced over her shoulder and couldn't stop the sound of surprise and dismay that burst from her. The teen had been doing more than weeping. She looked as though she'd been sobbing for hours. Her face was a mess, puffy and patterned by red splotches and scrubbed shiny.

"Please," she rasped, her arms wrapped tight around her waist. "I need to talk."

"You'd better sit down before you drop. I'll get something for your throat." Eve chose lemonade rather than iced tea, deciding Bree needed the sugar, as much as the lemon and coolness.

After downing half of the drink, Bree sat there like a ten-year-old in braces attending her first social. Glancing up to find Eve's gaze on her, her eyes filled anew.

"Take your time. Start anywhere," Eve suggested as Mama Lulu moved around the kitchen as if oblivious to anything going on.

"You need to understand, I never realized, okay? I never thought I was hurting anyone."

"Except yourself, right?" Sad, Eve shook her head. "It was acceptable to pour an endless stream of alcohol and drugs into your body?"

"No, I just… Okay, I suppose I was aware of walking a dangerous line, but I thought it wouldn't get to me. I believed I was in control."

Eve understood. Countless people, including a good friend, had died following that same logic.

Bree picked at already ruined frosted-pink fingernails. "All I ever wanted was—I thought I could make someone pay attention to me. Fall in love with *me*."

"Hate to know how you'd behave if you didn't like a body," Mama Lulu muttered. "No wonder my boy is dead."

Bree shot her a dark look. "I cared for Lem. But I, more than anyone, know that whatever happened the night he died wasn't because he was blameless."

"Don't you dare say nothin' more about my boy!"

Before they started screaming at each other, Eve decided to shift the line of focus to the immediate. "The person you said you had the date with the night Luther saw you, is that the man you've been seeing all along?"

She nodded. "But he didn't care, I realize that now. And so I'm through."

"How do you know?"

Bree looked up, her eyes haunted. "He took p-pictures!"

There was no need to ask what kind. Eve exchanged glances with Mama Lulu, who responded with a what-do-you-expect look. Sighing, she sat down in the chair beside the girl.

"I take it he's asking for money?"

"No. Silence. And for good reason. Don't you get it? He's the one everyone wants. He's the one who's been supplying the drugs to the kids around here. I think...I *know* he's one of the men Lindale saw."

"Good grief. Bree, how could you continue your relationship with him once you knew?"

"That's it, I didn't. Well, not all of it. I guess I suspected some things. When I let myself think about it. Mostly, I just liked the power and attention that came from— Oh, forget it. It sounds even more stupid when I hear myself say it."

And Eve had heard enough. "Then tell me why you came down here."

"I wanted you to understand, that's all."

"Tell me his name. I'll call Ben."

"Haven't you been listening? The pictures! He said he would send them to every journalist who knows us!"

"Let him try. We'll add blackmail to our list of charges against him."

"Eve." Bree gripped her throat as if having to force out the words. "Don't think he'll stop there."

"Then tell us who is he. A person who talks blackmail once isn't going to let you go. Give me his name, and I'll call Ben."

"Skeet. Skeet Blanchard."

Eve frowned. "Why is that familiar?"

"Because he's Perry's right hand."

Mama Lulu spun around from the sink. "Mr. Perry! Next door all this time and you said nothing?"

The housekeeper pressed her hand to her cross. "What did I do to you, to anyone, to deserve this?"

As Bree once again covered her face with her hands, Eve rose. She had to deal with her own emotional upheaval, even though Ben had tried to prepare her. "I have to call Ben."

She went straight to the study and dialed his private number. It took nearly a dozen rings to get an answer. As soon as he recognized her voice, he started rattling off orders.

"I want you to lock the doors, and when Luther comes don't let him in. If necessary, lock Mama Lulu outside, too. She can try to talk him out of it."

"Out of what? Why is Luther coming here now?"

"He said he would give me until he closed to get the name from Bree. Something must've set him off. In any case, Rae just ran over to warn me."

"I don't want trouble. I'll be happy to tell him, but—"

"No! All I need is a vigilante raid at Bellemere. It is Bellemere, isn't it, Red?"

"Yes. Skeet Blanchard."

There was a moment's hesitation. "Anyone else?"

"She didn't mention anyone else. But I have to think… Oh, Ben."

"I know. Stay put, honey. I'll—"

Eve didn't get to hear the rest because of the sudden commotion outside the study, then a crash. Seconds later Bree burst in.

"It's Mama Lulu," the shaken girl said, almost gasping. "She took Daddy's shotgun and your keys!"

Impossible. The woman didn't drive. "Did you hear that?" Eve said to Ben.

"Yeah."

Without further comment, he slammed down the phone. Eve took no offense; she was desperate to get moving, too. Hurrying around the desk, she squeezed Bree's arm.

"Don't fall apart now. I need your keys," she added, silently assuring herself that Ben's directives no longer applied. "It'll be faster than sending for one of the other vehicles."

The girl raced to the side table where the backup sets were kept for all the cars. "Eve, I don't think you should go after her by yourself. Does Ben know what you're doing?"

"He has enough on his mind right now. Besides, I'm sure Mama Lulu didn't get far. Hopefully, she's sitting in a ditch at the end of the driveway. If you want to help, lock the door behind me, and lock the back, too. Then run upstairs and warn Justin and help him keep Lacey calm. Have him phone Dewitt and tell him to have our people watch our boundary. If there is trouble, tell him we want to assist the police in any way we can."

"And if someone from Bellemere tries to come over?"

"Tell them to use their own judgment."

That said, Eve ran out to Bree's convertible. The sun was almost down and the warm ambers were giving way to the first hint of shadowy indigo. Eve sped down the driveway, noting where Mama Lulu had driven onto the grass a few times and barely missed a few giant pecan trees. But there was no sign of her off in the pasture or in the ditch at the end of the driveway. She didn't know whether to be relieved or terrified.

She'd driven almost a mile when she rounded the turn on the farm-to-market road and spotted the vehicle well ahead of her braking. When it turned into Bellemere, she recognized it as her own.

"No!"

An oncoming truck appeared out of nowhere and barely missed hitting the sedan. It braked, backed up and followed Mama Lulu into the drive. Eve knew that truck—it was Luther's!

"Let's move it, people, before we have a body count!"

Ben was grateful that Al, Buck and Dewey hadn't yet left for the day and that Ron Scranton and Norman Friedman weren't out on patrol yet. While they went to the gun lockers to get more ammunition and rifles to back up their handguns and shotguns, Ben had Dewey call for Sheriff Boyne, who informed them that he would contact the state police.

"Don't let people tie up the phones," he called to Dewey on his way out. "We'll be in touch by radio, but be ready to call for medical help."

His men were close on his heels as he strode into the serene evening. Al paired up with Ron; Buck could be heard arguing with Norm about who should drive. He shut that down by yelling, "We go in fast and quiet! Watch each other's backs!" and then all his thoughts turned to Bellemere and what they could be driving into.

They were almost there when Dewey patched in Cliff Boyne. Their ETA was ten to fifteen minutes behind them, but Ben felt fairly confident that they could manage until then and asked the sheriff to split his people to cover the dirt road separating Bellemere from Maitland Hall.

His confidence was blown the instant they turned into Ashworth's driveway and heard gunfire. "Christ," he whispered. "You'd better hurry," he added to the other lawman.

The scene that greeted him was worse than he could have imagined. Mama Lulu had apparently lost control of Eve's car three-quarters of the way up the drive and hit a tree. Luther's truck was stopped beside it, all but blocking any vehicle access to the house and barns. But what sent his heart plummeting was seeing Bree's convertible slightly behind the other two vehicles and Eve dashing from behind it to join Luther and Mama Lulu.

Now the three of them were pinned behind the sedan by gunfire.

"God almighty," he whispered as Eve dived beside Mama Lulu and added the shield of her own body. Beside them, Luther writhed and began desperately trying to tear off his shirt and press it against his right thigh.

Solar floodlights were coming on one by one and illuminated everything around the house, the stables and auxiliary buildings. Enough were directed on the driveway to keep them sitting ducks even after darkness. Ben parked beside the Mustang just as a bullet burst through his windshield and plowed through the headrest on the passenger seat…the seat he'd almost invited Al Jones to ride in.

Gunfire was constant, but seemed limited to only a

few guns. Hoping his men found cover quickly, he grabbed his rifle and got out. He crouched low and ran for Eve and the others.

Eve was soothing Mama Lulu, who didn't look well at all, but the quick gaze she shot him transmitted enough. Wanting only to drag her the hell out of there, he asked, "How bad is she?"

"We need EMS help. This looks like a heart attack, and Luther's taken a bullet in the leg."

Ben relayed the information to Scranton who was closest to a radio and turned back in time to see Eve reaching across Mama Lulu to Luther.

"Bleeding," he muttered, frantically wiping around the wound. "Bleeding too much."

She took the crumpled shirt and quickly folded it. "It's not an artery, Luther. Look, the color is dark. You're going to be fine. Keep the wound covered and apply pressure. No, Mama, don't lie back! It may make it more difficult for you to breathe. Stay still, Luther! The bleeding won't stop if you're agitating the wound."

Assured that Eve had things under control, Ben peered around the sedan to inspect the scene. An eighteen-wheeler was pulled up to the main stable, blocking most of the view of the area, but Ben could see a good number of men lying on the ground with their hands behind their heads. That was an unexpected but welcome sign. Apparently, not everyone wanted to give their all for a few extra bucks.

"Eve!"

At the sound of Perry's voice, Ben said, "Go ahead and find out what he wants."

"I hear you, Perry!" she called.

"Are you hurt?"

"No, but others are. Perry, you have to stop this!"

There was a long silence and Ben could only imagine what discussions were going on. How much control did Ashworth have over his men, or was Blanchard the real power broker?

"Eve!" Perry called again. "I'm coming out to talk. Meet me halfway."

Ben used one succinct word to let her know what he thought of that. "You stay put, honey."

"Not if it can stop more bloodshed."

She was, he decided, too brave for her own good. "Ashworth!" he yelled. "It's over. You're not going to get past us, and the sheriff's department and state police are on their way. We have civilians who need medical attention here, so do yourself a favor. Put down your weapons and come out with your hands up."

In reply, someone opened up with an automatic rifle. Bullets ripped up everything, hedges, fencing, shattered windows, and tore metal all around them.

Once it stopped, Ben muttered, "Well, that says it all. Regardless of whether or not Ashworth can be trusted, Blanchard can't. You're not going out there."

Luther grunted something that Ben chose to take as agreement.

"I count four rifles, Chief," Buck called from behind them. "The two automatics are gonna turn these vehicles into scrap metal if we don't do something soon."

"The EMS people will be under fire, too," Eve told Ben. She glanced around her side of the car. "He's coming. I have to go."

"Absolutely not!" Ben snapped. "Didn't you hear—"

She uttered an exasperated sound and quickly rolled away from them. Realizing what she was up to, Ben lunged after her, but she was faster.

"Eve!"

She disappeared around the left side of the car, and to Ben it felt as though she were taking a handful of his guts with her. For an instant, he couldn't breathe, his heart stopped beating. Only desperation had him collecting his wits and scrambling around a softly praying Mama Lulu and over Luther who tried to help, to the right side of the car where he brought the unfolding scene into the crosshairs of his rifle scope.

Perry, his hands raised, walked toward her. Eve, her hands at chest level, approached him. He smiled—not quite that confident, charismatic smile that worked so well for him, but engaging enough. Enough for Eve to keep walking. What had Ben sucking in a sharp breath, however, was the man appearing around the other side of the truck...raising his rifle...not in the direction of the sedan, but...

"Eve! *Down!*"

A shot rang out.

Ben pulled the trigger on his rifle a split second afterward.

In the reverberating silence that followed, one of his men yelled, "He got him! Go! Go! *Go!*" but he barely paid attention. Sirens announced the arrival of Boyle and his men, and Ben didn't respond to that, either. All that mattered was Perry and Eve together on the ground.

Neither of them was moving.

21

In his blinding rage and terror, Ben almost missed seeing the men behind the truck and, inside the barn, drop their guns and appear with their hands raised. But as his own men raced past him to take control of the scene, he understood what it all meant and charged toward Eve.

He dropped to his knees beside the still couple. They looked like lovers lingering in an embrace, indifferent to the world; however, one look at the expanding red circle in the center of Perry's back, and he knew it would be the last time he would have to endure the sight of him so close to her. Blanchard had killed his boss. Ben figured he'd been using a .30-06, and from this short distance the guy couldn't have missed. That had his heartbeat roaring in his ears for only one reason.

Pushing Perry to the side, he uttered a strangled sound of protest.

There was blood, a great deal more blood, and not just because of Ashworth's exit wound. As he'd feared from the moment he'd seen them falling, the bullet had gone straight through Perry striking Eve above her right breast. If the velocity of the fall, compounded by Perry's weight, hadn't snapped her neck or fractured her skull, the bullet probably...

"Eve." Refusing to accept his own knowledge, he checked for her pulse and found a faint flutter. "Where the hell are the ambulances?" he roared over his shoulder.

Sheriff Clifton Boyne ran up to him and gripped his shoulder. "Easy, Ben. Listen. Hear the siren? It must be the ambulance they had over at the clinic in Indianola."

"Thank God. She's alive, Cliff."

"That's good, son. We need you up front now. Let Deputy Ryce stay with her." The older lawman signaled the female deputy who'd been checking Skeet Blanchard.

The young woman ran over. One glance at Ben's face and the grim-faced woman said gently, "I'll take good care of her, sir."

Ben knew he had to get back to work, but it meant ignoring all of his instincts. Beyond the eighteen-wheeler he heard growing excitement around the barn and sighed. "I'm with you, Cliff. Let's go see what we have."

The next few hours were a blur, and it was past midnight before he finally made it to Greenville. At that point he was running on sheer adrenaline, but it never occurred to him to merely call for a progress report on her condition. Regardless of how tired he was, he knew he wouldn't sleep without seeing Eve with his own eyes.

The nurses didn't want to admit him into ICU, but he refused to be deterred. His next worst moment

came when he entered the glass unit and reality struck
him anew.

She looked worse than before. The blood had been
cleaned away, but she was, if possible, paler. He had
to convince himself that the machines wouldn't be
humming and beeping if she wasn't alive; even then
he took several deep breaths before approaching her.
Lowering himself onto the edge of the bed, careful
not to touch any of the wires and tubes, he stroked
her hair, caressed her cheek. He didn't mean to disturb her, but it would have taken a willpower greater
than his to resist some contact. When she opened her
eyes, he told himself it was nothing more than wishful
thinking.

"Why?" she whispered.

He thought it a blessing that she immediately
drifted back to sleep, because he had no answer for
her.

When he returned the next day, stealing an hour or
so instead of taking lunch, they'd moved her to a
private room and had removed some of the monitors
and life-support equipment. It would have been a less
scary scenario, except that she continued to look as
though she hovered on a precipice, unable to decide
whether to stay or go.

This time when she opened her eyes, he didn't
touch her. He couldn't let himself.

"Hope you're real this time," she murmured.

"You shouldn't talk. You need to rest."

"Been resting. But..."

"Are you in any pain?" he asked as a faint frown
drew her eyebrows together.

454 Helen R. Myers

"Drugged. Floating above it. Having...crazy moments." She moaned softly. "Perry."

Ben felt something sharp and long stab into his heart. "He's dead."

"I can't believe...waste."

"His choice, Red."

"He saved my life."

How could she defend him even now? "He didn't expect Blanchard to shoot."

"It was in his eyes. In the last...he moved me. Put himself..."

She closed her eyes and Ben used the opportunity to rub his. What she'd said had been preposterous. Ashworth had been in business with the man who'd killed his own father. He'd never loved anyone, certainly not enough to put his life on the line for her. Ben wanted to believe that so he could continue to hate the bastard.

"Mama Lulu. Luther."

Ben cleared his throat. "Fine. Both of them. It wasn't a severe heart attack. She's stabilized and resting comfortably. Luther was treated and insisted on being released last night. Skeet Blanchard is dead. Bowie Shay, the man who was with him when Lem was killed, is in the county jail, along with several others."

"Children. Ben, I need to—"

"Dewitt stayed with them last night, and one of the hands' wives came over this morning. I checked before coming here. Al Jones is out there, too, to make sure the press—or anyone else for that matter—doesn't try any funny stuff."

When she didn't respond, he drew nearer to the bed

and saw she'd drifted off to sleep again. About to leave, he saw something and bent closer. A trickle of moisture seeped out of the corner of her right eye. Eve Maitland crying. For whom?

Retreating, he paused at the door, rested his hands against it and struggled to bank the flood of emotion threatening to overwhelm him. Not since his father's death had he felt so much, and he hated it. Hated it.

Grim, but determined, he left without a backward glance.

By morning he was in control again, but he didn't return to the hospital, nor did he go at lunch, or after he left the station for the evening. The next day a concerned nurse called.

"Chief, she asks questions, and when we don't have answers for her, she gets agitated," the woman said, sounding concerned, and annoyed with him that she had to make the call.

"All right. Tell her I'll be there this evening." Once more, he thought with a fatalistic sigh after he hung up. One more time, that's all it should take to finish telling her everything he knew about what had happened. Then he could free himself.

There was clear invitation in her eyes when he arrived.

"I missed you yesterday."

"We've been swamped with paperwork and calls from the media and lawyers."

She said she understood, but her look told him that she only partially believed him. To escape his guilty conscience, he dived straight into updating her on what was unfolding back in Parish.

"Remember my curiosity about Hughes Hardware's excessive growth?"

"Yes. But there was the fire at Bellemere..."

"No. Think about it. It began even before. By the time of the fire, Perry had himself neck deep in trafficking."

Eve still didn't want to believe. When she looked away, Ben clenched his teeth to keep from exposing too much.

"He built a whole facility under the stables, Eve. Trevor Hughes knew he was ordering a terrific amount of building material over there, but his greed allowed him to close one eye. Think of the damage that could have been avoided if he'd said something sooner."

"What are you talking about? Under the stables...?"

"A cellar where he raised marijuana using growing lights. One of the guys from the Bureau of Alcohol, Tobacco and Firearms told me they found a similar operation in East Texas a couple of years ago. Maybe that's what gave Perry the idea. We'll never know, though, but that explains the trucks periodically showing up at odd hours."

"There was that much they needed an eighteen-wheeler?"

"It wasn't just about transporting grass. While the old man was alive, Bellemere was simply a transfer point for other people's stuff, laundered money, crap like that. Perry was accommodating because he was losing a good deal of money on his horse business and his old man was beginning to notice."

"But he was wonderful with horses."

"Maybe, but he wasn't so good at betting."

Eve winced. "Poor Vail. Maybe it was kinder that he died without knowing all that was going on."

"I think he died because he found out." He told her what they'd learned regarding Vail Ashworth's so-called "accident." "Apparently, Vail was becoming suspicious. One night he heard one of the relay trucks pulling in and went to investigate. With Bellemere's impeccable reputation, the operation could have gone on for years before anyone on the outside would have suspected. Unfortunately, Vail saw too much, so Blanchard struck him, then started the fire to make it look like an accident."

"The cigar," Eve whispered. "But Perry wouldn't—not his father and all those poor horses!"

"The insurance money must have helped him get over his grief. It certainly expanded their operation."

"Wait...wait." Eve pressed the heels of her hands to her eyes.

"Do you need a nurse? The doctor?"

She made a negative sound, then with a moan that ended with her touching her wound, she murmured, "I'm okay now. What I don't understand is how? How could they have kept it all secret? He had so many employees. People talk."

"Not everyone knew about the underground rooms. They were kept locked and fairly well camouflaged, and probably guarded. What's more, you saw the kind of people he hired. They were probably glad to have a regular paycheck. They weren't going to risk losing it."

"But there's always gossip," Eve said. "A resentful ex-employee...a customer who talks too much..."

"None that was ever heard from again. Perry left Blanchard in charge of such unpleasantness, and Blanchard made sure people learned quickly not to test him."

"Lem. Lem must have found out."

"I've been talking to Bree, too. She told me much of what I'd already guessed about Lem's own profitable little side business in bookmaking and whatever else earned him a buck. But he had a problem keeping a dollar, so whenever he was in trouble and needed a few bucks to pay off *his* bookmaker, he went back to Bellemere begging work.

"Shay says he was their worst mistake. A door was inadvertently left unlocked and unattended, and Lem was always the curious type. He probably went downstairs thinking he would find a crap game going full swing. You know the rest."

"Poor Lem. Poor Mama Lulu. I don't know that I would have reacted any differently had I been in her shoes."

Ben nodded. "She was thinking of all those kids who'd fallen prey to the poison coming out of Bellemere, all those parents who might have to go through what she went through. Something snapped inside her."

Eve clasped her hands and held them to her lips. "How's Luther and the family holding up?"

"Torn. They're relieved that it's over, but upset about the senseless damage and loss. Rae was allowed to take Mama Lulu home this morning, provided she guaranteed Lulu would stay in bed for the next few days and take things easy thereafter."

That surprised Eve. "I...see. She didn't stop by."

Her wistful, hurt tone did bad things to his resolve to keep his distance. "She has her hands full, Eve. Two patients, the boys, the business... Theo and Micah are trying to run the store."

"Of course."

"Don't whip yourself for something that's not real, Red."

"Perry and I were friends. Then there's Bree's relationship with Skeet Blanchard. Whether intentional or not, the Maitlands caused the Cobbs terrible pain."

"Blanchard did." Ben had spent most of his time back at the office piecing together that character's maneuverings, or at least trying to. Some things would remain unanswered, as they did with too many cases. "You also should know that he was the one who thought of putting the two grand on Lem. Shay was ticked at having to go back to take care of that. Blanchard thought it would add credence to the accident theory. Guess he didn't consider that the coroner would pay attention to the body being flipped over and therefore suspiciously dirty on both sides. All he thought was that the Cobb family would be eager to get their hands on cash, so much so that they wouldn't risk provoking an investigation that might force them to give back the money. Boy, he must have been burning when he found out they didn't get it."

"Is that why he was vandalizing the store? He thought they had it and was angry that they were supporting your investigation?"

"It's as good a hunch as any. Shay didn't know anything about that, and Bree— Well, you knew what condition she was in when she was around him. An interesting bit of information came through, though.

Those kids who roughed up Noah described a man who matched Blanchard's description. They were given money and certain 'treats' to scare the boy."

Eve reached for her plastic cup and sipped ice water through a straw. Her shaking hands gave away her distress. "I couldn't believe this if it wasn't you telling me, Ben. Even Noah... Bree has to be reminded that she's lucky to be alive. And to think it all began unraveling with Roy Lindale."

"Who never gave us any names," Ben added, pleased with how that had turned out. "The door's definitely shut on his future."

He'd finished. He'd told her everything he knew—well, what she needed to know. It was a relief when a nurse came in and told him visiting hours were over, because she'd figured out as much and was watching him with that calm confidence that drove him nuts.

"I have to be heading back anyway," he said, doing embarrassing things to the brim of his hat.

"I know it's a great deal to ask, but will you come back tomorrow?"

"It's pretty crazy at the station. There's a good amount of paperwork to get to the D.A.'s office so they can prepare for all those trials. I probably won't see you again until you're back at the house."

As expected, she was surprised, but she was also sharp. He could see she figured out what he wasn't saying and covered her feelings well by giving him a smile too bright for someone as ill as she was. "Running, Ben?"

"No. Telling you how it is. How it has to be."

"Of course. I do appreciate all that you did. Go on then. I'll see you—whenever."

The cheerful dismissal clawed at him as badly as the hurt in her eyes. That made him unreasonably angry, unreasonable since escape was what he told himself he wanted in the first place. "See you," he muttered, slamming his hat on his head.

They kept her in the hospital for over a week. When Dewitt finally chauffeured her home, Ben resisted dropping by, telling himself it was better that she got the message, and easier than tormenting himself with visits that just dragged out the inevitable. Besides, she had temporary staff to train, and interviews to endure to find Mama Lulu's replacement—the latest blow after the doctors advised the old lady that she would have to slow down.

He assured himself that she would be so busy she wouldn't notice his absence. Much. But because of where he lived, it soon proved inevitable that their paths would cross.

One evening, only days after her return, she was driving to the house in the cart as he was coming in. He was shocked at her frail appearance. Her clothes were beginning to hang on her like shapeless rags, and even her ponytail looked lifeless.

"What the hell's wrong with you?" he'd demanded.

She'd merely stared at him in reply—a fair response for such a stupid question. What was wrong with her was the same thing wrong with him. What's more, keeping up with two teenagers was tough enough, having a third around with special needs, and

then running a plantation, would be a challenge for a
healthy male, let alone one young woman who'd recently had a bullet dug out of her chest.

Even so, he couldn't keep his mouth shut. "You
look like a corpse in search of a casket."

"Thank you. That's exactly what every woman
wants to hear."

"Cut the wisecracks, Eve. Damn it, you can afford
more help. Hire some!"

She had him so furious with her, he cut a sharp
U-turn and drove back to the station to work until he
was ready to drop, himself. When all that happened
was that he got more irritable, he tried dating again.
An ex-girlfriend on the outskirts of town let him know
that she'd separated from her old man. She made it
clear on their dinner date that he could have her, have
anything he wanted. But when he closed his eyes and
kissed her, all he saw was a redhead who was turning
him inside out.

He considered quitting. Things in town were settling down, and in a way, his job was done—not that
he doubted somebody would start up another smaller
drug operation sooner or later. But many of the kids
with addiction problems were coming forward one by
one and getting help, going to a clinic here, another
to a distant relative there. Also, people seemed eager
to sweep the memories of this dark episode in Parish's
history under the proverbial rug, and he figured his
departure would make that easier for them.

When he had himself half convinced, he began putting out feelers for a position elsewhere.

* * *

"What's wrong with you two?" Mama Lulu asked Eve on the last day in August.

With her car still in for repairs, Eve had driven to town in Justin's van to pick up a few things at the market, and to check on how Mama Lulu was doing. She'd met the older woman leaving the store and on her way to sit with some lady friends under a giant magnolia tree a few dozen yards beyond the end of the building. They'd begun a sewing circle. "A nicer way of sayin' we're the new neighborhood crime-watch group," Mama Lulu had explained with a dry chuckle. But that was "old news" to her ex-housekeeper. It was clear that she wanted something juicy and new to bring to her friends for today's session.

As Eve took Mama Lulu's canvas tote of mending from her to escort the woman the rest of the way, she smiled. "You don't really expect me to answer that with six pairs of radar ears turned our way?"

"Half of 'em are deaf. You got time...but not for everythin'. He was out with that Sara Sue Tucker the other day."

"Good for him."

"I ask myself why? I know you two are in love."

"He doesn't want to be."

"Make him."

Eve didn't say another word until she had the old woman seated on one of the metal chairs Luther had set out for her and the rest of the group. "Ladies," she greeted with a smile as Mama Lulu fanned herself and caught her breath. Returning her concentration to the woman who had been her first friend in Parish, she murmured, "I'm not ignoring what you said, it's just not my way."

"I know that, child." Mama Lulu patted the hand Eve placed on her shoulder, her eyes eloquent, and showing wear. "I just want you to think about you for a change. Life is too short to put your heart aside and tell it to wait."

A cloud passed before the sun, leaving Eve suddenly chilled. Not wanting to accept what she saw in the dear woman's face, she nodded. "I will," she said, and bent to tenderly kiss her cheek. "And I love you for being you," she whispered into her ear.

It was a good thing she was a ways from the store. She needed the time to swallow the lump in her throat. She didn't want to enter the store with a long face due to worry and guilt. She and the Cobbs had had a long chat once she'd returned home, and they'd cleared the air, and she knew how necessary it was for them to put the past and their troubles behind them, to look toward the future, especially for their boys' sake.

"Here I am as promised. How's the leg?" she asked Luther upon entering.

He didn't exactly make good eye contact, but he almost smiled. "Fine. Fine. You doin' all right?"

"Absolutely."

"Don't know which of you two has the thicker head. Give him your list," Rae said, coming around the counter to glare at her, but also to give her a careful hug. "He'll get your things so he can prove he's stronger than every mule in this county, and we'll go sit down for a minute in the back so you don't drop from exhaustion."

Eve followed, but only to keep from arguing—and also so she could speak frankly. "Rae," she said once they were seated. "Should I take my business elsewhere? Was I wrong to think you forgave me?"

"What's wrong with you? If anything, he's embarrassed and doesn't know how to thank you for paying for both hospital bills. Remember what I said way back when? Southern men don't know how to deal with straightforward, strong women."

"Oh, hell. That wasn't an invitation to talk about Ben."

"Tough. His foul mood is almost harder to take than my man's pride. Here people are ready to throw flowers at his feet—"

"I know, I know, and old girlfriends are tossing their house keys at him. Mama Lulu didn't let the opportunity slip by to let me know that one. What can I say? He doesn't want me."

Rae's laugh brightened the steamy, dark room. "Eve Maitland, for a smart girl, you sure can be dumb."

"Rae!"

"I've changed my mind. I'm going home tonight and I'm going to sit Theo down and tell him if he brings home a college-educated girl, I'll disown him." Rae reached across the table and gripped her wrist. "Honey, he wants you."

"Sex. No feelings. I can't shut off mine. I wish I could, then there would be no problem. What does a girl have to do besides almost die to make a thick-headed lug wake up and admit what's going on inside him?"

"But he *does* know...in his own way. And you

know. So what difference do the lack of words make?''

They mattered. Ben Rader was a man of tremendous strengths and equally strong weaknesses, and right now he was letting himself be driven by those weaknesses.

"Sorry," she told Rae. "I guess I have discovered a selfish side in me, and I'm not going to settle for a half-baked relationship."

"Right. It makes more sense to walk around looking half-alive!"

She was right about that, and Eve did take better care of herself after their talk. Rae's lecture reminded her that she needed to stay healthy for the children—not so much Justin who was inching out of his shell thanks to his blossoming love for Lacey and the confidence that gave him, but for that vulnerable girl who needed female guidance and encouragement as she studied to catch up scholastically and emotionally with others her age. And also for Bree.

Bree was changing the most. Relieved as much as confused by the generosity of the Cobbs, who graciously forgave her, Bree was left speechless when Ben disclosed he'd searched everything Skeet Blanchard owned and there were no photographs. Recognizing that she'd been given a rare second chance, she had something of a breakdown. A few days later she asked to go away like some of her former friends had to better deal with her drinking and drug problem, and Eve gladly found a reputable clinic for her.

By the time Bree returned, college was well under way, and Roy Lindale's trial was about to begin. In another of the family meetings that were becoming routine in the household, Justin and Bree agreed it would be wiser to hold off a semester until all of their schedules were less hectic. In another meeting they decided they would like to attend the trial as a family unit.

Each day, the four of them attended court together, and Eve was filled with pride as she watched her step-children act as Lacey's buffer and support, especially when it was the girl's turn to testify through an interpreter.

As required, Ben showed up, too. Eve could barely sit through his professional yet poignant testimony. His effect on the jury proved second only to Lacey's.

He didn't approach them until the end, after the jury found Roy guilty on all counts. She envied Lacey the chance to hug Ben, and worried that the girl still saw in him a father figure. He would keep his distance more than ever after this, and that would hurt.

"Your wound...is it better?" he asked Eve once the teens moved on toward the elevators.

"Just about. Though I suppose my strapless-gown days are over." She'd rarely dressed so formally, but hoped it put him in a fine torment to think of her that way.

"Ah, Red. I'm sure you'll always be a vision in a bubble bath."

His fatalistic response left her disappointed and psychologically ambivalent about how to reach him. "Well, you'll never know, will you, Ben?" she whispered, and walked away to reach the others.

It came as no surprise that Lacey's grandfather passed away in his sleep only days later. The nursing home had forewarned them of his failing condition, and Eve arranged for him to be buried in Parish in a brief, private service attended by Lacey and the Maitlands alone.

Afterward, the teens headed for the car, but Eve lingered, seeing a woman standing by the grave she'd recently sought out herself and knew as Ben's father's. Hoping her hunch was right, she approached the woman with a tentative smile.

"Excuse me. You're Alice Potter, aren't you?"

Retiring, Quaker-plain, Eve could see why Ben would have wanted to reject such a woman for his virile, life-loving father. But Eve also sensed an inner strength in Alice, which gave her a quality of serenity. As far as she was concerned, that evoked its own attractiveness.

"Mrs. Maitland. I hope my presence here didn't intrude on your private moment."

So she did know her. Eve had guessed as much. "Not at all." She gestured to Coleman Rader's grave and the new roses. "You still take very good care of him."

"I will for as long as I can."

"Does it ever get easier? Missing him? The loneliness?"

"Death doesn't stop love. Conflict doesn't, either." At Eve's questioning look, Alice Potter nodded. "I've seen Coleman's son in town, I've seen him watch you when he thought no one was paying attention, and even when he didn't care if they were. Coleman used to look at me the same way."

"I see. You know, I've been suspecting that we had something in common." Eve had been keeping an eye on Alice, too. She'd seen the neat but poor cottage the woman lived in, had learned that she survived by doing odd sewing jobs and some crafts. This meeting gave Eve an idea. "Would you like to come for tea or coffee one day this week, Mrs. Potter? I'd like to talk to you about something."

Alice came the next day, the day Justin and Bree drove to Oxford to finish rescheduling their classes. With Lacey following like a puppy, Eve brought the widow to the sunroom in the back of the house, which was less formal and a favorite place of Lacey's. To Eve's growing satisfaction, the girl seemed comfortable around the woman, and Alice didn't find it too difficult to communicate with the girl. In fact, they were soon talking about the embroidery Lacey was working on that Mama Lulu had given her.

"My. This isn't enough of a challenge for you, dear. You have a lovely, patient touch. I'll have to share some of my own designs with you."

The meeting that Eve assumed would be a success if it lasted an hour, turned into an all-morning visit that stretched into afternoon. When Eve finally walked Alice to her car, she decided to follow another bold instinct.

"Mrs. Potter—"

"Please, call me Alice."

"Then you'll have to call me Eve, and I hope I'm not offending you with this question, but I was wondering if we couldn't help each other? You might have heard that our housekeeper, Mama Lulu, has been forced to retire due to failing health. I put off looking for a permanent replacement until we had the trial behind us. But I can't put it off any longer. It's not overly demanding work. We all pitch in—something you may have heard wasn't always the case. Of course, I'm not going to pretend we're some picture-perfect family, either. We do have our...personality warts, if you will.''

Alice eyed her soberly. ''Are you trying to talk me into or out of something, Eve?''

''I'm actually doing a very bad job of telling you that it would be important for whoever took the position to be someone desperately wanting to become part of the family.''

''A housekeeper who's not a servant?''

''Let's just say, the kids are on a crash course. Life 101. I'll be happy to explain in detail...as we go along.''

''But me? You want me?''

Eve didn't know what pleased her more, the woman's astonishment or the flicker of hope in her eyes. ''Oh, yes, I believe I do, very much.'' Her gentleness, her tolerance, her patience would be a timely gift to them all in ways that Alice couldn't begin to understand. Yet.

''Me.''

She was funny in her own sweet, shy way, and Lacey had taken to her already. So would Justin. Bree might take longer, or not at all—at least not like the others—but that was an acceptable risk. To be fair, Bree was maturing fast, despite an occasional flashback to ego and attitude.

''Won't you think about it? You'd have your own apartment next to the kitchen, and time off. Understanding how much you love your sewing, I don't see that you'd have to give up many hours of it.''

"I must admit, I do more of it than I often care to just to keep myself busy," the older woman replied. "I am concerned, though. Ben lives here, doesn't he?"

"He rents the old foreman's cottage. But—" Eve had to pause to keep her innermost feelings hidden "—you wouldn't know he was there if it wasn't for his truck parked out front. You won't have a scene. Please. Think it over. I do believe we might be good for each other."

Ben had a different opinion about that. As soon as word got around that Mrs. Sumner was in full stride again, uprooting lives and championing new causes, he'd driven straight to Maitland Hall to confront her. He knew this was a personal slap at him and he wasn't going to let her get away with it.

What he didn't count on was Alice Potter answering the door.

"Ben. Chief Rader, excuse me. Please come in."

"I...I'd prefer to stay out here. Will you tell Mrs. Maitland that I'm here. Please."

"She's not home. She and Lacey are in Greenville for their signing class."

Alone with his father's lover. Extremely uncomfortable with the idea, he backed away, "Tell her I need to speak to her."

Eve didn't call him. Even when he got home that evening and stayed up late to wait, she failed to phone or come over. The next day was no different, nor was the next. That irked, because she knew he didn't want to return to the big house. To add outrage to insult, Eve then showed up in town with Alice Potter in tow.

They shopped and visited everywhere, leaving behind an ant trail of gawkers who peered out windows or simply came out on the sidewalk to watch...them, *him*, as if waiting for a volcano to erupt.

He refused to give anyone the satisfaction of creating a scene. But inwardly seething, he made himself wait another day. By the next evening he'd reached his limit. As soon as he left the station, he stopped by the house. He could only stand there, incredulous, when once again Alice Potter answered the door.

"She's not here."

He heard voices—Justin and Bree's, and behind Alice Potter he had a glimpse of Lacey dashing across the hall with a trail of streamers. He supposed they were preparing something for the autumn festival that Eve had encouraged the PTA to organize as another fund-raiser for that damned library, which was back on the drawing board. He was already resigned to having to work at the thing himself, what with the out-of-town traffic said to be expected. The mere thought of having to mingle—especially since Dewey had let word get out about his job offer to return to Jackson—made him want to pack and leave now.

Nodding, he began to turn away.

"Ben."

He glanced over his shoulder.

"Don't you want to know where she is?"

"Does it matter? It's clear she's intent on ignoring me because she thinks I'm going to criticize her for hiring you."

"Were you?"

"Maybe. Once. Now..." He shrugged. "Anyone with eyes can see that you've helped her. If she's happy, then..." He stopped and wondered what the hell he was blabbering about.

Alice Potter's clear hazel eyes filled with emotion. It turned her into a different woman, almost an attractive woman.

"Young man, if you love her so much that you can stand seeing me in this house, then you find her, and don't invite fate to steal her away from you the way it stole your father from me."

Damn it, this was too much. "Stole? Fate didn't steal anything. My father was a fool."

"Your father was the noblest, most honorable man I've ever known. Don't you realize what he did that day? He took full and complete responsibility for us. He wouldn't let me bear an ounce of it, and it cost him his life because he underestimated the pride and anger in my husband.

"I've spent every day since honoring that love I was blessed to know, and if what you feel for Eve is anywhere close to that, and you walk away from her, then *you*, you're the pitiful one, young man. Not your father."

He stood there even after she shut the door firmly in his face. He summoned disgust for her pretense, her suggestion that her affair with his father had been something special. All that followed was shame, and debilitating fatigue.

On leaden feet, with his mind reeling, he returned to his truck and drove like a robot along the dirt road to his rental house. Once inside, he headed straight for the refrigerator and got himself a beer. The first, he promised himself, of as many as it took to obliterate the truth that Alice Potter had spoken.

His gun and holster hit the refrigerator door as he slammed it shut and, swearing, he wrestled it off. Then he ripped at his badge and flung it across the room. An impostor didn't deserve to wear it. Wishing he could strip off his own skin, he headed for the bathroom.

In the doorway, he froze.

She sat in the tub, her hair piled high in sexy curls, her body all but submerged in...well, more milky water than bubbles, but it was close enough to his fantasy to convince himself he was losing it. He didn't dare move for fear the vision would vanish.

"I guess my timing is off," she said mournfully as she watched the soapy orbs burst, exposing more and more of the swell of her breasts.

"It's my fault." Somehow he managed to cross to the tub and lowered himself onto the rim. Not surprisingly, his eyes burned as he took in the full, exquisite length of her. In the amber glow of the end of the day that spilled through various windows, she offered her own radiance. "I stopped at the house on my way here."

"Ah. I'd convinced myself that nothing could drag you back there. So I decided meeting you one hundred percent of the way was going to be my last compromise."

"Actually, I'd gone to say goodbye. But your new housekeeper forced me to reconsider."

"How did she manage that?"

"She called me a coward, or fool. Maybe both."

"Ouch. And here I thought she'd just earned herself a raise."

"Give it to her. I deserved that remark and worse.

I was willing to run away from you. You scare the hell out of me, Red. Then seeing you almost get killed..." He shook his head. "I didn't want any part of feeling that much."

"What's changed?"

"The realization of what the option is. Being without you makes me hurt as though I took a bullet, too. I figure I could still walk away from you...but I'd probably end up dying from regret." He leaned over and scooped her out of the water and onto his lap. "I love you, Red," he whispered and closed his mouth over hers.

She sighed and melted against him. Or maybe he was melting because of the warm water. In any case, he crushed her close and showed her that what he'd said was true.

There was a great deal he wanted to show her, tell her; and he ached to hear her say those special words to him. But there was time for all of that now, time for everything.

Because it was sundown. Their time.

A wonderful novel that continues what
Jane Austen's *Sense and Sensibility* began!

JULIA BARRETT

THE
THIRD
SISTER

In *The Third Sister,* Julia Barrett faithfully
evokes Jane Austen's style, characters and ambience
to tell just what happens when the youngest
Miss Dashwood meets two eligible suitors.
Which man will she choose? Which man will she love?
The gentleman or the scoundrel?

"Fans of [*Sense and Sensibility*] will enjoy...
a good new story, tight writing and a heroine
with brains and charm."
—*New York Times Book Review*

MIRA
BOOKS

Available in May 1998
at your favorite retail outlet.

MJB446

ALL THAT GLITTERS

by *New York Times* bestselling author

LINDA HOWARD

Greek billionaire Nikolas Constantinos was used to getting what he wanted—in business and in his personal life. Until he met Jessica Stanton. Love hadn't been part of his plan. But love was the one thing he couldn't control.

From *New York Times* bestselling author Linda Howard comes a sensual tale of business and pleasure—of a man who wants both and a woman who wants more.

Available in
May from
New York Times
bestselling
author

TESS GERRITSEN

He emerged from the mist, right in front of Cathy
Weaver's car—running from killers who were closing
in. Victor Holland's story sounded like the ravings of a
madman, but his claim to be a fugitive was confirmed
by the haunted look in his eyes—and the bullet hole
in his shoulder. As each house brought the pursuers
ever closer, Cathy had to wonder: Was she giving her
trust to a man in danger...or trusting her life to a
dangerous man?

WHISTLEBLOWER

Available in May 1998 wherever books are sold.